Icing

CHICAGO FALCONS SERIES
BOOK ONE

NICO DANIELS

ROMANCE AUTHOR

ICING

Nico Daniels

This is a work of fiction. All characters, locations, and entities are either products of the author's imagination, or used fictitiously.

✻ Created with Vellum

For our sky babies.
Never in our arms, forever in our hearts.
Love you to infinity.

Prologue
GAVIN: JULY

One cloud. The otherwise vibrant blue sky was clear and went on forever, the picturesque beauty marked by a lone white puff in the shape of a middle finger. The cumulus had positioned itself directly over the church and it seemed even the universe had provided commentary on the wedding.

"Can you at least pretend like you want to be here?" Asher's voice filtered through my daydream in which I saved the princess from the hairy beast she was about to marry. "I know you had some knight in shining armor fantasy worked up where you rode off into the sunset with Greyson, but it's her wedding day. You need to get it together."

"Would you shut your mouth?" I hissed as I pulled him away from the crowd. I looked around to make sure his obnoxiously loud voice hadn't carried to the hundreds of guests that milled around outside the huge brick church. "Someone might hear you."

Asher rolled his eyes and pulled a bottle of water out of his pocket. He downed half of it before he held the remainder out to me.

"Everyone knows Gavin. Most of us don't stay celibate pining for someone we know we'll never have. If you think people don't notice you never take a woman home, you truly are delusional."

"I'm not celibate, dickhead. I just don't feel the need to sleep with a different random person every day of my life."

"When was the last time you had sex?"

"Irrelevant," I grumbled.

I hoped it wasn't obvious to anyone but him. He was the one who had heard my rants for the last four years about what a complete and total dickbag KJ Sullivan was. The sun that peeked through the thick layer of leaves above our heads was a reminder that Mother Nature didn't share my stormy mood. The stagnant heat of the summer air suffocated me almost as much as our conversation.

"I get this is tough for you to swallow and I'm sorry. I know you believe in karma and signs and all that, and you really thought you were meant to be with her." Asher's tone softened when I dropped my eyes to my feet with a shrug. "Listen. Let's skip the reception and go get blackout drunk. In the meantime, you have to slap on a smile and pretend to be happy for your teammate on his wedding day."

The phrase 'wedding day' about the woman I shouldn't want made my tie feel more like a noose and I pulled at it uncomfortably. It was execution day for my chance at happiness. I'd rather be standing on the gallows.

A strong breeze lifted the leaves on the trees and a large gray cloud moved over the sun, like it was dropped straight from the belly of an angry storm. The temperature fell sharply, still not close to comfortable but noticeable enough that goosebumps rose on the back of my neck. Something had just shifted in the universe.

The guests simultaneously looked skyward to see if an unpredicted storm would unleash on us when the doors of the church flew open and smashed against the brick walls outside them. The groom-to-be was thrown down the steps, his pants wrapped around his ankles. The hulking monster of a man I knew was

Greyson's brother towered over him with so much rage across his face I was certain I was about to witness a murder.

"If you so much as look in the general direction of my sister ever again, I'll end your fucking shit life," Trevor growled, crouched over the pile of tuxedo and scared man on the sidewalk. His head snapped up and scanned the team who were gathered with wide eyes and slack jaws. When he landed on me, I shrank back in fear. Just a little.

"What the fuck just happened?" Asher's low voice was nothing compared to the thoughts that swirled through my head. My eye caught a flash of a wedding gown as it flowed down the steps of the church, surrounded by muted blue and rose pink. She was a frighteningly beautiful vision of heartbreak lined with hope. A broken winged angel in a white lace dress, Greyson stood calmly as her bridesmaids surrounded her like a shield. She looked dazed as her eyes lifted off the pavement and found mine. A flash of ... something ... ignited her soft blue irises for a split second before her attention was drawn to KJ at her feet. Greyson kicked away the hand he reached out in a desperate attempt to hang on to the life he'd almost faked his way into.

"Thank you all for taking the time to be here, but there will be no wedding today. Or ever. I can't pretend my fiancé isn't cheating on me now that I've seen it with my own eyes. I sincerely apologize that you've all wasted your time."

The hushed murmur that had been pulsating through the crowd increased into a full buzz after her speech. My heart pounded so hard against my chest it made breathing difficult as Greyson's brother zeroed in on me and stepped forward menacingly.

"You're the captain. Make sure this fuck gets as far away from my sister as humanly possible. Faster than yesterday. Otherwise, I'm going to arrest him for being a piece of shit and throw him in a cell," Trevor demanded as he stepped between her and KJ.

I fumbled for something to say when Greyson timidly moved closer to me. The lemony sweet smell of her skin filled my nostrils, and I closed my eyes with the need to collect myself. When I opened them again, I found her with her eyes on my mouth and a soft pink tinge crept up her cheeks.

"Ignore him. He's upset. This isn't your responsibility. Thank you for coming Gavin. I'm sure there are plenty of other places you'd rather be. Seeing you makes this a little easier," Greyson spoke so quietly I had to strain to hear her, and she turned away before I could respond. Her flock of protectors moved with her like a choreographed dance team. Trevor shot one more withering glare at KJ before he wrapped an arm around his sister and hurried her to privacy.

KJ wrestled with his clothes and tried to regain some semblance of dignity while we all stared at him with a mix of shock and disgust.

"Why are you all just standing there? Fucking help me!"

I squatted in front of him and called on all my self-control not to knock him out. "Get yourself together and get out of here. The Falcons don't need bad press because you refuse to keep your dick in your pants. At your own fucking wedding."

"I didn't plan it, Dad." KJ sat up as I attempted to shield him from the hundreds of cell phones pointed at the Chicago Falcon who had, very literally, been caught with his pants down. I bristled at the nickname my teammates used out of respect, but he managed to make sound like an insult. "But I was nervous, so I called a friend for stress relief. Really, it was for Greyson's benefit. I wanted to be my best self when I walked down the aisle."

I turned to my team and told them to disperse, that I would handle this mess.

"You're disgusting."

"Whatever. I'll have this smoothed over by tomorrow. She'll never have enough self-respect to cut me loose." KJ was so unbothered it was actually scary.

"I truly, honestly, hate you."

He grinned as he patted my cheek. I clenched my fists against my thighs, refusing to allow him to bring me to his level. At least not when there were cameras around.

"I truly, honestly, don't care. Have a nice summer, Gavin."

He didn't have the decency to be embarrassed by his actions or care about the hurt he'd just caused. I wasn't surprised, but I was still angry I had to fix yet another one of his screw ups. The media fallout from this would be a nightmare. I shot off a text to my coach so management could formulate a plan of action before it was everywhere. I wouldn't be surprised if I was already too late. The guys from the Biscuits in the Basket podcast were like wizards with how fast they got information. Asher's car appeared next to where I stood on the sidewalk and I hopped in the passenger seat and ripped off my tie. He raised his fingers to the sky and gave me his trademark grin.

"Well. There's that sign you were looking for."

Indeed.

CHAPTER 1
Greyson
OCTOBER

T revor squeezed my hand tightly while we stood in the darkened corridor waiting to be brought onto the ice. I didn't want to be there. When I stepped inside the Delta Center the memories swirled around me and overwhelmed my senses.

"Relax, RayRay. It'll be over soon," Trevor leaned in and spoke next to my ear while the Falcons announcer took his place behind the microphone. "What kind of cupcake would Grandpa want to represent him as a hockey player?"

It was sweet of him to try to distract me in the way that always worked, but even creating a recipe in my head wouldn't cut it this time. When the Falcons had reached out about doing a tribute to our grandpa during the home opener, I thought it was a great idea, until they requested his family be there for a ceremonial puck drop. I could sit in front of a video camera and talk about my favorite foods all day long to be broadcast on national television but standing live in front of twenty thousand people was a whole different story. I had only recently gotten to a point where I didn't cry the moment I woke, and I knew I wouldn't be able to keep myself together during the video that would play during the tribute.

"Jonah Park left an indelible mark on this organization. His work ethic and teamwork played an integral part in the creation of the establishment you all know and love today. He instilled those values into his family, and while he wore the Chicago sweater with unwavering pride, he was most proud of the accomplishments of his grandchildren. Please welcome Trevor and Greyson Park to the ice."

The baggy jersey I wore with my grandpa's number on the sleeves did nothing to provide warmth and I shivered while I clung to Trevor's arm. I didn't belong in this world anymore. I wasn't sure I ever had. My love of the Falcons games had slowly dwindled with each day KJ and I were together. I had powered through the sadness of watching him flirt with fans wearing his name on their backs so I could spend time with my grandpa. After he passed away, I had no reason left to go.

We stood together in the middle of the rink, all eyes on us as the clapping deafened before it trailed off to eerie silence. The tribute began with video clips of Grandpa from his early years in the league. They were interspersed with pictures and interviews, and I covered my lips with my fingers when his booming voice filled the arena. I missed the smile in every word he spoke and the laugh that shook his entire body. The photo from my pastry school graduation caught me off guard. It was a time when my chestnut brown hair was cut in a severe bob and colored a shocking shade of red rather than the soft balayage waves I now favored, and my makeup choices were more emo teenager than exhausted bakery owner who barely scraped a mascara wand through her lashes. I was mortified literally millions of people now had that version of me on their televisions, and I dug my nails into Trevor's hand.

"You gave them *that* picture? What the hell?"

"It's my favorite. Look how happy he was. How proud," Trevor spoke out of the side of his mouth without taking his eyes off the screen. When I looked back, I saw it from his point of view.

My eyes pricked with the tears I would do anything to hold in, and I tried to covertly dab them with the tissue that was crumpled in my fist. I looked up and noticed the team captain, Gavin Halstead, with his eyes on me. He held my gaze captive while the corners of his lips turned up into a sympathetic smile. I looked away quickly, embarrassed by the instant flush that covered my cheeks.

The willpower it took to not let his eyes pull my attention off the video was more than I had. By the time Trevor and I accepted handshakes from the former players who were lined up to pay their respects I'd snuck more than a couple glances at Gavin. Trevor nudged me and pressed the puck he had promised to drop into my hand.

"It should be you. Everyone expects it to be you."

As if he sensed my trepidation at the prospect of being the one responsible for the ceremonial puck drop, Gavin kept his stare locked on mine as he skated to his position in front of me. A gentle smile that was mine to keep was the last I saw of his face before he turned to the photographer poised for the photo op. Gavin and the captain of the visiting team posed with their sticks on the ice while I dropped the puck. My eyes followed the back of his neck as he bent over in front of me to scoop it up, and I caught the scent of salt and lime soap as he stood back up and pulled off a glove. He smelled like a margarita, and I knew what the cupcake special would be the next day. Gavin shook Trevor's hand first and then took mine as the warmth of his touch flooded my body. Goosebumps rose on my neck as the heat of his breath whispered over my skin. I fought to keep my eyes forward as I waited for his rough voice to invade my thoughts.

"It's really nice to see you back here."

I was shocked into stunned silence and turned my head quickly, met with his sparkling brown eyes and another half-smile. Gavin skated off like he'd been struck by a bolt of lightning, and I watched him until he had disappeared into the tunnel. I followed Trevor down the red carpet and through the bench, relieved to be off the ice. After a detour for drinks, we slid into our seats on the glass, and I relaxed for the first time since we had walked into the arena. Every time Gavin skated near us during warmups, I automatically looked down into my cup, annoyed by Trevor's immature taunting.

"You need to give him half a smile. He's starting to look pathetic," Trevor watched my awkward attempt to not humiliate myself with the man I'd had a completely inappropriate crush on for years. I looked up at exactly the wrong time, as Gavin skated towards me while his eyes dared me to look away. Just to shut Trevor up I ignored the heat in my cheeks and tried to smile. My mouth didn't connect to my brain, and I instead ended up in a pained grimace. Gavin smirked and a deep dimple showed in the corner of his mouth as Trevor threw his head back and laughed.

"This is the strangest mating ritual I've ever witnessed."

I shoved him hard as he lifted his cup to his lips and took pleasure as the golden liquid sloshed over the rim. He coughed up beer and held up a hand while he wiped the other across the back of his mouth.

"Alright, alright, truce," Trevor reached across me to the waitress who had appeared and ordered two more beers. "I thought it was weird the way he acted at the church. I get it now."

"What the hell does that mean?" I demanded. "He acted no different than everyone else."

"If you say so," Trevor gave me an unreadable look, and I focused my attention on the ice to avoid his questioning stare.

My engagement to KJ Sullivan had been a joke from the moment the ring went on my finger. Everyone knew it, including me. A small part of me had held onto the hope he would magically turn into a good man if we got married. That evaporated when half the city witnessed him get thrown out of the church by my brother. I was glad Trevor hadn't been carrying his gun that day, because I had no doubt the detective would have ended up the criminal. While I was utterly humiliated in the moment, the fact everyone I knew was there to see it happen eliminated any need for me to retell every salacious detail of the story. Anyone who wasn't aware just had to open the Biscuits in the Basket Instagram page, since they had reposted the video at least once a week the entire summer. I was aware of the Chicago based podcast before my wedding, since they seemed to be in *just* the right spot to catch my fiancé in compromising positions with puck bunnies *all* the time. But their celebrity had shot through the stratosphere once they posted a video of the entire scene. From right after Trevor tossed KJ down five stairs like he was a bag of marshmallows, right up to Gavin squatting next to him on the ground, looking like he wanted to rip his limbs off and beat him unconscious with them. Apparently, page views measured higher to them than human decency, and they'd become nationally known thanks to my devastation.

I wasn't ready to come back to the games. The only thing that made it palatable was the fact I wouldn't see KJ's cheating ass sit on the bench. I wasn't under any illusion his trade was because of me, but I did appreciate the swift response the Falcons took to his behavior. The Delta Center reminded me of my best and worst times, and I didn't want to face either set of memories.

The tension in my muscles relaxed the longer we were there. For the first time in months, I almost felt good. The freely flowing alcohol didn't hurt, even though I knew I would regret the decision to imbibe when my alarm went off at three in the morning. The lack of sleep part was manageable since it was my norm, but I really hated being hungover when I had to bake. Or even worse, still drunk.

My phone buzzed in my pocket, and I found an obscene number of messages from the group chat I had with my best friends. I scanned the discussion to see they had dissected how I looked on television and asked if 'Captain Canada' had almost kissed my cheek as it appeared from their living rooms. I'd replayed the moment a hundred times since it had happened. It was intimate and flirtatious, which excited and terrified me. But I'd met Gavin the same day I'd met KJ, and if he'd had any interest in me at all I would have jumped into it with open arms. If he had, I wouldn't have been humiliated and betrayed for years while I stayed faithful to KJ, and he stayed balls deep in puck bunnies. I couldn't keep up with Mila and Delaney's messages, so I shoved my phone into my bag as the team came back on the ice.

Gavin won the opening faceoff and my brain flashed to the first real conversation I had with him. When our relationship was brand new, KJ had brought me to an after party. He had deposited me at a table and promptly 'gone to chat,' which I'd come to learn was code for getting his stick waxed by a bunny in a bathroom stall. Gavin took pity on me and indulged me in a conversation in which I told him his faceoff percentage should be higher, which had completely mortified me as soon as the words had left me. He had laughed and told me he couldn't argue with facts, so I didn't think I had stuck my foot too far into my mouth. The years that followed told a different story however, since he avoided me like I was radioactive at every team event that I went to. His iciness almost hurt more than my fiancé's poison coated words and venom laced betrayals. I finally gave up any attempt at being a normal Falcons significant other and quit going to functions altogether.

I followed Gavin's movements on the ice and grew more animated the longer the game went on. By the final two minutes of the third period with a tie game, I was nervously glancing between the clock and the ice. I hated the anxiety of overtime and Trevor tried, unsuccessfully, to extricate his hand from my fingernails as the seconds ticked down on the clock. I had to put my nervous energy somewhere and apparently, that meant causing my brother open wounds. I had almost given up hope of a regulation win when Asher Tremblay stripped the puck from Anaheim and took off on a breakaway toward their goal, and he shot into a mostly unprotected net to win the game at the last second. The instantaneous deafening roar of cheers from twenty thousand people sounded like the most beautiful love song ever written.

I was officially back.

CHAPTER 2
Gavin

As I stood outside Icing, it was obvious this was not the typical bakery usually found in the middle of down-town Chicago. Decorative whisks were used in place of handles on heavy wood doors. Frosted glass windows shimmered against the sun with multicolored glitter reminiscent of sprinkles. A tiny sticker in the corner of the door caught my attention. '*As Seen On BAKED.*' If it were me, I'd advertise my business being on national television a lot more ostentatiously than a three-inch sticker on a door, but I wasn't surprised. She was nothing if not humble.

"I'm letting you go. I'm about to go in," I cut off my sister mid-sentence, and held the phone away from my ear when she cheered obnoxiously.

"Call me when you're done. Don't screw it up this time."

"Thanks for that stellar advice," I hung up and took a deep breath as I wrapped my hand around a whisk and pulled open the door. With just one foot in the bustling café, it was as if I'd been transported into a friend's kitchen.

Groups of people sat together on upholstered chairs covered in cupcake fabric and laughed over massive cups of coffee. The stools against the window were shaped like cupcakes, which made customers look like they were sitting on top of swirls of frosting. The light fixtures suspended over the tables looked like mixer paddles and hung in various lengths as they illuminated cookies and cakes in front of happy customers.

My eyes wandered to the large angel wings painted on the wall at the back of the cafe. A long line of patrons waited for their turn to pose in front of the insane piece of artwork. It looked to be a hand-painted mural of baked goods that melted together to form a giant set of wings. It was the most unique thing I'd ever seen, and Greyson's heart and mind started to settle into the cracks in my soul as I stepped up to the counter. Even that was on brand, the entire thing made of sprinkles, a thick layer of multicolored pastels under a coat of epoxy.

"Hi, what can I get for you today?"

A cheerful young woman smiled brightly at me from behind the counter as I scanned the cases. The rows upon rows of frosted cupcakes and sugar cookies were so detailed they looked like works of art and I was tempted to order one of everything.

"I think that's the hardest question I've ever been asked. What do you recommend?"

She leaned forward with a grin and folded her arms over the counter. "Are you a newbie? Our owner loves first timers. She'll know what you want after just a couple questions. Your pleasure is her main priority."

I bit back a groan at the idea of Greyson being focused on my pleasure. Only in my very vivid dreams. While I had never actually been inside the bakery, I had consumed plenty of her confections, since Asher had an insatiable sweet tooth. He bought enough to share with Cohen and me, and I was always blown away by the complexity of the recipes. But I would gladly feign ignorance if it meant Greyson would drop everything to come talk to me.

"I'd love to talk to her. Is she here?"

The girl with the 'Cake Dealer' t-shirt and headband that had chocolate chip cookies sticking straight up into the air rolled her eyes with a laugh.

"She's always here," she pointed at a secluded end of the counter where a 'Consultations' sign hung from the ceiling. "Prepare to be fawned over, as she pulls all your deepest wants out of the recesses of your brain."

As if on cue, Greyson appeared from the back and stepped up next to her employee. Streaks of flour dusted her forehead and purple frosting stuck in patches across the front of the 'Whatever Frosts Your Cupcakes' shirt that she wore very well. Her smile lit up her face, and when she realized I was the customer that commanded her time confusion crossed her soft features.

"Captain Canada," her eyes went wide, cheeks went crimson, and hands flew over her mouth. I had plenty of nicknames, but this was one I'd never heard. Although it was accurate. I kind of liked the idea she had her own for me. I raised an eyebrow as I fought to hide my smile.

"Queen Cupcake."

Greyson stared at me for a handful of seconds before she smiled slowly and rolled her eyes. "Clever. Thanks for attempting to soften my humiliation."

It was impossible not to smile back and when she nodded at the Consultation corner, I followed her like a puppy.

"I actually just came to talk to you about something," I threw out as Greyson pulled a pen from somewhere in her messy bun of hair. "If you have time, I mean. Otherwise, I can come back later."

She frowned, two little indents appearing between her eyes.

"Why? You never talk to me." She paused and looked at the sheet of paper in front of her, broken up into boxes with flavor profiles written in colorful font. "That sounded bitchy. I just mean, you've barely acknowledged me in four years. Is it about the tribute? Did the team send you? Did we forget to sign a form or something?"

I inwardly cringed at the unintentional dig she'd just thrown at me. But it made my reason for coming in even more crystal clear.

"No, nothing like that. I ... since I saw you the other night,

I've been thinking a lot about ... I really hoped I could just clear something up. If that's alright?"

"Sure, okay," Greyson hastily pushed the paper to the side of the counter and shoved the pen back into her hair. "Do you want to come back to my office?"

"That would be great," I said, as she motioned me behind the counter. I sidestepped employees that moved with practiced efficiency, cycling the endless customers through at an impressive pace. Greyson picked up a stack of boxes on the back counter and lifted her chin at the ones that remained.

"Do you mind grabbing those?" She pushed open the door with her backside and made quick eye contact before dropping her gaze to my hands. I picked up the boxes and followed her into the kitchen, where her personality bloomed even more brightly than in the dining room. The mixers were painted bright colors, an explosion of pinks, purples, and blues. The floor was covered in a bizarre glitter finish that was not something that should exist but, for her, nothing else would have worked.

"Wow. You really like glitter," my head moved in a swivel as I took in the surroundings and stepped over the threshold of her office into a galactic wonderland. It was like floating through the night sky. The walls were painted an inky blue and dotted with sparkling constellations and shooting stars. The mural of the infinity loop on the silver glitter accent wall also looked like a one-of-a-kind piece done just for her.

"Yeah." Greyson's eyes swept the room and lingered on the mural. "You said you wanted to talk to me about something?"

She took the boxes from my hands and a jolt of electricity passed through me as her fingers brushed mine. I realized in her quiet response that my statement could have come across condescending and tried to backtrack as I pointed at the sky wall.

"I like it. It's very sparkly."

"Did you come here to make fun of me?" Greyson asked softly.

"No, of course not. I'm sorry, I really do like it. It fits you."

"What does that mean?"

"I don't know. Can we start over?"

Greyson waved at the overstuffed chair opposite her desk as she moved around it and dropped into hers. "By all means, Captain Canada."

I took a seat and noticed the enormous white board calendar that hung on the wall to my left. Every day was meticulously planned and jammed full of activities, separated by different color ink. Even that sparkled.

"Do you ever sleep?" I asked. "Your schedule is insane."

Greyson waved away the question with barely a glance at her outrageously busy life.

"Sleep is overrated. When my brain is silent my demons scream. I can't handle that," she replied. Her throat bobbed with a hard swallow, and she shook her head. "Wow, that was embarrassingly honest and dark. My therapist will be so proud."

"I know you've been through a lot. That's why I'm here." I said, distracted by the Canis Major constellation depicted on the wall behind her head.

"Gavin? Are you okay?"

I forced my eyes off the wall and found her focused on me. I fought my way through the past to come back to the moment with the woman whose concerned expression was etched into her features. I realized she had been speaking, and I had totally blanked out.

"Yeah, sorry. That constellation just reminded me of something. Anyway, I wanted to say I'm sorry. I came to apologize."

"For?"

"KJ."

"Oh." Greyson sat back and sank into the plush piece of furniture. Her posture was familiar, the one I had grown accustomed to seeing when KJ pulled his standard disappearing act to get a blowjob in a bathroom. It reminded me of a turtle, pulling into its shell at the first inkling of danger. I wanted her to understand I wasn't a predator. "You sure know how to piss in a girl's icing."

"What does that mean?"

"It means I can think of about twelve thousand things I'd rather do than discuss my ex with one of his friends. So, if that's all, I'm going to get back to my insane schedule. I've got—"

"I am *not* friends with him," I interrupted in irritation. "He was my teammate and that was the extent of our relationship. I'm sorry I knew what he was doing and didn't try to stop it. You've always deserved better than him."

Her pinched expression softened, but I was starting to regret my decision to clear my conscience.

"You have nothing to apologize for. You didn't force him to betray and abuse."

I bristled at the word 'abuse,' as my fears of what he did behind closed doors seemed to have just been confirmed.

"No, but as you pointed out, I'm the captain. Integrity starts from within. Staying silent provides culpability. No woman should ever be disrespected the way you were. I should have stepped in."

Greyson's forehead furrowed and she tilted her head.

"Why would you have? Maybe I deserved it. Maybe I was treating him the exact same way."

"You didn't. You weren't," I replied gruffly, shifting as she sat back in surprise. "I know I never got to know you the way I did the other wives and girlfriends. It could be argued I was cold to you. That is not me, and it has weighed heavy on me for quite some time. It wasn't because of you."

"I don't understand," Greyson said softly. Her fingers dipped inside the collar of her shirt, and she came out with a small pendant that she rubbed methodically. "I thought I offended you that night at the bar. That wasn't why you got up and left every time I came in a room after that?"

Her words instantly shrank me, and I wasn't sure I'd ever felt like more of an asshole.

"KJ is a taker. A user. A pathetic excuse for a man who uses manipulation to attain his wants," I leaned forward and rested my forearms on her desk. "He made it clear I was not to know you. Under normal circumstances, I'd have told him to fuck off. But I've seen the man behind the mask, Greyson. I wouldn't put you in jeopardy by being selfish."

"What do you mean?" Greyson's voice barely carried across the desk. She knew what I meant. I saw it in the way she studied my face, chewing on her lip as if she were trying to divert words from coming out of her mouth.

"I saw how uncomfortable team events made you. You were always off to the side. Alone. I stopped myself a million times from sitting down with you because of how he would react. I can handle him. I didn't know if you could. I thought I was doing the right thing by keeping my distance."

"You were worried he would take his anger at you out on me," she said softly. She pinned her blue eyes on me, and I clenched my jaw with a nod. The pain that now covered her face hit me like an axe through the heart. "Well. Thanks. I guess."

"You're upset."

Greyson shrugged and released the pendant that I now saw matched the symbol on her wall.

"I thought maybe, just *maybe*, you were the one person who didn't look at me and see a pathetic woman who buried her head in the sand to avoid the proof that smacked her in the face every day for years." Greyson held up a hand as I opened my mouth to protest. "I'm sorry if I'm being rude. This just sucks. It sucks to be judged and pitied and made a spectacle of on some stupid sports podcast just because of your relationship. No one seems to understand or care that I'm a real person with real feelings. Everyone just sees me as the punchline of a joke."

Greyson trailed off as her voice quivered and I fought the urge to get up and hold her against me. She was like sitting in front of a bonfire. Entrancingly beautiful and radiated warmth, but quietly exuded the power of destruction and danger if you took a chance and got too close. I wanted to get burned.

"I see you as nothing but the beautiful person you are," I replied. "The last thing I would ever want to do is hurt you."

Her eyes widened and she opened and closed her mouth a few times before she finally spoke.

"I'm really confused by you, Gavin. You treat me like a non-entity for years, and then you come in here and tell me how beautiful of a person I am? I truly do not understand."

I blew out a heavy breath and raked a hand through my hair.

"The only way for me to be around you was to pretend like you didn't exist."

Her throat bobbed as she swallowed, and her top teeth came down on her lip before her whispered response.

"Why?"

"Greyson." My voice came out as a plea, desperate for her to see what I'd been forced to keep hidden for years. "Isn't it obvious?"

She pressed her lips together and as I held her stare, I watched the shade of her eyes change from sapphire to the color of the sky. A knock on the door startled us both, and I swung my head towards the sound, annoyed by the intrusion. A white-haired man with a top-knot and the most eclectic outfit I'd ever seen stood in the doorway. Greyson's guarded demeanor evaporated at the sight of him, and a true smile lit up her face.

"Eddie! Hi!"

"Happy hump day, sweetness! Am I interrupting?" He asked, raising and lowering his bushy white eyebrows while he looked between the two of us. Greyson blushed and dipped her head. She shot me a quick glance before standing to hug him.

"You could never interrupt. Eddie, this is Gavin. Gavin, this is one of my dearest friends, Eddie," Greyson bounced on the balls of her feet as I stood and extended my hand to Eddie. His grip was surprisingly strong and the tight squeeze when I attempted to release it sent a very clear message.

"Good to meet you, Gavin. What are your intentions, here, kid?"

"Eddie! What the hell!" Greyson squealed. "What if this was a customer?"

"Customers don't make it to the inner sanctum, sweetness. And the sexual tension in here is thicker than the humidity in the middle of July," Eddie said knowingly. Greyson's face was the color of my home jersey and I coughed out a laugh, holding my fist in front of my mouth to cover. "Come on, Gavin, help me with the boxes."

Greyson stepped between Eddie and me. She gave me a look somewhere between apologetic and mortified before Eddie got a full-on glare.

"Oh no way. I don't trust you alone with him," she said. "I'll help you, like I do every single day."

"What if I want to help?" I grinned. Greyson rolled her eyes and dropped her head to the side with a defeated sigh.

"Then we'll all go," she conceded. "I'm kind of enjoying talking to you, and he would definitely scare you away." She hitched her thumb at Eddie, who had an amused grin on his face and a sparkling glint in his eye.

"No one will scare me away again," I replied. Greyson turned to me in surprise and her eyes transformed again. The blue disappeared completely, and I was left staring into smoky gray pools.

"The air in here is practically dripping," Eddie cheerfully handed me a stack of boxes and I reluctantly broke the moment Greyson and I shared. We left the office and I followed them through the kitchen to the back door. Employees gave high fives to Eddie as he passed, and Greyson enthusiastically praised their decoration skills on the cookies laid out in front of them. It was shocking to see how different she was in an environment she was comfortable in compared to the Falcons events. Her cheerfulness was magnetic when she was surrounded by sugar and sprinkles.

Greyson stopped to talk with a stressed girl with tears in her eyes and a cake in front of her, and she waved me to follow Eddie when he kept moving. When we got outside, I helped him secure the boxes in the back of his van and gave him another handshake.

"My intentions are honorable, sir."

He twirled his keys around his finger and leaned against the door.

"That girl is one of the good ones. She doesn't need another smooth-talking jock promising her the world and giving her hell," Eddie looked me up and down. "I've heard your name before. You've darkened her smile in the past."

I had trouble processing the fact that my treatment had been enough for her to discuss it with this man. Enough to hurt her.

"Eddie. Stop talking," Greyson's voice was firm behind me, and I turned to see her in the doorway with her arms crossed tightly across her chest. "The shelter is waiting."

"Alright, alright," Eddie held up his hands and pulled open the driver door. "I'll be back tonight. Nice to meet ya, Gavin."

We watched him drive away before Greyson gave me a timid smile.

"Sorry about him. It seems like I'm always apologizing to you for the men in my life."

"They care about you. No apology needed," I said. I took a few steps closer until we were face to face. The wind caught the lemon that faintly radiated off her skin and bathed me in her bright and sunny scent.

"So, we've run into a caketastrophe with an order that's being picked up today. I need to get back to work, I'm sorry."

"Stop apologizing," I laughed. "I interrupted you at work. It's to be expected you have to get back to it."

"Yes, but I meant what I said. I like talking to you. I wish you could stay."

I absolutely wanted to talk to her more, to make up for the years I wasted.

"I could give you my phone number?" I asked. "Then you could talk to me whenever you wanted to."

Greyson swallowed hard. "My phone is dead. I wouldn't have any way to save it."

I moved into her personal space and reached behind her head to pull the pen out of her hair. Greyson sucked in a breath when I lifted her hand and raised my eyebrow in silent question. She barely nodded, and I flipped her hand and neatly wrote my number on the milky white skin of her inner wrist. She ran her finger over the purple ink as I reluctantly stepped back and handed her the pen.

"So it won't wash away before you can save it," I explained. "I'd really like for you to use it. Anytime. If you want to."

"I want you. To. I want to," Greyson shook her head. "I want to call you. I will use it."

"Good. I'll be looking forward to it," I said. She led me back through the kitchen with a promise to call soon. I was halfway home before I realized I hadn't gotten a cupcake.

I'd just have to go back tomorrow.

That's not weird.

CHAPTER 3

Greyson

"We're here! Begin downloading this conversation with Captain Clit Tease onto the best friend server *right now*," Mila's voice carried into the kitchen as the front door slammed behind them.

"Start from the beginning and don't leave out one second." Delaney didn't even set down the bottle of wine she carried before she picked up the opener. I started the replay of Gavin's visit, as I recounted the confusion that flared through me when I saw him with his hands shoved into the pockets of his jacket.

"It's not confusing. You want to take his big wood stick for a lap around the rink. It's called being horny," Mila responded as she poured half a bottle of wine into a glass and shoved it into my hand.

"It's not about that."

"That was not convincing in any form of the word."

"Three months ago, I was about to get married. It's not really appropriate for me to be thinking about being attracted to someone else right now," I took a long sip of Moscato. "But I swear, his beautifulness actually took my breath away when I saw him."

"You were about to marry a jackass who wouldn't go down on you. Wanting to hop onto Gavin is perfectly acceptable," Mila replied. I glared at her as Delaney changed the subject.

"What did your bizarre matrix tell you about his tastes?" Delaney asked. "What cupcake did he have to pop his Icing cherry? Or is he more of a cookie guy?"

I gasped as I realized I hadn't set him up with a sweet before he left the shop. That had never happened. Ever. One teaspoon of attention from him and I completely blanked.

"No way. You didn't do the thing? I don't believe it. You've never let someone come into your shop for the first time without filling out their report card." Delaney took her wine to the table and pulled my laptop in front of her.

"I started to, but then he said he wanted to talk to me. And when he was leaving, well he distracted me with this."

When I pushed up my sleeve and showed them the purple ink, complete with a smiley face incorporated into my infinity loop tattoo, they treated me to matching wide eyed looks of astonishment. Mila grabbed my arm and brought it up to her nose.

"Gavin Halstead wrote his phone number on your arm, like you're in an eighties rom-com? Why is that so sexy?"

"He told me he wants me to use it," I said. "Should I text him and ask him to come back for a cookie?"

"Oh, he would love to be offered your cookie," Mila replied with a wicked grin. Delaney rolled her eyes and turned the screen to show me the internet search she had done of photos of him. I pointed at a photo and Delaney clicked to enlarge. I remembered the game it was from, when he'd gotten into a fight that left his jersey half off and exposed miles of abs.

"So, what exactly did he come in for? What did he want to talk to you about?"

"He apologized," I said softly. I still couldn't wrap my head around that. Or the fact he didn't hate me like I'd thought for years.

"Apologize for what? You barely even know him outside of

the fact he was douche dingle's captain," Mila still refused to speak KJ's name, and came up with a different insulting moniker every time he was part of conversation.

"Exactly what I said. He said he was ashamed of the way he treated me. The way he ignored me. Because he was worried about how KJ would treat *me* if he didn't."

"That's honorable," Delaney said. "I always thought it was odd how rude he was when you were around. I obviously don't know him, but he doesn't seem like the asshole type."

Mila hung over my shoulder and zoomed in on the screen, so the entire thing was covered in pixelated abdominal muscles. Even blurry, the man was a masterpiece.

"Damn I wish you hadn't wasted so much time with Shitface Sullivan. You could have been riding this man like a Zamboni years ago."

I shook my head in exasperation. Sometimes I wished Mila could think about something beyond sex. Especially when I was trying to wade through whatever the hell that conversation was with Gavin and needing my best friends' input.

"We know this is still hard for you. It's only been three months since one of the biggest traumas of your life," Delaney murmured. "It's understandable if Gavin's flirtation makes you feel like you're doing something wrong. It's okay that you loved KJ."

On the scorecard of my life's worst moments, KJ's betrayal barely cracked the top five, but they didn't know that. I wished I could be open and explain why, even though it hurt, it didn't factor in the same category as a real trauma.

"No, it's not," I snapped. "It's not okay that I let some miserable jerk walk all over me for years because I was too scared to stand up for myself."

"We can't control our hearts, Greyson. Let yourself be sad and then move on. Don't wallow in the pain, but don't deny it either. You can't heal until you face it," Delaney said.

"He chose me for no reason other than to destroy me. Why

am I everyone's first choice for a human punching bag?" I finally gave voice to the question I'd held in since I walked into that room at the church. The sharp stab of failure at being face to face with his indiscretion had been my celestial punishment for daring to think I could have a normal, stable existence.

"He's a piece of shit, Greyson. I love you but you were no match for the masterful gaslighting of a narcissistic sociopath." Mila spit with venom. "You owe that bastard *nothing*. None of your time. None of your thoughts. You've always wanted it to be Gavin. Now it can be."

She clicked around on the computer until she found a photo that must have been snuck by a bunny after he was passed out in bed, only to be blasted on social media. While it was a huge invasion of privacy to post him in his underwear, starfished across the mattress on his stomach, I couldn't take my eyes off the screen. Mila ignored the wine on the counter and pulled martini glasses out of the cabinet, quickly mixing new drinks. She set an overflowing glass down in front of me a moment later, and I took one last look at Gavin's ass before I sipped the cocktail. My throat burned as the vodka made its way through my bloodstream and warmed my belly.

"Did you use a shot glass or a measuring cup for this?" I demanded with a cough.

"Sometimes the only answer to a problem is vodka," Delaney replied with a shrug as she took a hefty drink out of her glass. "The pricks with the dicks cause nothing but trouble."

Her own relationship had shattered since her husband threw down an ultimatum—him or her job. It hadn't worked out the way he expected.

"The dicks are all they're good for anyway," Mila said as she plucked an olive from her glass. "My two best friends are bad ass, successful females who were tethered to a couple of jerkoffs who couldn't see how lucky they were. Now you're free to find uncomplicated orgasms, and I *love* it."

Mila hadn't been in a relationship for as long as I'd known her, but that was completely by her own choice. She saw no use for the obstacles that came with feelings and deep connections.

"I'm proud of my accomplishments. I love that people recognize us and tell us they went to one of the restaurants we talked about on *Eat It*. And you know what? I love that we've got check marks behind our names on social media, okay?" Delaney slammed the remainder of her drink. "Did we get where we are because of a man? No. Fuck them and their disappointingly small dicks."

Mila and I exchanged a glance when Delaney took the vodka off the counter and took a shot straight from the bottle. I excused myself to make up the spare bedroom where she had taken to sleeping when she didn't want to go home to face her husband's absence. Their separation was just prolonging the inevitable. He was one of those men who couldn't handle having an accomplished wife. When we had been approached by the Baked Network about hosting their show *Eat It* he scoffed at the 'bargain basement' channel. But when we amassed a cult following he'd decided she was only worthy of his love if she was chained to their kitchen.

Delaney's chair was empty when I returned, and Mila was shaking her head at her phone.

"Bathroom," she answered the question I hadn't asked. "I need to run. There's a bachelorette party at the shop. Apparently, they ordered strippers and the entertainment are using their anatomy to stir the *cock*tails."

"That's disgusting," I shuddered, the thought of a penis flavored drink making my dirty martini a lot less desirable.

"And nowhere near legal, I'm guessing. That's got to be at least a handful of health code violations," Mila lifted her hair out of the collar of her leather jacket and slung her purse over her shoulder. "Before I go kick them out, I need to see what exactly I'm dealing with."

I could only imagine how involved she would be getting with her inspection. Her vulgar teashop by day/ speakeasy by night establishment was wild on the tamest of nights. If there was a party that her equally rowdy staff couldn't handle, I was sure I'd be hearing a great story tomorrow.

"Is there something in the water right now? The city is insane."

"It's Mercury. It's in retrograde or some shit." Mila kissed my cheek and waved down the hall at Delaney as she exited the bathroom. "We need to go out this weekend. After the game Saturday."

"Sure. If you let me wear my hockey clothes." I had barely waded back into the social pool after the summer and if she was going to force me to a club I would do it comfortably. Mila nodded with a grimace, undoubtedly already plotting my wardrobe change.

"Get some rest. Both of you. I'll talk to you tomorrow."

I turned the lock and watched out the window until she drove off before I flipped off the porch light.

"I can go home. I'm sure you're sick of me invading your space night after night," Delaney said behind me.

"You know you've always got a room here," I replied instantly. I'd be awake most of the night anyway, with or without a houseguest.

Delaney laughed quietly, a sad, muted sound. "How can our professional lives be so damn fulfilling at the same time our personal lives are dumpster fires?"

"Because it would be unfair to everyone else if we were this awesome *and* emotionally satisfied," I replied, a practiced smile plastered on my face. She hugged me and headed to her room, leaving me to retreat into my own. I locked the door and checked it twice before I crossed to the bathroom and turned on the shower. I took a long look at the ink on my arm before I washed it away, and the stress and emotion of the day slid down the drain with the soapy water. By the time I stepped out I was both exhausted and energized. I dressed quickly, and my heart pounded every time I looked at my phone. The urge was too strong, and I could barely breathe by the time his deep voice filtered through the line.

"Hello?"

All of my bravado evaporated, and I hung up before I had a chance to say something truly embarrassing. I'd barely had a chance to toss my phone across the bed when it rang ominously, and his number lit up the screen. I panicked and quickly declined the call as I closed my eyes and breathed deeply at the silence. I'd just about relaxed when the chime of a text made my eyes pop open.

GAVIN

> I know you're near your phone Greyson. I'm calling back in 3 ... 2...

I dejectedly answered as it rang again and figured the best way to deal with the embarrassment was to face it head on.

"Hey, Canada. Sorry ... I don't know why I called you. I'm sure you didn't mean for me to blow up your phone when you gave me your number."

"I think that's the point," Gavin teased, and I was glad he couldn't see the heat that his voice drew to my cheeks.

"Funny, smartass. How did you know it was me?"

"When you sent me to voicemail ... rude, by the way, I listened to the greeting to see who had just hung up on me. Imagine my surprise when I heard it was you."

"I'm sorry. I had too much to drink and since I had a brand-new phone number to drunk dial I figured why not," I cringed at my lame attempt at a joke. "Anyway, um, so the next time you're downtown stop into the shop and I'll get you something sweet. It'll be on me. I mean, not *on* me, like a dessert buffet and me as the table," I paused, mortified by the words tumbling out of my mouth. "Not that you'd be interested in eating me. Off me. Dammit. I meant, I realized after you left, I didn't get you a cupcake or cookie. You'd love my cookie. Cookies. Oh. Kay. Sorry to bother you."

Gavin was silent on the other end of the line for so long I was convinced I'd ruined any chance he'd ever pick up the phone again.

"I am certain you are correct. I'll look forward to your cookies." When he finally spoke, his voice was warm and smooth, with just a hint of rough timbre at the end. "I should apologize. I'm the one who barged in on you at work."

I smiled at the memory of looking up to find him in the middle of my bakery. The encounter would provide inspiration for days.

"It was a surprise, sure. But nothing that warrants an apology."

"Well, I'll make sure to stop in and bother you again sometime," Gavin said. "Is your drunk dialing a result of a fun night or a miserable night?"

"A little of both?" I sighed. "Can I ask you something?"

"Go for it."

"Did KJ ever love me?" I didn't miss Gavin's sharp intake of breath, and I tripped over myself to explain what I meant. "Like, was I always just a game, or did he ever care? Do you know? Maybe I don't want to know. Even though I think I already do."

"Why are you thinking of this now? Did I do this? Coming to see you, did I hurt you?"

I laid down on the bed with a heavy sigh and held the phone between my ear and the sheet. "Of course not. But I did start thinking of things because of your visit."

"I think he's just an immature guy, Greyson. He doesn't understand how to cherish a woman who deserves everything. He doesn't know how to put someone else first. It wasn't you. It was him. That I can promise you." Gavin artfully sidestepped my initial question, which gave me the answer I needed. "He's not the man you want to share your life with."

"He never was," I admitted quietly. Gavin went silent on the other end, and I wondered if he could read through the words, the confession I didn't have the courage to bluntly make. "Anyway. Thank you for clearing the air. I hated not knowing what I'd done to make you despise me so much. I'm glad to find out it wasn't me."

"It never was," Gavin replied. A knock filtered through the line somewhere in the background. "Hold on just a sec."

A feminine voice entered the space and asked him if he wanted cheddar or caramel popcorn with the movie. After he told her she should know it was *always* caramel, I was both inspired with a new popcorn cupcake and mortified I'd interrupted him on a date. Maybe a little jealous.

"I'm back."

"I'm sorry, I didn't mean to keep you from your date, you should have told me you were busy. I'll let you go. I'll talk to you ... some other time," I rushed through the words, never in more of a hurry to get off the phone.

"My sister would be disgusted if she knew you just called her my date," Gavin replied smoothly. His sister. That shouldn't have made me so happy. "But I do need to go. I've already put off watching this movie with her four times."

"Sure, yeah, of course. Sorry for calling. Then hanging up."

"Do you mind if I call and hang up on you sometime?" Gavin's question was laced with the smirk I could picture.

"I think I'd like that Canada. Enjoy your movie."

He groaned, clearly not looking as forward to movie night as his sister was. "Two hours of horticulturists solving crimes. It will be the highlight of my year. See you at the game?"

"Yes, I'll be there." I nodded as if he could see me, then shook my head in more private embarrassment.

"Good. It wasn't the same playing when you weren't there.

And Greyson? Don't give him anymore of your thoughts. He doesn't deserve them."

"Okay Gavin. I won't," I answered. The weight of the promise was heavy off my tongue. He made me feel a fresh, new hope that I didn't know what to do with.

"Have a good night, Greyson. Sleep well. Don't let him steal your happiness in your dreams like he stole it in the light."

CHAPTER 4
Gavin

Beep. Beep. Beep.

As I was pulled from unconsciousness, I slapped around in the dark to silence the alarm. Instead, I knocked it onto the floor and threw a pillow on top of it to drown out the obnoxious sound. It worked for three seconds, until my brain woke up fully and realized it was the day I dreaded the most. A date on a calendar shouldn't arbitrarily dictate a mood, but for the past fifteen years this one had. The one saving grace was the fact I'd see Greyson later. I hadn't slept well in the days since our late-night conversation and debated how stupid it would be to go back to the bakery, just to see her face.

When I'd emerged from my room after we hung up, Mattie demanded every single detail. My sister knew all about my almost decade-long crush. The first time I saw Greyson, I was a rookie and she was nothing more than a legend's granddaughter. The opportunity to speak to her hadn't presented itself until years later. When we'd been at the same event, I'd texted Mattie immediately to tell her the universe had finally given me a sign. Unfortunately, that sign turned out to be a dead end. I didn't have time to cross the room before KJ had moved in and my chance was gone. He was a piece of shit, but he knew how to charm women.

He said all the right things to convince them they were the best thing that ever happened to him. Then he yanked back on the leash and left them to dangle and wonder what they'd done to make him step out. Mattie had encouraged me not to give up, but I hadn't listened and spent the next five years beating myself up over the lapse in judgment.

I dragged my hands over my face before I swung my legs over the side of the bed and stretched my arms. Mattie would sleep until late morning if she wasn't disturbed, so I took care to move quietly through the hall and downstairs to my gym. By the time I was halfway through my twenty-minute yoga routine, my tension had melted from my shoulders. I moved methodically through the poses, centered and calm when I stepped onto the treadmill. I bypassed the stereo system for ear buds and slipped them in. I wasn't used to having anyone else in the house, and even though Mattie would never complain I still wanted her to feel comfortable during her visit.

I ran until my legs were weak and convinced myself the moisture that ran down my cheeks was more sweat than unconscious sadness as I hopped off the machine. My heart leapt painfully against my chest when I looked up to see Mattie in the doorway.

"Jesus Christ Matilda! You scared the shit out of me. Did I wake you?"

"Nope, I've showered already. I thought we could go grab breakfast before morning skate?"

"Sure. Everything okay?"

She smiled kindly and crossed her arms as she leaned against the doorframe.

"I know it's a hard day for you."

And now her surprise visit made complete sense. Why my nose prickled with emotion I wasn't sure. Mattie had always been the one to read me even when I thought my book was closed.

"That's why you came to Chicago."

"I mean, celebrating your birthday with you was a factor but yes. Asher wasn't as close to her as you were, so he doesn't get it.

I'm here so you can grieve openly, without any worry about being 'on' for your team."

"I feel guilty. She was the first thing I thought of when I woke up, but I'm not as...shattered as I usually am."

Mattie moved into the room and pulled me against her in a tight hug. "Because your mind is on someone else. That's a good thing."

"Why doesn't it feel that way?"

"Because you've always tried to carry the weight of the world on your shoulders. You've held yourself responsible for Olive's death since you were twelve years old, when there was nothing anyone could have done. Why do you feel the need to torture yourself?"

"It just isn't fair."

"You're right. But look at it this way. Olive taught you to pay attention to what the stars and the universe are telling you, right? So maybe she's trying to communicate something to you right now. This thing with Greyson—there's a reason for it, and maybe Olive is pulling some strings from Heaven."

Olive had been the most enthusiastic astrology buff I had ever known, and I thought it was lame until it was all I had left of her. The night sky became my security blanket and the stars told me the stories I could no longer hear from her lips. I had no doubt she would have ended up an astronomer or cosmologist, had the universe she loved so much not pulled a horrifying shift and taken her at eleven years old.

"That's a nice idea," I murmured as I ruffled her hair and headed towards the door. "I'm going to grab a shower, then we can head out."

Her eyes showed me she knew I wasn't as okay as I tried to let on but didn't press it as I made my way back to my room. After a quick shower I pulled out the photo album I kept pushed in the back of my dresser. The dark blue star fabric had started to pull away from the cardboard cover, brittle from being opened and closed over the years. The half full album was abruptly forgotten when Olive died. Since she was the one who had lovingly made it for me, it didn't feel right to add memories to it that she couldn't be a part of. I ran my fingers over the last photo, a picture of us taken an hour before she died. It was easy to see how tired she was. She was ready. The anniversary of Olive's death didn't hurt as much as the years went by, but it still crushed me when I thought of the last moments of her life. Now that I was an adult, I couldn't fathom the difficulty her parents must have had when they allowed me to stay with her and hold her hand as the last breaths left her lungs.

"Miss you," I whispered to the faded photo as I wiped away the tear that fell onto the protective plastic sleeve and tucked the album back into the spot it would stay until next year.

Mattie and I drove to my favorite restaurant, a small locally owned bar that served the best brunch I'd found in the city. After being featured on television, they were no longer the well-kept secret I'd gotten used to, but their pancakes were worth a longer wait. There was only one open table when we walked in and the owner, Shirley, held up a hand in a wave when she saw us.

"Hey Gavin! Go scoop up that seat. I'll be right with you!"

Mattie followed me to the booth in the back and slid in. She craned her neck to see the hanging plants and baskets of bright, fresh flowers.

"Gorgeous," she murmured, her eyes transfixed on the vibrant orange blooms of a flower.

I watched, fascinated by Mattie's adoration. "What is it? What's it called?"

"Sun Star," Mattie smiled softly, a private moment of appreciation for the beauty of the living thing in the window. "Or Star of Bethlehem. It's unusual for it to be blooming now though. Interesting."

Shirley appeared at our table and smiled brightly as she slapped down my requisite cup of coffee.

"Gavin has never brought a lady friend in here. You must be something special."

ICING

"Second time this week someone has mistaken me for his paramour. Disgusting." Mattie scrunched her nose up at me while I gave her an unimpressed eye roll.

"This is my little sister," I explained as I poured a packet of sugar in my coffee. Shirley grinned and handed Mattie a menu.

"Ah. I can see the resemblance now. It's about time he found a nice woman, don't you think little sister?"

"We're working on it," Mattie answered with a wink. She ignored my kick under the table and pointed up at the flower she was so mesmerized with. "That shouldn't be in bloom at this time of year. Is it a hybrid or something?"

Shirley looked up at the Sun Star and shook her head. "Craziest thing. She never blooms now, but a couple days ago I saw her peeking out. I guess she just decided to grace us with her stunning presence twice this year."

Mattie glanced at me pointedly.

"That flower symbolizes joy and optimism. Seems like a pretty clear sign to me." Mattie looked up at Shirley with a grin. "The woman he's been in love with for years is finally single and coming to watch him play tonight."

I threw up my hands in frustration, embarrassed at their laughter.

"She'd be lucky to have you," Shirley replied, as she took Mattie's order and verified mine before she left us alone at the table.

"Was that really necessary?" I grumbled into my coffee, the tips of my ears burning.

"Oh absolutely." Mattie laughed, as she blew the paper off the end of her straw at my forehead. "So, what's your plan with Greyson this evening?"

The thought of seeing her sitting on the glass, chewing her fingernails in adorable tension when the score was too close for comfort made me impatient to get to the arena.

"I don't have a plan."

"You need to. Call her after the game and ask her to come out

39

with you. Or call her *before* and make plans for after so she knows she wasn't an afterthought."

"I don't want to come on too strong." Greyson appeared fragile at first glance, but her intricacies were reminiscent of the most elaborate spider web imaginable. Looking at her, you would think you could destroy her hard work with one well timed swipe of a hand through her web. But try and you would end up tangled in her orbit. The first time I saw her was during my first NHL game. Jonah Park had held the same seats on the glass since he'd retired, and his grandkids were his without fail companions. She was bundled up in an oversized sweatshirt pulled up to her chin and hat pulled down over her forehead. All I could really see were piercing blue eyes that were so clear they were almost translucent. A lot of sadness swirled around in them and the one time they connected with mine it took my breath away. I spent the following years avoiding her eyes when she was there and missing her presence when she wasn't.

The Falcons Legacy event was the moment I had no choice but to speak to her when I literally walked into her and spilled my drink on her. It was one of the most awkward moments of my life to date and even now, I cringed when I thought about it. She had been gracious, repeatedly telling me it was fine and that no one would notice. Jonah came over and rescued me, officially introducing us. Greyson shyly extended her hand to me, mine clammy and wet when I took hers in it. When she reclaimed her own and tried to subtly wipe it off on her skirt, I couldn't have been more embarrassed and escaped as quickly as I could to call Mattie.

After a quick pep talk, I had worked up enough courage to ask Greyson out. But KJ had gotten to her and worked his magic in that handful of minutes. Two weeks later they were official. One day after that, I walked in on him screwing a random girl in our hotel room before a road game. He didn't seem to think there was anything wrong with it and I used my captaincy status to demand if Asher wasn't there, I'd have a room to myself. I had no interest in witnessing his infidelity on a weekly basis. The only way I was able to keep from beating the shit out of him was to distance myself from their relationship and pretend she didn't exist. Now that I was in the position to get to know Greyson, I wasn't going to do anything to screw it up.

"So, you're going to awkwardly stare at her and not speak like you've been doing for half of your adult life?" Mattie's voice brought me out of my reminiscing as our food was delivered to the table.

"What do you suggest?" I asked as I dug into the plate of pancakes piled high with bacon.

"Smile at her, flirt with her during the game. Then, after, call and see if she wants to meet you out. Make it friendly. There's plenty of time to make your move but start out as a male friend she can count on." Mattie reached over and snatched a stray piece of bacon, quickly retracting her hand before I stabbed her with my fork.

"Maybe. I just don't want to put any pressure on her. I've spent years ignoring her, now all of a sudden I ask her to come to an after party that I know for a fact she hates?"

"She called you mere hours after you gave her your phone number. She wants to get to know you. Trust me."

"The wedding aside, she lost her grandpa not that long ago. It's a lot for someone to handle."

"They were really close huh?"

"Yeah, she came to every single home game with him, when she wasn't away at school. They were inseparable."

Mattie pursed her lips and gave a slight shake of her head.

"That is a mountain of trauma in a short time. She could probably use a friend."

"I don't want to be another person who causes her pain," I replied as I reached into my wallet to pay for breakfast. Mattie methodically cracked each finger on both hands as she stretched her legs out under the table.

"You don't have it in you to be that person. Just be you. She won't even know she's falling in love with you until it's already done. I guarantee it."

My eyes flitted to the Sun Star, its beauty radiating and capturing the attention of people who might not usually notice a flower in a window. Quietly captivating, its presence was understated but magical and once it was noticed it was impossible to look away.

"I can always hope."

CHAPTER 5
Gavin

Every time I looked at her, she was laughing. She had kind of smiled at me when I came out for warmups, a timid turning up of half her mouth while she hid the rest of it behind her beer glass. She watched me, eyes following my skates with every slice of blades on ice. The only time she looked away was when I stretched. I had a clear view of her from my position and she didn't avert her eyes when I worked my back, but when I stretched my groin, her eyes snapped shut and she turned to the woman next to her so quickly it was like she'd been hit with an electrical current.

I'd seen her friends before. They accompanied her to games when her brother couldn't. KJ loved those nights, and he would sit on the bench going into explicit detail about what he'd like to do with his fiancée's best friends if he had the opportunity. The dark haired one kept looking at me, grinning until I met her eyes before pointedly moving her gaze over to Greyson. When warmups were over, I was relieved to have the chance to get my shit together before the game. When I glanced at her as I hustled off the ice and found her looking back, I was so surprised I tripped on the rubber mat and fell against Asher's back.

When we came back out for the start of the game, I managed

to keep my eyes forward during the anthem. That resolve weakened by the time I took center ice for the opening faceoff. Remembering our first real conversation I battled hard for the puck and skated past her after the play, holding up one gloved finger. She cocked her head to the side in obvious confusion but by my third faceoff win she had it figured out and laughed when I shook three fingers in front of her. When I lost one, she frowned and gave me a thumbs down as I shook my head with a grin, determined to win them all for the rest of the game. When I met up at center ice for the puck drop after we scored late in the second period Duff Rockwell, the captain for Nashville, sneered a toothless grin at me.

"You picked up where Sullivan left off, huh? Those pouty lips she just gave you would look great wrapped around my cock."

I didn't think before I threw my stick and ripped off my gloves. The instant eruption of cheers and yells from the fans not used to seeing their captain fight barely registered. Duff was always up for a battle and pulled off his gloves before he took a swing at the side of my face. I ducked out of the way and he caught my helmet, yelling an expletive. I took advantage and swung hard, landing the punch on the side of his jaw. His mouth guard went flying and if I wasn't mistaken, he was short another tooth.

"What the fuck Gavin!" Duff yelled, as blood sprayed from his mouth. The noise in the arena had become overwhelming and the glass vibrated under the palms of ravenous hockey fans.

"Talk about her again! I'll do this all fucking night!"

Duff charged at me and got me in a headlock, speaking into my helmet as we fell.

"I didn't know you were actually screwing her! My bad Halstead!"

"I'm not," I yelled, as we wrestled around on the ice. Duff wasn't a bad guy, and we usually got along pretty well, so this was definitely out of character.

"Then what the fuck man?"

"She's been shit on enough. I'll fight anyone who talks like that about her."

"You're not fooling anyone. Everyone knows you've wanted her for years." Duff caught my eye with an elbow, and I felt the skin split a second before warm blood hit my cheek. The fact he caused an injury pissed me off *almost* as much as him daring to have Greyson's name pass his lips.

"I'll kill you, you irrelevant piece of shit!"

The refs finally had enough and pulled us off each other. Duff chirped around spitting blood and my teammates bounced their sticks off the boards as I skated past to take my seat in the penalty box.

"Number 89 Chicago, number 3, Nashville, five for fighting," the referee thundered. He threw an arm towards the penalty box as the whistles and cheers of the fans became deafening. Asher skated by with my stick, and I slammed it violently against the bench when he handed it off with a grin. The towel I dragged across my face came away soaked red as I mopped up the blood. I knew it would need stitches, and that pissed me off more.

Greyson arched an eyebrow as she met my eyes across the ice. I lifted a shoulder in a shrug, already embarrassed by my asinine behavior. I was the captain of the team and prided myself on leading by example, in addition to the fact that she wasn't my girl-friend. Even if she were, dropping gloves over a woman during a game was ... not ideal. I had no reason to get so angry, but that didn't stop the rage when I thought of Duff mentioning her mouth on his dick. I threw a furious glare at the other penalty box and gave him the finger, which caused the crowd to again erupt in raucous cheers.

By the time the penalty ended blood had seeped through the butterfly bandage I'd been administered in the box. I caught her eye as I headed off the ice to the locker room and she bit her lip, looking so damn sexy I forgot to be angry. By the time the third period started I was calm and managed to get through the rest of the game without incident. As soon as I got to my locker, I texted her an invitation to the after party. She didn't respond, so I left irritated with myself for the way the night played out.

At the bar, I was lost in my own mind, and the dull throb in my head was nothing compared to the thoughts that swirled like a tornado. The stormy, powerful funnel of emotional upheaval was Olive. Guilt held me captive on this day the same way it had for fifteen years. My rational side still wasn't able to accept the fact there was nothing I could have done to save her. The eye of my storm was Greyson, just the idea of her causing an eerie stillness to claim my thoughts. It was confusing as hell and I was about to call it a night when my phone buzzed on the table. Asher craned his neck and looked at me with wide eyes when he read the screen.

"Greyson is calling you. Wait. Are you and her ...?

I dove for the phone and grabbed my coat, my mood significantly lifted. "I'm out, I'll see you later."

I hurriedly rushed away before Asher could pin me down and force the truth out of me. We didn't keep secrets from each other, ever. It had been that way since we were four years old. I'd never had anything I didn't want him to know. Until now.

"Hey, what's up?" I answered, weaving through the crowded bar.

"Canada. I didn't see your message until I was across town. I would have loved to spend time with you. I mean, I like to drink. Shit. What I'm trying to say is, if we weren't twenty minutes away, I'd totally come but Mila drove and she's working on a one-night stand, so she'd rather not abandon ship, you know? Thanks for the invite, but I won't keep you from the party."

I pushed through the door onto the sidewalk outside and shouted into the phone, misjudging the noise difference from inside to out.

"No! Don't hang up! I was just leaving!"

"You're leaving already? *Bo-ring*," Greyson teased.

"That's me. Boring Captain Canada," I answered, sliding into my truck. "Long day. I'd rather be home than at an after party if there's no one there to tell me how much my faceoff percentage sucks."

"Do you want to talk about it?" she asked softly. I did. About everything. With her.

"Where are you?" I asked. "Do you want to get a cup of coffee? I could pick you up."

When Greyson didn't immediately respond I inwardly kicked myself. It probably sounded like I was asking her on a date in the middle of the night. AKA: a booty call. I couldn't say the idea of her in my bed had never crossed my mind, but in this particular moment that was not what I'd meant to convey.

"I thought you wanted to go home."

"I want to be wherever you are." I dropped my head against the seat and hit my phone against my forehead.

Smooth.

"Oh! Um, I want to be with you, too. I mean ... I like coffee," Greyson groaned softly. "I'm so bad at speaking. I'm sorry. I'd love to get coffee with you. I'll get myself there. Where should I meet you?"

CHAPTER 6
Gavin

"Canada! You sure know how to party," Greyson's voice carried across the mostly empty diner where I was already waiting. She slid into the booth and shook off her jacket as the waitress came by to take our order. Greyson looked up at her after she lingered by my side of the table to offer me dessert. She smiled with a show of teeth, and the slight glassiness of her eyes gave away the fact she was more than a little drunk.

"He's good. He's got all the sugar he needs."

The waitress reddened and scurried away, and I laughed out loud. Greyson shook her head in disgust.

"I'm sorry, but how the hell does she know we aren't on a date? I mean, I realize I'm seen as the doormat of society after what my fiancé did to me but come on." Greyson drummed her fingernails on the scratched wood table and finally looked at me. "That was totally inappropriate of me. Maybe you want some of her desserts. Oh shit, I just screwed up your chances of getting laid by that bunny. I'm sorry Canada, I'll go smooth it over so you can make plans to eat her pie."

She started to get up and I leaned over and placed my hand over hers.

"I don't like pie. I'm more of a cupcake guy."

Greyson's eyes dropped to where I still had my hand on her.

"Cupcake guy, huh? Mine are the best. You won't find anything better to put in your mouth. But you would know that if I hadn't spaced when you came in and actually given you some. I can't *believe* I did that. It's never happened. You bring out the nerves in me, I guess. I've got a bit of a buzz on so consider this my pre-apology for the stupid shit I'm probably going to say."

"Out drinking something that's not coffee?" I asked as a different waitress returned with ours. Greyson must have successfully scared the other one away. I liked the idea of another woman thinking I was taken by her.

"Is it obvious? Am I being loud? Obnoxious? I lose control over my decibels when the vodka hits my bloodstream."

"No. You're perfect."

Greyson blushed and dipped her head, picking up her coffee before immediately setting it back down. "My bakery is closed on Sunday, so Saturdays are the only time I can have as much fun as I want without the repercussions affecting my job. I get to work around four in the morning, so it's not advisable to get wasted during the week. Tonight is the first time since ... the summer ... that I've gone out. It's apparently easier to drink too much when you're doing it at a bar with your best friends than at home on the couch."

So, she really hadn't left her house much after the wedding. I'd gone home to Canada shortly after it happened and had wondered how she held up after KJ got traded and life returned to "normal" for her. Asher had tried his best to get me information but there was none to be had. She had basically hibernated.

"Is that who was with you at the game?"

"Yes. Mila and Delaney. We met in pastry school and clicked instantly. We're really different personality wise, but I think maybe that's why we get along so well. Mila helps us remember to have fun. Not take ourselves so seriously all the time, you know?

Like tonight, for example, she met a guy and literally charmed the pants off him.

"Me, I could never do that. I'm more of a one man show, although the man I chose didn't feel the same. I'm surprised I don't have a disease after being with KJ. Of course, I wasn't having sex at all, including with him at the end, so I guess it makes sense. Well, and the seldom times we did, we used condoms. *Always.* Zero times unprotected, because I just had a feeling his semen was crawling with remnants of his infidelity," Greyson paused and shook her head as she whispered fiercely, arguing with herself. "Oh my God Greyson, *shut up.* "

I really didn't know what to say to that, since the thought of KJ anywhere near her made me sick to my stomach, and I couldn't very well tell her she was right about the particles clogging up his dick hole.

"I don't need to tell you. You knew all about it. Just like everyone. Anyway ... maybe this wasn't a good idea." Greyson drew out the 'a' in anyway as she clammed up. Her hands shook when she picked up her cup, and the dark liquid sloshed over the rim and onto the sleeve of her sweatshirt.

"His behavior is on him. You have nothing to be ashamed or embarrassed about." I kept my eyes on her as I stirred sugar into my coffee. She met them, hers full of uncertainty and sadness.

"I wasn't so oblivious I didn't know. I'm not sure why it's important to me that you know that. I just ... it was easier to stay," Greyson set her cup down and traced an invisible pattern on the tabletop with a pink glittered fingernail. "Damn, I sound pathetic."

"Don't do that," I murmured, as I interrupted her table drawing by dropping my hand in front of her finger. "You got out when it mattered. I can't stand that asshole, but I'll give him that he can be charming. People like him thrive on the game of deception. KJ is a chameleon. He turns into whoever he needs to be in a moment. Good people, caring generous people—people like you

—want to believe there's good in everyone. Unfortunately, it isn't always true."

"How did you get so smart?" Greyson asked with a small smile.

"Years of therapy."

"Well, we've got that in common," she said. "Do you still go?"

A waitress came by to refill our cups, but my attention stayed on the woman across from me.

"When I can. It's not as easy anymore, but I do make it a priority to check in at least once a month. I make sure my physical health is in order, I can't neglect the mental health. It's just as important."

"I think I love you," Greyson blurted out. I choked on my coffee and coughed loudly.

"I mean, not like in love with you. I hardly know you. That would be insane."

"Would it?" I asked with a straight face. I should not have said it. But the look on her face made it worth it.

"I *meant* it is so refreshing to be with a man who doesn't shame me for being in therapy," Greyson grimaced. "Not that I'm *with* you. Of course not. I just keep making this worse."

"I can't say I'm surprised to hear he was a douchebag about that, too," I replied. "I started therapy when I was twelve, and it was the best thing that ever happened. I can never say enough about the importance of taking care of yourself."

Greyson looked relieved I had maneuvered the conversation away from her unintentional come-ons. She let out a long breath, and the flame in her cheeks faded.

"That's when I started, too. My dad died in the line of duty, and it destroyed me. Then the hits just kept coming. When we moved in with my grandparents, they got me into therapy first thing. It saved my life."

"I take it you still go?"

"Oh yeah. My brother followed my dad into law enforcement. CPD rather than FBI, but the acronyms are all the same to me.

PTSD. Trevor is the most important person in my life. He's all the family I have left. If I didn't have a therapist to help me bring myself back from the edge about his job, I'd be a neurotic mess," she paused. "More than I am, anyway."

"I'm sorry to hear about your dad," I said softly. "I lost someone at that age, too. Not a parent, just a friend, but it was the first time I dealt with death. I can't imagine what you went through."

Greyson looked up and a sweet, shy smile covered her face. She reached across the table and gently squeezed my hand. "Thank you, Gavin. And I'm very sorry for your loss as well. I think losing a friend would be just as difficult, in a different way."

A shutter click of a phone camera sounded behind us, and Greyson's head shot up. She pulled her hand off mine so quickly it was as if I had burned her. We both realized the phone was not aimed at us, but the moment had been broken.

"Do you want to go for a walk?" She asked suddenly. "It's getting busy in here and I don't want to be the topic of a podcast tomorrow. I'm not ready to say goodnight, but I don't want to be all stressed every time I see a phone. Not that this is a date, but it's been a rough summer with my name on Biscuits in the Basket. Therapy may be helpful, but if they post a photo of me holding your hand and concoct a story about a secret affair between us, I might just lose my mind."

"Social media makes everything into something. You get used to it when you have to, but I can see why you're over it. So, yeah, let's go," I said as I dropped a ten on the table. She allowed me to help her into her coat and looked up at me.

"Thanks, Canada. You're quite the gentleman, but you're not getting in my pants. Thought I'd just go ahead and get that out of the way."

"What a coincidence," I held the door open as she stepped outside. "I was just about to tell you not to get any ideas. My jeans are locked up tight and can't be accessed."

Her gaze slid over my straight face and the side of her mouth turned up in a grin.

"You're wearing a very expensive suit, not jeans," Greyson murmured, her eyes doing a quick sweep down my body. "But seriously. No pants will be breached."

"I got it Greyson. It's just a walk. I'm not trying to sleep with you. I'm not a savage."

CHAPTER 7
Greyson

"So, I need to say this. Not that I think you'd ever be interested in me, but I'm not looking to be a notch on anymore Falcons hockey sticks. If that's what you're hoping for, we should just stop this right now."

Did that actually just come out of my mouth? Gavin pressed his lips together and tilted his head, taking enough time to respond I started to panic.

"Honestly, I don't have any female friends. Any woman I meet just wants to hop on my dick and then Snapchat a picture of me passed out in bed."

"Classy bunch of ladies you surround yourself with," I scrunched my nose in annoyance and flipped my hair over my shoulder. "I think I've seen one of those photos. Your bracelets gave you away."

Gavin raised his stitched up eyebrow at the same time I realized my slip. I had just admitted I not only looked at pictures of him online, but paid enough attention to his accessories to know it was him when his face wasn't showing.

"I didn't say I allowed multiple riders on the Halstead train, just that the women I come across only want that from me."

"You just referred to your dick as a train, Gavin Halstead. That is a clear implication there are multiple riders."

He shook his head with a smile, as he took a step closer to me.

"The train hasn't left the station in quite a while."

The thrill that shot through me at that statement was unwarranted, considering how I'd just told him I was not in the running to be a conquest. I froze and stared at him, an eerie handful of moments where neither of us blinked before I turned my focus to the angry waves crashing against the lake wall.

"What do you want from me?"

"Your friendship."

"Why?"

"The few times you and I have had real conversations I've left wishing I could talk to you all the time. I can be me, which is something I don't usually have the luxury to do. I want to be your friend; I want to call you to complain when I have a shitty day and have you tell me to quit being a pussy and suck it up. I want to sit at a bar and drink beer and critique the other teams in the league with you. I want your opinion on my game. I don't want to get in your pants."

Ouch. I had been the one to draw that boundary, but still. Ouch.

"I can totally give you that, Canada. Would be nice to have a man I can trust besides my brother."

We started walking again and I bumped his arm with my shoulder as I waved a hand at his face.

"So. What was that all about?"

"It was nothing."

"I've seen you play about four hundred games, give or take. You've never thrown down like that. Fights, sure. But that was extreme, and the view from where I was sitting didn't indicate any reason for it. What's the deal?"

Gavin averted his eyes and absently ran a finger over the bandage that served to make him hotter than he already was.

"Greyson, leave it alone."

Well that attempt at dominance was sexier than sin. And not going to work.

"Did he say something about me?"

Gavin stopped walking abruptly and shook off his coat when I shivered. My half-hearted protest when he dropped it over my shoulders earned me a stern look that left me feeling something unfamiliar low in my belly. He pulled it close around me and leaned into my ear.

"He did. Something I did not appreciate. I let him know."

Violence, generally, caused me to turn into myself and completely shut down. Growing up as I did has a tendency to do that to a person. But knowing he threw down, in the middle of a game, for me, did something strange to my heart. It felt like a thousand strings were pulling together at the same time. I boldly reached for him and touched the stitches above his eye.

"Thank you for defending me. I have never known what that's like, and I have to say, it feels really good," I said. "I can see your wheels turning, endlessly, about your lapse in judgment. It happens, Gavin. You *are* a hockey player. Fighting is kind of part of the job."

"Not for me. I'm a lover, not a fighter," Gavin grinned.

"I'm totally making that a cupcake," I exclaimed. I reached into my purse and came out with my notebook. "Lover Not A Fighter. It's going to be the special Monday. In honor of the captain losing control."

I took his sleeve, and drug him over to a bench. I pushed him down and dropped down next to him. The silence as I scratched out notes was comfortable, and I mumbled to myself in the way I never noticed until it was pointed out. Seeing as Gavin was not used to my work brain, I pulled my thoughts inward until I was ready for input.

"Would you rather eat a cupcake with flavors that traditionally go together or one with ingredients that aren't necessarily a match? Should I go with the 'lover' or the 'fighter' in terms of flavor?"

His confusion was clear, and I took a mental picture of the moment, in addition to a note on a new page. There was more than one inspirational recipe happening at once.

"You don't know what I'm talking about do you?" I asked, as I put a pause on my notes.

"Not a clue. But please teach me. Because whatever is going on in there," Gavin paused, and wiggled his finger at my forehead, "is beyond incredible to watch from the outside."

Every word he spoke hit so far into my heart it was like he had found a new dimension of my soul I didn't know existed. I had never felt like I was enough, and Gavin made everything I did seem like I hung the moon.

"My inspiration comes from everywhere. When it hits it's all I can think about, so I have to write it down in the moment or I won't be able to focus on anything else. That's why I carry a notebook," I tapped the pen against the glittered cover of my notebook. "The baking actually came out of therapy. I had nothing to focus on. I had a hard time trusting people, so I didn't have many friends. I had so many triggers I was afraid to read or watch movies, in case something hit me I wasn't expecting. Baking provided an outlet for all my thoughts and emotions that I couldn't put into words. It stuck, I guess. Every emotion I have comes out into a recipe. Every moment in my life that matters, becomes a treat."

"I love that," Gavin murmured. He caught my eyes and held me captive. "So, my fighting over you is a life moment to be remembered?"

My heart stuttered against my ribs, and I swore it stopped beating. Did I tell the truth? That every word he had spoken to me since he showed up at Icing was seared into my consciousness like a brand? That he had made me feel more loved in the week I had 'known' him than KJ did in the four years we were together?

Too risky.

"I guess you just need to come in on Monday and find out."

CHAPTER 8
Gavin

"Alright, they're on the way," I looked up from my phone, where Delaney had texted to let me know they had just left the Delta Center. In the month since our coffee date, I had learned quite a bit about Greyson Park. One being her love of a British pop singer who had gone solo from a now defunct boy band, and two that she was attending his concert when he was in town on her birthday. She told me about that with plenty of time for me to make a plan for a 'party' afterwards.

"I knew you were a romantic fuck, but this goes beyond even what I expected," Asher spun his old-fashioned glass between his palms.

"Shut up," I said under my breath, with a sideways glance at the bar, where Trevor sat with Eddie. They both heard Asher's loud mouth, judging by the smirks that turned up theirs. "Is this too much? It is, isn't it? She's going to think I'm psychotic."

"Relax, Halstead. It's actually pretty awesome. More thought than that jackass Sullivan put into her their entire relationship," Asher said.

"She's going to freeze," Trevor threw in. "And possibly shut down a little. Don't give up on her though."

I was stunned by his interjection, and the buzzing phone in my hand gave me a reason to look away.

"They're here," I said, as nerves and excitement battled for space in my gut. The small group gathered around the table and watched as Greyson descended the stairs into the speakeasy.

"SURPRISE!"

Her eyes widened as she took a step back and bumped into Mila, who grinned behind her.

"What ... why ... how is ... what?"

I moved forward and stood in front of her nervously.

"I thought you might like to have some drinks with your friends after lusting for Oscar Miles all night."

"I ... this is ... I don't usually celebrate my birthday. I don't know what to say."

"You say thank you, RayRay," Trevor appeared and gathered her into a hug. He whispered something to her, and her look of bewilderment shifted to polite acceptance.

I fucked up. She wasn't overwhelmed with excitement. She wasn't touched by my thoughtfulness. She didn't celebrate her birthday and I would know that if I hadn't pushed her away for years.

"Thank you," Greyson said robotically, a forced smile plastered across her lips. I was at a loss for words and ended up just staring awkwardly at her. Asher came up and scooped her into a bear hug.

"Let's get you a drink. I want to hear *all about* the concert. I heard Oscar's songs are all about a certain red lipped superstar. Do we think it's true?"

He winked over his shoulder as they made their way to the bar. His rescue was appreciated, and I made a bee-line to Mila and Delaney.

"Why didn't you tell me she hates her birthday? I feel like a jackass."

"Because she needs this," Delaney replied. "We aren't allowed to bring it up. But you're new. So, you can plead ignorance."

"You used me!"

"And it felt good, didn't it?" Mila winked. "Now, you're in my establishment, so I demand you get drunk on prohibition cocktails and find a quiet spot to give Greyson her present."

The drink part sounded wonderful, but after her reaction to seeing everyone who loved her gathered in one room the last thing I wanted to do was present Greyson with the gift I was now certain was way out of line.

Greyson moved through the room and mingled with her employees, Asher and our goalie Cohen, her brother, and Eddie, before finding her way back to her girlfriends. I sat with my back against the wall and nursed a bourbon while the rest of the men in the room gathered to play poker.

"Hey," Greyson's soft voice entered the space and her scent fell over me. "Mind if I pull up a chair?"

She didn't wait for a response and drug a seat up next to me. She unbuttoned her white suit jacket before she sat, revealing a bubblegum pink crop top covered in cherries.

"I love this outfit," I scanned her in a way I hoped wasn't lecherous, from the white combat boots and red jeans all the way to the pink handkerchief holding up her messy bun. Even in the dim lighting of the speakeasy, her blush was prominent.

"Mila picked it. I felt ridiculously out of my element but I actually love it, too. It was a fun night. The concert was amazing," she sipped from her drink and twisted the napkin underneath. "Listen, Canada, I owe you an apology. Delaney confessed that they left out a little detail regarding my feelings about my birthday when you texted them to set this up."

"No, I shouldn't have assumed. That's on me."

Greyson turned, and her front faced my side. I kept my eyes up, even though they wanted to drop to the exposed skin at her navel.

"I really do appreciate this," she looked around the room and smiled when her gaze landed on Eddie and Trevor. "It's just...my birthday has a history of being a really bad day. The day I was born was the first, and it just cascaded from there."

"How could the day you were born be a bad day?"

"That's a story for another time, Canada," Greyson sighed. "So anyway, my reaction was not about you, or your thoughtfulness. It was me. And I am sorry."

"So, I'm guessing you don't want a present, then," I said with a chagrined smile. She crossed one leg over the other and rested an elbow on her knee, chin in palm.

"You got me a gift? Gavin...you are...a treasure. You know that? Seriously. But you did not have to do that. I don't want you spending money on me."

"It's more of a homemade thing," I replied. "But I don't want to make you feel more uncomfortable or anything. Really, it's not a big thing."

I was cut off by her finger over my lips.

"I always accept gifts from the heart. Please, can I have it? I want it. From you."

"Okay," I spoke with her still pressing against my mouth. "But I had a little help."

I jumped off my chair and grabbed the small box off the booth that was piled with our coats. I slid it across the table into Greyson's waiting hands. She slowly peeled the top off and looked into the box in confusion.

"You got me a cupcake?" Greyson lifted the cake out of the box and held it in her palms. "Wait. You said homemade. Did you buy from another bakery?"

"I would *never* disrespect you like that. My loyalty is with you always," I growled, surprised by the intensity of my reaction to the joking question. She was just as taken aback, judging by her wide eyes. "And it is homemade. I made it. With a little help from your friends."

Greyson looked to Mila and Delaney, who were failing in their attempt to be discreet in watching us. She swung her gaze back to me as she inspected the cake in her hands.

"I don't understand."

"Since we took a walk by the lake and you told me about how you mark events in your life, I've been thinking about how there should be a cupcake for *you*. I'm no professional, but I hope you like it anyway. You're holding all the things that remind me of you."

A glimmer of a smile turned up her lips as she turned the cake and looked at it from all angles.

"It's beautiful," Greyson breathed. I scooted closer and my body brushed hers as a zing of need shot through me. "What is it?"

"The cake is blueberry, because Blueberries For Sal was your favorite book and is the reason you eat blueberries and cream, and they're your favorite berry because of how 'cute and unique' they are," I paused to gauge her reaction, relieved that her smile had grown. "The filling is cotton candy ganache, which Mila said, and I quote 'is completely absurd and going to taste like a unicorn's breast milk.'"

Greyson threw her head back and laughed.

"Sounds about right," she said. "Cotton candy ganache? I wouldn't even know how to go about that."

"It was a whole process and they were annoyed with me for it, but I wouldn't budge."

"I do love cotton candy."

"Exactly why I insisted on it," I murmured. "The frosting is blueberry lemon. Delaney refused to do just blueberry because that's 'entirely too much damn sweet' and I 'know nothing about balancing flavors', so I conceded. Plus, lemon is ... delicious."

"That it is."

"I made sure it was purple though, so it was like the sky at night. And the decorations are glitter, because, duh. A fluff of cotton candy because it looks like a cloud, star sprinkles and your infinity loop. Made out of chocolate. I know it looks like a toddler did it but I have never drawn with chocolate—"

Greyson jumped forward and wrapped her free hand around

the back of my neck. Her lips pressed against my cheek, danger-ously close to the corner of my mouth.

"I love this. I love that there are things that remind you of me. I love that you care enough to take time to do this. And I love that you just made me think my birthday might not be so bad, after all."

CHAPTER 9
Greyson

B y the time I'd showered and settled on the couch with a mug of lemon balm tea, I was so tired I wasn't sure I'd be awake to see the start of the game.

Donovan texted and let me know the bakery was closed, and the entire stock of Thanksgiving extras my team had baked were sold. I hated leaving them to handle a holiday rush alone, but with as sick as I was there was no way I could be responsible for other people's food. I downed a shot of alcohol masquerading as cold medicine and hugged my teacup against my chest as I flipped on the Falcons pregame. The commentary only kept half my attention and I dozed off before the game started. I woke two minutes into the first period, amazed I hadn't spilled the now tepid tea all over myself.

Gavin played well, and I managed to see him score before I drifted off again. I finally gave up and shuffled into my room before the third period, and was out long before the game ended.

I woke in the morning nursing a cold medicine induced hangover. If it was possible to feel worse than the night before, I absolutely did. The shower called my name and I let the room thoroughly fog up before I climbed in. The water was just this side of scalding and I dropped my head, soothed by the intense spray as it pounded the back of my neck.

The floor of the tub welcomed me when I sat down, and I let the steam envelop me until there was no hot water left.

It was strange to be alone on this day. Grandpa and I had always spent Thanksgiving cooking together, drinking screwdrivers and watching the parade. Since Trevor had to work, I didn't know what to do with myself having literally nothing to do.

It felt like I didn't have a whole lot to be thankful for this year, and I sighed heavily while I pulled on sweatpants and a baggy *Eat It* sweatshirt.

I turned the television on as the dancers were announced, and I knew my grandpa was with me, since the kick line was his favorite part of the entire parade. I forced myself to watch as they kicked through their performance, though my heart physically hurt in my chest. After it was over, I made a cup of the sore throat blend tea that Mila had made and had barely gotten back into the living room when there was a strong knock on the front door. I wasn't expecting anyone, so I chose to ignore it and stretched out on the sofa. The knock continued, louder and more insistent.

I set down my cup and peered through the glass, stunned to see Gavin on the other side. The hood of his sweatshirt was pulled over his head and he looked like a model for lazy day loungewear. There was no way for me to make myself look like less of a zombie, so I quickly said goodbye to any chance of Gavin ever being attracted to me and pulled open the door.

CHAPTER 10
Greyson

"Hi," I rasped, as I tried to clear my throat. "What are you doing here?"

Gavin dipped his head and shrugged as he peered at me through thick eyelashes.

"Thought you might like some company today."

He was the sweetest creature that ever lived. I wasn't sure why he decided I was worthy of his friendship, but I was going to hold onto it for as long as I could.

"That's really nice of you, but I don't want to keep you from any plans you might have. I'm not exactly great company."

"I'm Canadian, this holiday means nothing to me," Gavin replied with a wave. "So, can I come in?"

"Oh. Shit. Yes, of course. Come in."

Gavin stepped into the foyer and kicked off his shoes as he held up some bags.

"I know you aren't up for Thanksgiving dinner, but I thought soup might be good. It's turkey noodle. Pumpkin pie ice cream too. So, you still get traditional American Thanksgiving. Sort of."

I blinked hard and fast to make the moisture in my eyes dry before it fell down my cheeks. He again shocked me with his thoughtfulness and I didn't have the right words to respond. I launched into his arms and buried my face against his chest. Gavin stood with his arms at his sides before he leaned over me and set the food down. When his hands were free, he wrapped his arms around me tightly, allowing me to burrow into him. He was a champion hugger, and I wanted to live in his arms. He smelled like snow and sexy man. Sexy snowman. Interesting. That would be an amazing cupcake.

I reluctantly pushed off him and slapped my hands at my cheeks, impatient to get to a pen but really wanting to get back in those arms of his. Maybe I could fall apart later. He didn't seem to mind being my savior when the emotion struck.

"This is so unnecessary but so nice I can't even put into words how much I appreciate it," I said as I snagged the bags and waved him towards the kitchen. I needed to write out the ideas in my head about a snowy white cake that was spicy and warm at the same time. With my back turned I took a few deep breaths and tried to calm my shaking hands. I shoved the ice cream into the freezer after I examined the carton. It was from a small family-owned shop on the south side of the city. The soup was from a different mom and pop restaurant that I had never been to but heard great things about. "Are these places open today? How did you get this?"

A slow blush crept up Gavin's ears and he shook his head while he tossed his coat over the back of a chair and took the soup from my hand. He deposited it into the fridge and pulled out a beer.

"I got them before we left town yesterday." Gavin was quite blasé about the fact he'd thought ahead to do this for me. He held up the beer. "Do you mind if I have one of these?"

"Of course not," I replied. Gavin twisted the cap off the bottle and tilted it up to his mouth. I watched his lips hit the opening as he took a long drink of the amber liquid.

"Have you ever put a cherry in this? It's my favorite way to drink it. Makes it taste completely different."

Gavin's question snapped me out of watching his mouth, and

when he held up the bottle I was hit with another idea for a cupcake.

"Shit. I need a piece of paper." I quickly scrawled a few words on the back of a napkin regarding the Sexy Snowman I'd forgotten to document, which had *never* happened. That should have been an indication of how important he had become in my life, but whatever. He came up behind me and looked over my shoulder at the words '*coconut milk and curry?*' '*sweet cream and Chai*' '*smoked white chocolate and cranberries.*'

"What just made you think of a new cupcake?"

"What you said about the beer. Putting a cherry in it. Like ... butterscotch beer cake with Amarena cherry filling ... or cherry cake with wheat ale buttercream. Yeah?"

"Both sound incredible but that's not even close to what you've written." Gavin stood close, and my body temperature notably spiked. I couldn't very well tell him the Sexy Snowman was yet another cupcake inspired by him, so I folded the napkin and finished writing notes for the cherry beer cake on the other side.

"Just something I was thinking of earlier. I forgot to write it down. Your beer reminded me. No big deal. Anyway, should we sit? Do you need another beer yet? Maybe I'll make a hot toddy. Might as well day drink on Thanksgiving, right?"

My cheeks burned, so hot I felt it in my lips. I could not make my mouth stop moving. Gavin smiled softly and regarded my pitiful red nose and watery eyes with sympathy.

"Do you have any maple syrup? I'll make your hot toddy for you."

"Maple syrup? I mean, I know you practically IV drip it but come on Canada. Hot toddies are made with honey."

"Don't shut down the idea of something new without at least giving it a chance," Gavin replied with a curve of his eyebrow. There was something behind the words that assured me he was talking about way more than maple syrup.

I took the syrup out of the refrigerator and had to consciously keep myself together when our fingers brushed as he took the bottle from me.

"Vermont? Seriously?" Gavin scoffed with a haughty roll of his eyes as he inspected the bottle like I'd just given him rat poison.

"Sorry my syrup isn't up to your standards, but I don't have a direct pipeline to Canada," I replied, my voice like sandpaper as I turned on the teapot and pulled out the whiskey.

"You do now. I'll make sure to keep you stocked so you don't have to use this swill."

"Those are some pretty combative words over a bottle of liquid sugar," I watched him mix and pour, enraptured by his preciseness. When the kettle whistled Gavin moved around me to grab it from the flame, and his hand skimmed my hip in a friendly and subconscious move of comfort. My skin lit up under his touch and I swallowed hard, grateful for the pain in my throat to divert my attention away from my hormones.

"Here you go," Gavin turned. "Even if it is subpar syrup, it's still better than honey."

He passed me a mug, which I begrudgingly admitted did smell phenomenal, and we made our way back to the living room. Gavin took a seat on one end of the couch as I took a sip of the hot toddy he had prepared. That was all I needed to know I would never again be able to drink one without maple syrup. I made an appreciative groan which caused Gavin to turn his head with a smirk that had 'I told you so' written all over it.

"Alright. I concede the battle of the hot toddy to you," I admitted as I took another sip and welcomed the burn of the too hot liquid as it coated my throat like fire. "But really. Why are you here?"

Gavin stretched his legs out onto the ottoman in front of him and slouched down into the couch cushions.

"I wanted to hang out with you."

"That is bullshit."

He took a long pull from his beer.

"It is in no way bullshit. When you told me Trevor would be working today, I couldn't let you be alone. Then when you got sick there really was no question."

"You always seem to appear when I need support the most. Even if I don't realize it."

Gavin held up his drink and clinked it against mine with a smile that warmed my insides.

"That's what friends are for."

"I'm not sure I was fully prepared for how hard it was going to hit me today," I admitted softly, my throat thick with the sadness I tried to keep inside. "I'm happy I don't have to be alone. I'm happier you're the one keeping me company."

Gavin set his bottle on the table and slid down the couch. He dropped an arm over my shoulder while he used his other hand to pull a soft blanket over me. I couldn't make myself do anything but sigh and let my head fall onto him. He wanted to take care of me, and for this day, I was going to let him.

"I'm all yours until you kick me out, but don't worry about being a good hostess. If you're tired, go to sleep. I make a good pillow."

"Lucky for you I don't use pillows." I bit my tongue so hard I tasted blood, relieved he didn't acknowledge the unintended admission. He adjusted his position and I held out a corner of the blanket, which he tossed loosely over his legs. "I appreciate the offer, but I won't fall asleep with you here."

"Well don't stay awake on account of me, okay?" Gavin flipped through channels on the remote. "So, what should we watch? You cool with football?"

I could not be less interested in football, but I'd be fine with watching paint dry if it meant more time I could lay on him and absorb his warmth.

"Sure, yeah, football is great."

We fell silent and Gavin drew circles on my arm with the tip of his finger. When I opened my eyes however long later, I was confused to find myself horizontal with my head on something soft. I quickly realized it was a pillow. In Gavin's lap. And my hands. Oh my God. My hands. My head was on a *pillow* and my hands were shoved up underneath it, curled against his inner thigh. I jumped up so quickly my head spun and startled Gavin when I turned to face him as panic bit my throat.

"How did I end up in your lap? I cannot believe I fell asleep. I never sleep. I mean, around people ... with people. Where did that pillow come from? I'm so sorry, I'm so embarrassed. I *swear* I was not trying to cuddle your penis like a stuffed animal. Was I touching it? Holy hell. I just mentioned your penis. I don't even think about you having a penis."

Gavin's mouth dropped open before he chewed the inside of his lip, unsuccessful in his attempt to hold in his smile.

"You really don't need to keep telling me how *not* interested in my dick you are. I get it."

"That's not what I said."

"So, you are?"

"Gavin. Please, I'm begging you to stop. My humiliation level is already almost at the breaking point."

Gavin laughed loudly and laced his fingers into a forward stretch. "I had to go to the bathroom, so I tried my best not to disturb you and just laid you down with the pillow that was on your rocking chair. When I came back you kind of found your way back to me and ended up on my lap. It's not a big thing."

"I'm sorry," I whispered, horrified that my unconscious state got closer to him than lucid me ever could. Gavin put his arm around me and pulled me back to him, and I couldn't shake the feeling of safety that just being near him provided.

"Stop apologizing. I like taking care of you and I like to cuddle." Gavin's hand came around my mouth and covered it before I could protest. "We can cuddle as friends. Doesn't have to mean I'm trying to sleep with you."

I peeled his fingers away from my mouth, quickly inhaling and hoping my response to his hand on my face wasn't picked up on by him.

"Really? You're fine with me using you as my personal mattress?"

"Anytime you want," Gavin licked his lips and dropped his gaze to my mouth. "Have you never had a guy friend before?"

"Not really. I've never had a lot of friends, period."

The silence that fell over us was heavy with the weight of confession. Gavin lifted his eyes to mine and held them long enough to make my pulse pound against my throat.

"You do now."

I hesitantly reached out and cupped his jaw as he closed his eyes and inhaled deeply. The thoughts in my head swirled and moved dangerously close to the tip of my tongue. I wanted to kiss him, and I could tell he wouldn't stop me if I tried. We could not do this. Gavin's eyes popped open when I scrambled off the couch.

"I'm kind of hungry. I'm going to get some soup; do you want any?" I escaped the room before he could answer and had the soup on the stove when he sauntered into the kitchen. Gavin didn't speak, but his presence behind me was strong and forceful. When I turned, he had his palms on the granite and his back against the counter. The way he looked at me was unsettling, something I wasn't sure I would ever get used to. It was like he could read my thoughts and emotions a split second before I had them, leaving him prepared to debate any of my protests. I was constantly off balance, like my entire being was suspended in emotional vertigo. But the thrill of the rollercoaster outweighed the terror, and I knew I'd never get tired of the ride. After a weak smile I turned back to the counter and gasped when I felt him a moment later. He was closer than I'd consider friendly, and I fought every cell in my body to not fall against his chest and let him take my pain away.

"Can I help with the food?" Gavin's voice was low and rough in my ear as his hand came around me and took the knife I clutched tightly. I wanted this so much. Almost as much as I needed it to stop. I nodded vigorously and cleared my throat as I pointed to the cutting board.

"Sure ... can you slice up some bread?"

We stared at each other as tension crackled between us like a live electrical wire jumping across a sidewalk. I backed away and bumped into the corner of the counter when there was nowhere else to go. He was magnetic. If I was in the halo of his pull, I was powerless. He broke eye contact first and focused his attention on the task at hand, which allowed me to breathe again.

"Do I make you nervous?"

My hands shook as I pulled down soup bowls and I hid my reddened cheeks behind the cabinet door. "Of course not. What a ridiculous question."

Gavin finished with the bread and set the knife in the sink. He turned and stood in front of me before I knew he had even moved.

"Are you sure? You seem a little uncomfortable."

"Yes," my voice betrayed me, and I tried to clear away the uncertainty as I got lost in his warm eyes. "You make me feel a way I don't know how to verbalize. But nervous or uncomfortable is not it."

"Is it a good way?"

"Yeah. It's a good way."

There was so much being said between us without words that I couldn't hold in the emotion, and it fell warm down my cheek. Gavin tilted his head and whispered against my cheek as he cupped his hand against the other side of my face.

"I'm part of your life now, okay? You're safe. I want you to be yourself, always. Completely. No need to hold back."

"I want that, too. But I'm scared."

"What are you scared of?"

"Losing you for it."

He moved closer, his hands pressed against the counter on either side of me.

"I've been waiting ... hoping ... for years that I'd have this chance to get to know you. KJ would have flipped shit if I'd said anything more than hello to you then. So, I didn't, even though I wanted to. Now that I have … well, let's just say I'm here to stay, okay Lemon Drop? It doesn't matter what you spew in your stream of consciousness babble, or how adorably awkward you are. I'm not going anywhere."

My nerves and needs gave way to confusion at the bizarre term of endearment, and I narrowed my eyes.

"Lemon Drop? What kind of nickname is Lemon Drop?"

Gavin pushed off the counter and grinned as he went to the stove to turn off the flame.

"If you don't want to tell me what you were really thinking about with those cupcake flavors earlier, I don't need to tell you the reasoning behind that nickname. Someday. I promise you that. Someday it will make sense."

Gavin held out a hand for the bowls and dished up the soup while I arranged bread and butter on a tray. As an afterthought I grabbed another round of beers out of the fridge. I dropped cherries into the bottom of two pilsner glasses and poured the golden liquid over the top. The frothy wheat swirled around, and the foam turned light pink when it mixed with the cherry juice. Our fingers brushed when I handed him his glass and it made me want to take it back so I could do it all over again. His eyes followed my lips as I took a timid sip of the concoction he was so fond of and his Adam's apple bobbed with his hard swallow when I moaned in appreciation of the subtle cherry notes.

"Well? Incredible, eh?"

Eh. I would never get tired of that little word. How something so small could be so endearing I had yet to figure out, but he had the market cornered in adorable Canadian speak. Gavin kept his eyes trained on me as I nodded and took another sip, and by the time he drank out of his glass I was fully turned on. The man had magical libido powers, and that could be extremely dangerous.

"Ready for dinner?" Gavin finally broke the sexually charged moment as he picked up the tray and led us back into the living room. He arranged the meal on the coffee table and waited for me to take a bite before he started eating. I wasn't actually hungry at all, but since I'd used food as an excuse to escape the emotional moment, I forced myself to attempt. One bite was all I managed before my attention settled on Gavin. He hunched over the table with his forearms on his thighs while he dragged the bread through the thick soup and took a hearty bite. Even the way he ate turned me on, and I got lost in the flex and release of his jaw as he chewed.

"What? Why are you staring at me like that?" Gavin caught my adoration of his perfect face. "Do I have food on my face or something?"

"Yeah, a little." I was embarrassed to get caught and grateful he presented me with a legitimate reason. "Just, right here." I pointed to his cheek and he dragged the napkin across his mouth and against his face, which left me with no excuse to stare at him anymore.

"Thanks for looking out for me."

"It's the least I can do," I replied quietly. I tried another bite and regretted the decision immediately.

"Hurts to swallow?" Gavin asked, and I realized, this time, he was the one staring. He witnessed my last attempt, and my grimace gave away my discomfort.

"A little," I admitted, relieved when he reached for the spoon and stuck it back in the almost full bowl. Gavin tucked my hair behind my ear and brushed his thumb under my chin, as my heart pounded painfully in my chest.

"Don't push it. It will be here later. I'm going to go clean up and then I'll head out so you can rest."

"You don't have to go," I protested as I quickly grabbed hold of his wrist. I didn't want to spend the rest of the day alone. I wanted to be with him. "Unless you want to. I mean, if you have somewhere to be, I get it."

Gavin stood and picked up the bowls, then leaned over and pressed a kiss against my forehead.

"I have nothing planned, or anywhere to go. I just didn't want to overstay my welcome with you feeling so poorly. If you're sure you want me, I'd love to stay."

"I want you," I blurted out quickly. His eyes flared in a way that sent a shot of heat through my core.

"I'm very happy to hear that," Gavin answered, his voice rough. "Find something to watch. I'll be right back."

I watched him disappear into the kitchen. Dazed, I ran my fingertips over my forehead, as if the impression of him would still be there for me to physically touch. Gavin reappeared a moment later and flopped comfortably next to me. He pulled me into him with no hesitation and shoved the rogue pillow behind his head.

"I might fall asleep this time, just warning you." He grinned and stretched his legs out on the oversized ottoman in front of him. "What are we watching?"

"Well, my grandpa and I always watched White Christmas together Thanksgiving night, but if you'd rather watch something else—"

"No way," Gavin cut me off excitedly. "My mom *loves* Bing Crosby. We watched that movie every holiday season until I left home."

"My grandpa sang along to every song," I paused with a smile. "He bought me a blue ostrich feather fan for Christmas one year. That was our favorite scene."

My voice broke and I tensed when Gavin sat up and turned to me.

"Thank you for sharing this with me. It won't be the same, but I'm honored that you chose to let me in on such a special tradition," he said softly.

My tension melted from my shoulders as I fell into his arms. I turned my face into his neck and breathed until my heart calmed. I had never told anyone about our Thanksgiving movie night.

Gavin understood the importance in a way I hadn't realized even mattered. *He* mattered to me.

It scared me to death.

Because when people started to matter, that's when they could really do damage.

CHAPTER 11
Gavin

Mattie was the picture of holiday spirit as she danced past me with an overflowing martini glass. Vodka sloshed all over her garish Christmas leggings and clashing Santa sweater while she giggled.

"Come on Scrooge, come get a drink."

I followed Mattie into the kitchen to see Asher draped across the counter with my mom and other sisters. The spread of food was outrageous, even though there were ten of us, and it somehow seemed to keep multiplying. The only thing missing was dessert. Cupcakes would be great.

Fuck I missed Greyson.

I thumbed through my notifications, disappointed but unsurprised to see nothing from her. She had worked twenty-hour days for a solid month, and we hadn't spent any substantial amount of time together since Thanksgiving. The holidays were one of her busiest times of year at Icing, which meant no time to hang out. She always made a few minutes for me when I'd stop into the bakery unexpectedly, which had become so often her employees now had a cupcake waiting before I even made it to the counter. I should stop, I knew that. But I didn't want to.

Asher slid a bourbon down the counter with a half-drunk

grin and held his up in a silent cheer. I mirrored the gesture and welcomed the fiery burn of the expensive liquor as it coated my tongue. I wasn't in the holiday spirit. The team had struggled since the second week of the season and half of them had already given up. Greyson had been my cheerleader since that night on the beach, but she had been so busy it felt selfish to add my burden to her already overloaded plate. I'd spent a lot of time talking to the sky, but even that hadn't cooperated. The city had been so dark at night I searched in earnest for any star to direct my feelings to, but there had been none. Every night that passed with no sign from above sent my mood into a further spiral.

The chime of the doorbell rang as I took another long drink.

"Are any of you expecting anyone?"

There was a chorus of 'no' and Asher smiled with his face buried in his cocktail. I narrowed my eyes at his lazy shrug as I started towards the front door, all too familiar with the look on his face. It usually meant an orchestrated plot with me as the main character.

"Hopefully it's someone bringing cookies," he called down the hall as I pulled open the door to Greyson. She bounced on the balls of her feet with an enormous tray balanced in her hands. I stared at her in shock, certain my mind had played a vicious trick on me and she wasn't really there.

"Um, hi," Greyson finally said meekly, her eyes focused on the tray in her hands. I realized I hadn't even greeted her and recovered too quickly. My shouted response caused her to jump in surprise.

"What are you doing here? I mean ... hi. I've missed you." My ears heated at my pathetic greeting and she smiled weakly as she locked red-rimmed eyes on me. "Hey, are you okay?"

She nodded and shifted the tray to swipe at a tear on her cheek.

"Seriously, what's wrong? Come inside."

Greyson shook her head quickly and stepped back. "No, I'm not ... I mean ... I'm here for Asher. Is he here?"

"You want Asher?" The sharpness in my question physically affected her and she shrank into the unzipped puffy black coat that swallowed her. She shivered and rolled her eyes at the porch ceiling.

"No, gross. I don't *want* Asher. I need him. No. Shit. Okay, he ordered this." Greyson lifted the tray. "He told me he'd pick it up at the shop and then at the last frigging minute said he couldn't and asked me to bring it here. I hate to bother you with your family here, but he paid for it, so I *had* to deliver it. I'm sorry."

It took everything in me not to quiet her babbling with a kiss, and I reached for the tray. Her hands were icy, so I took advantage of the opportunity to warm them with my own. My stomach grumbled as I assessed the variety of cupcakes, decorated cookies, and fruit tarts artfully displayed.

"I told you to stop apologizing to me. I'm so happy you're here. Please come in. At least for one drink. I know you're spending tonight with Trevor, so I won't try to get you to stay all night." I was alarmed when a fat tear escaped her makeup free eye. Greyson quickly swiped it away.

"He got called in. Crime doesn't stop for Christmas, even when you've got an emotionally unstable sister who really needs you."

"You're telling me you're alone on Christmas Eve? After you were alone on Thanksgiving?"

"It's not his fault," Greyson snapped, her tone acid. The protectiveness over him was instantaneous and fierce, and it was weirdly hot. They were an army of two, soldiers in their own war that no one knew the reason for. "He can't really tell the mayor of Chicago he's unable to work a case because his sister needs someone to watch Home Alone with her."

"I wasn't implying it was Grey," I said gently as I moved away from the door to make room for her to come in. "I am, however, not taking no for an answer now that I know you'd be alone if you weren't here with us."

"I can't Gavin. Look at me." Greyson waved her hands over her leggings, furry boots, and '*I Did It All For The Cookies*' Santa face hoodie. Her face was scrubbed clean of any trace of makeup, cheeks pink from the cold.

"What about it? You look incredible," I blurted out. She did. Her eyes seemed bigger without the glittery eyeshadow and the faint freckles that were dusted across her cheeks and nose were like a starry sky on a cloudless night. "It's freezing. Please come inside. Don't make me beg. I mean, I will. I'll get down on my knees right now."

I started to lower myself to the floor in front of her, which earned me another eye roll. She timidly stepped through the door and put her hand on my shoulder. Her fingers danced across my collarbone and she curled them against the collar of my sweater.

"What if they don't like me?" Greyson whispered, as more tears glistened on the verge of letting loose. "I know how much their opinions matter to you. If I make a bad impression ... I mean, not that it's like, meeting the family as in a potential mate. Because you don't want to mate with me. I mean, I'm ... dammit."

I abandoned the tray on the table and pulled her tightly against me. Her hands were so cold the chill cut straight through my shirt, but it barely registered.

"You really have no idea how incredible you are, do you?"

"I don't know why you think that." Her voice was muffled against my shirt and I pulled back to look into her eyes as I smoothed her hair away from her face.

"You have this fear that people are going to reject you, when you captivate everyone from the moment you arrive. It's how you've managed to save restaurants by telling people on television you like to eat there. People listen to you."

She scrunched her nose in confusion, successfully looking more delectable.

"What are you talking about? I'm on *Eat It* because of my last name. I'm a legacy. It's business. I'm not some big-name celebrity chef that people care about."

"Your legacy didn't get you on Chicago's 25 under 25 last year. Your talent and charisma did that. Hate to tell you, Lemon Drop, but you actually are a big-name celebrity chef."

Greyson chewed her lip.

"You knew I was on the list?"

"I did. Because I care about you."

"But that was before you and I ... that was when I was with—"

"I know," I said hoarsely. My hands still framed her face, and she turned her cheek into my palm. "I shouldn't have, but I cared then, too."

She stepped further into the house and I reached one hand around her to push the door shut.

"I wish I had known that. Known you. Then," Greyson said softly.

"Actually, your recommendation on the brunch episode of *Eat It* brought enough business to my favorite place they were able to stay open."

"How do you know what I recommended?" Greyson asked.

"Because, Greyson," I murmured, as I tucked a loose hair behind her ear. "I have a lot of down time on the road, and food channels calm me. I watched you long before I could talk to you. You captivate me. I listen to you. You matter to me."

"You just gave me the best gift I've ever been given," Greyson whispered. "I've never mattered to anyone outside of my family. Some of them anyway."

"You make it easy to care about you," I replied. "Can I take your coat?"

"I really don't want to intrude. You and I can spend time together later. I should go."

"You should stay."

One more stare down that left me uncomfortably turned on

and she shook off her coat and passed it to me to hang in the closet.

"One drink." Greyson lifted the tray of desserts and held it away when I tried to take it from her. "Please, let me, I need to have something to do with my hands."

"Whatever you want, Lemon Drop. Are you ready?"

"Um, no, but I guess I have to be."

She took a deep breath and fell into step next to me. When we got to the kitchen all activity stopped and everyone stared at her in surprise. She tensed and leaned into my side, and my arm automatically wrapped around her waist. When my fingers brushed her sweatshirt, she relaxed into my touch.

"There she is!" Asher rushed forward and plucked the tray out of Greyson's hands. He handed it off to me as he scooped her off the floor.

"I hate you so much right now," she growled against his cheek. Asher laughed as he spun her around the kitchen. She caught my eye in a silent plea before he set her down and peeled the lid off his secret order of Christmas treats.

"Surprised, eh Halstead? Getting Greyson here is your Christmas present. You're welcome!"

If my mom wasn't right there, I would have junk punched him. Greyson's cheeks burned bright red as she stood awkwardly in the center of the madness. I moved next to her as Mattie cleared her throat and stepped forward with a welcoming smile.

"Hi there, it's so nice to finally meet you. I'm Mattie, Gavin's sister."

Greyson timidly held out her hand and Mattie covered it with her own. The rest of my sisters clamored around her, vying for her attention as they all talked at once.

"Well, now that she's here you think you could stop acting like Santa jizzed in your stocking and actually enjoy Christmas?" Asher asked as he finished his third cookie and roughly hit his shoulder against mine. While I was grateful for his meddling, I was still so shocked I wasn't ready to thank him.

"You really shouldn't have done this," I replied, as I watched everyone gush over Greyson's baking as she explained every item. "Or at least talked to me first."

"I love you but you need my help. You two are the biggest cockblocks to your own relationship. Honestly, it's pathetic."

"You think I wouldn't like to have it another way?" I lowered my voice when Greyson peered over her shoulder with a look of curiosity. "I'm happy with whatever she wants to give me. And since friendship is what she's offering, friendship is what I'm taking."

"Okay, but I haven't seen you this happy since we were kids. Since before Olive."

"Right. So why would you want me to destroy it by telling her how I feel?"

"You don't know she'd shut you down," Asher argued. He nodded towards the living room when all four of my sisters glared at us. There was no chance Greyson hadn't heard that.

"She's not ready. She may never be. If she's not, I'll live with it. Having her know she can count on me to always be there for her means way more to me than getting her in bed for a night. I won't ruin it on a maybe."

Asher paused and focused his attention on the huge Christmas tree in the corner. The blue and white lights twinkled against the flickering fire.

"Life is fucking crazy," he finally spoke. I followed his gaze to the kitchen, where the women were gathered around the island. Their conversations were animated with talking hands and marked with spontaneous peals of laughter. Our dads were at the table, relaxed and happy to have their families together. The room seemed brighter somehow. "Five months ago, I was watching you fall apart when she was about to get married, and now she's sitting in your kitchen on Christmas Eve, looking like she's always been there."

Greyson did seem comfortable with my family, and the fact she hadn't noticed I wasn't in the room to be a protective buffer was proof. I was still trying to figure out the nuances of her personality, since the two versions of it were so different it was almost impossible to believe they came out of the same body. I imagined the desperate fight to keep people out came from losing her parents at such a young age.

As if she felt my thoughts, Greyson slowly turned and smiled sweetly when our eyes met. She said something to Mattie and picked up a cupcake as she walked my way. Greyson ignored Asher as she presented me with what I knew was a brand-new recipe by the way she lovingly cupped it in both hands. I grinned at the look of trepidation on her face as she softly placed it in mine, as if there was any chance I wasn't going to love it.

"Hey, where's mine?" Asher interrupted, and she threw an irritated glare at him.

"I'm still mad at you."

"Keep telling yourself that," Asher replied. He kissed her cheek as he took his cue and left the room. "Merry Christmas, Gigi."

Greyson bit her lip and looked between us. Her gaze settled on our hands, still entwined after the cupcake was handed off. She hesitantly moved her thumb against the outer edge of my pinky before she pulled her hands back and shoved them in the front pocket of her hoodie.

"Your family is amazing," she said quietly as she took in the stockings lined up on the mantle and the pile of presents that spilled out halfway across the living room floor. "Four sisters, huh? Your ability to handle mood swings makes so much sense now."

"Yeah, it was a stressful life of dodging estrogen land mines, but I made it out alive."

Greyson turned back with a small smile.

"Their names are so interesting. How did you end up as Gavin when theirs are all vintage?"

"It's my dad's middle name. Trust me, they did what they could to come up with nicknames that would avoid anyone ever using their real names. Not that I cared. I took full advantage of embarrassing them."

"Trevor's middle name is Hudson, which was my dad's name. First born males never get to be original," Greyson replied with a sad smile.

"What about you?" I asked as I took a bite of the cupcake. I groaned in appreciation as the taste of whiskey and maple hit my taste buds. She made this specifically for me. A hot toddy in cake form. "What's the background of Greyson? Family name?"

She started the transformation into protection mode and folded her arms over her chest. I'd clearly hit a nerve, but I didn't know how her name could possibly be a point of contention.

"It's not a nice story."

Confused, I cocked my head and waited for her to elaborate. When she didn't, I debated changing the subject but ultimately decided to press just a little.

"I don't understand."

"My mom went into labor when my dad was working. A major case that he was ensnared in for weeks. He couldn't get away before the birth. They had agreed on a name together and then she changed it when they put me in her arms. She said '*the weather, my mood, my daughter. All devoid of color and light. All grey.*'"

It was impossible to comprehend the terrible connotation of her explanation. She had just swung open the door to her past and smacked me in the face with it.

"That's..."

"Awful. I know." Greyson laughed self-deprecatingly and shrugged like it didn't matter. I did not buy it. "I don't mind it now. Regardless of the reason behind it, I grew into it. Trevor calls me RayRay. Has since we were kids. I obviously hated my name once I knew the story, so he made it into something cheerful that was ours. He says I'm a ray of sunshine that breaks through when everything else is grey."

I tried to speak but found my throat dry and the words stuck in the back of it. I cleared it quickly and fought to keep my composure when all I wanted to do was hold her against me and protect her from that memory. "What about Grace? That's nice too."

"No," Greyson shook her head with finality. "Do not call me that. *Ever.*"

"Okay. No problem. I won't," I backtracked as my mind raced with a ridiculous number of scenarios of how the story of Grace could possibly be worse. "What about your middle name?"

"I don't have one. She didn't give me a middle name, so I had no choice but to go by the name that showed how she felt about me from birth. She wanted to make sure I had no other options." Greyson's tone was flat, as if the conversation had completely exhausted her. She started to fidget, and the way she rubbed her pendant gave away how deeply the memory still hurt her. "Can we talk about something else? Do you like the cupcake?"

"Of course. It's incredible, like always," I answered. Her defeated posture made me wish the entire conversation had never happened.

"I made it for you."

"I know."

She stepped closer and watched as I finished the cupcake. My heart pounded as she settled her cheek against my chest, her hands still stuffed in her sweatshirt.

"You've become my inspiration in a lot of ways." Greyson sighed when I wrapped my arms around her. "I'm working on communicating better. I've never cared about that much ... until you. I want you to understand me."

"And that's the best gift *I've* ever been given," I replied. She tilted her head up and parted her lips, a quiet invitation that I had not expected to receive. She left no room for question when she bit her bottom lip and dropped her gaze to my mouth. Blood pounded through my ears as I lowered my head and saw her close her eyes. This was going to happen.

"Dinner's ready, come on you guys!" Winifred bounced into

the room and froze when she read the atmosphere. Greyson jumped out of my arms and stepped back until there was at least a foot of space between us, and I instantly missed the warmth of her body fitting against me like a puzzle piece.

"Thanks Freddie. We'll be right there," I replied tightly. My lips tingled with the kiss I didn't get the chance to give Greyson, and when she covered her mouth with a shaking hand, I knew the moment was gone. Winifred backed out of the room with a nod.

"I'm going to go," Greyson said hoarsely. She rubbed her lips together furiously and inched towards the closet to retrieve her coat.

"Why? We want you to stay. I ... want you to stay."

"If I stay, I'm going to spend the entire night wondering how it would have felt if *that* would have happened. Hoping for an opportunity for it to happen again. I don't think I'm ready for that."

"Greyson, I'm—"

"The way I feel *every* time I'm near you is something I have never felt in my entire life before," she interrupted. "It's scary, and exciting, and safe. It's like the sun has broken through the clouds that live inside me. But *every* time I'm in front of you, I worry I'm going to ruin it. I always bring the storm, Gavin."

"No. You don't. You quiet mine. The tornado in my head calms when you appear. I'm not going anywhere," I replied.

"Please keep that promise," Greyson whispered. She came forward and brushed her lips across my cheek. I followed her into the kitchen as she said goodbye to my family and gratefully accepted packages of food to take with her. When my dad handed over two full bags of meals for Trevor and his team, her eyes filled with tears. By the time I walked her to her car she had started to cry.

"I'm sorry I'm such a mess, Gavin. After meeting your family, I totally see why you're the amazing man that you are. Thank you so much. For including me. For caring enough to make me feel like I'm not alone."

"You'll never be alone again," I assured her as I leaned into the driver's window as she buckled her seat belt. "And for the record, you and your glittery personality are the most colorful and bright I've ever had the pleasure to know. A name does not matter. But if it did, yours is beautiful."

CHAPTER 12
Greyson

I missed Gavin. Even if he could perform some magic there was no way he'd be home in time for me to *not* ring in the New Year solo, since the team played on the west coast. It was probably for the best, since the midnight kiss scenario would leave no reason not to follow through on what we had almost started on Christmas Eve. In the week since, I'd thought of the moment no less than ten thousand times. Three new cupcakes had been born. The man was a creativity fountain. As frustrated as I'd been by his sister's interruption, she'd done both of us a huge favor. As soon as the friend line was crossed, things would change. Something would inevitably go wrong.

Gavin had been the only thing to keep me together on Christmas, which was hilarious considering I had hyperventilated into a piping bag when Asher called. I forgot I was dealing with a millionaire when I said a last-minute delivery fee would be an extra one hundred dollars, since that amount, to me, was ridiculous. I was shocked when he agreed and added a hundred-dollar tip. While it was true I didn't want to interrupt Gavin's time with his family, I was more than a little excited to have a legitimate reason to see him.

After Thanksgiving it felt like we had turned a corner, but

since I barely had enough time to breathe in that month between then and Christmas, I didn't have the energy to spend the time to deepen our friendship. I loved that he came into the shop whenever he had a few extra minutes, and I wasn't sure if he just really liked my baking or actually wanted to see me. Jemma was convinced he was in love with me, which was a lovely thought to entertain regardless of the improbability. His soul was too beautiful to be interested in mine. I was battered and broken, a dull shade of grey, while he was bright and glowing, a rainbow of positivity and all the most vibrant colors on the wheel.

A full week after I met his entire family and crashed their Christmas Eve dinner, I was still shocked that I had told him the story of my name. He had obviously picked up on what I didn't say. I saw it in the intense way he watched my mouth while I spoke. I had started to prepare myself for the questions that were sure to come, certain he would eventually ask what happened to my mom. The thought of it filled me with a level of panic I hadn't known for quite some time. I wanted to tell Gavin the truth, but I didn't want him to look at me differently. It would be impossible for him not to if he knew the uncut version. It would be unconscious, but it would be there. He would try to fix me. Mend the invisible cracks. But he couldn't. No one could. I had accepted the fact I was irreparable. But he made me feel like I wasn't a lost cause. When I was with Gavin, I was someone else. Someone who could be happy. I liked her, and I wanted her to exist in my place.

I was startled out of my reverie by four quick knocks on the front door and the turn of the knob.

"RayRay! Where are you?"

"Dining room. Can you hurry up? I need help with my nails."

"Seriously? You do her nails?"

The deep male voice of Trevor's partner brought an instant smile to my face. I looked up as they entered the room and nodded at the counter where Trevor's contribution to the New Year's Eve party waited.

"What is all this?" Trevor asked from behind me. I jumped up and smacked his hand when he tried to pull a cake pop off the covered tray. I learned long ago to keep a plate of overflow close, or there would be conspicuous holes where the treats he sampled had originally been. There weren't many things I hated more than my vision being altered by an impatient brother with an insatiable sweet tooth.

"Champagne cupcakes, red velvet cake pops, French macarons and chocolate covered strawberries," I replied, as I held out the plate of samples. He and Jace devoured every crumb before I forced Trevor into a chair and held out the sheet of black and gold glittered nail strips.

"Come on RayRay, why do you always make me do this?" Trevor whined, completely for Jace's benefit. He was generally the one who set our manicure dates so he could come over to catch up on reality television and drink spiked seltzers. I played along, since I found it adorable when he lapsed into tough guy mode in front of his friends.

"You know I can't apply them evenly on my left hand and you happen to be the only person available, so it falls to you," I answered sweetly, while I held out my hand for my free manicure.

"So, Greyson. I hear you're dipping your toe back in the dating pool with a certain hockey player." Jace dropped his chin into both hands and fluttered his eyelashes like a true gossip queen. "I want to hear *everything*."

"Trevor, really? What are you telling people?" I demanded with irritation. The last thing I needed was my brother starting rumors that would inevitably spread like wildfire with Biscuits in the Basket holding the match. They somehow knew about everything in the city ten minutes before it happened, and I was sure they had hidden microphones planted every ten feet around Chicago. I wasn't even out of the church before they had posted the video of Trevor throwing KJ down the stairs.

Trevor shrugged while he applied my nails, his refusal to meet my eyes proof of his guilt. But I couldn't be upset. Jace knew everything there was to know about Trevor, including the one major thing we kept private from almost everyone. Jace waited expectantly and left me no option but to spill. He could wait me out, and he knew it. Years of questioning suspects left him much better equipped to wait for someone to tell him what he wanted to hear.

"Contrary to what you've heard," I started as I glanced pointedly at Trevor, "there is no dating on my horizon. Do I have a new friend who happens to have a penis? Yes. Will I be seeing it? I will not. Any more questions?"

"Do you want to?"

"Do I want to what?"

"See it. His penis. I mean, I'm not into dudes and I wouldn't turn down the chance to see Gavin Halstead's dick," Jace replied with a careless shrug. I shook my head repeatedly as I tried to talk down the blush that threatened to creep across my cheeks.

"No," I answered firmly. A little too quick. A little too loud.

"I can see your nose growing RayRay," Trevor muttered, his face buried in the final nail application.

"You do remember we're detectives, right? It's our job to sniff out liars." Jace stuck his nose in the air, as if he could smell my deception. Asshole.

"So maybe I do. So what? It won't ever happen so there's no point thinking about it." I didn't need to tell them I did think about it. A lot. Trevor and I were closer than most siblings but discussing my sexual fantasies with him was where I drew the line.

"From what Trev has been telling me about this guy, I don't think that's necessarily true," Jace replied. "Sounds like he's into you, and patiently waiting for you to throw him a sign."

"Let me know if you need a designated driver later," I answered as I inspected my completed nails. It was my not-so-subtle way to change the topic and the detectives took the hint.

"Come with us. It's just some people from work. You know most of them. It'll be fun."

"No thanks. I've got a hot date with the couch and a bottle of Moscato," I said. I tried to hide the shudder that rolled through me at the idea of making small talk for hours with a bunch of cops who liked to trade war stories. I knew the streets of Chicago were a dangerous place, but I enjoyed life in my little bubble where I could pretend it was so removed it could never touch me. I also didn't necessarily love to spend time with people who reminded me that Trevor's life was on the line every day he slipped his star around his neck.

"I don't want you to be alone for another holiday," Trevor protested as he handed Jace the sweets. I smiled softly and thought of how the past two holidays had been saved by an angel in Falcons clothing.

"This is the first one where I'll be by myself," I murmured, comforted that I'd at least be able to see Gavin through the television screen. "Besides, I abhor New Year's Eve, and you know it."

"If you're sure, we're going to head out," Trevor replied as he paused at the front door. "You'll be okay?"

"I'm good Trev. I promise. I'll be asleep before midnight anyway."

"I'm proud of you. You know that, right?"

"You always make sure I do."

"Happy New Year, RayRay. I have a feeling this will be the best one yet."

The game had just started when I made my way into the living room after I locked up. I settled in with a glass of wine and bowl of popcorn and rang in the new year watching the Falcons win with an energy I hadn't seen much of this season. I texted Gavin to congratulate him and was surprised when he responded almost instantly.

GAVIN

Thanks, Lemon Drop. Happy New Year. I hope you're enjoying it.

I replied with a photo of my slipper clad feet propped up on the ottoman next to an empty wine glass, and his response made my heart pound in nerves and anticipation.

GAVIN

Wish I was there to be your pillow. Coffee and
a walk by the lake tomorrow?

Maybe Trevor was right. Opening January on a date with
Gavin Halstead was a solid start on the way to the best year of my
life.

CHAPTER 13

Greyson

I 'd tried on every combination of clothes in my closet by the time I heard the knock on the door, and I rushed down the hall as I pulled a soft cashmere sweater the color of rose petals over my head. Gavin always teased that it made my blush more pronounced when I wore it. If he only knew it was him that did that. I opened the door to see him with a smile so big his dimple disappeared into the side of his mouth and my stomach dropped into my furry boots.

"Hey, you ready? You look great." Gavin's voice had that husky quality it took on when he was going on too little sleep, and his eyes gave away the fact he probably wished he were still unconscious under piles of blankets instead of on my porch when it was eleven degrees.

"Thank you," I replied shyly as heat crept up my cheeks. He smiled and took in the color of my shirt that now matched the color of my face. "Are you sure you want to do this? We can rain check for when you've had time to rest."

"I'd choose time with you over a few hours of sleep any day," Gavin assured me. He guided me to his truck with a hand on my lower back and helped me climb inside the vehicle. Small talk flowed easily as Gavin drove us to a locally owned coffee shop near the lake. He held my seatbelt in place when I reached to unclip it.

"If we go inside, I'll have to divide my attention between you and the fans. I'd rather be cold with just you than warm surrounded by people. That's why," Gavin answered the question I didn't ask. I nodded, unable to speak around the lump lodged in my throat.

I waited in the truck while he went to collect our drinks and ran my hands over the buttery leather of the seats. The backseat was bigger than my entire car, and my mind went to an inappropriate place. When Gavin returned I was fanning my cheeks, and he looked me over with concern.

"Are you hot? I can turn down the heat," he offered as he reached for the control.

"No, I'm good. I was just ... I had a thought ... I ... hot flash. Not that I'm going through menopause or anything! Plenty of eggs left in this basket."

My heart thudded so loud with embarrassment that I was sure he could hear the drumline of humiliation that played out in my chest. Luckily, Gavin was too polite to call me out. Directly anyway.

"I really like the color of that sweater."

That made the intense fire of humiliation mixed with desire burn out of control, and I leaned my forehead on the window as we headed towards the lake. Gavin pulled into a parking spot near the water and met me on the sidewalk. He passed over my coffee as we started our stroll and a jolt of sexual energy travelled through my gloves when our hands touched.

The city was quiet with the muted tones that came with snow. Even the traffic noise was muffled, like the serenity of winter would not allow the chaos of honking horns and squealing tires to permeate the peace. Gavin and I bumped into each other as we walked, and I looked forward to the quick grazes enough that I started to do it on purpose.

"So, your New Year's Eve was crazy exciting, eh?" Gavin

turned his head away from the wind and presented me with the full power of his beautiful smile.

"Absolutely scintillating." I was so desperate for his touch I lost my inhibition and threaded my arm through his as we walked. His eyes dropped to where we were connected, and he tucked his elbow tightly against his side, which made it impossible for me to extricate myself. "Yours was good though. You played great. Very impressive with those face-offs."

Gavin laughed and sipped his coffee. "It was alright. Winning was nice, but I'd have much rather been home. With you."

He loosened his arm so mine slid down his side, only to immediately capture my hand in his with a possessive grip. I was so stunned by the move that I stumbled forward and almost lost my grip on the cup of coffee.

"I made champagne cupcakes yesterday. If you don't mind day old, we can toast to the new year with cake when you drop me off."

"That's an offer I'm definitely taking you up on," Gavin said. He shot me a bashful grin. "Midnight countdown and all?"

I froze, and my heart skipped enough beats it was mildly concerning.

"Uh ... if you want ... I mean ... it's not midnight. So that would be ... is that bad luck?" I begged my brain to stop my mouth from moving. I wanted pretty much nothing more than to kiss him. But I was not at all prepared for him to suggest it so blatantly. He shrugged carelessly and took another drink out of his cup.

"You might be right. A kiss for a dictated reason isn't necessarily the greatest way to do it."

"Do you remember your first kiss?" I wasn't sure where the question came from, other than attempting to steer the conversation of us kissing in another direction.

Gavin smiled sadly; his gaze fixed off into the distance. "Olive Russell. I was twelve."

It was clear from his expression it was a memorable moment, one that he had carried into adulthood.

"Olive. That's a cute name. Do you still talk to her?"

We stopped in front of a bench, and he motioned for me to sit.

"I wish I could. She passed away."

Guilt rushed through me for dredging up a memory that might be difficult for him to relive. This must be the loss that got him started in therapy.

"I'm so sorry. I didn't mean to bring it up."

"Don't be." Gavin's lips moved in a loop from a smile to a frown. I wanted to take the sad part of that cyclical expression away, so he was left with only the good part of the memory. "I'll never turn down the opportunity to talk about her."

"If you don't mind my asking, what happened?" I asked tentatively. When Gavin remained silent, I quickly backpedaled. "I'm sorry. Never mind. It's none of my business. I used to get so mad when people would want details about my dad's death. Like it was an entertaining story and not a painful thing to recall. I don't want to be that person to you."

Gavin lifted his head and looked sideways as he squeezed my thigh. The warmth of his palm soaked through my leggings. When he moved to pull his hand back, I stopped him and dropped my gloved hand over his.

"She had cancer. Lymphoma. It was just a couple days before … she asked me … she didn't want to die without knowing what it felt like to be kissed."

"Was she your girlfriend?"

He leaned back and stretched his legs out on the sidewalk with a shake of his head. "No. Just a friend. One of my best friends. When we started kindergarten, she followed us around and just never left. Asher thought she had a crush on me, but it wasn't like that. She was just part of the group. I'm not sure why she asked me when it came time for that."

I knew why. Gavin was soft and good. He gave everything he

had for the people he loved. It was obvious why a sweet little girl who wanted to feel desirable for just a moment would turn to him. I was a grown woman and doing the same.

"I'm so sorry for the fact you had to navigate that loss at twelve. I know how difficult it is to accept death at such a young age. Cancer is how I lost my grandma too, but she had the opportunity to live a long and happy life. Fall in love. Have a family. It's not right when it happens to a baby."

His eyes dropped to where my hand still covered his. It could have been my imagination, but I swore he curled his fingers around my thigh with a soft squeeze.

"I was pissed off for a long time. It wasn't fair. She was the sweetest girl; the purest soul. It was a lot to swallow as a kid. I've spent my entire life comparing first kisses to that one. They all come up short—they don't carry that level of importance. How could they?"

"Adult problems aren't meant to make sense to children's brains. I get it," I replied softly, as my own memories drifted back to the sound of the doorbell the day we found out Dad would never come home. We had been waiting on pizza delivery. Trevor and I raced to the front door, as we tried to beat the other to the slice with the bubble. Neither of us ate. I still wasn't much of a pizza fan.

Gavin sighed and gently pulled his hand from under mine as he stretched it across the back of the bench and absently brushed his fingers over my shoulder. He turned his attention to me, and his eyes came into focus as I fought the urge to look away from his intense stare.

"It's so screwed up right? But really, the tough spots have shaped us into the people we are today. I think I'm a pretty good guy. You're beyond amazing. Silver lining or something."

"There isn't always an explanation for things, Gavin. Sometimes shit just happens and it sucks and that's that."

"I disagree."

"Well, I'm sorry, but that's how I see it."

Gavin pulled his legs up as he turned towards me.

"A difference of opinion isn't a need for an apology. You're allowed to have your own thoughts."

"I'm not used to that," I admitted softly.

"You will be," Gavin licked his lips before they stretched into a smile and the dimple to the left of his mouth deepened. It was one of my favorite things about his face. Most people's dimples rested in their cheeks, but that wasn't good enough for Gavin. Like everything else about him, he had to be different. Special. He had a freckle in almost the exact same spot and when he smiled big it disappeared into the dented curve of skin.

So sexy.

I really needed to stop with those thoughts before I accidentally said them out loud.

"What are you trying *not* to say right now?" Gavin asked, with an expression that let me know he saw deeper into my brain than I was necessarily comfortable with. I jumped off the bench in a desperate attempt to break the spell he had over me.

"Not one single thing! I need to get back to the shop, can we go now?"

Gavin tilted his head to the side as I tapped my foot nervously, ready to escape the situation that had gotten too personal.

"Nope."

"What? Nope?" I squeaked out, so high pitched I barely recognized my voice.

"You didn't tell me about your first kiss. We aren't done here."

"Gavin." My attempt at authoritative came across as more of a childish whine and the laugh he gave me in return showed how much he was *not* threatened by it.

"Greyson." He pushed off the bench and entered my space as the warmth of his scent filled my nose. "It's only fair. I showed you mine, you show me yours. Plus, the shop is closed today."

"There's nothing to tell," I replied breezily. I pushed against his chest until he backed up a step. I started to walk away but stopped short when his fingers closed around my wrist.

"Come on, tell me," Gavin had lost the playful tone. Now that I knew the story behind his first kiss, I really didn't want to share mine, but I had already learned Gavin didn't give up when he wanted something. I heaved a defeated sigh and stared out across the frozen lake.

"It's not a nice story." That seemed to be the way all my stories started out. "I was an unwitting participant in a mean game. He was popular and I wasn't, but I was too naïve to see how unlikely it was he actually liked me. When he kissed me in front of the entire school and the rest of the cool kids bowed down to him, I knew."

Gavin's frown was etched deeply into the lines of his forehead. Silence stretched between us, thick and heavy.

"Are you serious?"

"Yeah, but it was good. Shaped me into the person I am today, right?" I failed miserably in my attempt to laugh it off. "Taught me early I'm perfect prey for assholes who want to publicly humiliate me."

Gavin turned me to face him and held my cheeks in his hands. Being so close, I found the underlying tones of cinnamon and spicy ginger in the cologne I knew was expensive by the way it laid on his skin. An idea started to form in my mind of a heavily spiced cinnamon cake studded with candied ginger and vanilla peppercorn buttercream. The pepper would bring out both spices and create a balanced cake I *knew* would be a hit.

"That guy was a douchebag," Gavin said roughly. "That bullshit doesn't reflect on you."

"I was an easy target. I was a mess after my dad died. Then what happened with my mom ... I was barely lucid half the time. Being Jonah Park's granddaughter made my score higher. It is what it is. Do you have a pen?"

"Score? What score?"

"Doesn't matter," I mumbled as I rummaged around my purse for my notepad. I quickly scribbled notations, measurements and ingredients before the moment passed. "Would you order a cupcake that had black pepper frosting on it? Like, would you try it? Or is that too weird?"

"Is it a cupcake *you're* making, or just in general? Tell me what you meant by 'your score.'"

"Me. My cupcake. Would you eat *my* cupcake with that frosting?"

"I'd eat your cupcake however you gave it to me." Gavin's face flushed and I stopped my recipe creation long enough to lock eyes with him. The flash of sexual tension that crackled between us was so electric I was surprised I didn't get shocked. He blinked furiously and pulled his jacket across his middle while he clenched and unclenched his jaw.

"Well anyway. What's the score about?"

"Why do we have to talk about this?" I waved the question away. "It was forever ago. It doesn't matter."

"I think it does matter. I want to know. Tell me."

"Your alpha male tendencies are kind of frustrating, you know that?" I grumbled as I finished my notes and shoved my notebook into my bag. "The guys in my school had a point system when it came to the girls. It was like some fucked up sport. Their game started the first day of school and went on all year. Dates were x points. Kisses were y. Double for oral. Sex was more. Taking someone's virginity was most. Apparently, I helped Clint win since I not only had a famous name, but I was damaged. They got higher scores for the traumatized girls. Even though he didn't get my virginity all his points combined got him the trophy. Look, can we please go? I need to work on this new cupcake for the case tomorrow."

Gavin frowned deeply; his anger palpable as he stepped closer and placed his hands on either side of me.

"I'm sorry that happened to you, Greyson. It's unacceptable behavior."

"It really wasn't that big of a thing." I was breathless, dizzy with warring emotions. Gavin was intense. He was gentle and kind, but when the switch flipped, he was protective and commanded attention. His force field was stronger than the most dangerous storm you could ever encounter. Lately all that energy was focused on me. I hated it and never wanted it to stop at the same time.

"Your first kiss is supposed to be special. Something that matters, that makes you smile when you think back on it. It shouldn't have been stolen from you under false pretenses."

"I absolutely love your view of the world, Canada. You show me positivity in a way I've never felt before. But it was just ... boys being boys," I replied, safe inside the protection of his arms. I had never felt this way with KJ, even at the beginning when I was too wrapped up in attraction and star gazing to see what I had gotten myself into.

"I hate that fucking expression. We shouldn't get a free pass to be dicks just because we have them," Gavin growled, his voice low and rocky. He closed his arms tighter and took another step towards me. "Someday you'll have a first kiss that makes all the ones before it irrelevant."

It seemed more like a promise than a statement. I hoped it was.

"You sound pretty certain about that."

"Mark my words. Your next first kiss will erase that memory. Your next first kiss will be your *best* first kiss. Maybe it'll even be your *last* first kiss," Gavin paused to let his words find their mark and settle like dust after a tornado. "Ready to go?"

He pushed away from the railing, clearly aware of what his statement had just done to me. It had become impossible for me to ignore the feelings I'd developed for him, and since I was never the greatest at hiding my emotions, I was sure he could see it too.

CHAPTER 14
Greyson

The door opened and Dr. Thomas stood with a smile, waving me towards her office.

"Happy New Year!"

"It's February, doc," I said, dropping into my usual chair and shaking out of my coat. Doctor Thomas sat in her chair with a good-natured roll of her eyes.

"Yes, but I haven't seen you since before Thanksgiving," she paused. "On that note, let's not get into the habit of three months between appointments."

She was so right, especially now. There was no excuse for blowing off therapy other than I didn't want to be told things I already knew. Not to mention, whatever was going on with Gavin was deeply personal and I knew she would dig down to figure out all of my reasons for trying to keep him at arm's length.

"The holidays are so busy—"

"Which is exactly why you need to maintain your schedule," Doctor Thomas interrupted. She had been my therapist for almost fifteen years, in my life longer than most people I knew had been. Her stern tone was nothing new, and I found myself feeling guilty that I had disappointed her.

"I'll book my next three appointments before I leave," I

conceded. She gave me a victorious look and settled back into her chair.

"So, how did the holidays go? The last time we saw each other you were nervous for the emotional toll of the firsts."

Once I started talking, I was glad I had booked two hours for the comeback session. Wading through how I had made it through the two most family centered holidays, the first ones without my grandpa, the first ones since my wedding fell apart, without Trevor's support, took almost an hour on its own.

"How did you do navigating those days alone?"

I flushed, wanting to hold onto Gavin, keep him to myself. Once he was spoken into therapy, he became part of my life. Not that he wasn't already, but telling my therapist about him made it real. That would make the conversation start, about whether or not he was someone who would become important enough to learn about my past. But I couldn't lie. Otherwise, what was the point of even coming?

"I actually wasn't alone. I've ... met someone."

"Oh?" She asked. "A male someone? Met as in, a romantic suitor?"

"No! He's just, he's a friend. I mean, I've known him for a long time but KJ wouldn't let me get to know him, know him, so it was kind of like just meeting. He came to spend Thanksgiving with me because I was sick, and then on Christmas I went to him and that's when we almost kissed. But his sister interrupted us and thank God for that, because if she hadn't, I definitely would have tried to swallow his face. So, okay, I guess we spent New Year's together, too, and technically I guess we went on a date—"

"I think we've skipped a bit of important information," Doctor Thomas interrupted. "This man knows KJ?"

I broke eye contact and turned my attention to the aloe Vera plant that I always transferred my energy to whenever she asked me a question I didn't like.

"Mmm," I answered noncommittally, as I rubbed the end of one of the leaves. "They ... worked together."

I snuck a look at her. Her usually carefully neutral face had slipped long enough for me to catch the look of surprise.

"He's a hockey player?"

More than one session had revolved around my gravitation to hockey players due to my love for my grandpa. Since he was my safe space after the traumas I suffered in childhood, I subconsciously expected anyone in a hockey jersey to provide that level of love and protection. I had made a hard line in the sand after KJ; no more NHL players. Ever again.

"He's a person who makes money playing hockey, yes."

Her eyes went slightly squinty as she regarded me closely.

"Have we talked about him before?"

Dammit.

I blew out a hard breath and looked at the ceiling, sliding down into the chair. Doctor Thomas knew about Gavin, from before. My feelings of guilt for having an attraction to a man who was not the one I was engaged to. My innermost wish that he spoke to me, ever. The way I would replay any accidental eye contact or curt 'hello' over and over and over until I made myself insane. How the way he treated me hurt worse than every new woman I found out about my fiancé sleeping with.

"Yes. I'm seeing Gavin Halstead," I admitted. "Not seeing, seeing. Seeing, as in, hanging out. Going on walks every night."

I smiled to myself at that. Since New Year's Day, we had fallen into a routine of coffee and walks by the lake. I looked forward to that hour as if it were the energy that made the rest of my day possible.

"This is quite a turn of events. If I recall, he's been quite standoffish with you for years."

The picture of his face when he explained himself in my office crowded my memory, and I reached for my pendant.

"Apparently KJ told him not to talk to me, and Gavin was concerned about what the fallout would be for me if he ignored that," I paused. "Like he wanted to."

Doctor Thomas raised an eyebrow and crossed her legs, pushing her glasses into her hair.

"It sounds like his reasoning for his behavior towards you was honorable, even if it wasn't adequately communicated at the time."

I waited for her to continue, to point out that I was doing exactly what I said I wasn't going to do by getting close with another Falcons player. But she just sat, quietly watching the expressions move over my face.

"He's exactly the man I thought he was. Kind. Funny. Generous. Thoughtful. He makes me feel safe," I said softly. She nodded but kept quiet, a sign for me to keep talking. "I don't trust it, though. I'm waiting for him to realize I'm not worth his time or his affection."

"Why is that automatically where your mind goes? That you're not worthy of cultivating a healthy, happy relationship with a good man?"

I dropped my head and shot her an exasperated look, then checked my watch. I still had twenty minutes left. No way out.

"You know why," I muttered. Doctor Thomas folded her hands into her lap as she leaned forward.

"I want to hear you tell me."

I debated shutting down, staying silent the rest of the session. I was fidgeting after a minute, and after two I couldn't stand it anymore.

"My mother didn't love me. The one person who was supposed to love me unconditionally instead tried to get rid of me. My fiancé didn't love me. He worked to keep me a shell of a person, so I would know that no one else would ever look at me as anything but a damaged, pathetic excuse for a woman. Why the hell would someone as wonderful as Gavin even look twice at me?"

Dr. Thomas passed me a box of tissues, and that's when I realized I had started to cry. I was certain Mila, Delaney, and Trevor saw through my continued denials about my true feelings for

※ 110 ※

Gavin. They never called me on it, since they were all aware of how deeply KJ's indoctrination had hooked into my brain. I remembered every comment about my weight, my looks, my career, and my desirability. I latched onto the past insults as if they were life rafts every time Gavin got too close. The walls I had built through KJ's emotional abuse were thick and impenetrable, and I didn't know how to knock them down enough to let Gavin in. You can only be told you're a waste of a human being so many times before you start to believe it. Since my mom had given KJ a head start, it didn't take as long for him to completely break me down as it might have otherwise.

"It seems to me that Gavin has held some feelings for you the same way you have, all this time," Doctor Thomas said. "He's letting you set the boundaries and the pace of your relationship."

"We don't have a relationship," I protested. Yes, we spoke every day, and saw each other twice a day when he was in town. He came to Icing in the morning, and we went for a walk at night. I was going to every Falcons game again, keeping track of his face-offs and discussing with him later. When he was on the road, I watched on television and texted with him afterwards.

"A friendship is a relationship, Greyson. I think it's smart of you to take your time, but I want you to focus on being open with him. He's obviously happy in your company, and you seem happy, too."

I was happier than I could ever remember being. Which scared the living hell out of me. He hadn't been able to crack my walls, but he was doing a steady job climbing over them. Once he got inside, I wasn't so sure he would like what he found.

CHAPTER 15
Greyson

Winter was ruthless, the bitter cold determined to make sure everyone knew who ruled. At the first hint of warmth, the city bloomed and everyone came out of hibernation. Save for one. I loathed spring, the scent of mud and bizarre weather that dipped between chilly and unbearably humid ensuring I stayed indoors as much as possible. The constant rain that had gone on for over a week dampened the city, the bakery, and my mood. I should have been excited over the fact I was headed to South Carolina to film a special for *Eat It*. The weather alone was a bright spot. But there was one major negative.

"You're seriously going to be out of town for the playoffs?" Gavin tried to cover the disappointment in his question, but I heard it. I hated it. Almost as much as the wet that clung to the bottom of my yoga pants.

"Just the beginning," I promised. "I'll be home to watch you raise the cup."

Gavin laughed and squeezed my hand. He kept hold of it until he spotted a couple walking towards us in the opposite direction, and took an additional step away as we walked past them. Our nightly walks along the lake weren't as interesting to

Biscuits as they had been in January when we had started them, but we were still careful not to touch in any way that could be misinterpreted. Not that there was anything to tell, aside from a dozen or two close kiss calls and awkward almosts. My heart demanded I tell him how I felt more than a few hundred times, but my head stepped in before I could make the move that would change everything.

Gavin moved easily back into the spot right next to me once we were clear. There were no other people anywhere along the water, and as much as I loved the one-on-one time with him every day he was in town, I longed to be one of the people warm and dry in their condos.

"I love your optimism," Gavin said.

"Someone has to have it," I replied sternly. The Falcons had gotten into the playoffs as the wild card team, and none of them seemed to think they would get far.

"So how long will you be gone?"

"Three weeks," I rolled my eyes at his over exaggerated groan, secretly thrilled he would miss me. "I'll still watch every game. I just won't physically be in front of you doing it."

"That's why I'm worried about winning. I'm only good when I can lay eyes on you while I'm playing," Gavin said. I stopped walking and tugged on his sleeve. When Gavin turned to look at me, I saw everything I'd ever hoped for in his eyes.

"Listen Canada. I need you to hear something, okay?" I moved into him, aware of how close our bodies were. "I'm always with you. Just think of me. I'll be there."

Gavin's arms slipped around my waist and his hands settled just above my backside.

"There haven't been many moments I *haven't* thought of you in the last six months," he said softly. "Have you felt it?"

"Yes," I whispered. "I don't want to leave you."

Gavin took a step back, and framed my cheeks in his hands. I savored the warmth of them, shivering for reasons that had nothing to do with being cold.

"I'll make sure we stay in it. So I can celebrate the win with you. On the ice. For everyone to see."

"What do you mean by that?" I asked. Blood rushed through my ears at the boldness of the question, and I barely registered the mist that had begun to fall.

"You know, Greyson. You might not accept it, or want to let yourself believe it, but you know."

CHAPTER 16
Gavin

The atmosphere inside the Delta Center was electric. Excitement buzzed through the air like a current, and I couldn't keep still. My body shook with nerves as the anthem ended and the lights came back up. We had worked all season to get to this point, and now that it was here, I was vibrating.

The series opened at home, which was always a positive in terms of headspace. Hearing our fans go nuts during the playoffs made us better and being matched against Nashville for the first round—one of our most vicious rivalries—made any edge we could get important. Duff Rockwell hadn't forgotten about our fight at the beginning of the season, and the way he circled me before the opening faceoff set the tone.

This game was going to be ugly.

"Ignore it," Asher warned, as he skated close. "Not now. He's going to goad you. He's going to say something about Gigi. Don't take the bait."

It irritated me that he felt the need to caution me. I knew I had fucked up with Duff the second it happened. I didn't need a reminder.

"I got it," I replied shortly.

"Make sure you do," Asher slapped my helmet with a grin. "Leave the fighting to me, dad."

The team fought hard to get where we did, and I was already proud of the performance. Nashville won the opening faceoff, which infuriated me. At least Greyson wasn't there to see it. When I had glanced quickly at her seats when I came out for warmups, I saw Trevor and his partner Jace occupying them. Greyson had been in South Carolina for two days, and I was feeling her absence in my performance. I was going to do every-thing I could to make sure she was smiling at the game in her hotel room.

Seven minutes into the first period, Nashville stripped the puck from Asher and took off down the ice towards Cohen. He was blocked by Frost, one of our defensemen, and ended up pushing Cohen into his net. Frost took offense, and he and Marshall, the Nashville forward, dropped their gloves. This was not how I wanted the game to go. Frost had wrestled him to the ground by the time I made it down the ice. They were both assessed five-minute majors, and when they came back out onto the ice it was clear the issue was far from over. Every time Frost and Marshall were near each other there were shoves and chirps. Tensions had mounted by the time the second period began and penalties were handed out like Halloween candy throughout the entire twenty minutes. A face-off of in the third period found me opposite Duff.

"Greyson—"

"Nope. Don't go there," I snarled. "Off limits."

"Heard she's got a tight little—" Duff shoved forward, hitting my shoulder.

The official blew his whistle and waved Duff off the circle. I smirked since I'd hoped the linesman would catch the intentional cheat. His replacement had a terrible face-off win percentage and I easily slid the puck back to Asher. As he set up a shot, he was slashed and we managed to convert on the power play to finally get on the board.

Nashville got even more aggressive after that. We were exhausted and pissed off, fighting to hold the lead. Duff hauled back on a shot that whistled as it left his stick, and I watched in horror as it hit Cohen directly in the forehead. He went down instantly, and the arena went silent the longer he was motionless on the ice. I dropped my stick as I took off towards him, pushing through the linesman and falling onto my knees next to him.

"Co, are you okay? Talk to me."

His eyes were closed, and he didn't respond to my voice. Even though he had his helmet on, when a puck hits you dead center in the face at upwards of eighty miles per hour, it's going to cause an injury. Our trainers crowded around him, and when I saw the stretcher come out, I talked down the panic clawing at my throat. Asher and Frost stood quietly next to me as he was loaded on. He didn't even lift a hand to signal he was alright, so I skated to the doors with him, looking down into his blank stare.

"We're kicking their asses for you, Co. You're going to be good. I promise."

Our focus was shaken, but since I had made that promise we were going to keep it. We scored two more times before the game was over and held Nashville without a goal. The excitement over the win was dampened by the fact we didn't know how our goalie —our friend—was doing. We ran down the tunnel into the locker room and were told Cohen was alert but was being evaluated for a concussion and would very possibly be out the rest of the round. By the time I got home, I was so drained I could barely drag myself into my room.

My phone rang as I fell into bed, and as tired as I was, I answered immediately.

"Is Cohen okay?" Greyson's worried voice trembled. "That looked so bad. Is he awake? Fucking Duff Rockwell!"

Her outrage brought a smile to my face, and I stretched out with my arm behind my head.

"He's in concussion protocol. It could have been a lot worse, but it wasn't great."

She blew out a breath and I heard her relay the news to Mila and Delaney. A door opened and closed in the background, and I got a notification she had switched to a video call. As soon as I saw her face, my tension melted.

"Now that I'm alone, and we've established Cohen is okay, you can tell me the truth. Are you worried about the rest of the series? Since your backup is also coming off an injury, and Cohen is probably out?"

I pulled my knees up and settled the phone against my legs, as I leaned forward to adjust a heating pad behind me.

"I shouldn't care about that," I replied, a groan escaping me when I leaned back. Greyson watched me closely, and she chewed her lip as I fluffed a pillow behind my head.

"The Cup is the reason you play the game, Gavin. You can be disappointed while still caring about your friend's well-being," Greyson said. She gave me a small smile. "Can I do anything to help?"

"Tell me about your day," I answered. "Listening to your voice will help."

She did just that, and an hour later we were both stifling yawns to keep the connection. Greyson sighed with a sleepy smile.

"You played so well tonight. I hate that I'm not there, but I'll be at every game the next round."

"Home games," I corrected. My heart pounded when she shook her head with a bashful grin.

"I was thinking I'd do both. If you don't mind. I mean, maybe that's weird. It's weird, isn't it? We aren't dating, so following the team around for the playoffs is—"

"I'll give you one of my player edition shirts to wear," I interrupted. Greyson's mouth snapped shut and her eyes widened, clearly understanding the implication of that. No number of protestations would quiet Biscuits in the Basket's speculations if she was spotted out of town in one of the shirts that only players owned.

"As long as you don't expect to ever get it back," she replied, a crimson stain creeping up her cheeks.

"I can't wait to see you in it."

"Me too," Greyson murmured. "Goodnight, Canada. Sleep well."

"I will. Cause I'll be thinking about you."

CHAPTER 17
Greyson

The plane had barely landed, and I was out of my seat. The trip to South Carolina had been great—if not longer than originally planned—but I was ready to be home.

To him.

After Cohen's injury, the team had fallen four in a row and got knocked out of the playoffs in the first round. Gavin was in a foul mood after that, not unexpectedly, but it had been difficult to even get him to smile. I had grown accustomed to his easy laugh, and the permanent grin that seemed to be his resting expression, so for that to be absent affected me in a way I hadn't expected. He had barely even answered the phone the last few days, and when he did his voice was guarded and short. Since I was so good at assuming everything was my fault, I had wondered what I did to make him so upset with me.

Now that I was home, I was going to make it my mission to bring a smile to his face. I headed straight for his house once I got out of the madness of airport traffic, nerves and excitement battling for space in my stomach.

I practically skipped up to his front door, tapping my foot impatiently as the seconds went by without an answer. The blinds were drawn in the front windows, which was strange. I took a step back and noticed the overall aura of the house, settled and quiet. He obviously wasn't home, and it felt like he hadn't been for some time.

Disappointed, I headed back to my car. Gavin's neighbor locked eyes with me with a hand held in a wave, as if he were waiting for me to ask where he was.

"Hiya Greyson. He's not there."

Obviously.

"Do you know when he'll be back?"

The neighbor scratched his chin, glancing at the dark house before his eyes settled back on me.

"Uh, he made it sound like he was going to be gone all summer. He asked me to keep an eye on the place. He didn't tell you?"

If he had thrown a bucket of ice water on me, it would have shocked me less. But since I had heard his neighbor listening to the Biscuits podcast when he was washing his car, I didn't want to give him any ammunition he could send to them in terms of our relationship. I carefully rearranged my face, replacing my hurt with a bright smile.

"I've been traveling the last few days. Cell service has been sketchy. I'm sure it was a miscommunication! Thanks!"

I didn't stick around long enough to see if he bought it.

I broke quite a few laws speeding home, incessantly dialing Gavin's number. Even though it went straight to voicemail, I never gave up. Until I got a better idea. Asher picked up after one ring.

"Gigi, hey, you home? How was South Carolina?"

"Where is he?"

Asher was quiet, long enough for me to squeal at him in frustration.

"*Asher.*"

"Have you been home?" Asher finally asked. I turned onto my street and slammed to a stop in front of my house.

"I just got here. Why does that matter?"

"Check the mail," Asher paused. "I'm sorry. I told him not to go."

I scrambled out of the car, abandoning my luggage and pulling the overflowing mail out of the box. Thumbing through the bills and junk mail, I found what Asher was referring to. A light green envelope with no postage, just my name printed neatly across the front in block letters.

"I gotta go," I whispered, hanging up on him before he could respond. I dropped onto the porch and ripped it open, tearing the paper in my haste. Gavin's slanted handwriting stared back at me as I began to read.

Lemon Drop,

Let me start by saying I'm sorry. I know this was not the right way to handle this. I had to get out of Chicago, and if I told you—if I heard your voice—I wouldn't have been able to leave. This loss gutted me. Not just because we lost, but because of ... well, I really wanted people to see you, at the playoffs, for me. It's immature and selfish, I know. But you aren't here, and the fans are, and I just need to go where I'm left alone.

I'll be off the grid for a while. I'm going home to Canada. I've got a cabin that's pretty remote, and I need to go there to recharge, to get back to the Gavin you deserve. I promise I'll call you as soon as I'm back online. Just please know—this has nothing to do with you. I won't ask you not to be upset with me. If you did this to me, I would be livid and heartbroken, so I don't expect a different response from you. If I can ask one thing; don't give up on me. On us. I'm begging you.

Love,

Canada

My breathing had slowed as I read his words, his scent all over the paper that was now wet with my tears. He was gone. In another country, in a place he had purposely chosen to go so I could not reach him. Regardless of his words, I couldn't help but take it personally. I had no way of knowing exactly when he had left town, but our last telephone contact was only two days earlier. He had already been gone when I was gushing about how excited I was to see him. And he had said nothing.

Idiot.

I was so stupid. I had truly thought I was something to him. Something important.

As I cried on my porch, I realized it had happened again. I had been fooled by a Falcon.

May 28

GAVIN

Hey...

June 2

GAVIN

I miss you

June 7

GAVIN

You know how sorry I am...don't you?

June 11

GAVIN

Please just let me know you're okay

June 12

GAVIN

I'm going to call the police if I don't hear from you

GREYSON

Weird how communication is only important when it suits you.

GAVIN

I deserved that

June 15

GAVIN

Can we talk?

June 16

GREYSON

No, thank you. Your letter said all I needed to hear.

GAVIN

Please don't shut down on me. I fucked up. I own it. But I'm not going to push you. Call me when you're ready. I'll leave you alone until then.

CHAPTER 18
Greyson

The splashing from the back yard made it clear the party was already going. I spotted Asher's car parked next to Delaney's and leaned into the back seat of my own to grab the tray of desserts. I walked right into Mila's house, depositing the sweets onto the table that was covered with assorted snacks. After I tossed my purse onto the couch, I slid open the back door, and grabbed a beer from the cooler.

"Gigi! Happy 4th of July!" Asher swam to the side of the pool and pulled himself out, running at me and dripping wet.

"Asher, no."

My protest fell on deaf ears as he scooped me into his arms and spun me in a circle, his standard greeting. The longer I knew him, the more he reminded me of a human version of a golden retriever. When he set me down, my cotton sundress was soaked, and I shot him an annoyed look.

"It's a pool party," he grinned. "The whole point is to get wet."

I shook my head and dropped onto the edge of the pool, leaning into Mila's side-armed hug. While the group that was gathered had become close friends, I had never been super comfortable in a swimsuit. Especially around men. Undeniably good-looking men with rock hard bodies. Of course, the only one whose opinion mattered to me was noticeably absent. Oddly, if he had been there, I would have had the confidence to shed my dress and spend the day splashing around. As it was, I was content to sit on the edge, swirling my feet and watching Asher, Cohen, and their baby teammate whom they had taken under their wing, Nate Frost, continually jump off the diving board. I had been moping and depressed since we had returned to Chicago and getting together with the guys for the 4th of July was Mila and Delaney's idea to bring me out of my funk. Unfortunately, spending time with his friends made it even more difficult not to miss him.

I drowned my sorrow in Blonde Bomber and finally waded into the pool, making sure I was halfway covered by water before I pulled my dress off my head and tossed it on the edge of the pool. Delaney was stretched out on a unicorn float and Mila met me next to it, where we talked until Asher swam up to us.

"Mind if I steal her away for a minute?"

Delaney lifted her head and raised an eyebrow, dipping her hand into the water and splashing it towards his face.

"If she comes back here upset, I *will* drown you."

Asher waved her off and pushed her float towards the deep end, then turned back to me with his huge smile.

"I don't want to do this, Asher," I said. I already knew where the conversation was going, and it hadn't even started.

"I know, but I promised him I'd talk to you," he drug his hands lazily through the water. "He's miserable, Gigi."

As hurt as I was by Gavin's actions, it hurt more to hear that he was unhappy.

"I'm not exactly dancing on rainbows, myself," I answered. Asher shook his hair, droplets of water flying.

"Right. You're both having a hell of a time. You're both sad. Depressed. Wasting the summer. For what? Pride? Stubbornness?"

"No, Asher. Try fear. At least for me."

His face softened and he stepped closer, water rippling around us.

"What are you afraid of?" Asher asked softly. I couldn't believe I was having this conversation with Gavin's best friend, knowing it would be going straight into his ears as soon as Asher left.

"This, I guess. This situation."

I could see his confusion, so I hurriedly continued before I lost my nerve.

"I don't know how to trust people. Opening my heart makes me vulnerable to getting hurt, but when we started getting close, I *wanted* to let him in. I suck at it, and it's been a challenge, but I've tried my hardest. I guess I never considered I would have to protect myself from him, too. It never crossed my mind Gavin could make me feel this way."

Asher frowned, a darkness shadowing his face.

"It would kill him to hear this."

"That's why I've been avoiding talking to him," I admitted. "I don't begrudge him going home. If anyone knows what it's like to want to escape, it's me. He has the right to deal with his mental health however he needs to, but the way he went about it triggered my own past trauma, and I—"

I trailed off, fighting against the tears gathering in my eyes. Asher pulled me into his arms, his hand settled on top of my head, and in that moment, I felt like I had another brother, the move so familiar from Trevor I instantly relaxed.

"My feelings aren't his responsibility," I continued. "But I can't just stop being hurt, you know? I've got a big issue with being lied to, and that's what he did. That's how I see it, anyway. When my trust goes, I just shut down."

Asher stepped back and looked at me earnestly.

"So, here's the question. Is this the end of the road? Something you can't get past, can't forgive him for?"

The thought of losing Gavin from my life made my throat close in panic.

"No! Of course not."

"Then text him," Asher scratched his chin and held up his hands. "You're probably going to get pissed when I say this, but we're pretty good friends now and my friends hear what I'm thinking whether they want to or not."

I tensed for whatever was coming.

"KJ conditioned you to be afraid to stand up for yourself. You weren't allowed to express your emotions, so when he would fuck around or be awful to you, you just swallowed it. You don't have to do that with Gavin. He doesn't *want* you to do that. He wants you to talk to him. About the good, bad, ugly, and everything in between."

By now, tears were sliding in twin columns down my face. Asher was a whole lot more in tune to my past with KJ than I was aware, which meant Gavin understood me, too.

"It's been so long now I don't even know what I'd say to get the conversation going," I said weakly. Asher threw his head back with a loud laugh and signaled Frost to toss us beers.

"Literally anything, Gigi. He's waiting for any communication. You could tell him to go fuck himself and he'd probably smile, because it meant you reached out."

Asher caught both cans as Nate launched them, presenting one to me with a flourish.

"I want you two to figure your shit out. It's obviously not happening organically, so I'm going to push it because I love you both and I don't want you to waste any more time when you could be happy."

I took the beer with a sigh, giving him an exasperated smile.

"Thanks, Ash. For caring this much. I'm really lucky to have a friend like you," I took a sip and wiped my mouth. "You win. I'll text him tonight."

. . .

July 4

GREYSON

I'm ready. Talk?

GAVIN

I'll call you in 10 seconds.

CHAPTER 19
Gavin

"Whose idea was this?" Cohen growled from the backseat. His leg extended across the space as he kicked the back of my seat in an annoying rhythm. Asher pushed his seat back as far as it would go to ensure there was no spare leg room for our monstrosity of a goalie to have a comfortable ride.

"Pretend you're on a tractor, Cowboy," he taunted.

"You didn't have to come," I reminded him as the entrance to the outdoor theater approached. I paid the attendant at the gate and rolled the truck into a spot at the end of a row. I turned my eyes to Asher, unable to tamp down my nerves. "You're sure she's coming?"

Cohen tumbled out of the backseat and made a huge fuss as he stretched his legs and immediately put Asher into a headlock. He wrestled away and let out a low whistle as two women walked towards us. One was dressed in cutoff jean shorts and a baggy green tank top, the other in a navy blue and white polka dotted romper thing short enough to send my imagination in an interesting direction. I'd know those legs anywhere.

"I can confirm she is," Asher grinned. He ducked away from my fist as I stood up straighter and nervously smoothed my hands over my shirt. Asher ran at them with his arms open and lifted each by their waists as he swung them around with one on each arm. Greyson and Delaney shrieked in laughter at his impromptu swing ride. Asher deposited Greyson on the ground in front of me, and she smiled shyly.

"Hey." Her hair fluttered around her shoulders with the strong breeze. Loose strands blew across her mouth and stuck against the light pink gloss that smelled like cotton candy.

"I'm so glad you're here. I missed you," I replied honestly as I got a solid hit of the sweet smell of her skin. That was the hardest thing to get used to while I was in Canada for the summer. I hated it. She blushed so hard it made her physically hot, judging by the way she pressed her hands against her bright red cheeks and waved them in front of her face feverishly. I decided to ignore the plan I had, to let her guide the evening, and instead moved against her and wrapped my arms around her tightly. She melted into me, and her arms came up behind me on either side of my shoulders, nails pressed into my skin.

"I really, really missed you." Her muffled voice was only for my ears. When I had gotten back to town, she was still protecting her heart, telling me she was too busy with new episodes of *Eat It* to hang out. After my disappearing act, I didn't want to do anything to tip the precarious balance, so I stayed away. Even though I had wanted to go to Icing to pop in on her, this was the first time we'd set eyes on one another in months. I dropped my head and whispered my response. Goosebumps rose on her neck when my lips brushed her ear.

"I promise I missed you more."

I could have stood with her for another hour, but Asher ruined it when he loudly cleared his throat and passed out beers. I reluctantly untangled myself from her and watched her roll the can over her cheeks and across the curve of her chest. It was torture, and I was certain she did it on purpose. Greyson leaned against the truck and held my eyes as she cracked the Blonde Bomber beer and took a long drink. When she swiped her tongue over her lip to collect the froth left behind, I knew for sure she was trying to get a rise out of me. It worked. In more ways than one.

"It's nice the gang is all back together. Mila was bummed she couldn't make it tonight," Delaney cut through the sexually charged moment and I blinked back to reality. "How was your summer, Gavin?"

"It was ... needed," I replied carefully. Listening to a crying Greyson on my voicemail, so hurt that I had left town without telling her, had me fully regretting the way I had left. When she had cut off all contact for over a month after, I received her message loud and clear. It ended up being more stressful than if I had just stayed in Chicago, and it was still a thorny subject. I glanced at her as I continued. "But I'm very happy to be back."

"He'll barely get settled before we leave to go back," Asher threw in. Greyson stood up straight, her languid posture replaced with tense confusion. I hadn't yet told her I was on the World Cup team for Canada, and the way I had left after the regular season made me hesitant to tell her I was going to be gone again. Her smile fell instantly at Asher's revelation and the dents between her eyebrows gave away her displeasure.

"What do you mean? Why? You just got home. The season will be starting." Her protests made me feel like an asshole for not telling her and the hurt in her eyes when she searched my face for an answer was like a knife through my gut.

"We got asked to be on the Canadian team for the World Cup," I replied. My mood took a nosedive at the disappointment that washed across her sunburnt cheeks. "Asher and I will be gone for the first couple weeks of September. We'll miss training camp."

"How long have you known?" she asked quietly.

"A month," Asher piped up, oblivious to the tension.

"Oh," Greyson stepped away from me and lowered her eyes to her feet. "That's exciting for you. It will be fun for you to play with some of the guys who are usually your opponents."

I had no excuse for the fact I had kept it from her. I couldn't feign ignorance or pretend it slipped my mind.

"I'm sorry. I was going to tell you."

Her shrug was full of closed off emotion. This was not how I wanted our first night back together to go.

"Your life is yours. You can choose who gets the important information, and you don't have to apologize to me because I'm not one of them," Greyson turned to Delaney. "You want to go get some food before the movie starts?"

That was a clear indication our conversation was over, and I clenched my jaw tightly. She didn't look at me again as they walked away, and as soon as she was out of earshot, I shoved Asher roughly against the side of the truck.

"What the fuck Gav?"

"Why would you tell her about Worlds now? Was that done on purpose to make her feel like she can't trust me? You two got so chummy over the summer, is there something I should know?"

Cohen looked between us in disbelief while Asher glowered at me.

"I'm not going to apologize for not turning my back on her friendship when you tucked tail and ran away. She needed to lean on her friends, and that's what I am," Asher fumed. "Fuck you for implying I'd betray you for a woman. Especially her. Aside from the fact she's like my sister, you're my best friend. Tell her how you feel about her, you jackass. Enough of this stupid ass dance. You've both been doing it for way too long."

The blinding rage I had felt faded as quickly as it came on and Asher and I stared at each other for another minute before my total embarrassment settled around me. I shook my head in embarrassment as his completely valid irritation dissolved from his face.

"Sorry," I grumbled and held my hand out in apology. Asher slapped it away and pulled me in for a hug as he kissed my cheek with a flourish.

"How did you not tell her about this?" Cohen climbed into

the truck bed and opened a chair as he sat down against the back window.

"It took a month and a half for her to talk to me after the last time I kept something from her. I knew this would upset her, and I hate doing that. So ... I didn't."

"Worked out well for you," Cohen lifted his feet as I laid out blankets.

"Seriously man, she's into you. When I ran into her a couple weeks ago, the only subject she was interested in was you. She told me she had the date you would be back starred on her calendar," Asher had zeroed in on a woman a car over. "Shoot your shot. It's been a year."

Fourteen months, to be precise. Fourteen agonizing months since I watched KJ get thrown out of a church and I embarked on a frustrating journey to control my hormones and not go in for the kiss that might destroy everything.

"What's been a year?" Greyson's voice behind me made me jump. I flushed, unsure of exactly how much of that she had heard.

"Oh, you got a pretzel? Nice. Can we share? You need another beer? I'm really sorry about the World Cup situation. I swear I was going to tell you. Tonight, actually. I found out when I was away, and it was right after we started talking again. I wanted to tell you face to face. After the way I left after the playoffs ... I never want to make you unhappy; you know that right? The thought of being away from you even longer is torturous. Seriously, I'm—"

Greyson's finger was pressed against my lips and a smile tugged at her mouth a moment later. I swallowed hard as her eyes moved down my face to my throat before they came back up to mine.

"You're babbling as awkwardly as I usually do," she teased. Her hand left my mouth and found my fingers as she squeezed my hand. "You don't have to tell me everything about your life. I was just looking forward to having you home. Me being upset doesn't constitute you doing anything wrong."

Another step forward had our thighs touch and my lips hovered over hers.

"I want you to know it all. I hate that I hurt you. It was not intentional. It would never be intentional. I promise I'll make up for the time away."

Greyson's breath hitched as her hand flitted to her throat and pulled at the infinity pendant. She licked her lips and gave me a smile I had never seen.

"I'll look forward to that make up," she murmured softly before she put a hand on my chest and pushed me back to accept Asher's hand to help her into the truck bed. Greyson declined Cohen's offer to vacate his chair and chose the spot near me. I took it as a good sign.

One night a couple weeks prior something shifted between us during a video call, and I would take every sign that arose that I had read it correctly. She had called the night she ran into Asher, and I was dead asleep when the phone rang at four in the morning. When I saw her face on the screen I woke instantly. I picked up with bleary eyes, and she giggled and whistled with wide eyes.

"Hot damn, Canada. Why don't I get to see you with no shirt more often? It's so hot."

"You're drunk."

"Maybe. But I know what I'm saying."

"Would you say it sober?"

"Of course not. No way I can let you know how often I think of you in a very unfriendly way without a snoot full of vodka. And by unfriendly, I mean ... you know. Sexy. I think of you in a sexy way. A lot. A lot a lot. And don't bring it up tomorrow. Pretend it didn't happen. Kaythanks."

So that was exactly what I did. When we talked the following afternoon there was no mention of the possible exposure of true feelings, and it was not acknowledged again. But I knew it was there, and I would wait patiently for it to happen again. Hopefully tonight was the night.

Greyson patted the blanket next to her when I climbed into

the truck, and we relaxed into easy conversation. I barely paid attention to the theater announcement of a change in the first movie. I wasn't there for what was on the screen anyway. Greyson settled into the curve of my arm with a contented sigh, and I glared at Cohen and Asher when they made immature gestures in our direction. I caught Delaney's amused smirk, and if I'd been under any delusion Greyson's best friend wasn't aware of my feelings for her that flew right off into the summer air like the fluff off a dandelion.

Every few minutes Greyson burrowed deeper into me, and the bulb finally clicked why she had barely looked at the screen. The change to an FBI action film didn't matter to anyone besides the woman currently trying to climb into my shirt. The last scene was particularly difficult, judging by the way she dug her fingernails into my thigh.

"You okay?" I leaned down and spoke quietly as I pulled her closer. Greyson turned her head away from our friends and nodded against my chest. She was a terrible liar.

A handful of minutes later she jumped out of my arms and scrambled out of the truck bed after an incredibly violent scene.

"I'll be right back," she muttered softly. Greyson half jogged away as Asher and Cohen exchanged confused glances and I locked eyes with Delaney. She chewed her lip and nodded around the truck. When we rounded the front, she shoved her hands in her pockets and rocked back on her heels.

"If she had known there would be a movie like this playing, I'm certain we wouldn't have come. I'm going to go find her and we'll go. Stuff like this flips her switch and there's no pulling her out of her memories. The rest of the night would be a bust for everyone," Delaney said.

"Do you mind if I try?"

Delaney sighed heavily. "Look Gavin, I'm going to be real with you here. You've become one of the most important people in her life, but she's terrified to get hurt. She keeps you at arm's length because it's safe, even though that's not what she wants.

You're a smart guy. I know you see it. And we all see that you feel the exact same way about her. She doesn't have to worry about losing you if she won't let herself be in a position to have you. Your patience with her is incredible."

"I'll always be there for her. However she needs. Or wants." I really wanted to tell her that I was completely in love with her best friend, but she obviously already knew that. "Would you be okay riding back with the guys in my truck if I took her home?"

"Sounds good." Delaney reached into her jacket and pulled out the keys to Greyson's car. She held them just out of reach. "Please take care of her."

I followed the creaking chains of the swing set to find Greyson. She sat alone and slowly rocked on the old plastic seat. When I stopped at the swing next to her, she dragged her toes through the dirt at her feet to stop her movement.

"Is this seat taken?"

Her eyes glistened as she looked up to meet mine, and her tear-stained cheeks told the story of her memories.

"The spot next to me is always yours."

"If that's the case you'll never have to worry about it being empty." I wrapped my hands around the chains as I lowered myself into the swing. "You want to talk about it?"

Greyson stared at the sky; the inky blackness dotted with stars of varying size and intensity.

"Did you know the North Star is stationary?"

My eyes moved off her and up to the vast expanse over our heads as I focused on the star that shone the brightest. My heart stuttered hearing her talk about the subject Olive loved so much, and I wanted this conversation to go on forever. It was as if they were both there, talking to me at once.

"I think I had heard that," I replied as I remembered Olive's full presentation from her hospital bed on the star called Polaris because of its relation to the north celestial pole.

"I mean, if we're getting super technical, it does move a little, but it's the grounding force of all the other stars in the sky. Everything else spins and this star stays where it's meant to be. Holding court. Being reliable. Helping you navigate and always there when you need to find your way home." She paused and pointed at the Big Dipper, then moved her finger to the tail of the Little Dipper. "It can be hard to see sometimes, but you know it's always there."

"The sky can tell you a lot, if you care to listen," I replied softly as I clutched the rusty chains of the swing. She smiled sadly with her eyes on the sky.

"You're my North Star, Gavin. My shining light in a world full of darkness."

I swallowed hard as Greyson stood and stepped in front of me. She looked down and spread her fingers over my cheek.

"I'll always be here to guide you when you need help finding your way."

"I love you. You can never tell the girls I said this, but you're my best friend. I don't know when or how it happened, but you became the person I need the most. When you were gone, I realized how much I need you. I never want to risk losing what we have. My North Star can't blow up into a supernova. You know?"

Unfortunately, I knew. I knew she just told me what we were was all we would ever be.

CHAPTER 20

Greyson

I was tipsy when I showed up unannounced on Gavin's doorstep the night before he left for Montreal. If I were totally drunk, I wouldn't have had the nagging thought in the back of my mind that it was a huge mistake. Since the night at the drive-in, he had very obviously pulled back. He had barely come into the bakery and was full of excuses on why he couldn't hang out. I finally gave up asking. He was a terrible liar, and it hurt more to hear him tell an untruth than it did to hear nothing at all. I knew it was because something changed that night. I also realized I didn't like it. At all.

Gavin was slow to answer the incessant chime of the doorbell. When he pulled open the door, he was dressed only in low cut, baggy gray sweatpants, and I tried unsuccessfully not to stare at his bare chest. He stepped back and made room for me to enter as he flipped on the lights. As my eyes adjusted to the sudden brightness, they were drawn to the defined v-cut of his abs and the deep scar that ran in tandem, a memento from a skate to the gut in a game long passed.

"What are you doing here?" Gavin's sleep filled question was laced with confusion and I didn't want to waste another second fighting feelings I knew were real and were never going to go away. "I thought you were having girls night."

"I didn't want you to leave without seeing you again. I wanted to ... tell you ..." I couldn't force the words out of my mouth. The speech I had rehearsed in the ride share was stuck in my throat and Gavin stepped forward. He waited patiently, but no matter what I tried, I could not get my brain to let me tell him I was completely in love with him. Gavin cupped his hand behind my neck and pulled me into him, which I took as a sign he read the unspoken declaration of my heart. I took my chance before I lost my nerve and tilted my chin up as I moved towards his mouth. To my complete mortification he pulled back at the last second, just enough that his lips were out of my reach.

"Not like this," he whispered into my mouth. Tears stung my eyes as I nodded in humiliation.

"You're not interested. Of course you're not. I can't believe I thought you could be," I replied, as regret coursed through me like molten lava. I had to get out of there, immediately. "I don't feel anything for you either, I just, I was ... stupid. Good luck at Worlds, okay?"

Gavin narrowed his eyes and did that sexy nostril flare thing I always saw when he was frustrated by me. He sighed heavily and grabbed a hoodie and pair of shoes out of the closet.

"I've got a lot to say about that statement. But not when you're full of Bantam Brewing courage. Let me take you home," he reached for my elbow at the same time I immaturely pulled it away. As I fled the house and down the sidewalk, I lifted my hood over my head and pulled the strings tightly in a desperate attempt to hide my feelings.

"Perfectly capable of finding my way home, Supernova," I yelled over my shoulder as I considered actually running away.

"You can't walk home from here," Gavin called, a few steps behind me. "Please, Greyson. Face this."

Shit. I hadn't thought this through. I'd call Trevor, but that would still leave me standing on the sidewalk for, at the very least, fifteen solid minutes.

"I've been needing more exercise," I threw over my shoulder, as I broke into a jog.

"Dammit Greyson, stop!" Gavin's feet pounded down the sidewalk and his continuous attempts to capture my attention fell without landing until I heard the name that made my blood turn to ice before it boiled. "*Grace.*"

I froze and clenched my fists at my sides before I spun around and charged him. I surprised both of us when I shoved him hard enough to knock him off balance and step off the sidewalk into the grass.

"I told you to never fucking call me that!" I screeched, blinded by fury as I pushed him again, both palms flat against his chest. Gavin's mouth dropped in shock, and he held up his hands.

"I'm sorry! I was just trying to get your attention. I didn't ... I mean ... fuck Greyson I'm sorry!"

My chest seized as I stared at him with a level of hurt I didn't know was possible. I wanted to punch him over and over until the awful churning in my stomach subsided, but instead I tore my eyes away from him and located Trevor with the GPS app I forced him to use. It was a little pointless since he disabled it when he was at work and in the places that were the reason I needed to know where he was, but he humored my anxiety by leaving it on the rest of the time. This wasn't the kind of neighborhood he would generally have business in, but I just thought it was my lucky day that he was only a block away. I called him as I walked down the sidewalk, away from Gavin, who continued to throw apologies from the spot he was rooted.

Trevor pulled up less than a minute later and nodded at Gavin as I climbed into the car and slammed the door. I stared straight ahead as we took off out of the neighborhood and pretended I didn't notice Trevor's repetitive glances. He knew me well enough to not force me to explain what the hell had just happened. When he pulled up in front of my house he leaned over and kissed my cheek before I jumped out and ran inside to break down in private.

I was in a violent mood when I woke up for work three hours later. After two full pots of coffee and a bottle of electrolytes, I didn't feel quite as homicidal, but I did tell my staff that if *anyone* came into the shop to see me, they were to say I took a sick day. The withering death stare Donovan got when he asked if that included Gavin made everyone shift uncomfortably in their chairs. I hid in the kitchen all day and baked my humiliation into a cupcake I wasn't sure anyone would want to eat. When Donovan came in for the first tray, he read the description card with pity before he assured me whatever happened would work itself out.

THE TASTE OF EMBARRASSMENT:
spicy chili cake that covers your tongue and heats your face, filled with lime curd that puckers your cheeks before showing you its sweet side. Finished with vanilla milk frosting that cools you when the fire subsides, it's perfect for those days when you can almost taste your mistakes.

I was surprised they sold well, but glad something good came out of the destruction of the best relationship I had ever had. By the time I left for the afternoon I was exhausted from the storm of emotions I had fought the entire day. When I turned onto my street and spotted the matte black truck parked outside my house, one thought loudly broke through my emotions.

He hasn't given up on me.

I had no gas left in my tank to take on this conversation, so I took my time parking, as if that would help. When I finally emerged from my car, I shrunk at the beams of anger he shot at me out of his eyes.

"Feeling better?" he asked sarcastically as he pushed up off the stoop and folded his arms angrily over his chest. Donovan was not happy with me after Gavin had come into Icing and he had to lie about my being there. "Must have been one of those nonexistent bugs, huh?"

"Fantastic." I breezily brushed past him to hop up the steps as he reached out and caught my hand. Gavin pulled my body against his and buried the fingers of his other hand in my hair as we stared each other down in a fierce battle of emotions.

"I'm sorry I called you that name," Gavin said. The hand that held mine moved down, skimming my ribs before it settled on my hip. "I just wanted you to talk to me. I can tell there's a story behind it you don't want to share, and I've never pushed it, because I will never do anything to purposely hurt you. But do not shut me out, Greyson. And don't you dare have your employees lie to me. If you don't want to see me just fucking say so. I deserve better than that."

He was *pissed*. He had never been anything close to angry with me and my throat burned with hot emotion when I tried to swallow.

"You're right. I'm sorry. But you've shut me out too. You know that right? I told you how much I needed you and then you cut me out. It took everything I had to admit how much you mean to me, and then you treat me like I'm nothing. This summer was so hard. On us, on our relationship. I wanted things to move forward, I wanted us to figure it out. But this time, you were the one who backed away. You stopped talking to me after I told you you're the most important person in my life. I reacted like a child last night, and I wish I could say it was just the alcohol, but it wasn't. It was ... pure heartbreak."

Gavin's jaw ticked and his eyes softened as he brought my hand up to his mouth. When his lips brushed over my knuckles my heart leapt against my chest. I could do nothing but stare at him as he flattened my fingers against his cheek and held them captive with his palm.

"At the drive-in, what you said on the swings, it hit me really hard. I know I was distant, and there is no excuse for that. I'm here for you now just as much as I was then. I always will be," he murmured softly, his lips brushing over my cheek. Gavin moved another step closer, and I could barely breathe.

"I couldn't face you today. I made them lie to you because I had no clue what to say and it was easier to avoid. Which my therapist sternly reminded me is not the way adults handle conflict." I paused and bit the inside of my lip to stop the tremble. "We aren't ... you don't see me as ... I'm your friend. I am so sorry I showed up at your house in the middle of the night like a crazed bunny. I'm sorry for the drive-in. I'm sorry for last night. I'm sorry ... for me."

Gavin's fingers swept over my lips, settling on the corner of my mouth. I truly felt like I was in an alternate universe; he never touched me like this, so forward, so intimate. We were always so cautious and unsure with our physical contact. This ... this was different.

"Don't ever compare yourself to a puck bunny. And do *not* apologize for being you. If you had shown up sober and tried to kiss me, the night would have ended very differently. But I will not ruin our friendship over something you might regret in the morning. I know what I want. Until I'm sure you feel the same, I won't say yes to a drunken offering. You mean too much to me. I'd rather have you as a friend forever than a lover for one night," Gavin said softly. He squeezed my hand as he lowered it from his face. "I need to go. I'll text you when I get to the airport. When I get back, it's time to have the conversation we've both been too scared to have."

He pulled me in for a hug and held me against his chest long enough to melt away any residual fear that I had created an insurmountable rift between us. The fact he had just laid down the gauntlet and confirmed there was a conversation that needed to be had made me cautiously hopeful. I reluctantly dropped my arms from his back and let him go. Gavin was almost to his truck before he stopped and jogged back to where I stood. I held my breath as he dropped his head.

"Don't call me Supernova ever again," Gavin hovered next to my ear. "I'm not blowing up your atmosphere. I'll always be your shining star." His breath drew goosebumps to my neck and he turned his head as he dropped a long kiss on my cheek.

CHAPTER 21

Greyson

E veryone cheered so I figured I should too. I jumped up and slapped hands with the people around me as I joined in the excitement over the Grizzlies win. It was a shame such a good seat was wasted on me since my football knowledge ended at the word 'touchdown', but when Trevor wanted a sibling date it didn't matter what we were doing. I would have gone to a farm and shoveled shit if it meant I got his undivided attention for a full night. More than once I had caught him staring at me in a way that said he had something big on his mind. Each time he got that look, he smiled too big and asked if I wanted another beer, which resulted in me being drunk off my ass before we left the game.

As we fell into the flood of people, I gripped his hand tightly and followed behind as he did his aggressive detective walk. Once we were out of the throng, I fell into step beside him as we bypassed the car and detoured into our favorite neighborhood bar. After we ordered I sat back and folded my arms accusingly.

"Well? What the hell is it?"

He popped his gum with zero intimidation and raised an eyebrow.

"What do you mean?" Trevor's gaze shifted to the television behind my head and I grew even more impatient.

"You know what I mean, asshole. What do you want to tell me?"

"I don't know what you're talking about."

"Trevor. It's been obvious all night long there's something on the tip of your tongue. Spit it out."

A slight drop of his infuriating smile let me know I'd pegged the reason for this impromptu Thursday night hang out session and I waited for the explanation I guessed wasn't going to come.

"Can't I just spend time with my baby sister?"

"You could, but you never do."

"Whoa. That's a deep cut RayRay. You're the one who's become Miss Fancy Pants with your famous friends, flitting around town and being featured on Biscuits in the Basket with Halstead."

The heat that spread through my cheeks and down my neck was almost painful. I hated the way he could turn a serious conversation focused on him back on me and make me forget about the original issue.

"I've been involved with the Falcons my entire life, thank you very much. Biscuits slapping a picture of me with Gavin on top of a poorly written post doesn't constitute being 'featured' either," I grumbled, grateful for the waitress who had returned with our food.

"How long until Halstead is home?" Trevor spoke around a mouthful of mozzarella stick while I dipped an onion ring in ranch and took a very unflattering bite.

"Ten days," I replied, too quickly. Trevor grinned knowingly while I sputtered and tried to cover my flub. "I think. I don't know. Haven't talked to him today."

"This is me. You don't have to pretend. Did you tell him how you feel yet?" Trevor put me out of my misery in the matter-of-fact way he always did.

"No. Not really. Kind of tried to the night before he left but it turns out he wasn't interested in a drunk bakery owner trying to kiss him after showing up at his door in the middle of the night."

"Ah. So *that's* why I had to scoop you up at one in the morning."

I cringed at the memory of throwing myself at Gavin, only to be rebuffed, followed by an epic temper tantrum. "Yeah, I guess I'm no good at seduction. Or simple flirting. Or being, you know, open and vulnerable."

"Not true at all," Trevor argued. He finished his food and tossed his napkin on the table. "He's the kind of guy who would put his coat over a puddle so you wouldn't have to get your shoes wet walking through it."

"Not following. What does that have to do with this?"

"Everything. He's not going to allow you to do something you might not be completely behind doing, under the false confidence of too much alcohol."

"As I've had too much alcohol this evening, I'm going to need you to spell out your point in bold font."

"My point is you were drunk, and he won't take advantage of that. He didn't say no because he doesn't want you. He said no because he does."

"I really appreciate you trying to make me feel better. Regardless of my feelings, it's safer to stay in the friend zone. Even if he thinks he wants more, as soon as he knows everything, he'll run. I need to just accept that and move on."

"Dammit, Greyson. Stop this. Stop sabotaging yourself. You deserve to be loved by him. Let him do it."

If only it was that simple. Laying my heart on the line was not something I had ever found the courage to do.

"I need to get home. Early morning."

Trevor sighed and paid the bill, and I was home and in bed before I realized he hadn't told me whatever was on his mind. The shrill ring of my cell phone pulled me out of sleep a few hours later and when my exhausted eyes read the name on the screen, I answered quickly.

"Gavin? Is everything alright? Why are you awake?"

He didn't respond, the only sound a low hum of an air conditioner and intermittent heavy breathing.

"*Gavin.*"

When he finally spoke, his voice low and seductive, the sound went straight between my legs.

"Greyson. My beautiful, perfect Lemon Drop. I miss you so fucking much."

My body woke up with a snap at the slight thickness of his tone and the slur that finished his words. Any sleep or alcohol haze cleared my head. I wanted to remember every second of this conversation. Gavin rarely drank enough to even catch a buzz, since he took his leadership role for the team very seriously. So, to hear him so obviously drunk was more than a little concerning.

"I miss you, too. Are you okay? Why are you calling in the middle of the night?"

"No, I am not okay. You aren't hearing me. I *miss* you. Everything about you. Your face and your mouth and your pretty hair. Your eyes and the way your body fits in those novelty t-shirts. Your body period. Fuck."

My heart pounded uncomfortably with each word he spoke, and my brain wanted to stop him, extend him the same courtesy he'd done for me when I tried to express my feelings under the cover of alcohol.

"Stop. You don't know what you're saying."

"Oh yes I do. Maybe I'm drunk off my ass and I'll regret it tomorrow, but I don't give a fuck. Cause you know what? I got drunk on you the first time I saw you and I was chasing that feeling tonight. I ordered Lemon Drops because I wanted to taste something that smelled like you. I kept drinking them, licking the sugar off the rim and wishing it was you. I know you'd taste sweeter."

Heat gathered between my legs the longer he talked, as his

speech gained speed and intensity, like a dam of feelings that broke with the first word spoken. He just told me he tongue fucked a martini glass pretending it was me and I was legitimately at a loss for words.

"What, uh, why ... you think I smell like lemons?"

"You smell like a sun-kissed tree of fresh lemons covered in a sugar shower. All the time. I love it. I crave it. I *need* it. I need *you*."

I rarely wore perfume due to the fact some ingredients absorbed smell easily, especially royal icing which I was elbow deep in for the decorated cookies every single day. I was beyond confused as to where he came up with this very descriptive version of my unique smell. He continued, and I was stunned into shocked silence.

"And then your hair is all smelling like a strawberry daiquiri and hell if I didn't get one of those too. All that whipped cream. Everything—every single thing—about you makes my world spin and fireworks flash behind my eyes. Drunk. On you. That's me."

"Gavin ..." my voice shook menacingly and threatened to give way to the year of denied emotions and hidden feelings. I should not do this. Not now, when he was in another country and so drunk I wasn't even sure he'd remember the conversation. But I had to. "I don't want to be friends anymore. I mean ... not *just* friends."

I was met with silence. Not even a surprised intake of breath or a heavy sigh. I pulled the phone away to see if we were still connected, which was a yes, and instantly regretted saying it. By the time I was convinced I'd scared the hell out of him he snored softly.

"Are you freaking serious?" I asked incredulously, as I listened to him breathe before I whispered goodnight and disconnected. I laid back down and stared at the ceiling, unsuccessful in my half-hearted attempt to go back to sleep. After I rushed through a shower and filled an extra large cup of coffee, I arrived at the bakery a full hour earlier than usual. Gavin's bombshell had left me with an insatiable need to create a delicate new cake and merge the things I now knew reminded him of me. It had never occurred to me he could have his own notebook of inspiration with me as the muse.

The recipe flowed easily from my mind and I handled the batter with more love than I could remember ever giving to a cake. Even the wrappers were specially selected, navy cups splattered with gold specks reminiscent of a starry night. I deposited them safely into the oven and had three other batters mixed when Trevor pounded on the back door. I grabbed the hockey stick I left in the kitchen for protection and slid the door open an inch, met with a bearded mouth next to my eyeball.

"How many times do I have to tell you not to open this door at ass crack thirty?" Trevor yelled through the sliver of space I'd made available.

"You do understand that I wouldn't be opening it if *you* weren't banging on it, right?" I stood firm behind the heavy door as he bitched and moaned on the other side.

"Come on RayRay, quit busting my balls. I need some fucking coffee," Trevor whined theatrically.

I rolled my eyes and leaned the stick against the wall as I pulled open the door the rest of the way and he barreled inside. I yawned into my sleeve and gave him the finger when he motioned for me to get him a cup of coffee. He laughed and filled a travel mug as I dumped a scoop of raspberry cupcake batter onto the worktable instead of the tin. I was a mess, cruising on emotion and possibly still drunk.

"How do you feel after last night?" Trevor peeled the wrapper off the pumpkin muffin I'd already set aside on a plate for him. He finished it in two bites and washed it down with a giant gulp of coffee. "You hammered down more Blonde Bomber than I've ever seen anyone consume."

"That was your fault. On that note, are you ready to confess your sins, big brother?"

Trevor lowered his eyes and unwrapped his second muffin with way too much precision.

"You're off your nut."

"And you're disgusting. Do you even taste your food or just swallow it whole like a python?" I watched as he shoved it in his mouth and the crumbs caught in his beard.

"Lay off. I didn't have time to eat this morning," Trevor wiped his face with a napkin and tossed the empty wrappers into the trash.

"Do you ever? How are you not hungover?" I demanded. The timer on the oven buzzed and the shrill noise made my unhappy head pound in protest.

"If you would start listening to me and drink electrolytes *before* you pass out, you wouldn't be either," Trevor replied as he filled a bag with muffins. I roughly shoved him away from the table when he emptied almost my entire stock of pumpkin and half the blueberry.

"Save me one of those, would you?" Trevor nodded at the tray of Gavin's cupcakes, which sat safely in the cooling rack. I rolled my eyes in exasperation, not ready to tell him about the events of the early morning and the particulars of that specific cake.

"I'm sure glad I'm not trying to run a business here, you know, where people actually pay for what they eat so I can keep the doors open."

"You have personal police protection every second of your life. That's worth way more than a couple of baked goods every week." Trevor wiped off his shirt as he stood and grabbed his to go bag. "I gotta go. I'll stop by after work. We'll talk."

He kissed my cheek as he headed to the door.

"Don't get murdered," I called loudly, already immersed in the icing for Gavin's cakes.

"Don't get robbed and manhandled." Trevor covertly snagged a cupcake off the cooling rack as he passed.

I got back to work and forced myself to focus on cranberry white chocolate oatmeal and peanut butter and jelly cookie doughs, when all I wanted to do was perfect the cupcake that now owned my heart. When my phone dinged with a text from Trevor, I finished the dough and got the trays in the oven before I peeled off my gloves and picked up the device. My heart rate kicked as I glanced at the words in front of me.

TREVOR

I'm pretty sure I just saw KJ. Here. No idea why, but keep your guard up. Do not engage him if he comes into the shop. Call me immediately.

GREYSON

Preseason is going. He's in Dallas. You must have been seeing things...

TREVOR

Greyson. I'm serious. I don't like it at all. If he's here it's because of you. Be aware.

The idea he lurked around outside caused me to drop my whisk and run to the door to verify it was locked. I'd gotten complacent, taking advantage of the fact KJ had been shipped off to Dallas. Or maybe it was more that I knew I was safe now. Gavin would never let anything happen to me. Although Gavin didn't know about the worst parts of my relationship with KJ. The times when he reminded me so much of my mother I'd meekly agree with whatever insult he spewed until he decided he was bored and took off. I'd come to look forward to the explosions, because it meant I wouldn't see him for a few days. When he returned, he was caring and loving for a few weeks, until the cyclical behavior found its way back to abuse.

A key scraped in the locked door and I grabbed the hockey stick, ready to pummel KJ if he walked through it. Relief and embarrassment fought for space inside me when Jemma and Donovan stepped inside.

"Morning!" I waved the stick with false cheeriness and ignored their shared look of concern. "Today's menus are on your stations. Your recipes are highlighted!"

Trevor had barraged me with texts during my unwelcome trip down memory lane. His explicit instructions told me to call the police and report KJ for harassment when—not if—he showed up at the bakery. My first instinct was to call Gavin and let the smooth assurance of his voice lull me into a sense of calm only he could provide, but that thought left almost as quickly as it arrived. There was literally nothing he could do, and I knew him well enough to know he would obsess over his inability to provide protection.

Instead, I finished the cupcakes of emotion and carried one carefully to my photography table. I arranged it lovingly before I switched on the light above and snapped a handful of photos. I chose the shot that highlighted the glistening sugar that enrobed the fresh strawberry with candied lemon peel twisted around it like a hug and sent it to Gavin with no explanation. It didn't take long to regret the text. He probably wasn't awake considering he'd professed his love of my scent less than four hours earlier. Besides that, there was the very real possibility he wouldn't remember what he had said, or be so humiliated he wouldn't want to talk about it. He'd been kind enough to pretend I'd never spewed word vomit everywhere the night I'd basically drooled on his shirtless chest through video chat, so I shouldn't call attention to his declarations by way of a new recipe. Of course, there was the chance he would think it was just another cupcake since I sent him pictures like this almost daily.

I frowned at the incredibly beautiful tray of cupcakes in front of me. I chewed my lip furiously and read the description card as I alternated between wanting everyone to taste them because they were so damn good and the desire to protect them with my life because they were *ours*.

THE DAIQUIRI DROP:
For those times when you can't quite decide if you should go

for what you want. Fresh lemon cake soaked in vodka simple syrup, filled with strawberry curd and finished with light lemon whipped cream. Garnished with a rum soaked strawberry dipped in a sugar shower and candied lemon peel. Cake of your dreams, decision of your life.

Jemma appeared at my side. She read the card before she lifted one of the cupcakes to her nose and inhaled.

"Damn Grey. This cupcake is sexy."

"Yeah." My cheeks heated as I stared at them and thought of Gavin's tongue on that martini glass. "I'm not sure I want to sell them."

"Why? They'd sell out in a hot minute."

"This one is really personal."

Jemma arched a brow and set the cupcake down gently. "Gavin?"

"Now why the hell would you assume that?"

She grinned and rolled her eyes as she picked up a different tray and balanced it on one hand with her fist propped against her hip. She looked like she belonged in a 50's diner with her high curled pink ponytail and ruffled apron. I was immediately hit with an idea of a retro cupcake flight, with old school flavors offered as a set. I scribbled the idea onto a piece of parchment paper and stopped when she started to talk. "We've been taking bets on how long it would be until you two finally admitted your feelings to each other. Donovan was convinced it would be after the season started. Luna doesn't think it's ever going to happen."

"This is what I'm paying you all for? To gamble on my love life?"

"I mean ... yeah." Jemma turned and shook her hips at me as she headed towards the dining room.

"What was your bet?" I called, annoyed but intrigued.

"I said there was no way he'd be able to contain it until he was back. Was I right?"

"Maybe. I don't know. Drunk people say things they don't mean."

"Wrong. Drunk people say things they don't have the courage to say sober."

The chime of my phone distracted me enough to allow her to escape and my heart jumped with the text from Gavin.

GAVIN

The only thing I've ever seen more beautiful than that cupcake is you.

GREYSON

I had some pretty serious inspiration.

He started to type, and I watched the three dots on the screen bounce for what felt like an hour until they went still and then disappeared completely. He obviously didn't know what to say, and I could picture him in his hotel room as he typed and erased a message that would let me down gently. The dots finally started to move again, and I waited impatiently for the response.

GAVIN

I'm so sorry for that phone call. It never should have happened. I'm mortified by the things I said to you. I shouldn't have gotten so drunk, there's no excuse. I hope you can forgive me and we can move past it. I wish like hell I could take the whole thing back.

So, there it was. It was a mistake. Never should have happened. I tried to craft a response that didn't make me appear hysterical. The result was questionable.

GREYSON

Oh lol! We both know I say and do stupid shit all the time that I don't mean!!! No worries!!!!!!!!! Hope you don't have too big of a hangover lol. The cupcake was a joke ... anyway, have a good day!!!

As soon as I sent it, I knew I was screwed. He'd see right through it, with my excessive use of punctuation and internet slang. It took all my courage to look at his response.

GAVIN

Greyson. I meant every word of it. I just wish that wasn't the way I told you I have feelings way deeper than friendship for you.

CHAPTER 22
Greyson

Holy. Motherfucking. Hockey pucks. I had to read the message five times before the words fully absorbed into my brain, and he wasn't done.

GAVIN

Hang on. I'm at breakfast with the guys. I'm going up to my room so I can call you and we can talk about this in private. I'll call you in 5 minutes.

GREYSON

No! We can talk when you get home! It's cool, really!!!!!

There was less than zero percent chance I'd be able to coherently form sentences without completely humiliating myself. I did not want a conversation that could possibly alter the course of my entire life to happen when I had a bad case of mumble mouth and was spitting out insanity.

GAVIN

> You started this conversation with that little piece of cupcake pornography. It's happening. And don't even think about dodging my phone call.

Cupcake pornography? I liked it. It was almost like he heard the thoughts I wasn't speaking out loud.

GAVIN

> I don't like that you said those cupcakes were a joke either. I know you made them because you feel it too.

Now I was convinced he was inside my mind. The peal of my phone made my heart pound painfully against my chest and I took a deep, shaky breath before I connected to the man I couldn't believe wanted me.

"Do not sell those cupcakes, Greyson. Those are ours." Gavin's voice was deep and demanding with a hint of hangover roughness, and it was easily the sexiest thing I had ever heard.

"What am I supposed to do with them if I don't sell them? That is so wasteful," I said softly.

"Do you have a pen?"

"Of course I do. I always have a pen. What does that have to do with this?"

"I'm going to give you my credit card number. I'm buying all of them. Every single one of those cupcakes are mine." The possessiveness of Gavin's voice was something new. Something had *finally* shifted between us. And it was hot.

"You couldn't afford it," I replied. His unamused growl bounced through the phone and settled in my core.

"Wrong. No one tastes you but me."

"You mean no one tastes the cupcakes," I half moaned, as the fantasy of Gavin's mouth on me grew more vivid.

"I mean both."

I could not believe we had actually gotten here. Having a conversation about him *tasting* me.

"I already stopped Jemma when she tried to take the tray to the case. I couldn't stop thinking about the lemon tree and sugar shower, especially the sugar shower. That would be so sticky. The strawberry daiquiri and the whipped cream, I just ... I can't get it out of my head," I honestly could not stop the words as they tumbled from my mouth, and I welcomed Gavin's interruption.

"Baby. Relax."

Well, that did it. Shut me right up. He called me baby. And I liked it. Really, *really* liked it.

"I'm sorry for this conversation happening over the phone when I'm a thousand miles away. It's not how I pictured it. But after my drunken declaration I couldn't leave you thinking I didn't mean it. I do. I always have," he paused. "I thought a friendship was the only thing that would ever be on the table and that was fine; you in my life in any capacity was better than nothing at all. But since you came to my house that night, I haven't been able to stop thinking about the fact you could possibly feel it too."

"Gavin..." I whispered. The emotional flood that roared through my veins was so strong I almost couldn't breathe. He kept talking, and for once I just listened.

"I've been lying to you. I don't think of you as just a friend. I've completely fallen for you. I know that wasn't the deal and being with another hockey player might put you back on Biscuits but I'll protect you. If there are any photos or mentions, they'll be about how completely taken I am with you."

"You wouldn't want me if you knew how fucked up I really am," I blurted out. The self-sabotage was easier than the idea I deserved to be happy.

"Stop doing that. Stop trying to push me away," Gavin replied seriously.

"I'm not! Well, not purposely," I miserably wished we were face to face so I could smell him, see him, *touch* him. "I've kept so much from you, Gavin. The things that would explain why I am the way I am. The things no one knows except Trevor. If you knew them, you'd run."

"I understand your need to keep some things private. I wish you felt comfortable enough to fully open your heart to me, but I know you—whatever it is will not change the way I feel about you. I'll be standing by your side waiting patiently until you're ready to share your secrets."

"I'm scared." Two words. Complete honesty.

"I'll protect your heart, Grey. And every other part of you. Give me the chance to prove you don't have to be afraid anymore."

The totality of the change in our relationship settled, and I gave voice to the other side of my concern when it came to being intimate with him.

"I know your soul Gavin, and I know my heart is safe in your hands. But I'm not the kind of woman you're used to. Like ... in the bedroom. I don't have the best track record when it comes to keeping my boyfriend satisfied, and I'm not sure I can handle you. Especially since I've heard a lot of rumors about your ... well I just mean I'm kind of afraid of your ... your ... manhood."

Silence.

Naturally, I had to try to smooth it over.

"Not, like, afraid of getting a disease! I've seen condoms in your wallet, I know you're responsible. Although the thought of you using them with anyone makes me feel stabby. I just meant afraid of the size. I've had my head on it and seriously, I felt it *through* a pillow and that's just crazy."

Still nothing from Gavin. Why not make it worse?

"I haven't been with anyone for a year and a half. Well, longer. I kind of lost track. I mean unless you count Purple Rain. I've been in a committed relationship with him for *years*. I suppose you could say we've been having a threesome, since it's your picture I look at when I'm ... wait. What did I just say? Oh my God, I wish I was dead."

Gavin finally made a noise. Was he laughing at me? Probably. It had to be comical on his end. For me I just wanted to lock myself in the walk in and wait it out until I froze to death.

"You've thought about my cock?" His voice had changed, gotten deeper, raspier. The sexual tension in the question sent goosebumps rushing over my skin.

"I ... uh ... I mean, I ..."

"And is Purple Rain your vibrator? Actually, don't tell me. Because if it is, the mental picture of you using it is going to make it impossible for me to focus on anything else all day."

"Okay, I won't..." I nervously paced as I imagined him running those giant hands over the rumored giant piece of equipment. "But it is."

Gavin sucked in a sharp breath. I finally realized he wasn't laughing at all.

"Are you touching it?"

"No! Of course not!"

Of course not. How the hell had *that* question just come out of my mouth?

"I mean ... if we're being honest, I most definitely will be later, now that I know you think about my cock when you're using your vibrator on yourself."

My body pulsed with need every time he said the word. It should not be such a turn on. No doubt about it, the friend line had been obliterated with my expression of worry over his size.

"Will you tell me? When you, you know, so I can too?" I cringed as I asked, horrified I had just told him I wanted to simultaneously masturbate.

"Greyson. You're killing me." Gavin sounded like straight sex. The day had just begun, and I wanted to go home and jump under the covers with the vibrator I was more than a little mortified I had just told him about. Especially the fact it had a name. Not even a good or original name. I needed to get back on track, fast.

"I want you too, Gavin. More than friends. I want to know

what your hands feel like on my body. All of my body. And your lips. Especially your lips."

There was a knock on the door of his hotel room and he rudely yelled at whoever it was to go away. If he was being less than polite to anyone, I knew this conversation was serious.

"But more than all that I just want you. As mine. Not my friend. Well not only my friend. My man. Just mine."

"Are you serious? Don't fuck with me, Greyson."

"I'm all yours. If you want me."

"I've literally been dreaming of this for a year. Standing by the lake the night we got coffee I hoped I was convincing when I told you all I wanted was to be your friend. I kind of feel like this isn't really happening. I've never been so grateful for a hangover."

The night by the lake? That was the first time we had gone somewhere together, when I was buzzed after a game and told him he would never get in my pants. The night he got into a fight over me. When we barely knew each other and he defended my honor, after my fiancé had spent our relationship destroying it.

"I need to tell you something Trevor told me this morning," I started, unreasonably nervous. Gavin was going to explode, and I wanted to bask in the new relationship afterglow for a bit longer. The knock on his door started up again, more insistent this time.

"Shit sorry, hold on baby," Gavin said. I could really get used to that term of endearment. Maybe he'd call me that while we were naked.

We were going to be naked. Together.

"Earth to Greyson. Did you hear me?"

"Huh? Oh! Sorry, no I didn't hear you."

"Were you thinking about my cock again?"

Well, I was now.

"Actually, I was thinking about the fact we're going to have sex. Someday. I mean, even though we just started dating five seconds ago it's kind of like we've already done all the infant relationship stuff so we can get right into it, right? I probably shouldn't use the word infant when I'm thinking about you putting your dick in me. I really want it. Soon. Why can't I stop talking?"

"Fuck. I'm going to need a cold shower when I get to the arena with you talking like that. But that's what I was saying. I need to go. You said you need to tell me something? Is it quick? Otherwise, can we talk about it later? Sorry to rush, but I'm pretty late."

"It can wait, it's nothing," I said. It was not nothing. It was the farthest thing from nothing.

"Alright, I'll call you later. Have a good day," Gavin paused, and I heard the smile in his words when he spoke again. "Beautiful girlfriend of mine."

Oh how I could get used to this.

I boxed up the Daiquiri Drops and got them into an overnight package, as excited as if it were Christmas morning. I wished I could see the look on his face when they were delivered to him at his hotel. I couldn't hope they would play badly in the finals, but I was ready for my man to come home. As soon as word got out about us there would be rumors that I would rather not navigate alone. The fact KJ was possibly in town added an additional layer of uneasiness, and I decided I would tell Gavin we needed to stay low key until he was home. I was going to protect this with my life.

CHAPTER 23
Gavin

I was so late to the bus I was prepared to get my ass chewed when I stepped on.

"For fuck's sake Halstead. What were you doing up there? Did you hold us up so you could buff the banana?" Drake called out, which drew all attention to my dick. I punched him in the shoulder as I dropped down into the seat beside him and ran an unsteady hand through my hair. The events of the morning had me as jacked up as if I'd snorted cocaine, and I couldn't get the mental image of Greyson touching herself out of my head.

"Shut up dickhead. I was talking to Greyson. Since I decided drunk dialing her in the middle of the night was a fantastic idea, and she had some questions in the light of day. I told her how I feel. Everything. And you know what she said?"

Drake's face fell and Asher looked like he expected to hear terrible news. As my two best friends since childhood, they'd both been up my ass to tell her the truth. However, they also quietly worried she really wasn't interested in me.

"I'm almost afraid to ask," Drake ran a hand over his beard as I paused.

"She told me she wants me. That I haven't been just her friend for a long time. That she was my girlfriend if I wanted her to be,"

I dropped my voice. "Oh, and that she's afraid of the size of my dick."

Drake's mouth dropped and Asher choked on his energy drink.

"Shut the fuck up she did not. She actually said that?"

I tried to bite back the smile as I recalled the quiver in her voice at that revelation. I knew Greyson would rehash the entire conversation with Mila and Delaney, so I didn't feel too bad telling my friends. It was also an ego boost.

"So, you're official now?" Asher asked. "Captain Halstead is off the market?"

I nodded an affirmative with a moronic smile.

"HOT DAMN!" Drake jumped out of his seat and faced the bus. "Ladies, can I have your attention, eyes up front. It's time to take a moment of silence for all the puck bunnies out there, whose collective cries of anguish may cause a nationwide flood later today when it becomes known that the 'dreamiest Captain in all of hockey' is officially coupled up. The idiot finally got Greyson to notice him, so they'll have to settle for all you losers now!"

I gladly took the good-natured ribbing from my teammates, and by the time we got to the rink my cheeks hurt from the smile plastered on my face.

Practice was rough, and I needed it. I could not get her off my mind. The nervous way she stuttered when she said something that could be interpreted as dirty even though it wasn't her intention. The way she had zero filter and was incapable of stopping herself from saying things that were hideously inappropriate, deliciously sexy, and supremely embarrassing. How she bit her lip when she wrote out a new recipe and talked to herself when she made changes to measurements and ingredients. She was so worried about the things she hadn't told me about herself, but the past wasn't who she was. It may have shaped her, but she was not stuck in the mold.

As soon as the final whistle blew, I hustled to the locker room to shower and change. When I checked my phone, I found multiple messages from Greyson, random thoughts interspersed with dirty promises followed by embarrassed apologies. If she kept it up until I got home, I was going to be in blue ball hell. I sent her a quick message and told her I welcomed all the sexually explicit messages she wanted to send, and as I stepped on the bus my phone rang.

"Gavin? Okay ... I can't believe I texted you about how wet I ... oh it's worse actually saying it," Greyson murmured. I looked sideways at Drake and shifted my body, so I faced the window of the bus. I chose to believe this meant he couldn't hear our conversation. "I don't want to talk about that. I just wanted to hear your voice."

"Don't ever apologize for telling me your fantasies. I mean, you're killing me with it, but don't ever stop. It's a mental picture I fully welcome."

"I can't even tell you how worked up I've gotten myself the last year thinking about you. Now that Greyson Falls will be open for business when you get home ... let's just say it's going to get slippery," Greyson abruptly stopped talking and shrieked quietly. "Why don't you stop me when I get like this? This conversation is over."

"Because it's sexy as hell. Greyson Falls? It's really like that?"

I imagined her flaming cheeks and wet panties, and my dick tried to make a break for it out of my jeans.

"It never used to be ... until it was you controlling the fantasy. Seriously, Gavin. No more. I can't talk dirty when you're with your entire team. I can't have other men hearing me."

"It's for me?" I barely heard her, my need to know her thoughts so strong. "You get that excited for me?"

"I mean ... yeah. Your face turns me on like a faucet ..." she trailed off with a grimace. "Please Gavin. Stop saying things that let people know what we're talking about."

I was now in physical pain from the erection that throbbed in my pants and when the bus slowed to a stop, I groaned in relief.

"Let me call you back in a minute once I get upstairs. We just got back to the hotel," I ground out. "You can finish telling me all about this."

"No Gav, I need to go, I have a meeting with a supplier and then have to go see my accountant. I'll talk to you later. Bye."

After a moment of silence, I realized she had hung up on me.

"What the fuck just happened?" I asked out loud as guys exited the bus and stopped to talk with fans. Drake looked over with a raised eyebrow.

"Trouble in paradise already? You suck at this."

"She just hung up on me and I have no fucking clue what I did wrong."

Drake shook his head and stood. I followed him off the bus and into the hotel while Asher straggled behind to sign an autograph.

"What did she say?"

"She was unintentionally dirty then said the conversation was over because I was on the bus, and after I responded a couple times she hung up," I replied.

"For being a smart dude, you can be pretty fucking stupid sometimes," Drake pushed the button for the elevator and absently picked at his fingernails.

"Am I missing something? I literally didn't say a word."

We stepped onto the elevator and he turned to face me, as Asher jumped in as the doors slid closed.

"You *did* say a word. You said a lot of words. I'm guessing those words were after she said she was uncomfortable. You pushed her to keep talking because you liked the topic."

The picture had cleared up and I hated the fact I hadn't put it together without help.

"I obviously have no frame of reference here as far as relation-ships go. But that guy is a fucking twat. I've had a front row seat to the way he treats women he barely knows," Drake, who now played with KJ, continued. "I truly can't imagine the mental damage he did to Greyson for years. Trauma doesn't just leave the theater because the movie's over, you know what I'm saying?"

"She probably feels like you just treated her like he used to," Asher added. He held up a hand as I opened my mouth to protest. "She's resisted the truth we've all seen. That you two belong together. Is it fair? No. But you shoulder it because you're the fixer and you live to show there are good people out there. Greyson couldn't get hurt if there were no romantic intentions. She finally gives in to it and you kind of act like a domineering asshole, demanding she tell you how desirable you are."

My stomach rolled as I opened the door to our suite. I dialed her number, not surprised to get voicemail. When she felt like she could get hurt she retreated into herself and sealed away her emotions. I didn't like that she thought she needed to do it with me. I left a message asking her to call me, and by the time she responded two hours later I was convinced I'd given myself an ulcer.

"Gavin, I'm sorry I was abrupt. I just had a flashback of my private life being shared with an entire team and went into shut down mode, even though you aren't him, obviously, and would never put me in a position like that. I promise I'm going to work on my reactions; not shut down at the first thing that brings up a bad memory. Are we okay?" Greyson asked quietly.

I remembered, in that moment, the time KJ stood up on the bus and read a string of messages between him and one of his bunnies, explicit detail of their encounters. He then told everyone on the team how Greyson was impossible to get wet. I'd almost choked him out when he laughed about how he dumped a bottle of water on her to 'speed up the process.' Asher had been on the phone with his then wife during that particularly vile charade and she had immediately made sure Greyson knew her fiancé referred to her as Sahara. It was under the guise of friendship, but now I knew it was because his ex was a miserable cheating bitch.

"We're great. I appreciate the apology, but I get it. The thing is, I've wanted this—wanted you—for so damn long. When you tell me you've thought about it too I just lose my mind. I didn't mean to ignore your feelings. I'm really sorry."

She sighed softly and then inhaled deeply.

"Okay, I have to be completely honest. Knowing I turn you on talking about how you turn me on is ... very hot. I loved that conversation, even if the timing made me feel a little uncomfortable. My weird behavior was because Trevor told me he was almost one hundred percent sure he saw KJ here. Today. I guess it has me a little freaked out."

I sat up straight as my muscles tightened like an over coiled spring. "He's there? Has he come to Icing? To your house? Is Trevor with you?"

"In order. I don't know if he's here. He hasn't tried to make contact with me. Trevor is working, but Delaney is spending the night. I'm fine. I think Trevor must have been mistaken, I mean preseason has started. So, he must be in Dallas. Right?"

The underlying fear in the question made my senses prickle with awareness.

"You know what? Hold on. I'm going to ask Drake. He can find out."

"I'm sure it's fine. It's fine. You don't have to ask him. Really."

"Are you afraid to know the answer?"

She was quiet for a moment, so I knew. I forged ahead with a question I never would have asked before, but her safety and security were now my responsibility as her boyfriend.

"Did he hit you?"

"We're just diving right into the hard stuff now that we're together, huh Canada?"

"Tell me," my voice was hard, gruff, and demanding. She might take offense, but I really didn't give a shit.

"Listen up. I don't respond to demands. But on that note, your authoritativeness right now is seriously hot."

The fact I wasn't there to protect her when I now wondered if KJ physically abused her during their relationship had me rip open the door of my bedroom. Drake and Asher looked at me with narrowed eyes when I tilted my phone away from my mouth.

"Call whoever you need to, but find out right now if KJ is at training camp." I turned and went back in my room to force the truth out of Greyson as I paced like a caged tiger. "I'm not trying to be hot. Did he?"

"He did a lot to break me down."

"So, yes. That's a yes. He did," I legitimately growled into the phone when Drake appeared and showed me a text from his team-mate Noah.

NOAH

> Nah man he got clearance for personal leave. He's not even in Dallas. Said he had business in Chi. Left two days ago, supposed to be back in a week. Why, what's up?"

"Not exactly ... more like ... implied abuse?" Greyson's voice shook. I shouldn't push, since I wasn't there to smooth over any of the emotional upheaval this conversation caused. But now that I knew he prowled around the town where my girlfriend was currently alone, and I didn't know the details of his truly disgusting behavior, I wouldn't stop until I had the facts.

"What the *fuck* does that mean, Greyson? I'm freaking out here, especially since Drake just confirmed that KJ is, in fact, in Chicago, where I am not. Please. Tell me it's not as bad as I'm imagining."

"It wasn't good," Greyson's whispered admission felt like someone had just pummeled me in the heart with a bag full of bricks. "I can't do this right now, Gavin. He never physically laid hands on me. He stopped himself before it got there."

"So, what then? What did he do to you?" I hadn't thought I could hate him anymore than I already did. I was wrong. Her life was a series of broken promises, lies, and pain. Now that I was finding out more about the deepest wounds, I couldn't blame her for trying to cover the scars with glitter.

"He knew I was already cracked, so he made it his mission to shatter me. Words that were sharper than knives. Threats that kept me in line. Every day was worse than the one before."

I had gotten so hot I truly wondered if spontaneous human combustion was a possibility. The man was dead.

"You know that reflects on his issues, right? You can't take responsibility for that. It's not on you."

"I let him disrespect me because I felt I deserved it. I know you've picked up on the fact my childhood wasn't fantastic. My whole life was conditioning to be used and abused. I was told over and over no one would ever love me. That I should be grateful for any attention, because I deserved none. So, I believed it." Greyson fought to keep her voice clear, but I heard the tears. She had no chance to come out of her formative years without lasting wounds, but this was beyond extreme. "It's why I've spent the last year trying to talk myself out of my feelings for you. I don't—didn't—believe I was good enough for you."

"You're more than good enough. You're all I've ever wanted."

"I'm going to work on believing that," Greyson promised. "I want to, I just don't know how."

After we said goodbye, I told Drake and Asher what was going on. Since Drake now played with KJ he understood my incessant bitching for years about his work ethic, relationship ethic, and overall shit stain status on the fabric of humanity. He said he couldn't remember the last time anyone on the team got clearance for leave so it must be something actually worth the time away, at least in the eyes of the front office. That did not make me feel better.

CHAPTER 24
Greyson

The following day Gavin posted the Icing box on his Instagram story and tagged the bakery with the caption 'Special Delivery.' He agreed not to confirm our relationship until he was home, but refused to hide it. Eagle eyed fans, or rabid podcasters, could easily figure it out if they tried hard enough. Surprisingly, I hoped they did.

Gavin sent me a video of himself as he tried the Daiquiri Drop, and if he hadn't been fully clothed, I would have considered it pornographic. I now had a confirmed visual to go with the mental fantasy of what his tongue could do, and I snuck away to watch it over ten times over the course of the day.

Evidently his social media was a direct pipeline to new customers because less than a half hour after my bakery was featured on his story people flocked the doors. By the time we were ready to close there was still a line out the door and I refused to turn people away. We stayed open until the last customer was served, and I was officially exhausted. By the time I was ready to leave, it was two hours later than usual. I was so tired I decided to pick up dinner at the sandwich shop down the street rather than cooking when I got home.

A blast of chilly air hit me when I pushed out the door and

turned to lock up, but that wasn't the reason my blood ran cold. It was the voice, and the man attached to it, that had materialized behind me. He was close. Too close. My fingers closed tightly around my keys, shoving one up between my index and middle. If I wasn't so scared, I would have laughed. A year ago, I was about to pledge my life to this man and now I was creating a shank with a bakery key.

"Greyson." KJ's voice was low and tired, and I wanted to pretend I hadn't heard him and just walk away, but the last thing I wanted was for him to follow me.

"Do I know you?" I spun around with an exaggerated glare. The courage I had surprised me, considering how deeply KJ's emotional trauma had implanted in my brain.

I took great satisfaction in the fact he looked like complete shit. He'd lost quite a bit of weight and he looked more skeletal than muscular. His wavy blonde hair was longer than I would have liked if we'd still been together and fluttered across his shoulders under the baseball cap that made him look like any other asshole. Trying to blend in was not like him at all.

"I deserved that."

"How kind of you to agree," I muttered as I ran my fingers over the phone in my pocket. If I managed to get to the call screen, I knew I could dial Trevor without looking. "Were you just hovering outside the door like a stalker?"

"No, it's called waiting patiently. You look great," KJ started. He reached out as he stepped forward, and my heart tripped as I backed away.

"Don't. Don't touch me or give me your fake apologies."

"I'm not trying to get you back. If I thought there was any chance of that I would have been here a long time ago, trust me."

"Trust you? That's a hilarious choice of words coming from the king of deception," I replied.

"Can we go inside? Talk?"

"Absolutely not."

"Coffee? Dinner?"

"Are you delusional, KJ? What do you want?"

I might have been more shocked than he was by the words as they came out of my mouth. I had never stood up for myself. He'd conditioned me to blindly accept his words without question. KJ gaped at me and his wheels turned as he realized I was no longer the woman he had manipulated and degraded for years. He couldn't control me anymore, and he knew it. He hesitated and the silence dragged on between us uncomfortably.

"I'm in therapy. A program. For my addiction," KJ answered. I came back into the conversation on the tail end of his declaration and blinked a few times, as if that would help me understand what I'd just heard.

"What addiction?"

"Sex."

The word had the same effect on me as if he were a cobra that had just sunk his fangs into my heart and dispensed the venom of self-loathing.

"Sex addiction," I repeated, as the past came back in an avalanche of bad memories. He had never been faithful, even from the start. I had never been so clueless I wasn't aware, but I wanted to be in a normal relationship more than I cared about being respected, so I just tried to ignore the signs and proof that stared me in the face.

"Greyson?"

"Yeah. Sorry. I was just ... sex addiction? Are you for real?"

"I know it sounds like bullshit. I'm not just making it up, it's a real thing."

"I mean, I know it's a real thing. Is this your way of trying to hide behind an excuse and not just accept the fact you're a shit human being?"

KJ winced, and I internally high fived myself before the split second of immature happiness gave way to pity.

"I deserve anything you want to say to me, and I understand why you aren't so quick to believe me. I don't have the greatest track record on telling you the truth," KJ replied as he pulled the hat off and ran a hand through his unruly locks. He half laughed at my shudder when he pulled a black hair tie off his wrist and gathered his hair into a low bun. "I'm sure you want to take a pair of scissors to this."

"It's not your best look," I agreed. I reminded myself not to believe a word he said as I asked him a pointless question. "Were you ever honest? About anything?"

"Yes," his voice broke on the one small word and hot tears gathered in the corners of my eyes. I would not give him the satisfaction of seeing me cry. He'd done it enough to last a lifetime. "I loved you. Whether you believe it or not."

"How could I believe it?" My voice was louder than I expected, and I shrugged apologetically at the surprised pedestrians who jumped at my tone as they passed by. "Love isn't lying. And cheating. And abuse."

"I'm sorry."

I advanced on KJ menacingly as I fought to control the rage those two words brought out of me. It was satisfying to see him step back.

"You're ... *sorry?* Is that a joke?"

"The program—"

"Oh. Of course. This is the part where you're supposed to make amends. The almighty KJ Sullivan still can't take responsibility for his own actions."

"I am taking responsibility, Greyson. That's why I'm here."

"Well, you can take your apology and shove it up your hopefully massively infected dick hole."

KJ scoffed. "You really think I'm stupid enough to open myself up to disease by not using condoms?"

This was the most ridiculous conversation. I was too tired to pretend I cared about his pseudo apology.

"Great. You've apologized, you can check it off your steps. I'm done with this," I turned to leave. KJ blocked me, and a spike of adrenaline coursed through me.

"I really am sorry. For everything. Part of me wishes I had just left you alone the day we met."

"Why didn't you?"

He grimaced and scrubbed his fist over his eyes. "Since we're finally being honest—"

I cut him off. "*You're* finally being honest. I always have been."

"Right. Since I'm being honest," KJ paused and lifted his hands to the back of his head. "Fuck. This makes me sound like an even bigger asshole."

My stomach churned with the possibility that what he was about to say could be worse than what I already knew about him.

"I knew he wanted you, so I made sure he couldn't have you."

"Who? Who wanted me?"

"Gavin Halstead."

Gavin had barely spoken to me that day. If he had shown a tenth of an ounce of interest, I would have kicked KJ out of his chair with both feet.

"Elaborate. Now," I demanded as I took another menacing step forward.

"Do we seriously have to do this?" KJ whined. "I'm here for us. Not that douchebag." The more I stared at him the more disappointed I was in myself. There was nothing redeemable about the man I'd wasted so much time on. But Gavin, who shined so brightly with a soul full of stars, was kept at arm's length for over a year by no fault of his own. I owed him a massive apology.

"Yes. We do. Your amends don't end with I'm sorry. Not with me. You think two words fix what you've done to my life? And now you're telling me you only asked me out because someone else wanted to? Do you realize how fucked up that is?"

"I'm here, aren't I?" KJ snapped. The transformation into the man I remembered had begun. His false remorse and honeyed words weren't having the effect he expected, so he was lapsing into his real personality.

"Tell me the story behind our fairytale first meeting."

KJ rolled his eyes and threw his hands up in irritation. "It wasn't like I planned it, but he'd chewed me out at practice earlier that day and I was pissed. So, when I saw him try to run game on you, I decided to take you for myself. You weren't ugly so I didn't mind."

"Why would you do that?" I shrieked, as I drew more attention to the conversation. Without the hat it was obvious who he was, and the covert second glances our way assured me people had begun to recognize him.

"Because. He's a jerkoff. Everyone in this city thinks he's some fucking golden boy. Oh, Gavin Halstead, the Falcons' dad, the most relatable player in hockey." KJ was irate and his voice had climbed to one octave below a full yell. "He acted like he was better than me because he was a young little punk with an undeserved C on his sweater. He was *twenty* when they gave him the captaincy. I had been on the team five years, and this asshole who can't even buy a drink is trying to lead me? *Me?*"

I saw a cell phone pointed our way by someone on the street. This I recognized. This was the KJ I knew. If he was about to snap, I was glad it was being recorded, even though the nosey assholes who controlled the video weren't doing it to help. As I took a step to the side, KJ moved with me, and a tingle of real fear sparked in my chest.

"So, you used me as a pawn in your pathetic little game to try to beat him?"

"Look, I figured I'd fuck you a few times, sneak some nudes I could show around to piss him off, and move on."

Pure shock forced my mouth to drop as I learned the truth behind four wasted years of my life. I also had a vague understanding that this conversation would definitely end up on Biscuits in the Basket, with as many people who were recording it.

Awesome.

KJ continued his confessional, and I tried to cover my ears with my hands. His meaty paws pried them away, and my heart leapt to my throat.

"But then, damn, it was so awesome how bothered he was. You let me do whatever I wanted and never left, and being committed to someone with a name like yours made me seem like a solid dude. So, I went with it."

"You are actually a psychopath, KJ," I hissed. "Normal people don't think that way. They don't do those things."

"Oh, fuck off, Greyson. I played a game and I won. Don't make it deeper than it is."

"Sorry to break it to you but you're playing checkers and he's playing chess. You're not even on the same board."

Although I should have been prepared for the shift in his behavior, it took me completely by surprise. KJ clenched his fists and moved forward too quickly for me to react. I was pinned against the door of the bakery and his body that, while less muscular than a year ago, was still a lot stronger than mine.

"Oh, you're a tough girl now, huh?" KJ sneered, so close his breath heated the cheek I'd turned away from him. "I'm fucking talking to you, bitch."

"Despite your efforts, he still won."

KJ roughly grabbed my chin between two fingers and jerked my face hard enough to immediately make my neck scream, which gave me no option but to look at him.

"What the fuck does that mean?"

"It means I'm his girlfriend. It also means he's going to fucking *end* you when he sees this video."

KJ laughed coldly and slid his hand from my face to my throat. That was when my bravado faltered, and icy fear shot through my veins. I'd pushed too far, and I was seeing the side I always knew was there, but had avoided by keeping my mouth shut. He tightened his other hand around my upper arm as he squeezed my neck enough to show me he was in charge. I clawed at his fingers, which seemed to excite him, and he flashed me the most terrifying smile I had ever seen.

"I wish you had fought like this before. Maybe then you wouldn't have been such a useless screw," KJ leaned down and ran his tongue across my cheek. Tears filled my eyes as I fought the nausea that accompanied them. "You're not recording shit. He can have you. He'll get sick of you just like I did. You're a waste of a fuck."

A commotion to my left drew his attention long enough for me to pry his fingers off my throat, and I gulped a deep breath as three vaguely familiar men surrounded us.

"Get your hands off her, you sick fuck." One of them roughly shoved him back as the other two surrounded me in an attempt to shield me from the rows of cellphones that recorded the altercation from different angles. My vision was fuzzy as the guy in front of me asked if I needed an ambulance.

"No. Please. I just want to get out of here," I gripped the front of his jacket so hard my knuckles turned white as my teeth chattered violently.

He looked around and grabbed my hand, pulling me away from the crush of people. We hurried down the street as he helped me escape the chaos, and a police siren wailed through the night as we ducked into the lobby of a hotel.

"Are you alright?"

When I focused on the concerned man in front of me, I had a flash of recognition at his golden eyes and crooked nose. My terror ebbed, replaced with shock.

"Only me. Only in my fucking life would the people who used my humiliation to get famous end up being the ones who come to my rescue," I groaned, face to face with Camden Reynolds, one third of the podcast that was the bane of my existence.

"We never once said anything distasteful about you." He tried to be covert in his sweep of my neck, but I noticed. Pain radiated when I reached up to my pendant and rubbed.

"You and I have a different understanding of distasteful if you truly believe that."

He glanced over to the door and waved his friends over as they rushed into the lobby. I pawed through my purse, looking for a napkin or anything to wipe away any remnant of KJ. All I came up with was a bottle of hand sanitizer. Good enough.

"I'm sorry. Sometimes humanity falls by the wayside in the day to day. I'm Cam, by the way," he said as the two men who made up the rest of the Biscuits team appeared. As I smeared hand sanitizer all over my cheek, I was officially introduced to Tommy Redman and Jay Montgomery, and I couldn't hate them as much as I wanted to when they relayed how they'd neutralized the situation. KJ took off after the crowd of rabid Falcons fans had started to close in on him, and I was relieved I wouldn't have to deal with the police. At least not yet.

Shit. Trevor. His head would explode when he found out about this.

"Can we call someone for you? You really should report this. Press charges or something. There's plenty of evidence." Tommy waved his phone. "We've had twenty-five people send us their videos in the last two minutes."

I blew out a heavy breath and pulled out my phone.

"It's like I've got my own publicity team," I said sarcastically. "Since you guys posted the last video of KJ and me, you might remember my brother. He's the only one I need to report to."

Trevor's phone went straight to voicemail, so I left a message that told him KJ had shown up and he might want to avoid the police scanner. I tapped my phone against my lips as I waited nervously for him to call back.

The Biscuits team stood around me and tried to ignore the incessant dings of their phones. Cam looked at me apologetically when he reached into his pocket to silence the notifications.

"So how does this work? You post the video to your account and record an emergency episode tonight? I'm not naïve enough to think you won't take the opportunity to record a first hand account of this shit show, even though I do appreciate you stepping in," I said softly. "No one else did."

"We will post it, and we will record an episode tonight. Because that bullshit was despicable and we're going to show everyone what kind of a man Sullivan is. Let us make up for the last time." Cam's eyes had hypnotic powers, and I nodded in oblivious agreement.

"Can I call Gavin first? He can't see this before I talk to him." My head pounded and my throat burned, and I pressed the heels of my palms against my eyes, desperate for a shower.

"Sure, of course. But does that mean you and Gavin Halstead really are dating? It wasn't just something you said to get Sullivan pissed?"

I sighed and dialed Gavin's number, even though I knew he was in the middle of a game and wouldn't answer. "No, it wasn't just something to say, but it's brand new. We weren't saying anything until he was back from Worlds, but I guess that cat is out of the bag."

When his voicemail picked up I turned my back on them and used all my power to keep my voice even.

"Hey. You're probably already going to know about this fiasco with KJ before you hear this message. Just know I'm okay. Call me as soon as you can, please. I lo—" I gasped in surprise when I caught myself about to say the L word a day after we officially started dating. "Um, okay then, bye."

I turned around to find wide grins on the men I no longer had the energy to despise.

"What? What is funny?"

"You trying to act like you didn't almost say 'I love you' for what I'm guessing is the first time to Gavin Halstead." Tommy laughed.

"That is ... no, I did not. That's beyond ridiculous."

"Okay, whatever you say."

"Look, post the video, say what you will on your podcast. But if you could leave that little nugget out, I'd be in your eternal debt," I paused with a wave of my hand. "Go ahead. Post it now."

Cam kept his eyes locked on mine, calming me inexplicably as Tommy uploaded a version of the madness to their official account. It took less than one minute for their phones to be dinging so obnoxiously with notifications that the concierge sent them a disapproving glare. I'd had all I could take and spoke while Cam and I were still stuck in a staring contest.

"I'm not feeling so hot, I'm going to head home."

He shook his head and folded his arms over his chest.

"You're not driving. We'll give you a ride. Maybe to the hospital? Get checked out?"

"Oh, are you my dad now, Cam?"

"Let's go with overprotective big brother."

"She's already got one of those." Trevor's voice thundered through the lobby as he pushed through them and cupped my cheeks in his hands. I gripped his wrists and let the tears slide down my cheeks that I'd managed to hold in up to that moment.

"How did you find me?"

"I'm a detective, RayRay. And I tracked your location," Trevor gently tilted my head back and his eyes darkened with rage when he saw my neck. He turned to my saviors and pushed his jacket back to expose his gun.

"I saw what you did for my sister and you've got my gratitude for that. But that doesn't erase all the shit your podcast has put her through. If you make her cry again, I promise you will regret it. That isn't a threat. It's a guarantee," Trevor growled. I wasn't given a chance to say goodbye, so I shouted my thanks as I was pulled out the door and shoved into the passenger seat of Trevor's SUV. I was pissed by that point, and when he climbed in next to me, I reached over and punched him.

"Don't treat me like a perp you asshole."

Trevor ignored me as he took off away from downtown. "I *told you* to call me. I fucking *told* you, RayRay."

"I had it under control."

The way he laughed immediately raised my hackles. It said 'yeah fucking right' and I wished I could make him swallow it with my fist as a chaser.

"Have you actually seen the video that's *everywhere*?" Trevor replied shortly as he turned off the road that would take me home. "It's already on TMZ, for fuck's sake."

"Where are you taking me? No, I haven't seen it, but I know what's on it considering I was the one actually living it."

He glanced over and his iciness melted when he saw me shaking. Without the spike of adrenaline, the dull throb in my neck couldn't be ignored, and I knew my arm would boast a bruise in the shape of KJ's fingers when I took off my coat.

"You're spending the night with me. There will be no argument or discussion about it. You're also giving me an official statement and a report *will* be filed."

I slumped against the window as I opened my text thread with Mila and Delaney. Since I hadn't heard from them, it was obvious they didn't know about any of this, so I asked them to come to Trevor's house ASAP. "Okay. Whatever you say."

Trevor fell silent but reached for my hand, holding it tightly until we got to his house. I shook off my coat and headed straight for the kitchen to make a cup of coffee. He caught up to me as I dropped the pod in and turned me into his arms.

"I knew he was here, and I didn't protect you. That's twice, RayRay. Twice your life has been in danger and I haven't stopped it in time."

"Don't you dare try to shoulder this. I'm alive because of you. The first time, you did stop it in time. This ... I wouldn't have known he was here at all if it wasn't for you. Yes, he was verbally abusive our entire relationship, but a physical attack wasn't on my radar. I tried to handle my own problem for once. It's my fault." I sobbed as the closure I sought wrapped around me like a dark night that swallowed the stars.

"None of it has ever been your fault. Not him, not mom, not anything. It is my job to watch out for you, and I'm never going to stop doing that. I promised Dad I would step up if it ever came to it." Trevor coughed away the emotion that clogged his words.

"That never should have been on you," I replied. "You were just a kid."

"And you weren't? You've been through too much, Greyson. Being your savior is my greatest accomplishment. You may not need it, and I may be overbearing and overprotective, but I'm never going to stop. Because the night I almost lost you was the night I realized I can't live without you. Annoying you is way better than burying you."

I squeezed him tightly, the man who had given me everything. "I don't want you to live your life for me first. I want you to be happy."

Trevor smiled for the first time since he picked me up and whispered against my forehead as he pressed a kiss to my skin.

"You're with a good man who can protect you *almost* as good as I can. Don't worry about me."

He grabbed a beer and took a long pull as the doorbell rang and Mila's loud voice filtered through the glass. He didn't have time to get to it before Delaney screamed at him to tell them what was going on as she pounded relentlessly against the wood.

"Nice to see you too," he said sarcastically as they shoved past him into the house and tackled me. I was bound to end up completely black and blue before the night was over.

"Not cool, Greyson! You send a text like that and then go radio silent? We were terrified the entire drive," Delaney scolded, still on top of me. Mila untangled herself and pulled me into a sitting position. She inspected me closely and held up my arm, where the expected bruise had begun to show.

"What the fuck is this? What happened? Were you in a fight?"

Trevor waved to the living room and pulled out his phone. "Go settle in and tell them. I'll order dinner and then I'm going to shower."

I picked up my coffee and dropped softly into the overstuffed couch. As they settled into seats and popped open beers, I pulled a blanket over my legs.

"KJ is here," I started as Delaney's eyes traveled the roadmap of his anger. I tugged the blanket higher, an attempt to hide what they had already figured out, and I was about to tell them anyway. "We had a ... discussion. It started out promising."

"How did it end?" Delaney's question was pointed, sharp as an arrow.

"Not as promising."

My two best friends started to talk at the same time and their voices clashed and fought for space in the tension filled air.

"Were there witnesses? Please tell me there were witnesses," Mila said loudly. She gripped her beer bottle so tightly I was surprised I wasn't covered in glass.

"There were," I confirmed. I opened the Biscuits Instagram feed and passed over my phone. I sat in silence and sipped luke-warm coffee as they played and replayed the evidence of the assault. Every time I heard KJ's voice I shrank a little more. By the time they looked up from the screen I was fairly convinced I was just part of the couch. Delaney brought her hand over her mouth and her wide eyes threatened tears, while Mila's flashed fire. The lamb and the lion, and I was somewhere between the two of them.

"Of course these fucking Biscuits assholes would be the ones to do this," Mila fumed. "Do they just follow you around waiting to humiliate you?"

"No, actually they were the ones who stepped in and stopped it. The guys at the end who took me away. That was them."

Delaney scrunched her nose and played the video on her own phone a handful more times. "I'm confused. They're the ones who posted it."

"A bunch of people that were there sent it to them. They said they were going to make him look like an asshole. Since it was going to be everywhere anyway, I said they could control the story. I'm guessing the podcast episode will drop before the night is over. They're not what I thought."

"You want *them* in charge? Did you hit your head, too?"

"Mila," Delaney scolded. "If that's how Greyson wants to

play this, that's how we play it. If she trusts them, we trust her. Always."

"I never said I trust them, but Trevor said it's already on entertainment news sites. If that's true, it's only a matter of time until other outlets pick it up. The Biscuits guys were an active part of it. They have perspective no one else does."

Mila shook her head in exasperation and held her beer up to her lips as she drained half the bottle.

"What did Gavin say?"

I winced and checked my phone, even though he was still playing and there was no chance he had responded.

"He's actively playing in a game; there's no way he can even know yet."

"He's not going to accept this 'let Biscuits in the fucking Basket handle it' bullshit narrative you've decided on, you know that right?"

"Shut the fuck up Mila," Delaney finally exploded. "You're being an asshole. Have you stopped to consider how traumatic this probably was for Greyson? He put his hands on her. He *licked* her. Your attitude is completely unacceptable right now."

Trevor strode into the room at that moment, and I was certain he was shirtless for no purpose beyond distracting their argument. It worked. They both stopped talking when he walked between the two of them to pick up the remote and switch on the end of Gavin's game. Delaney's cheeks blushed as she objectified my brother and Mila did nothing to hide her overt ogling. He folded his arms and looked sternly between them, focused on Mila. She didn't mind the fact she was being scolded. She loved every second of it.

"While I appreciate your frustration, Mila, you're out of line. I don't love it either, but it's her choice and it's done. Being rude isn't going to change the fact it's already out there."

"I'm not being rude. I am *pissed*. I'm sorry I'm taking it out on you, Grey, but KJ doesn't get to do this. He doesn't get to come in here a year after he emotionally knocked you out and do it again—physically this time!"

"Well, if they want to make up for how they handled the wedding they're doing a good job of it," Delaney said as she provided current updates. "They've tagged Chicago P.D., the NHL, The Diablos, and every major news or sports station you can think of. Even the reality network fan accounts. Your name is trending. They want the world to know."

"I don't care," I replied, focused on the television where Drake had just scored to beat team Sweden in the first game of the finals. Warmth flooded my cheeks when Gavin skated up and embraced one of his best friends with so much pride it made my heart ache. "I just want the KJ Sullivan chapter of my life to be closed for good."

The three of us fell silent and watched as after-game interviews began and Gavin filled the screen. He dragged a towel over his face and a hand across his eyes, his exhaustion palpable. I felt guilty he wouldn't get much rest once I got him on the phone. I could already picture him pacing his hotel room, jaw clenched in anger while he made never-ending phone calls to people who could provide more information about what the hell KJ was doing. It was going to be a messy cleanup, and I was not looking forward to one second of it.

CHAPTER 25

Gavin

Nothing could kill my mood as I stopped in the hall of the locker room to talk to the reporters lined up. I was buzzed with adrenaline and wiped my face off with a towel as they started to hurl questions at me.

"The defense really stepped up tonight, how will you keep that intensity going into the next game with Team Sweden?"

"Will the lines for game two stay the same? You guys were really cohesive out there tonight."

"With so many members of the Falcons on Team Canada are you using this as a preseason practice opportunity, since the season will be gearing up by the time you get back?"

I chose the last question I heard to respond to.

"We use any chance we can to work out kinks and tighten up our lines. But Team Canada is also full of all our opponents so the real work will start when we get home to Chicago," I replied. I scrubbed the towel across the back of my neck as sweat trickled between my shoulder blades. The thought of going home, to Greyson, caused a smile to want to pull across my lips.

"Will the incident between KJ Sullivan and Greyson Park cause a conflict on the ice between the Falcons and the Diablos now that the two of you are dating?"

I was caught off guard by the question since we hadn't gone public, and I didn't know how they knew. Or if they knew. It could just be a soft toss to see if I'd swing, but it had been months since the media tried to make our friendship into something more, and it was odd for this to come up now. Especially since KJ was in Chicago. I didn't like it.

"That was over a year ago and we've played through an entire season with no problem. I'm not going to comment any more on that situation."

The reporters gathered around me exchanged uncomfortable glances, and hot fear crept up my spine. I was missing something. Something important. Topher Jones, the biggest pain in the ass reporter I had ever encountered, crowded me and shoved his phone so close to my mouth it practically hit teeth.

"I think they were referring to what happened in Chicago tonight. When KJ Sullivan assaulted your girlfriend outside her bakery in the middle of Michigan Avenue." He paused and bared his teeth as he went in for the kill. "Do you care to comment on *that* situation?"

My vision left me, replaced by straight red fury. I'd always thought seeing red was an expression. I didn't realize it could actually happen.

"I'm sorry what? What did you just say?"

Drake's arm was around my shoulders out of nowhere and he held up a hand to the gaggle of reporters as Asher stepped between Topher and me and firmly moved his still outstretched hand to the side.

"Interview is over. Thanks for the questions everyone, see you next time!" Drake said loudly as he pushed me into the locker room.

"What the fuck was he talking about?" I ripped open my locker and grabbed my phone as my hands shook violently. I had numerous missed calls from Greyson and a couple from Trevor, in addition to Mattie and Cohen. There were also a shit ton of text messages from apparently everyone I knew, and more social media notifications than I could even comprehend. Nothing made sense as I fumbled the device and sent it skittering across the locker room floor.

"He assaulted her? What does that fucking mean exactly? I'm going to fucking kill him. I have to get to her." I furiously punched the locker in front of me until Drake stepped in.

"There's a video." He handed over his phone while Asher hung over my shoulder to watch. My hands shook as I took it from him and watched as that piece of shit insulted her, degraded her, and put his hands on her.

"You need to check the anger, Gavin. There's nothing you can do from here. Relax." Drake took the phone back and ignored my heated glare.

"How do you expect me to relax? You were watching the same thing I was right? You, of all people, are telling me to relax when a man put his hands on a woman? On *my* woman?"

Drake's face screwed up in annoyance when I snapped at him, and I knew if I hadn't been so fucked up, he would have punched me.

"I agree he needs to get a beat down. Save it for the ice. Get yourself a penalty and be done with it, at least until the next game. You go after him now you'll fuck up your whole season, maybe even your career."

"Her safety is more important than my fucking career. You think an on-ice fight is good enough? After what he did to her?"

"He'll get taken care of," Asher assured me. "Trevor probably already killed him."

He peeled off his jersey and leaned down to snag my phone off the floor as it began to ring. Greyson's face lit up the screen and when I answered the video call, I heaved a relieved sigh.

"Gavin? I'm so sorry you found out that way! You legit looked like you were going to snap that reporter in half. I tried to call you; I wanted to explain before you saw the video. Did you see the video? I'm guessing you did by now. I'm sorry." She talked so fast I could barely understand her and I caught a glimpse of Trevor as he passed behind her in a room I didn't recognize.

"Where are you? Are you safe? I'm so sorry I'm not there. This wouldn't have happened if I was there."

"I'm at Trevor's. He's being absurd," she said the last word louder as she lifted her chin to speak at her brother. "He won't let me leave, keeping me like a prisoner."

"As he should."

"I can take care of myself, Gavin."

I bit my tongue before I could respond in a way that would piss her off. In this case I did not feel she could. Apparently, Trevor agreed.

"Well, he's worried about you, and I'm personally glad he's being absurd," I replied gently.

"I know. I feel so stupid. I listened to KJ at first. I let him in, and then his switch just flipped completely and he, well, you know."

She chewed on her lip and shook her head as embarrassment clouded her delicate features. Asher and Drake grabbed their bags and moved to the other side of the locker room so I had some semblance of privacy, and I sat down on the bench with a heavy sigh.

"You didn't do anything wrong. I'm just glad you got out of there when you did."

A doorbell rang and I saw Trevor again, followed by Mila. Greyson stood up, and when the phone jostled, I caught a glimpse of her arm, where purple fingerprints were clear. The evidence of his hands on her filled me with a murderous rage I'd never experienced. She walked through the house and passed the kitchen where Delaney, Mila, and Trevor pulled takeout boxes from paper bags. Greyson moved into a bedroom and closed the door. Her whole demeanor changed when she was away from the people who held court over her, as if she were a tire that had finally gone flat.

"I'm not sure how closely you watched the video but ... the

guys who came in and took me away, they're from Biscuits in the Basket."

Greyson's statement hung in the air, and even though I was alone at the end of the locker room her voice carried enough for Drake and Asher to look over in surprise. It was no secret I thought they were all pieces of shit, and her dealing with them *and* KJ in one night made me feel like a failure as a boyfriend.

"Why would you go with them?" I demanded, more sharply than I intended.

"They took me away from the cell phones and the man who was trying to choke me out. The one who left his fingerprints on me. The one who gave me whiplash. Forgive me for accepting their help without considering how it would make *you* feel." Greyson waved her arm and showed me the bruise that filled me with a concerning amount of rage. "They were the only people who stepped in to stop it rather than record it for internet fame."

The rest of the guys were finished dressing, so I set the phone up on the shelf in my locker and hurriedly pulled off my jersey and pads, shedding all my gear down to my underwear. I was about to peel them off when I realized Greyson had stopped talking and watched with wide eyes.

"Holy mother of gorgeous, Gavin." She blinked rapidly and pulled at her pendant. "I'm not sure if you're just trying to distract me, but I'm begging you not to get completely naked where I can see. Like, move the phone or something because if the first time I see your dick is when you're literally in another country and I don't get to immediately touch it, that's just not cool, you know?"

A few of the guys tried to swallow their laughs, and the rest didn't even attempt it.

"I'm not alone, Greyson," I reminded her as I flipped the phone upside down while I quickly changed into clean clothes. "But I very much appreciate your excitement for certain activities."

"Fuck. Of course you're not. How many men just heard that?"

"More than a few, less than a ton," I answered. As I turned the phone back towards me her cheeks darkened multiple shades. "I've got to get on the bus, but I'm not done talking to you. Do you want me to call you back when I get on, or a video call when I'm at the hotel?"

"Video call for sure. Preferably sans clothes."

"Still not alone, Gigi!" Asher crowded into the frame and laughed as she rolled her eyes. "How are you doing? We'll take care of him on the ice, don't worry about that. If he doesn't get suspended, anyway. Or arrested."

Greyson sighed and smiled weakly. "I'm alright. Sore, tired, humiliated. Better now that I got to talk to Gavin."

"He does that to people," Asher grinned and blew a kiss at the phone. I gathered the rest of my things and told her I'd call back soon as I jumped onto the bus and settled in next to Drake.

"How's she doing?" he asked, while I pulled up the Biscuits website and watched the full video. They had also written a blog post on the incident in which they rallied around Greyson which made me despise them a little bit less.

"If I had to guess, I'd say she's in shock," I answered, watching repeatedly until I knew I was going to lose my shit if I saw KJ touch her one more time. By the time we made it back to the hotel Drake had talked to his teammate, Noah, and found out the shit had hit the fan in the Dallas front office. I had déjà vu back to when I got called into an emergency meeting two summers earlier about Sullivan's behavior at his own wedding. It wasn't the image Chicago wanted associated with them, and I was more than happy to add my opinion into the mix.

"I can't believe this happened," Asher said as we got to the hotel and stepped into our suite. "He was always an arrogant prick, but I never saw him going this far. Do we know why he was there?"

"Not yet. I mean, she hasn't told me the whole story. The

video only shows part of their conversation. I'm sure it wasn't interesting enough for the vultures behind the phones until he got violent," I replied with a growl, pissed again. Or still. I wasn't even sure what the emotion I felt was. It was a mix of rage and sadness, with a little inadequacy thrown into the mix. It was close to the same feeling I'd had when Olive died, but this was more violent. The moment I'd lost her the day before my thirteenth birthday was the worst pain I'd ever felt. The most helpless, the angriest. Until now. Rationally I knew I couldn't have done anything for either of them, but it didn't stop the weight of failure from crushing me. I was supposed to keep Greyson safe, and barely a full day after that became my most important job, I failed miserably.

After I ran through the shower, I settled into bed and dialed Greyson. She picked up almost instantly. Soft light illuminated her face and created an angelic glow around her head. Her eyes were red and wet, but her lips stretched into a smile when her gaze landed on mine.

"I thought I said sans clothes," Greyson teased as she propped her head on a stuffed toy. I leaned forward and pulled off my shirt while I tossed the blanket back so she could see I was wearing her favorite shorts. The way she looked at me through the phone made it difficult to keep myself under control. Greyson sat up and started to unbutton her shirt, and I coughed in surprise when I realized she had started to undress.

"No. Don't."

Her fingers froze on the third button, and I saw just the hint of a soft multi-colored bra that reminded me of rainbow sherbet. I wanted a lick. Badly.

"You don't want to see me ... I mean ... okay. Yeah, of course. Sorry," she fumbled, as embarrassment tinged her words. Which made me feel like more of an asshole.

"Fuck yes I want to. I just want it to be special, you know? The first time we see each other that way, I want to be able to do something about it. If you take your shirt off right now, you're going to see me spontaneously come, and I'd like you to think of me as more manly than a fifteen-year-old who just saw his first boob."

She laughed and nodded in agreement, or just to make me feel better. Either way, she seemed to understand my reluctance and stopped torturing me with my own private striptease. She didn't re-button the ones that were already popped though, so my eyes were glued like lasers to any glimpse of what was under her shirt.

"I can't argue with that," Greyson sighed wistfully. "I missed your whole game. I watched some highlights. You were impressive with your face-offs."

"You should come to Montreal. Stay for the rest of the tournament."

"I couldn't possibly leave the shop for that long on the fly," Greyson murmured softly. "I'd love to though."

"What the hell happened out there?" I wasn't going to beat around the bush. I needed details.

"He was waiting outside when I closed, which was really creepy because I left late. So, he was just ... there. For who knows how long."

"He came to Chicago to assault you?"

"No, he came to apologize."

I couldn't help the snort at the idea of KJ ever apologizing for anything. Especially for being a pussy chasing fuck hound. "Sure, he did."

"He's in a program, so it was time to make amends. For sex addition."

"Oh, give me a fucking break," I couldn't help the involuntary roll of my eyes at the idea. He wasn't a sex addict. He was just a piece of shit.

"I know it sounds like an excuse for being a cheating asshole, but—"

"But nothing," I interrupted. "He doesn't get a pass for what he's done."

"I know, and when I pointed that out to him things went to

shit," Greyson's voice broke, and I could see she was most likely reliving the assault.

"Do you believe him? The sex addict part?"

She sighed, and it was full of painful memories. "It makes sense, I guess. Maybe. But it just feels like a convenient way to not take responsibility. I just want him out of my life once and for all. I feel like this was a pretty solid goodbye."

"I'll make sure he gets my farewell note, too, when I beat his ass."

"That won't accomplish anything," Greyson protested. "I'm pressing charges, according to Trevor. So, he will have consequences."

"If he's not suspended when we play the Diablos, I *am* going after him. You can be mad, but I'm telling you now, it's going to happen."

Greyson snuggled back into her bed and laid sideways. The angle of her body caused her cleavage to spill out of the bra and gave me a clear view of her milky white skin. I considered a retraction on my 'keep your clothes on' stance.

"The way you protect me, I kind of love it," she said on a yawn.

"Get used to it," I replied, entranced by how she wrestled sleep for me. "Go to sleep, Lemon Drop. I'll call you in the morning."

"Do you mind staying on the phone? Until I fall asleep? Mila gave me a gummy, so it hopefully won't be too long."

"Of course. I wish I could actually be there to hold you all night."

"I'm not a good sleeper, especially around people, but I just really need you right now."

I stayed on for an hour after she closed her eyes and dropped the phone. Her shallow breaths told me the story of her dreams. Twenty minutes after she first fell asleep, she whimpered slightly, and I wished the camera was aimed at her face so I could see her expression. Ten minutes after that she started talking, fear cutting

through the 'No, stop' and 'please don't do this' that tumbled
from her mouth. She didn't wake, but she definitely didn't rest
comfortably. I would have done anything to be in that bed to
show her nightmares that they held no power over my love. I was
angry to know KJ invaded her mind even in sleep, and I only hung
up after she had been quietly asleep for half an hour.

What a way to start the rest of my life.

CHAPTER 26

Greyson

"So, he's hot? Like, hot enough for me to slip off my panties before we go in?" Mila asked with a grin as I chose the most beautiful assortment of pastries to add to the 'Thank You for Saving My Ass' box I put together for my new friends.

"Do you ever stop thinking about the next dick you might hop on?"

Her look was disdainful.

"No. Why would I? Seriously, I hope Gavin uses his talents to show you why riding dick is the greatest American pastime, because it pains me to see you not understand."

I still hadn't fully grasped the idea of Gavin and I being naked together in the very near future, and the thought of it filled me with equal parts excitement and anxiety.

"I don't know what to do with it. Please teach me your ways," I mock begged as I put the finishing touches on the package and waited impatiently while Mila reapplied her blood red lipstick.

"There's so much to learn. We can't waste any more time. First lesson: edible panties."

"Hard pass. I watched a video of these guys trying on edible underwear, and while hilarious, the consensus was not good. The statement 'it looks like my dick is bleeding' was uttered, and that's not something I ever want to hear out of Gavin's mouth when I'm trying to be sexy."

Mila shook her head and stared at me in disbelief. "Lesson two: don't talk about weird shit that's going to make him think of anything except you naked."

"I can't help it."

"Try," Mila answered with pity. We got in my car and I typed in the address to Biscuits in the Basket's office. It turned out the Falcons backup goalie Evan was friends with Camden Reynolds, and both the hockey and social media teams had tightened around me. The minute it was known I was their captain's girlfriend, the entire team turned into protective older brothers. They honestly believed I didn't notice the fact there was always at least one of them occupying the table next to the front door of Icing, as if they were waiting for KJ to come back so they had a legitimate reason to beat the shit out of him. It had only been two days, but the constant presence of Chicago Falcons at the bakery had spread across social media and brought in an unending string of customers from open to close. It was great for business, but it was also completely asinine. No matter how much I begged him to call it off Gavin refused to acknowledge he knew anything about it, let alone dictated the entire thing. Even though he was thousands of miles away, his presence was known and felt by everyone who came near me. I'd never felt more safe or more loved. After Mila had a chance to read up on all of Biscuits' posts since the confrontation and my back-and-forth conversation with Camden, she'd decided they weren't total assholes.

We pulled up in front of the understated building, and I read the address four times to confirm we were in the right place. I wasn't sure what I expected, but a rundown brick two story in a questionable neighborhood was not it.

"Are you sure this is it?" Mila asked with a curl of her perfectly sloped nose. "This is ... not pleasant."

"This is what Evan said," I replied more confidently than I felt. This felt like an episode of Dateline. "Let's go. It's fine."

"It's the farthest thing from fine, but whatever you say."

"Trevor knows we're here. I wouldn't be surprised if he was around the corner. We're good."

Even so, I ran up to the door and darted inside faster than I'd moved in probably ten years. There wasn't anyone around, so Mila took it upon herself to walk down the hall peering in doors. I hovered around the front when she came back with a lanky blonde. He was clearly in awe of her and would have done anything she asked, so when she demanded he take us to Camden Reynolds he just nodded in compliance and led us to the elevator. On the ride up he stole a few glances at the box in my hands and I ended up offering him a cupcake, even though it would completely throw off the aesthetic I'd created. I was relieved when he declined.

The elevator doors slid open into a space that didn't feel like the same building. The floors were gorgeous, finished hardwoods and there was a basketball court along one side. Plush armchairs were scattered throughout the space and each wall was a mural to the Falcons. My eye was drawn to a life-sized artist's rendition of Gavin and his reaction when Cohen stopped the shot that secured their Cup win three years prior. I was so impressed I texted a photo of the wall to Gavin. He had slowly accepted the idea they weren't total vultures after he talked to Evan and found out more about the men behind the microphones. His protectiveness still hovered on the brink, ready to come out and battle at the first inkling they weren't the nice people I was convinced they were.

The employee had taken off to let someone know we were there, and when Jay and Camden emerged from a closed-door office Mila's eyes widened in appreciation.

"Care to retract your hatred?" I asked under my breath. Jay would be a notch on her headboard by the end of the weekend. Camden grinned at me and came forward for a half hug, which I awkwardly accepted by using the box of cupcakes as a buffer.

"Hey, Greyson. What are you doing here?"

"It's not enough, but I just wanted to bring you a thank you. This is my friend Mila." I nodded over at her as she shook hands and held onto Jay's long enough to solidify her one-night stand status. "This office is ... not what it looks like from the outside."

"Yeah, we chose someplace that was less on rent so we had more money for charity donations and stuff like that," Cam replied with a shrug.

"Seriously? I wouldn't think you cared about that." I cringed as soon as it was out of my mouth and shoved the box into his hands. "Sorry, that came out wrong."

"No worries." He laughed and surveyed the contents of the box. "We have to prove ourselves. I get it."

Cam chose a cupcake and set the box on the hockey rink shaped conference table as he motioned for the rest of the employees to help themselves. He took a huge bite and smiled around a mouthful of caramel icing. "You didn't have to do this, but I'm glad you did."

"It's the least I could do. You really saved me, and I appreciate it more than you know."

Cam shrugged with a chagrined smile.

"I mean, we would have done it for anyone, but seeing as *you're* the reason our podcast blew up, it was the least *we* could do."

After the video and corresponding podcast episode that outlined the disaster of my wedding day, they had gone from a small time hockey podcast to being signed as an offshoot of one of the biggest sports entertainment brands in the world.

"Well, I'm glad you recognize that. You're welcome," I paused. "Do you have some time to talk? I have a business proposition for you."

Jay and Camden exchanged a look and led us to a vacant conference room. Mila unsurprisingly chose the chair next to Jay, and I saw her hand graze his thigh under the table as Tommy joined and closed the door.

"So, what's up?" Cam asked once we were all settled. I assessed the cords on the table and held one up in front of their faces.

"If I plug this in will it project up there? There's a camera in here right?"

"Yeah. Why? Are you doing a presentation or something?" Tommy asked in confusion. He grabbed the remote and turned on the screen as I plugged in my phone and watched the camera spin and point at us.

"Sort of." I dialed and let out a long breath of relief when Gavin answered. The men gathered around the table gasped in shock to see the Falcons' captain on their big screen.

"Hey baby, are we ready?" Gavin asked, his full attention on me. I still wasn't sure this was the best course of action, but he seemed pretty set on it, so I just sat back with a nod and watched him command the room.

"I just want to start by saying thank you, and tickets to the home opener are on me for how you stepped in to help my girl," Gavin said as his mouth lifted into a smile that was all mine. "I can admit I wasn't happy when she told me she was trusting you guys with this story, but you've proven me wrong."

They stared dumbly at the screen and it was entertaining to see Gavin elicit this reaction from someone other than me. He waited a moment without a response and looked at me again with a raised eyebrow.

"Anyway, I've been getting bombed with requests to talk about this, and I've turned them all down, but it's become bothersome. I'm going to do one interview only and do it on your podcast, if you're interested. Greyson trusts you, and I trust her."

This finally got their attention and Camden jumped out of his chair, like his legs didn't know what to do with the energy Gavin's offer had given them.

"Are you serious? Holy shit!"

"Is that a yes? You're interested in handling this, and putting out my statement?"

"Yeah. For sure. A million times over. Thank you."

"Don't thank me. Thank her." Gavin pointed at me. The guys finally got their voices to work and solidified the timing of the interview, which would happen later that afternoon once they had time to formulate some questions and get themselves under control. Gavin winked at me before he disconnected the call. My phone was still connected to their screen when he immediately texted to tell me how sexy I looked in my flannel shirt and that he was counting down the days until I could be his 'personal lumber-jill' and 'handle his wood while wearing that shirt and nothing else.' I ripped the cord out of the phone as the three men looked over at me, and Mila pointed at the screen that was now black.

"See? Gavin knows what he's doing. I can't wait for you to get under him."

"On that note. We're going to go," I could barely speak through my embarrassment. "Oh, and I'd advise you against bringing up that text during your interview."

Cam nodded vigorously as he walked us to the elevator.

"Thank you, Greyson. I've been trying to get an interview with Gavin Halstead for five years."

"What can I say? I make dreams come true, one humiliating experience at a time."

CHAPTER 27
Gavin

"I can't believe you're doing this," Drake talked around the lollipop shoved up into his cheek. He stretched his legs and tossed a stress ball into the air as he lazily caught and alternated hands.

"Do you have a better idea?" I wasn't sure I loved it either, but it was the easiest way to have a lot of people hear what I had to say. There had been a time I respected their reporting and liked how enthusiastic Camden was for the team, but that flew out the window with the first mention of the way Greyson looked in her wedding dress. Seeing the real-life fallout of their words had soured me.

"I mean, no. I'd have already done it if it was me, but you're not like me."

"What does that mean, exactly?"

"It means Drake is impulsive and does things without considering consequences, and you calculate every possible outcome down to the slightest variance before you make a fraction of a move," Asher replied.

"Fuck you, ass wipe. I consider things." Drake threw the ball across the room and caught Asher on the side of the face. The welt it left behind was instant and angry, and Asher retaliated by slapping him directly across the face.

"Did you consider that?"

"Knock it off," I barked. Once again, I wondered how we were the same age when most of their lives they acted like children. "Can you focus on me for a minute, please? I need you in the background telling me if I'm getting into territory that's going to make the office pissed at me."

"Just talk. Tell him you have the final authority on what makes it into the episode or you aren't doing it," Asher rubbed his face where the imprint of the ball was still fresh.

"This is just stupid. Why is there so much interest around my relationship? No one ever cared about your marriage like this."

"People get cheated on every day. True, they don't always discover that infidelity the day the child they *thought* was theirs is born, but still. My situation was just an unfaithful wife. He got caught with his dick in a bunny at his own wedding and then tried to choke out his ex a year later railing about how much she sucks in bed."

"Thanks for that," I cringed. Guilt washed over me again for not being there when she needed me. "I talk about hockey. I don't talk about my women."

"Not totally true. Have you forgotten the Entice article, where you talked about your love of big titties and how your favorite way to fuck is from behind so you can watch asses bounce?" Drake threw out, which made me want to smack him too.

"That was a lapse in judgment by a twenty-year old idiot," I grumbled, as my ears burned in shame about that damn interview. It was the one thing about my past I regretted. The only people who continued to bring it up on a regular basis were my best friends, who liked to use it as proof I wasn't the boy scout everyone made me out to be. It made me sound like an arrogant dickhead who took full advantage of the legion of puck bunnies that swarmed in droves, and my mom wouldn't talk to me for a full week after it came out. It was also where my distrust of reporters started, since all the worst bits were supposedly off the record.

The alarm on my phone buzzed so I dialed the number I'd been provided and was met with Camden Reynolds looking like he was on the verge of vomiting. The other two were in the room and kept their heads down as they fiddled with their laptops. It was clear I was completely in control of this interview.

"Hey, right on time," Cam's voice was full of nervous energy, as if he expected to be bitched out. Might as well give him what he wanted.

"Since Greyson isn't listening this time, I'm going to talk to you man to man. I don't trust any of you. She feels some kind of way towards you and that's why I'm doing this. If you even *think* about talking about her physical appearance in any way, shape, or form, I will beat you so hard your own mother won't recognize you, and I'll make sure you never have any connections inside the Falcons organization for the rest of your career," I paused, pretty sure his testicles shriveled. "Do I make myself clear?"

"Crystal."

"Good. Now let's do this."

The interview flowed easily for twenty minutes before Cam asked how I'd handle having KJ in front of me during a game. The response I gave was less professional and more threat on his life. Drake caught my eye from across the room and chopped his hand across his throat. He was right, that probably wasn't the best thing to say, and I was sure the front office wouldn't appreciate it.

"Is that a challenge?"

"You can interpret it however you want."

"I mean, it gives the fans something to look forward to if it's a challenge."

"It is what it is, man. He put his hands on a woman, one I happen to be very fond of, and if anyone thinks I'm just going to let that slide they're part of the problem."

A half hour later, after we'd discussed the world tournament and the start of the new season, Cam stopped recording and took off his headset.

"Again, thanks so much for taking time to do this, Halstead."

"I wasn't expecting you to ask me about hockey. I was all amped up to defend Greyson for an hour. It was a pleasant surprise. Thanks."

"Like I told her when she was leaving, I've wanted to interview you since I started doing this. You're one of my idols in the game. So when the opportunity came up I had to throw in some of what I really wanted to talk about," Cam answered with a shrug.

"I respect that. Sorry about how harsh I was when I first called in, but your team hasn't been what I'd call professional in the past when it comes to her, and I'm always going to protect her first and be a nice guy second."

"I get it. We've all made some mistakes in our stories, and we're learning as we go. Unfortunately, we can't take it back once we realize how awful it is," Cam replied. "But you have my word, there will be no more episodes like that about her, or any women for that matter."

"That's all I ask. Everyone has stories they regret. Drake likes to remind me of mine every chance he can."

"Entice?"

"Damn man, you too?" I laughed for real, and decided I'd give them the benefit of the doubt. "But for real, hit me up closer to the start of the season and I'll hook you guys up with game tickets."

"You don't have to do that, but we won't turn it down," Cam said with a nod. "Your girlfriend is a pretty amazing person, Halstead."

"That's never been in question," I replied with a tip of my chin. "She's kindness in a box of talent, wrapped in beauty and finished with glitter."

"Can I quote that?"

"Please do."

CHAPTER 28
Greyson

I realized after the same table of customers had looked up at me when I paced past their table for the fourth time I might be making people edgy. Gavin would be home in the next hour and even though we had spoken a ridiculous number of times since we had become a couple, I was so nervous to see him my stomach rolled. I didn't know how to act around him now that my status in his life was elevated beyond friend, and I'd been anxious over how to greet him for a full day. Did I run into his arms and lay the kiss on him I'd dreamt of for a year? Or did I wait patiently and awkwardly for him to direct the movement?

After the confrontation with KJ, the city of Chicago had become a whole lot more interested in me, and my relationship with Gavin. It was great for the bakery, since everyone who had ever watched a Falcons game apparently felt the need to come buy cupcakes. Not so fantastic for my anxiety and temperament in general, since I'd worked really damn hard to get my name off of Biscuits in the Basket radar after KJ and I split and now I was right back in the bulls eye. But Camden Reynolds was a lot more of a human being than I originally thought, and they had kept to their word to make KJ look like the piece of shit he was. I actually started to like him. Hell had officially frozen over.

It was only after the volume level in the shop dropped significantly that I stopped pacing and looked over at the door, where Gavin stood with a grin. A wave of heat rolled over me as I took in the sight of my boyfriend. The hat that rested backwards on his head looked like it was made for him and him alone, and I swallowed hard as my eyes swept quickly over the rest of him. He was effortless perfection, and I mentally froze the sight of him in my mind. His dark jeans rode low on his hips, held in place by the worn leather belt that had seen better days. A gray t-shirt had a black jacket thrown over the top. I reminded myself to breathe as he slowly moved towards me. I couldn't do anything but shuffle a few steps forward and wait for the moment I'd imagined for days. When he got to where I stood he stopped on the other side of the counter and surveyed the case with his thumb on his chin.

"Do you have any of those Daiquiri Drops today?"

The blush was instantaneous and consumed my body like a spark in a dry forest. I lifted the counter for him to walk through and eagerly curled my fingers into his when he reached out his hand and leaned into my cheek.

"Can we go in the back so I can kiss you in private?"

I swallowed down my nerves as I led him through the kitchen and into my office. Gavin closed the door firmly as we made it to privacy and turned the lock while his eyes never left me. I nervously clasped my hands in front of me as he hooked a finger in the loop of my jeans and pulled me against his body.

"In all the time I've known you, this is the first time you've had literally nothing to say," Gavin murmured, his fingers pressed firmly into my hips as my heart punched against my ribs.

"I don't want to mess it up," I whispered, my eyes drawn into his with the force of a million magnetic pulses. Gavin's thumb moved over my jaw and across my lips as his mouth twitched into a half smile.

"Remember New Year's Day when we talked about first kisses?"

"Of course."

The emotion that coursed through me as I recalled the moment he promised my next first kiss would cancel out the first almost knocked me to the ground. It had the same effect on me then that it was having on me now.

"What I said ... I meant it. I knew it was going to be me giving it to you too."

"Pretty cocky, don't you think Canada?" I asked breathlessly as Gavin grinned confidently and pulled me even closer. I was positive my heart was going to leap out of my chest with the intensity of the moment and I wanted it to be frozen in time.

"It's not cocky when you know you're right. It's just the facts. Now, are you ready for me to change your life?"

I rolled my eyes so hard I made myself dizzy with his arrogance and lost my breath when he softly lowered his mouth against mine. When his lips pressed against mine, I saw fireworks and parted in anticipation for more. His breath smelled like cinnamon and he tasted like marshmallows. My mind raced with thoughts that competed for space. One side of my brain was in overdrive with thoughts about the cupcake I would put together to commemorate this moment, a heavily spiced cinnamon cake with fluffy, sticky marshmallow frosting. The other side grasped at every sensation and tried to hold on for dear life in case this was just a figment of my imagination.

Gavin took advantage of my sigh into his mouth and slid his tongue into mine, his hands tangled into my hair. Heat built between my thighs as I dug my fingers into his neck, greedy, needy, and desperate. Gavin's guttural growl woke up my soul and he backed me up against the wall as he pulled back. His lips moved across my jaw and down my neck. He inhaled deeply and the warmth of his breath on his exhale sent a wave of goosebumps over my chest. I brought him up to meet my face, impatient to make up for lost time. Gavin rested his forehead on mine and trailed soft lines down my face.

"Now that I have you, I'm never going to let you go."

"Until you realize how crazy I am and decide I'm not worth

your trouble," I said, regretting the words even as I said them. Gavin narrowed his eyes and clenched his jaw tightly as he pressed his body against me aggressively enough to make the bulge in his jeans a very prominent reminder of the way he felt about me.

"Maybe you are crazy. But it's beautiful to me."

"I think you stole that line from a song."

"Well, you stole my heart, and your crazy makes you who I fell in love with, so I don't care."

I froze against the wall and searched his eyes to see if the words he had spoken were purposeful or just a slip of the tongue. "Fell in love with? Are you saying you ... love me? Like, really love me. Not the best friend love I already knew about, but boyfriend love. Real love?"

The more I tried to get my mouth not to say the L word the more it tumbled out.

"I mean ... yeah," Gavin mumbled at the floor, his eyes on my shoes. I could not believe it. He was embarrassed. I lifted his chin and leaned down to meet his gaze.

"Could you maybe look at me while I tell you I love you back?"

His eyes lit up as his head shot up and he cupped my cheeks. "For real?"

"Nothing in my life has ever been more real. I love you, Canada. In a way that terrifies me. In a way that thrills me. In all the ways."

Gavin tangled his hands into my hair and kissed me with the intensity that proved he'd waited as long as I had for this moment. He was right. He changed my life with his kiss.

"If you can do this to me with your lips, I can't wait to see what you can do to me with your dick."

Gavin's eyes sparked and he flicked his head towards my desk.

"While the caveman in me would like to show you what my dick can do right here in your office, I'm taking you out before I take you to bed. I will not make love to you before I take you on a proper date. I won't do it."

"So serious," I murmured as I traced my index finger down the scrunched-up spot between his eyes. "We'll do it your way. This time."

"I want to make sure you're treated right, Greyson. Getting you in bed is not my first priority. It may be what I think about every night when I'm alone, but I don't expect you to be naked five seconds after I get home."

"You've treated me more respectfully as a friend than he ever did as a fiancé. The four days I've been your girlfriend have been better than four years with him. You've never treated me like anything but a lady. And there have been times ... you should have."

"Even when you're ... challenging ... I'll still respect you. You can count on that," Gavin promised. "I'll pick you up at seven and we're going somewhere nice. Sorry to crush your dreams but your sweatshirt gets the night off."

"I have to wear a dress?"

"Your whining is so adorable." Gavin dropped another kiss on my mouth, which turned into a handful of minutes of hardcore making out. When we finally broke, he pressed his thumb against my bottom lip with a deep sigh. "If I don't leave now, I won't be able to stick to my own rule about taking you out first."

He took my hand and led me into the dining room, where he stopped to sign autographs for star struck little kids with frosting covered cheeks. He tossed a smile over his shoulder when he reached the exit and all the blood in my body rushed straight to my clit. "Dress and heels. I'll see you at seven."

I waited until the door closed after him before I escaped back to the kitchen. I grabbed a notepad to scribble down measurements for the cinnamon marshmallow cake I couldn't stop thinking about, then played hooky for the rest of the afternoon, to give myself ample time to prepare for my date.

His kiss had sent a shockwave through my body that I still felt in my toes. He took over the second we were alone, assertive and dominant in a way I'd only seen a fraction of in our time as friends. Boyfriend Gavin was way different than best friend Gavin, and I was beyond impatient to find out how far he took that alpha attitude when it was just the two of us.

I stepped into my dress and inspected myself in the full-length mirror. I looked good. Even I could see that. I snapped a picture and texted it to Mila and Delaney for confirmation, since I could never trust my instincts. Their ego boosting responses came as a strong knock echoed down the front hall. After one final deep breath, I swung open the door. Gavin stood with his hands in his pockets and his slow perusal of my body left no question where his mind was.

"Wow." He stepped into the house and placed a protective hand on my waist. "You look unbelievable."

I nervously clasped my hands in front of me, then pulled my arms together across my stomach. Gavin took both hands in his and brought them to his lips.

"I know you're uncomfortable, and I won't tell you to relax, because that's not helpful for you. What I will say is that you're gorgeous. I've never seen someone more beautiful than you in this moment."

I dipped my head and bit my tongue to hold back the retort to the compliment. I wasn't used to them. It would take time to accept them openly.

"I love you for that. And a lot of other things," I finally replied as I leaned into him for a kiss. The realization I could kiss him whenever I wanted to was slow to sink in, and I was ready to take advantage of that perk in a big way. He held my jacket after we separated and took my hand as he led me out the door.

Gavin helped me into his truck and I watched him walk around the front and slide behind the wheel. "Seriously. You look too amazing for words."

"You don't have to say that," I murmured softly as I rubbed the infinity symbol around my neck. The nervous tic was something I'd tried to abandon, but my fingers automatically reached for it whenever I felt unsure.

"Yes, I do. I've got a year's worth of compliments I've kept in my head to catch up on. You're gorgeous and I'll never stop making sure you know that."

"Thank you. For everything. You never gave up on me, even when you should have."

"You don't give up on your dreams. Being able to love you like this has been mine for a pretty long time." Gavin brushed his lips softly over mine and pulled out of the driveway.

We were seated immediately once we arrived at the restaurant, and our table was situated in a private corner. There weren't chairs, rather a plush purple velvet couch against the wall complete with purple and cream throw pillows. The black marble table was adorned with a lavender runner down the middle and candles that artfully dripped in their own protective bowls. It was breathtaking. It was also most definitely not my scene. After the hostess left, I shifted against the couch to meet Gavin's eyes after I pushed the pillows to the floor.

"Alright Canada, what's the deal? This is not us. We're beer and nachos, aren't we? This is duck liver and champagne."

Gavin smiled and lazily drug his tongue over his top lip.

"I've never been to this restaurant. I admit it's a little over the top, but I wanted to take you somewhere special. Tonight, I want to focus on nothing but you. But if coming here means you're going to wear that dress more often, then this is our new regular spot."

"I feel ridiculous in this dress." I glanced over the drink menu as the waiter approached the table. "I've really been craving a Lemon Drop. I think I'll have one of those."

Gavin licked his lips and made a 'heh' sound under his breath before he ordered a whiskey neat. As the waiter walked away he reached for my hand and ran his finger across my palm.

"You're not making it easy for me not to take you right here on this table," Gavin said. He lifted my hand to his mouth and traced my knuckles with his lips.

"This dinner was your idea," I replied breathlessly, relieved and annoyed when the waiter reappeared with our drinks. I lifted the glass to my lips and flicked my tongue across the sugared rim. Gavin's eyes went dark and hungry, and as he took a sip of his whiskey, he dropped a hand under the table to run across my thigh. My skin tingled in his wake, and I was close to begging him to reconsider date night so we could just get to what we both wanted.

By the time our food arrived I'd realized nothing had changed between us as far as the ease of conversation. This was just like any other dinner we'd shared aside from the less comfortable clothes and way more expensive food. Which, I hated to admit, was incredible.

"Thank you for making me feel so special tonight," I murmured softly as I watched him take the last bite of steak and wipe his mouth. A slight blush crept up his cheeks and settled in his earlobes when he wrapped his fingers around his glass and spun it in half circles on the tabletop.

"I hated seeing the way you were treated before. How much he took advantage of you. While I've never treated *any* woman that way, it especially pissed me off to see it happening to you."

"I truly don't understand why you cared about me. We barely spoke."

Gavin turned on the couch and ran his hand over his mouth as I raised my drink to my lips. "The truth is, I wanted to ask you out at the Legacy event."

I legitimately choked at that tidbit of information and coughed up the vodka I'd just sipped. It was true. KJ told the truth. For once in his miserable life.

"I don't believe you." I was flustered and dabbed at my dress while Gavin scooted in closer.

"I was so embarrassed after I spilled my drink on you, I had to call Mattie for advice. She convinced me to ask if I could sit next to you during dinner. By the time I came back...."

I remembered the exact moment KJ approached. He had confidently dropped into the chair next to me and thrown his arm over the back of mine. He didn't ask for permission—he just took what he wanted. I should have known then. My memories brought back the vision of Gavin as he strode back into the room and stopped short at the sight of my full table. I didn't think anything of it at the time. Now though, I realized it was a look of defeat in his eyes when he pulled out the chair next to Asher at the table across from mine.

"He told me. When he came to the shop that night. He said he only asked me out because he wanted to get back at you."

"Of course, he did," Gavin replied with a shake of his head. "I never wondered *why* he zeroed in on you. Look at you. Anyone would. But KJ was never the boyfriend type. It makes sense that he had an angle."

I was saddened and enraged to learn, without question, I was nothing more than a big *fuck you* in the world of male posturing.

"The day of the wedding ... why did you come? If you truly felt this way, why would you want to be there to see it?"

"I didn't want to. I was quite childish about it honestly. Asher had to literally drag me to the car. Being the captain put the responsibility of team camaraderie on me, so I had to be there for a teammate's wedding. I didn't want to see it."

"He's what I thought I deserved. So, I took the life I thought was my penance."

Gavin swallowed a gulp of whiskey and squeezed my hand.

"I hope you know you can tell me anything. Your past, whatever happened to make you believe you don't deserve happiness, you can trust me with it."

The deep moment was interrupted by the waiter as he brought our desserts, and I was grateful for the momentary reprieve. The pounding of my heart was so aggressive it hurt. I was going to have to tell him. I would. Just not now.

Gavin ignored the sweets while I picked up my fork and dipped into the soft cake. When his thumb slid over my lip my breath caught. He lifted his finger to his mouth and licked off the frosting that hadn't made it into my own.

"I don't want to disappoint the expectation you have of me," I murmured around the lump in my throat. "I'm nothing special, and for you to have held this vision of me in your periphery for this long, I'm not sure the reality of me can live up to the version in your mind."

"You already have," Gavin replied softly. We ate in silence, and it took all my concentration to hold in my tears at his revelation. I couldn't and would probably never be able to understand what he saw in me that kept his attention this long. It didn't make any sense to my fractured mind.

"These are alright, but they've got nothing on your cupcakes." Gavin raised his spoon to my lips with the last bit of his dessert. His eyes followed my mouth as the velvety custard coated my tongue.

"I've got some cupcakes at home for you," I lowered my voice, even though there wasn't anyone around. "A brand-new recipe."

Gavin blew out a heavy breath and curled his fingers around my hand before he guided it onto his leg. I wasn't sure what I was supposed to do when we got home, and I had never been one to be aggressive in the bedroom. I timidly moved my hand further towards his inner thigh, and the outline through his pants assured me he was as endowed as I expected.

We were both quiet on the drive back to my house. The reality of what was about to happen had set in. I nervously drummed my fingers on the armrest while the lights of buildings blurred as we flew down Lakeshore Drive. I noticed Gavin cast a sidelong glance at me as he reached for my hand. It wasn't the feverish passion we'd exchanged back and forth all night. It was softer, as if he were expressing his understanding of my mood through touch.

"We don't have to do anything tonight," he said gently.

"I want to. I *really* want to. I'm just ... I don't know what to do with," I waved my hand over him, "that."

He laughed loudly and squeezed my hand. "It's not *that* big. It gets the job done, but it's nothing to be afraid of."

I threw a glare at him. "I'm not really interested in hearing about all the jobs it's gotten done, thanks."

Gavin braked at a red light and turned in his seat to face me.

"I've got a past. There's no denying that. I ran around a lot. I partied. I enjoyed plenty of time with women I wouldn't introduce to Mom. But since I've gotten close with you the only job it's gotten done is with my own hands."

"You mean since we started dating."

"No. I mean since the first night I skated past your seats and we made eye contact. Since I went to Icing and was so fucking awkward, I couldn't believe you ever called me. Since you got drunk and told me I was never getting in your pants. Since *then*."

I stared at him in disbelief as he turned his attention back to the road.

"You haven't had sex in over a year?" I asked incredulously. Impossible. The man was gorgeous. Literally thousands of women would jump him at any given time without a second thought.

"To be completely honest, I can't actually remember the last time. No one else has interested me. I'm not going to go to bed with a random woman just to get off when I'm perfectly capable of handling it myself. Especially when my mind would have been on you. But I plan on making up for lost time starting tonight."

CHAPTER 29
Greyson

We walked quietly side by side up the walk when we got to my house, and Gavin stepped back so I could unlock the door. He took the keys and gave me a sweet smile after my hands shook so badly, I dropped them on the porch. Once we were inside and he'd helped me out of my coat we stared at each other in charged silence.

"So, do we just go at it then?" I finally asked. I immediately shook my head in embarrassment, my eyes trained on the floor. Gavin laughed as he took a step forward and closed the gap between us. Heat radiated off him and he smelled spicy, a mixture of whiskey, expensive cologne, and man. My breath caught in my throat as he gently laid a hand on the side of my neck and stared down at me as a year's worth of pent-up lust and imagined moments flashed through his eyes. He brought his lips to meet mine as he softly ran his fingers down my shoulder to settle on my hip. My hands rested on his chest before I slipped my fingertips under the collar of his jacket. Gavin shook it off his shoulders and paid no attention as it fell to the floor.

"I should put that on a hanger. It looks expensive. It shouldn't just be thrown on the ground," I babbled, almost incoherent with desire. Gavin grabbed my wrist and pulled me into him hard.

"Fuck the suit. I need you. Now."

He tilted my head to the side and nestled his lips into the curve of my neck as he kissed his way to my earlobe. I pulled my head back and stared into the chocolate depths of his eyes as I recalled the first time they had met mine after I'd thought my world had fallen apart. When I'd been a broken woman, crushed by the humiliation of a horrible man. Gavin helped put me back together and I hadn't realized it. His friendship helped me find myself. For the first time in my entire life. And now he was here and wanted me as much as I wanted him.

"Are you okay?" he asked softly. I nodded slightly and laced my fingers behind his neck.

"Perfect."

Gavin's hands slid up my back and found the zipper of my dress. His fingers brushed my spine as the garment fell open under his hands and he pushed it to the floor. As it slid down my body and pooled at my feet, his eyes followed. I stepped out of it and kicked it to the side as I stood in front of Gavin in nothing but black lace and heels. I'd never felt so exposed and it took every drop of my self-control not to pull my arms across my body and hide the flaws I imagined he saw in the soft light. His jaw clenched and he stepped back as his gaze swept every line of my body. He reached out and ran his finger over the tattoo between my cleavage as he slowly traced the stars with his fingertips. His hooded eyes caught mine and the intensity that flashed through them was so powerful it took my breath away.

"A cupcake constellation? I couldn't even conceive of something more authentically *you.*"

I moved my hands down the buttons on his dress shirt as he crushed his mouth against mine and helped him push the sleeves off his wrists. He was impatient, and as I pulled the edge of his undershirt out of his pants, he reached one arm behind his head to toss it away.

He lifted me and swept my legs around his waist as he carried me to my room and laid me gently on the bed. Gavin hovered over

ICING

me on hands and knees while his eyes continued to roam my body.

"Why are you staring at me like that?" I gave voice to the question as my inability to live in the moment fought to the front of my brain. He looked at me in surprise as his hands ran down my chest and settled over the thin lace that covered my breasts.

"I'm in awe of you, Greyson. You're a work of art." Gavin lowered his mouth and sucked my nipple between his teeth. It didn't matter that I still wore my bra. He was ravenous, and I was under his complete control. His hum against my chest caused me to writhe against the sheets and beg him to take me further.

Gavin reached around me to unhook my bra and tossed it away as he dipped his head back to my chest. His hands went lower and when he slipped a finger inside me, I bit my tongue to hold in the moan.

"You're so fucking wet," Gavin groaned.

"I told you. This is what you do to me."

He withdrew his finger and pressed it against my lips as my eyes widened in shock.

"You know how much I love that, right?" He kissed his way down and slid my panties off. As he moved lower, I could no longer ignore my demons and pushed his forehead back as I sat up quickly and pressed my knees together.

"What is it? What's wrong?" Gavin looked up, concern etched over his face. If I wasn't so mortified, I would have laughed. All the conversations and prep with the girls hadn't prepared me for the moment when this actually happened.

"I just ... um ... well the thing is ... no one has ever ... I mean, I haven't ... done this before," I finished miserably. His face showed confusion, followed by shock when he realized what I'd just told him.

"You mean to tell me, in the four years you were with that asshole, he never once went down on you?"

I could not believe I had just told him I'd never been on the

231

receiving end of oral sex. I would have laughed again. If it wasn't so pathetic.

"No. He said I was disgusting. Before him I wasn't experienced at all. I guess I'm still not, since he was always out banging other people and not me. I was always afraid of getting attached to someone and having them leave, so I just never did. Before him I was a total virgin, unless you count my vibrator, I've got *tons* of experience there. I mean, I'm always horny, but I don't have much experience with actual human dicks, you know?

"I bought a sex toy once that looked like a tongue since no one had ever been down there with their mouth. I figured maybe it would be a good stand in, so I'd know what it was like. It was super weird. Then I thought if the real thing was anything like *that* I wasn't missing out on much." I shuddered at the memory of the rubber tongue as it buzzed against my clit.

Gavin's expression was a cross between confusion and horror as I realized I'd probably just murdered the mood. I wanted to sink into the bed and wake up in the morning to realize the entire conversation had been a hideous nightmare. Judging by his narrowed eyes and the way he roughly rubbed his hand over his nose and down his lips this was not a bad dream. Gavin crawled back up the bed and kneeled before me.

"I wish you had told me all this before. I don't want you to feel rushed into anything. We have forever. We can go slow," he said. "Also, you will never have a need for a fucking fake tongue ever again, I guarantee that. Why in the hell is that even a thing?" His complete disgust by the idea of a simulated tongue made me want to show it to him, since it was still in a basket under my bathroom sink.

"I don't want to go slow Gavin. I want this. Now. Tonight. I'm just terrified of disappointing you."

He opened his mouth to protest and was met with my finger to silence him. "Please let me get this out. Even if you weren't captain Gavin Halstead, you'd still have women throwing themselves at you, because you're the total package every woman dreams of finding one day. I can't compete with all of them. Not even a little. Case in point, I don't know what it's like to have a tongue on my cupcake even though I'm more than halfway through my twenties. I'm not good enough for you."

"There's nothing to compete with. It's no secret that I've been with more women than I'm proud of. But that was a long time ago because I'm in love with *you*. The fact you just told me I'm the only man who will ever know what your pussy tastes like actually turns me on more than I've ever been in my entire life."

"Okay, but how could it possibly taste good? Why would you want to get your tongue all covered in ... me?"

He sat back, his tongue pressed to the corner of his mouth, an arrogant smirk surrounding it.

"Do you want to go down on me?"

"Obviously," I clucked, with a sharp eye roll.

"Why?"

"That's a ridiculous question. I'm in love with you. I've literally fantasized about your dick for like a year. Why wouldn't I want to go down on you?"

"Exactly. So why wouldn't *I* want to taste *you*? I know you're going to taste better than the Lemon Drop. I want my face *drenched* in you." Gavin slowly slid back down my body as he left a trail of kisses down my overheated skin. He kissed up both my thighs and inhaled deeply before he looked up.

"Are you ready to know what a real tongue feels like?"

I was so nervous I could barely nod but Gavin got the confirmation he needed. The first sensation of his tongue on me was so unbelievable I thought I might black out. The longer he spent between my legs the more I relaxed, and I stopped worrying about if he actually liked it. His skill and intensity proved he was serious about his quest to satisfy me.

With every flick of his tongue, Gavin brought me closer to the edge. He did things I couldn't have imagined in my deepest fantasies, and when my climax crept through my core, my thighs quivered. Gavin steadied my legs with his hands as the first wave washed over me, and I cried out his name. Orgasms with simulated, factory manufactured man parts were not comparable to those with the real thing, and I thought I might cry because he had just given me my first ever orgasm from a human being. I didn't have the chance to work up a tear before the *second* climax hit me like an oral sex freight train. Two orgasms. Or maybe it was just an extension of the first. I didn't know, and I did. Not. Care. As I came back to reality, my eyes focused on Gavin as he sat back and wiped a hand across his mouth. He was flushed, his cheeks as pink as if he'd just gotten off the ice after a long shift. He had a self-satisfied half grin on his face, and the muscles in his neck and shoulders were tight as he crawled back up to me while his erection strained his pants. The smell of me was on him as he nuzzled my cheek.

"I knew it. You taste so much better than a Lemon Drop."

"I know that's not true," I said, turning into his face. He smiled lazily and dragged his tongue over his lips in a way that was not at all innocent.

"Completely true. Your pussy might taste better than your cupcakes. You've just made sure my sweet tooth will never be fully satisfied."

I wasn't sure what color my face was, but after that statement I had to believe it was closer to the purple side of red. Automatically my brain flipped through the fruits that looked suspiciously like vulvas. Tomorrow's signature cupcake would definitely be something on the list. Peach maybe, or grapefruit, or even strawberry. *Fig!* That was it for sure.

"Your tongue is nothing like the falsie. Your tongue is pure magic. Is it okay if I kiss you right now? Is that weird? It is, isn't it? Since you were just ... with your mouth ..." I didn't have a chance to finish the thought. He captured my mouth with his and I tasted myself, the moment so erotic I clung to every sensation. We kissed contentedly for what seemed like hours, until my lips were raw and the hardness of his cock against my leg couldn't be ignored. I felt a little guilty he'd waited for so long to get a release when he'd already taken me to another planet with his mouth. The least I could do was return the favor, even if it meant I would choke on his huge penis.

I maneuvered us so he was on his back and timidly moved my fingers over him from outside his pants. Gavin dropped his head back against the bed, and when his low groan of a muttered expletive reached my ears it made me want to do anything to get him to say my name in the same tone. I took a deep breath before I unbuttoned his pants, grateful for the help he provided by pushing them down his legs. Then I was left face to face with a bulge in black boxer briefs, and I really started to question my ability to do anything with it. After another steadying breath I pulled the waistband away from his skin and the soft cotton down his legs.

"Oh. My. Fucking God." I gingerly wrapped my fingers around him. When they didn't even come close to meeting, I started to panic. Gavin watched my movements with amusement as I looked up at him with a slack jaw. "Not that big? You consider this *not that big?* Are you kidding me? How is this," I paused and tugged on him for effect, "going to fit in here?"

Using my other hand to run over myself and prove two of my fairly small fingers were a tight fit he narrowed his eyes and growled like an angry dog.

"Well between you playing tug of war with my dick and giving me a private show, it won't be an issue because I'm going to blow before I have a chance to get it in you. Haven't had sex in over a year, let's not forget."

"Sorry!" I dropped him and was amused to hear it smack against his stomach with a thud. "But what, you want a medal for not indulging in a puck bunny? I've been without sex for years. Years. Plural."

Gavin laughed and again watched as I twirled my thumb around the tip of him, closing his eyes. "Same for me, Lemon Drop. It's not that big. I'm telling you."

"I've only seen one other penis. To me it's the Holy Grail."

Gavin popped open one eyelid and quirked an eyebrow.

"What do you mean you've only seen one other penis? Are you saying you were ... he was your only ... you never ..."

"I told you this. I was a virgin before him. It's not a big deal. I just never got there with anyone else."

"But you got *nowhere* with anyone else? You said you've only seen one other dick. So, nothing?"

I flushed, embarrassed again by my lack of experience when he was a veritable expert in comparison.

"Nothing. I was a loser." I had lost all enthusiasm for what I thought would be the best night of my life, and debated being the girl who dramatically escaped into the bathroom. Gavin's fingers under my chin startled me, and he forced me to meet his eyes when all I wanted to do was close my own and forget about all of it.

"Choosing to keep that part of yourself private does not make you a loser. It makes you an inspiration."

"It makes me a twenty-six-year-old woman who doesn't know how to please her boyfriend because she might be a little afraid of his big dick."

Gavin shook his head and leaned forward, his lips a whisper away from mine as I realized the dick in question had brushed against my opening. I no longer cared how it was going to fit, I just wanted him inside me.

"It makes the path of this evening change direction, and it makes you even sexier to me than you already were, which I truly didn't even think was possible."

"How could the fact I'm going to make our first night together a disaster make me sexier to you? I have no clue how to satisfy you. What if you feel like KJ did about my abilities in bed, and start to look elsewhere?"

"First of all, never say his name when you're naked. Ever. Secondly, I've waited for you for how long? Now that I can make love to you all the time, there's no chance in hell I'm looking anywhere besides this room. Finally, you're not making anything a disaster. But you're not giving me a blow job."

"I definitely can't satisfy you if you won't let me try."

"Oh, you'll have plenty of opportunities. Maybe even tonight. But not until I reclaim your virginity." Gavin rubbed his lips together as his eyes dropped to the space between us, where he could have already been inside me if he tried at all.

"I know I'm no expert on the subject, but I know enough about sex to know you can't get your virginity back," I replied. My breath caught when he shifted and almost entered where only one very inept man had been before. He took me with him when he fell back against the bed and then turned us so I was on my back.

"Not technically. But I'm going to make it a memory not worth going back to, and you'll feel like the first time was with me because nothing before me was anything you care to remember."

"You're beyond arrogant, are you aware of that?"

"I am very aware," Gavin's voice was muffled against my skin as he kissed his way down my neck and across my chest. He got all the way down to my belly button before he made his way back up and reached for the wallet he had the foresight to toss on the nightstand when his pants left his body. He quickly rolled on a condom while I laid in nervous silence and my heart pounded painfully in anticipation. "Are you ready for me to change your life?"

"Twice in one day? You're some kind of wonderful aren't you, Canada?"

Gavin hovered over me in a pushup. After a handful of seconds, I was confused enough to raise my eyebrows in silent question.

"You didn't say you were ready."

"I think it's obvious I'm ready."

Gavin lowered his head and whispered against my ear. "I'm not taking anything until it's offered."

The man was a dream.

"Please change my life with your dick, Gavin."

That was all he needed. Gavin positioned himself and dropped his mouth onto mine as he pushed inside me. He paused when I sucked in a sharp breath as my body stretched to accommodate him. I felt inadequate to handle him, and the tears were unintentional and humiliating. Gavin kissed them off my face, his fingers in my hair.

"Are you in pain? Do you want to stop?"

"No. I want it all. But I don't have enough room. I mean, I know there's room. Like, you may be hung but you're not as big as a baby's head. If that can come *out*, logically you can go *in*. But if I was in labor, I'd be on all the good drugs and wouldn't even feel how stretched I was—" I trailed off with a grimace. I had just alluded to pregnancy when I had barely gotten his dick in me for the first time.

Gavin bit his lip and tried unsuccessfully to hide his laughter. He moved slowly and each thrust took him deeper.

"Let me do the work, okay Lemon Drop? You just focus on feeling good. Can you do that?"

I hesitated and closed my eyes to try to hide from the intimacy of what really did feel like the loss of my virginity. My breasts heaved against the pounding of my heart and Gavin's mouth found my nipple. He grazed his teeth before he pulled off and blew against the wet skin, all the while rolling into me until I felt his hips hit mine and I realized he was fully inside. The sensation of him wasn't painful, rather a fullness I'd never experienced, and he stilled once he was in all the way.

"See? Not that big."

When I laughed, I felt it against him, and his face transformed from gentle lover to ravenous hunter. I moved under him and caught him in a kiss while I sucked his lip into my mouth. Gavin groaned and nodded as we found our rhythm and quietly learned each other's bodies until he moved us so I was on top of him. The gentle tingle that began in my thighs quickly snaked its way up and caused my legs to quiver. I didn't want to lose the orgasm working its way through my core, but the fact it was so close distracted me. Gavin caught my attention as he held my hips tightly against him and rolled us over again.

"I ..." I panted, sliding my fingers through the damp hair at the base of his skull while he nodded in agreement. I couldn't get the words out, but I didn't need to. Like every other aspect of our relationship, he knew from what I didn't say. The only sound in the room was the rustle of the sheets against our bare skin.

"I know. I see. Let me take you to the stars," Gavin ground out, his focus on my mouth as I blew out a breath and licked my lips. I obliged and relaxed against his hips as pulsing began deep inside me.

Gavin pushed up, one arm supporting his weight next to my head while he brought his other hand down my body to rub against my clit and instantly brought a wave of sensation I had never experienced. Ever.

Wrapping my fingers around his wrist I clung to him as I allowed myself to fall through the waves of pleasure as my breath threatened to give way to whimpered cries. Gavin clenched his jaw as he continued to move, a bead of sweat dripping off his nose to settle on the corner of my lip. I poked my tongue out to collect the exertion, causing him to let out a guttural expletive as his movements slowed. His heart thundered as he lowered his head and dropped a long, soft kiss against my forehead before he traced every line of my face with his lips.

I didn't want it to be over, but he slowly slid out of me and rolled to his side, pulling me into the curve of his arm. I knew where he had been, sore and content and already missing the ache of my body accommodating his. He was home, and wherever he was is where I wanted to be.

CHAPTER 30
Greyson

When I came back into the room, I was surprised, but not at all bothered, by the fact Gavin was still sitting on the bed without any clothes on, the sheet tossed halfheartedly over the best parts. He was propped up with his head against the headboard and one very muscular leg hung off the side, swinging slowly. He cracked one lid when he heard me and a slow smile crept across his face as his eyes swept over me in nothing but his dress shirt.

"That shirt looks a lot better on you than it ever did on me." He grinned as I boldly climbed on top of him and straddled his legs. As much as I wanted the sheet gone between us, I throbbed down below and couldn't handle anymore. His groan was low against my chest as he sat up and circled my waist, pressing his mouth against my skin. "I'd like to take you to the stars again, but I think I'm all empty right now."

"I actually agree," I replied, as I scratched my nails across his shoulders. "I'd need an ice pack down my pants for a few hours before I could even think about going again."

We had spent two hours discovering each other, taking breaks for cupcakes and wine, experimenting with said cupcakes, and resting some more. Pure heaven.

"You're not wearing any pants." Gavin rolled me off him and pinned me against the mattress. "I'd like it if we could keep it that way until morning."

"I always sleep with pants on. What if there was a fire? I'm not running outside flashing my bits to the whole neighborhood."

"Very good point. We'll just keep a pair close, how's that?"

"I'll stay without them until you go home," I conceded.

"Perfect, so I win. No pants until morning," Gavin murmured triumphantly as he looked around the bed and scanned the floor. "Where are the pillows? I'm beat." My sex haze had my brain so clouded I didn't realize the implication until that moment.

"You're staying the night?" I hadn't intended to sound so panicked, and he tensed at the high-pitched question.

"I thought you wanted me to. I guess we never talked about it," Gavin trailed off and shifted against the mattress. "Sorry, I'll go, I shouldn't have assumed."

"No! It's ... it's not that. I just ... I don't really..." I blew out a hard breath and smoothed shaky hands over his shirt. "I don't sleep very much. I have nightmares. So, I don't sleep with people because I'd feel guilty if I woke them up with my screaming. Night terrors. It's dumb."

Gavin narrowed his eyes as he dug his fingers into his biceps, crossed tightly over his chest. "I wouldn't care if you woke me up. I'd sit up all night comforting you. But I can go."

Of course I had to go and screw this up. Why hadn't I considered this very possible scenario when preparing for this evening? Bring in a few pillows from the spare bedroom and make it look like I was a normal person, rather than sit in awkward, half naked silence with my boyfriend who now thought I didn't want him around.

"I don't ever want you to go," I replied softly as I batted away the tear that had escaped my eye. "Being asleep next to another person is the most vulnerable you can get. I've never been comfortable enough around a man to break through that fear."

"Except KJ."

There it was. He was jealous. His jaw was clenched as tightly as his arms over his chest and I half laughed, half sobbed in reply.

"No, actually, not even him. Especially not him. I never slept in his presence."

Gavin's arms fell slightly as he shot me a sidelong glance.

"You never spent the night together? You were engaged."

"That's right. I know people had plenty of opinions on why we didn't live together, but that's why."

Gavin reached over, and his icy posture melted the more I spoke.

"I was obviously going to have to get past it when we got married, but I think part of me expected it to fall apart. I never planned for cohabitation, and he never pressed it because he loved the freedom."

"I had no idea."

"It's not something I generally bring up in conversation. I'm sorry I reacted poorly." I took a moment to force out the lie. "I do want you to stay, I just didn't consider it. I'd like you to take my sleeping virginity."

"I already have Lemon Drop," Gavin pulled me against him and pressed a kiss into my hair. "Maybe it wasn't overnight, but you've slept around me before. Remember Thanksgiving?"

I had been so stuffed full of medication on Thanksgiving I couldn't keep my eyes open regardless of how hard I tried. That was the day I'd woken up in a panic with my head in his lap on a pillow. I'd spent the next month trying to figure out how I'd not only slept with him in my house but been comfortable enough to use a pillow.

"I'll never forget it. That's the day I started falling in love with you."

"I thought so. Or rather, I hoped the feelings I had were reciprocated. Something changed that day."

"I'm sorry it's taken me so long to open up to you," I murmured, cuddling into him as he yawned loudly. Right. The pillows. "I'll go grab some pillows for you from the guest bedroom."

"Wait, you really don't have any pillows on your bed?"

I turned away quickly and scrambled off the side of the bed, waving off the question as I reached the door. Shit. Shit, shit, shit. How was I going to explain this? While I was certain I trusted him with the truth, I didn't want to ruin the night by giving it to him.

"Think Greyson," I muttered to myself as I entered the guest room and snatched up an armful of pillows. I could always lie down on one until he fell asleep and then get rid of it. My chest tightened at just the thought of my head on a pillow and I knew it wouldn't work. Not to mention it didn't answer the question of why I didn't have any in my bedroom to begin with. I turned to find Gavin in the doorway, surprise causing me to squeak and drop them all at his feet.

"What's going on?"

"I don't know what you mean." I gathered the fallen pillows and brushed past him into my room, throwing them on his side of the bed. His stare burned against my back as I peeled off his shirt and replaced it with my own before I crawled under the covers. "Are you coming?"

Gavin slid into the bed and laid his head on the mound of pillows, pulling me into him wordlessly. When the moisture left my eyes and fell down his chest he sighed and kissed the top of my head. "Whatever it is, I'm here when you want to talk about it."

I loved him in a way that terrified me. He could tell there was a story behind the lack of pillows on my bed, but he didn't press, and he assured me I was safe in his arms. If he really looked around my house, he'd notice there weren't many pillows at all. The one solitary throw pillow that my grandma had crocheted, and I couldn't bear to get rid of was the one he'd found to cradle under my head on Thanksgiving. The guest bedroom had them, but even those were locked in a closet unless I knew they needed to be out.

I wanted to bare my soul to this man who already knew more

about me than most, but the fear that held me captive for most of my life still reigned supreme. He was a fixer. He worked through problems and found solutions. I didn't want to be a puzzle to be solved. I wanted to be a woman loved by a man. As simple as that.

It wasn't long before his grip on me relaxed, followed by the shallow breaths of sleep. I attempted to close my eyes and relax but tossed and turned with the endless stream of thoughts I couldn't quiet, and panic eventually set in with the darkness. Gavin was a sound sleeper and didn't stir when I rolled off the side of the bed and slipped into the hallway.

I started a pot of coffee and paced the kitchen as it brewed. I had to tell him. He deserved it, and the burden of the secret had started to weigh me down. The trauma was mine to hold, and I had never wanted to let anyone help lessen the load. Gavin wanted to carry me and my baggage, but I just didn't know how to let him.

I poured an oversized cup of coffee and shuffled into the living room to jot down cupcake ideas. Memories of the night made it easy to create multiple recipes, but I narrowed them down to a peach cake with brown sugar buttercream and an olive oil fig cupcake with honey cream icing and pistachio crunch. Out of all the fantasy scenarios I'd worked up in my head over the past year about what being with Gavin would be like, the reality took down every single one.

When I couldn't fight the exhaustion a second longer, I dropped my head against the back of the couch. I had only had my eyes closed a moment when softness covered my nose. My scream pierced the silence, and the sharp cut of my fingernails scratched my neck when I clawed at something that wasn't there.

"Holy shit, Greyson! It's me! Calm down!" Gavin's alarmed voice cut through my panic and I forced myself to breathe as I slowly realized what I had felt was him bending over the back of the couch to kiss me.

"Sorry," I gasped, as I held my hand over my racing heart. "I thought you were asleep."

He regarded me with suspicion, his arms folded over his bare chest.

"I was. I woke up and realized you weren't there." Gavin's eyes swept over me and settled on the table with my half full cup of coffee. "It's beyond clear you didn't really want me to spend the night. I'd appreciate you just being honest rather than agreeing to what you think I want. I think I should go."

There was no more time for internal debates. He deserved the truth.

"I want you here. I never want to be without you. But you deserve to know the reason I can't sleep with people around me. I didn't think I was ready to tell you because..." my voice trailed off. The trepidation threatened to take my strength, but for once I wouldn't allow it. He was worth fighting for. "I love the way you look at me. How you touch me. I'm afraid it will be different when you know. But if telling you will erase any doubt you have over my feelings for you, then it's worth it."

"Greyson, you don't have to do this. Seriously. I don't want to be the person who pries into your difficult memories." Gavin came around the couch to hold me when the tears started. He had immediately put aside his feelings to help me sort my own. But I didn't want him to live as second most important. The way he felt mattered just as much as how I did, and I didn't want to start our relationship on uneven footing.

"I can't guarantee I'll be able to get this out without completely losing my mind. But if you'll let me, I'd like to try."

"If you're sure," Gavin's voice broke, and he cleared his throat while he took a seat. "If you're not ready, please don't do this for me."

I smiled sadly with a shake of my head.

"If I wait until I'm ready I'll never tell you. There will always be a secret keeping us from being truly open."

Gavin chewed his lip, a deep furrow etched between his eyes.

"I don't want secrets, but I'd rather you keep them than hurt yourself for me."

"That right there is why I want to tell you. You've never pushed me. You let me realize things on my own and come to conclusions on my terms. Even when my silence directly affects you. I don't want to do that anymore."

"I'll never push you into anything you aren't ready for."

"It's time for me to push myself." I blew out a heavy breath and waited for my heart to settle before I turned to him. "Here we go. So ... I didn't have a good relationship with my mom. I know you picked up on that last Christmas. And I truly appreciate the way you left it alone."

"It wasn't my place to demand an explanation," Gavin replied softly.

"She never wanted me and made sure I knew it. My dad was the one who wanted two kids, but she was happy with just Trevor. She would do anything to keep my dad happy, though, so I was created as a concession."

"That's not true," Gavin interjected. When my eyes met his, he clamped his mouth shut and swallowed hard. He saw in my sadness it was absolutely true.

"I might have had a fighting chance if I was a boy, but she had this hyper fixation on being the only female in my dad's life. She felt like she had to compete with me for his attention. After he died, she blamed it on me."

"How the hell could that be your fault?"

"In her mind he couldn't retire because he had to provide for a child she never wanted. He was forty-two when he died. Retirement wasn't even on the horizon. But she found every way possible to destroy my mental capability to be a normal human being."

Gavin leaned his elbows on his knees and steepled his fingers against his mouth. He stared at the fireplace as his jaw worked, and I knew he was doing everything in his power not to explode. I smoothed my hands over my legs, running them up, down, up again. My throat was thickening with every word, trying to force me into giving up.

"He protected me. Doubled the love he gave me to make up for her hate," I couldn't force my voice above a whisper, and he leaned closer to hear without asking me to speak up. "As soon as he was gone, it was like game on. She started leaving me at school, ignoring their calls after I'd been sitting there for hours. We lived five miles away, and I would eventually just walk. Rain, snow, it didn't matter. If I wanted to come home, I had to figure out a way to get there."

I paused, remembering the blisters that never seemed to go away. My fingers absently rubbed over the spot on the arch of my foot that constantly bled through my shoes. I finally got smart and packed an extra pair of socks in my backpack, as prepared as I could be.

"That's awful," Gavin's voice was barely audible, and it was clear he had no comprehension of the possibility of this. He came from a large, loving family. Parents who celebrated every accomplishment and helped learn from every failure.

"I wish that was the worst of it," I replied sadly. "I got locked in my room without food a lot. Years of therapy have helped me realize that's why I maybe enjoy it a little too much now. Even though I can eat whenever I want to now, my brain still tells me to fill up, just in case I can't get any for days."

Gavin dropped his head, both hands clasping the hair at the back of his scalp. Was I losing him?

"Weekends were the worst. I feared Friday, because I knew I would be trapped, locked up like a prisoner, until Monday morning," I stared blankly at the fireplace, the manufactured flames jumping against the glass. "I had no one, no friends I could confide in, nobody to trust this situation with."

The pain of the story overwhelmed me. I couldn't stay seated, the proximity to Gavin too much. Jumping up, I paced in front of him with my hands clenched tightly at my sides.

"Then, one day, everything got better. She smiled when I walked in the room, she made my favorite dinner, and she let me pick a movie to watch before bed. She even let me stay up late." I choked back a sob at what I knew was coming next. My pace increased as I walked in front of him.

Back and forth, back and forth, my heart rate increasing with my footsteps. "When she tucked me in—which she never did— she asked me what my biggest dream was out of life."

Blood rushed through my ears the longer I spoke, the realization that I had to finish the story almost sending me to my knees.

"What did you say?" Gavin's voice was thick with emotion. He chewed roughly on his bottom lip and bounced his leg nervously while he waited for my answer.

"I wanted to make people happy," I sobbed, remembering the manic look in her eyes when she leaned over my bed as her hands obsessively fluffed the pillow behind my head. I knew enough to be scared, but not enough to protect myself.

"She just laughed and said 'have the sweetest dreams' and left the room. I thought maybe things would change. That she was finally ready to love me."

"But she wasn't."

"No, she wasn't." I fell to the floor and pulled my knees up to my chest, closing up. This was the part I couldn't say. I danced around the words in therapy, using creative alternatives that let me avoid the words that tasted like poison. Gavin wordlessly closed the gap between us, sliding to the floor in front of me.

"Do you need me to give you physical or verbal support right now?"

I blinked away the pain, bringing myself back into the moment. The understanding he showed was the strength I needed. My face crumbled as I found his hand and squeezed tightly.

"I woke up in the night super confused. I couldn't breathe. When I tried, I just inhaled fabric. The more I panicked the tighter it got over my face. Once I was oriented, I realized it was a pillow. She was ... my mom ..."

I cut off with a scream, collapsing against his chest as the waves of pain, terror, and inadequacy consumed me like a spark in a dry forest. He held me so tightly I almost couldn't breathe as I rocked on the floor like an infant.

"She ... tried to ... kill me," my words came out in stunted half breaths as I attempted to take in enough air. I was on the verge of hyperventilating, dizzy from the lack of air and the totality of my words.

Gavin pulled me into him tightly, as if his arms were a shield from everything outside of him. I let the silence calm me and breathed in his warmth as we wordlessly embraced. Now that I'd said it, I found myself with a need to finish the story.

"Trevor woke up. He found her holding a pillow over my face. He had to wrestle her off me. She was determined to not let go until I was ... gone."

Gavin's handsome face was a mask of pure horror and a glassy sheen covered his eyes. A light pebbling of gooseflesh covered his bare chest and arms as the story caused a physical reaction.

"He was strong for fifteen, but she was powered by hate and was too much for him. She kept yelling at him to let her get rid of me so they could go back to being a happy family. He went and got his hockey stick and just hit her. Until she went still. He grabbed me in his arms and got us in the car and drove to our grandparents' house. I remember telling him he didn't have his driver's license yet and his school permit didn't cover going out at night. Obviously ridiculous."

Silence enveloped the room and Gavin stared blankly at my mouth, not focused on anything. I let him ruminate for a solid five minutes before I got concerned I'd laid too much on him too soon.

"Say something," I pleaded as I nervously chewed on the skin around my thumb. The pain of the hangnail I created was a nice distraction from what I'd just confessed. He finally looked up, slowly, like he was slogging through a pool of maple syrup.

"He killed her?" Gavin's question was tentative, laced with something between fear and hope. The question pulled me out of my tailspin and I leaned back, searching his eyes. Then I did the only thing I could.

I laughed.

"No, he didn't kill her. We aren't *that* much of a Lifetime movie," I said.

Gavin's forehead bunched and he ran his hands down my arms.

"Okay, babe, I've taken in a lot of information here. I need you to clarify. She's alive?"

"Last I heard. Trevor keeps track of her whereabouts. As long as she isn't here, I don't think about her more than once a year. I haven't spoken to her in fourteen years."

"I'm so sorry. I never would have guessed anything even close to this."

"Well, no." I laughed quietly as I wiped my hand across my face. "Most people wouldn't think *my girlfriend doesn't use pillows because her mom tried to murder her with one*."

Gavin flinched at my blasé statement. I'd just told him the messiest part of my entire life and he was still here.

"I'm really sorry I pushed to stay here tonight," Gavin murmured. He tucked a loose strand of hair behind my ear and just stared at me. "I hate that you felt pressured into this because of me."

"I've wanted you to know me, all of me, for months. But the shame has kept me paralyzed. First my mother, then KJ. I accepted that I'm worthless as a person, and as much as I wanted to open myself to you, I was too scared. I haven't been able to accept that I'm good enough for you." I felt lighter, as if the weight I'd carried had been cut in half. It wasn't gone, but it wasn't nearly as heavy. "Do you have any questions?"

He only hesitated a moment.

"Did she call you Grace?"

I dropped my eyes with a nod, as Gavin squeezed my thigh in a protective show of solidarity.

"She would tell me that my dad's love for me was my only

saving grace. When he died, she started saying *'your grace can't save you now.'* She taunted me, calling me Grace constantly. That's what I heard through the pillow. *'Nighty night Grace. Bye-bye Grace.'* That's why when you said it, I lost my mind. You didn't deserve it, there's no way you could have known."

"I'm sorry, but I fucking hate your mother," Gavin spat. He leaned back against the couch, dropping his head against the cushions.

"I don't expect you to be clear headed about any of this. I've had years to process and it still makes no sense to me. If you need some time without me, I get it."

Gavin turned to me with a fierceness I'd never seen. "Your life has had more storms than most people could weather, and you've come through with rainbows. I'm your umbrella. You'll never be left in the rain without protection."

While I was relieved it was all out in the open, I had reached my devastating childhood trauma quota. Completely talked out, I straddled his lap without hesitation and spoke against his mouth.

"I love you so much. Thank you for not giving up on me."

"I would have waited forever. I spent years trying to talk myself out of my feelings because you weren't mine to covet. But you're impossible to forget. One conversation was all it took for you to steal my heart, Greyson. All the ones since then have just solidified what I already knew. That I love you with everything I've got."

"Take me to bed, Gavin."

"You don't have to try to sleep for me," Gavin murmured as he cupped my jaw.

"I wasn't talking about sleeping."

CHAPTER 31

Gavin

The desk sergeant looked me over suspiciously when I approached before the look of recognition replaced the one of irritation.

"How can I help you?" his voice carried across the bustling police precinct.

"Uh, yeah, I'm here to see Detective Trevor Park."

"He expecting you?"

"Halstead," Trevor's voice was more like a bark, and I turned to see him standing on the stairs with his hands shoved in his jacket pockets. "Get up here. We need to talk."

"Good luck," the desk sergeant muttered, as he waved me towards the staircase. I made my way to Trevor, and put a lot of effort into appearing more confident than I actually felt.

When I got the text from him, requesting a meeting at the precinct, I didn't know what to think. Aside from the fact it absolutely had to do with his sister. Trevor led me up the stairs and past a group of desks. The plain clothes detectives seated around them didn't even look up as we passed, and I followed him until he stopped outside an interrogation room.

"In there," he pointed, as he unholstered his gun and secured it in a locker.

"Why are you locking up your gun?"

"Can't take it into an interview," Trevor replied, with a nod to the room. "Go."

"Wait. Is this ... an interrogation? Why am I here? Am I *under arrest*?"

"Did you break the law?"

"Of course not," I replied, as I pulled out a chair and dropped onto it.

Trevor stood with his back against the mirror, one booted foot on the brick wall below it. He pushed off and grabbed the other chair, spinning it around as he straddled the beat-up metal. It was almost comical, how the reality of him at work lined up with the cop shows I was convinced couldn't be real. Interrogation scenes were so dramatic on television, and I'd always assumed most of it was complete bullshit. But being on the other side of the table was terrifying, and I hadn't done anything wrong.

"This morning when I visited my sister at Icing, I expected to hear all about her night with you. What I wasn't prepared to hear was that she told you about our mother. So now you and I are going to talk about it."

I wasn't exactly surprised she had told him, but the speed with which it had happened was shocking. I'd left her house barely five hours earlier.

"Does she know we're meeting? I don't feel comfortable talking about her business if she's not aware it's happening," I drummed my fingers on the steel tabletop.

"Then you can sit there and listen while I talk," Trevor replied. "I know how much you love her. It's obvious. Always has been."

I nodded and folded my hands into my lap.

"She makes it easy to love her."

Trevor raised an eyebrow and shot me a sad smile.

"She does and she doesn't. But it's not her fault. She has a hard time believing she deserves happiness. So, she does what she can to sabotage anything that seems like it could be good."

"I would have waited forever," I said.

"I know that, too," Trevor said. "The fact of the matter is this: if you had any doubt that she trusts you with her life, that doubt should be gone now."

I swallowed hard, the image of her face as she shared the worst moments of her past seared into my brain.

"I'll protect her with *my* life."

"I don't doubt that," Trevor sighed. "But don't expect everything to be fine now. She's not going to magically lose her fear of pillows or start wearing scarves."

"Scarves?" I asked in confusion.

"Something you didn't notice? I'm shocked," Trevor grinned. "She can't have anything covering her face. At all. She can't handle scarves in the winter. Hell, half the time she won't even zip up her coat. The anxiety of the zipper touching her face is too much. She would rather freeze."

I sat back in the chair, as realization swept over me. I had noticed. But I hadn't understood.

"Where is she? Your mom. Greyson said she has no idea where she is. Do you?"

Trevor hesitated, a pause that said a lot.

"I know that she is not in violation of the restraining order."

"Restraining order. She didn't tell me about that," I shifted uncomfortably. "This feels like I'm invading her privacy."

Trevor waved away the concern.

"I'll tell her we met. And the fact you've mentioned twice now how you aren't comfortable talking about her without her knowledge makes it even more clear you are the right person for her," Trevor said. "Every two years on her birthday, I take Greyson to renew the order of protection she has on our mother."

"Her birthday," I repeated. Things were falling into place, and my stomach churned with realization. Trevor watched me; his expression grim as I put the pieces together.

"The original emergency order of protection was put into place three weeks before her birthday, fourteen years ago. That's when we told our story to a judge and were immediately placed with our grandparents," Trevor began. "The final order was signed at the hearing, three weeks later. On her thirteenth birthday."

Bile rose in my throat as I recalled the look on her face when she came down the stairs into the 'party' I had set up the prior year.

"How do people not know about this? How is this not public record?"

"It is," Trevor replied. "If anyone cared enough to hunt it down, it's all out there. Just because she hasn't told anyone doesn't necessarily mean they don't know. But this happened before the internet was quite what it is now. She was a minor. Her name wasn't published in the original filings. Now, people could definitely find it. If they were so inclined."

The information coming at me was slow to absorb, and I sat in horrified silence.

"But how did she get away with this? A restraining order is all well and good, but it's a piece of paper. She literally attempted to murder her. Did she go to jail? Any consequence *at all*?"

Trevor leaned against the chair with a nod.

"There was a deal made. She went to a facility to get help with her mental issues. Part of the agreement was signing parental rights over to our grandparents. And staying away from Greyson."

The entire situation was nothing short of completely insane. I was ashamed of my behavior the previous night, snapping at her about spending the night when her heart was at war with her head.

"And she has no remorse?"

Trevor's phone trilled, and he fished it out of his pocket, glanced at the screen, then back to me.

"She's tried to reach out. I sent the letters back as soon as they came. I won't put RayRay through that," he stabbed a finger at the table. "My sister has the purest soul of any person I have ever met. She deserves to move on. The woman who birthed us doesn't get to dull her shine ever again."

I swallowed down my emotion as his phone rang again and he moved to push back his chair.

"I just wanted to see you to say thank you," Trevor said. "I've never seen her happy. Not really. That all consuming happiness that radiates out of a person has always eluded her. Until she met you."

"I will do everything I can to keep her that way," I promised. "I've loved her for a long time. But now ... now I'm beginning to understand her, too."

Trevor nodded and knocked on the table.

"One more thing. If you hurt her, I promise I will kill you."

"You won't need to do that."

"I hope not. I kind of like you."

CHAPTER 32
Greyson

It was amazing how time melted when your soul wasn't restless. It had been a month since I'd shown my dirty laundry to Gavin and waited for him to tell me there wasn't enough soap in the world to clean my past. Nothing had happened besides more love than I thought possible and more sex than my body could handle.

Okay, that was a lie.

My body was greedy when it came to intimate moments with Gavin and every time we were done I immediately asked for more. I was exhausting him. He'd told me so, right before he got me naked again and took me straight to the stars. We had fallen into a comfortable rhythm of coupledom. I hadn't realized it was possible to feel so free and content, especially after dropping a bomb of childhood baggage squarely on him. But he said he'd rather carry the weight since he had broader shoulders, and I fell into trust and love rather than fear and hiding.

We hadn't spent the night together again. He hadn't pushed it even though I knew he wanted it. It wasn't that I didn't want to be with him at night. I did, so badly it hurt. But the thought of lying down to sleep with another person in the bed was still too much for me to handle, and he patiently told me he'd wait as long as it took.

I slipped an apron over my head and set to work with batters for pumpkin, apple cobbler, and caramel crunch cupcakes. I'd been working nonstop, which was nothing new, but I was getting burnt out. I'd always been a workaholic, finding it easier to quiet my inner demons when I was surrounded by butter and sugar, but I had started to toy with the idea of delegating some of the day to day operations so I could spend a little more time focused on other things. Mainly, Gavin. In my bed.

I walked trays of cakes to the oven and paused to look through the kitchen to the wings painted on the wall in the shop. The memory of their birth caused my throat to tighten.

"I don't believe in God."

"Don't give me that, girl. Everyone believes in something."

"I don't understand."

Eddie leaned on the mop and tilted his head, narrowing almond shaped eyes that were the color of a calm ocean on a summer day.

"So, you don't believe in the quote unquote God waiting at the pearly gates. Do you believe in Mother Nature?"

"I mean, I guess so. Nature is just … it is. It's beauty incarnate. There's not a regal woman in a couture dress of leaves watching over the trees on Michigan Avenue though."

"For being heaven sent you sure are cynical, Greyngel," Eddie teased, flashing his sweet lopsided grin.

"I'm neither heaven sent nor an angel," I protested half-heartedly, secretly loving the nickname he'd bestowed on me the first night he cleaned the bakery. Besides Trevor, no one had ever cared enough to give me a nickname.

"Okay then, you keep pretending that's the case. Back to the question. What's your almighty power? The thing that gives you the faith to keep going. The thing that makes your days worthwhile?"

"Baking," I replied without hesitation. "The way you can add flour and sugar and eggs to a bowl and create a beautiful pastry. A

*cupcake that makes you want to cry. A brownie that unlocks a
memory of a backyard barbecue, back when life was simple. A
cookie that reminds you of baking in Nana's kitchen, watching your
grandpa scoop up the errant sprinkles to drop in his mouth before she
can see and scold him. That's it. That's my God."
Eddie was nodding, staring at the wall, his fingers tracing invisible
lines on the naked space. "Can I paint a mural? As a thank you for
saving my life?"
How could I say no to a question like that?*

I was shocked when a warm tear slid down my cheek as I came
back from the memory. I loved that I could see the angel wings
from the kitchen, the mural so breathtaking it made me gasp
every time it caught my attention. Eddie had been bashful and
nervous when he pulled the sheet off the wall to unveil his art. I'd
fallen into a chair and thanked him repeatedly through my tears.
It was like he'd tapped into my soul and pulled out the bits no one
else understood. My customers all seemed to feel the same, and I
loved scrolling Instagram every night looking at the photos of
people in front of the wings.

I'd convinced Eddie to let me display a few paintings in the
shop, and after the third person had asked if they were for sale, I'd
told him he had a real talent that should be shared. I helped him
set up an online shop and secured a space for him at the farmer's
market. He was famous now. Real deal, art gallery famous. Yet, I
couldn't seem to get him to stop pushing a mop around the
bakery at night.

"Earth to Greyngel," Eddie's voice filtered through my
daydream. I was confused to see him in the kitchen, since it was
early morning, and he didn't come in until the afternoon to get
the day old deliveries for the homeless shelter. I didn't mind,
though. He was one of my favorite people.

"Sorry, I didn't hear you come in," I murmured, pulling out
the cakes that were close to being overdone. "On that note, why
are you here?"

Eddie pulled back his long silver hair and nabbed a hairnet. He washed his hands in the sink at the corner of the kitchen before he snapped on a pair of gloves over his weathered fingers. He was the first person I'd ever allowed to help with the baking before I'd gradually added employees, and I lit up to see him hunch over my list for the day and take over blueberry muffins.

"Trevor commissioned a piece. He said he'd pick it up here on his morning visit, but I didn't want to leave it last night," Eddie explained, and I bit back a smile at the protectiveness he felt over every canvas he covered with love. No one would have been in the bakery after he finished cleaning, but he wouldn't risk anything happening to the piece.

"I'm surprised he told you to bring it here. He's been missing a lot of mornings," my voice cracked on the admission and I cleared my throat, willing away the lump. Something was off with my brother, and I couldn't get the truth out of him. Every time I asked what was going on, he waved me off or rolled his eyes and said I needed to take a vacation. He was a lying sack of shit, but I couldn't force him to tell me. I knew he would on his time, but that didn't make it any easier in the interim.

Eddie clucked his tongue and headed to the oven as he balanced four trays on his arms. How he managed to put the batter together that fast I had no idea, but I didn't doubt it wasn't exactly right. The man was a master of all the things.

"I hear wistfulness mixed with jealousy in that melted butter voice of yours, girl. Spill it." Eddie moved gracefully around the kitchen and crossed blueberry off the list as he started on lemon poppy seed. He saw *me* because we were kindred spirits—different pieces of the same torn quilt.

"He's hiding something from me. He's been super secretive lately, and that's not at all like him. He only comes in maybe two mornings a week now, and even then, he's always late. He keeps his phone face down when we're together, and he never wants to hang out. Or rather, he 'can't.'"

"Sounds to me like big brother has a lady friend."

"No way. Absolutely not," I sputtered indignantly. "He wouldn't hide that from me. Would he?"

"Would it really be so bad? He's so grouchy," Eddie replied with a laugh. He'd known Trevor long before he knew me, when he'd repeatedly get himself hauled into the station on a stupid charge so he'd have a warm place to sleep and a meal for the night. Trevor was a patrolman at the time, and always secretly slid Eddie a twenty so he could eat for a couple days after he was released. They'd formed a bond, and Eddie had become the father figure we no longer had.

"He's not grouchy. He's ... overwhelmed with unnecessary burdens." I held myself responsible for Trevor's happiness—or lack thereof—and would never stop berating myself for the growing up he was forced to do to handle me. "What's the piece he ordered?"

Eddie glanced at the brown paper wrapped canvas propped against the wall.

"A cross."

I looked up sharply and narrowed my eyes in confusion. "A cross? Are you sure?"

Eddie rolled his eyes as he went to the oven to swap trays. "I painted it, pretty damn sure. It's Celtic. Irish knots and stuff like that."

That made zero sense. We weren't Irish, and we sure as hell weren't religious. Could he be right? Was Trevor seeing someone? The pounding at the back door announced his arrival, and I stomped over to wrench it open with as much force as I could muster. Trevor earned my fiercest glare before I turned my back on him and carried on with sugar cookies. His face betrayed nothing as he slowly looked between Eddie and me and took in the situation he'd walked into.

"Good morning, RayRay. Eddie." Trevor nodded at him and held out an envelope for the piece I was now sure was for a secret girlfriend. "Thanks so much for this. Appreciate it more than you know."

"Anytime Trev. You know I'll do anything for you." Eddie pocketed the envelope and peeled off the gloves, staring at me for a handful of seconds.

"I'll see you later, girl. I expect the scowl to be gone before I return."

With that he was gone, and I was left with a brother nervously bouncing on the balls of his feet.

"What is going on with you?" I demanded as I threw my piping bag on the table and folded my arms. "And don't give me some bullshit line you think I'll just swallow because I'm too naïve and stupid to know it's a lie."

"I would never do that, Greyson." Trevor was clearly offended, and he kept his eyes on me when he lowered himself onto a stool. "There's nothing going on."

"See, and there's a fucking lie." My hysterics had started to push through, and the way Trevor clenched his jaw gave away the guilt he felt at not telling me the truth. He might be the detective, but I knew all his tells. "Why did you have Eddie paint you an Irish cross?"

Trevor's confident façade slipped, but he recovered quickly. Not fast enough, though.

"It's a housewarming gift. For a colleague."

"Try again."

"Excuse me?" Trevor plucked a blueberry muffin out of the spread in front of him and kept his eyes on the wrapper.

"Eddie's lowest priced pieces are way more than you would spend on a colleague. And that canvas is not small. Try another lie."

I caught the almost imperceptible intake of breath, and the bob in his Adam's apple when he swallowed down his trepidation at being caught.

"It's an important colleague."

I glared at him and slapped the muffin out of his hand.

"Are you mad at me? About Gavin? For being happy? Do you feel like he's replaced you or something? Is that what this is?"

Trevor jumped up and rounded the corner of the table as he gripped my shoulders with a slight shake. "Halstead is the best thing that could have ever happened to you, and there isn't *one second* I don't thank Dad for dropping him into your life. This has nothing to do with Gavin."

"Great, so what *does* this have to do with? How can you think I don't know you're hiding something? You're acting psychotic."

Trevor threw out a heavy sigh. "You're right. Let's get dinner tonight. I'll tell you everything I can, okay?"

"Why can't you tell me now?"

"Because I have to go. We're tracking something big and I've got no free time. I just came in—"

"To get your important colleague's fake housewarming gift, that's definitely not for a girlfriend you haven't told me about," I interrupted, as I turned back to the cookies. "I'll see you when I see you, I guess."

Trevor silenced the phone that had begun to ring in his pocket. "I said we'll have dinner tonight."

"You did. Except I know it won't happen. If it's that big of a case, you'll have to cancel. I get it. You belong to the City of Chicago and the badge."

"That's not true," Trevor's protest fell flat, and the endless chime of his phone made it known that was exactly the case. The people of Chicago came first. I was being immature, but I really missed my brother and if he wouldn't tell me what was going on, I was forced to come to my own conclusion.

"I'm sorry. I just miss you a whole hell of a lot. That's all. I miss you."

Trevor pressed his lips together in a thin line. He reached out to grab me around the back of the neck and pulled me tightly against his chest. The sharp outline of his shield cut through my t-shirt and cold dread settled in the pit of my stomach.

"I will do everything in my power to make dinner with you tonight, RayRay. Everything. We do have a lot to talk about."

"Are you safe? Are you going to have to go under for this?"

Trevor released me and rubbed his hand over his chin as he closed his eyes. There was my answer.

"We can talk about it tonight."

"Why is it always you? Jace never has to do this. It's not fair!"

"Jace doesn't have the backstory built that I do. People on the street know each other and it's just easier for me to go under."

"Exactly. People on the street *talk*. You're in the most elite unit in Chicago, which means the scumbags know you. You have no idea what it's like to wonder, every single time, if this is the time you're found out. If someone you've arrested happens to be in the same bar you are when you're playing Ryan or Todd or Carson or whatever the fuck your undercover name is, and then what? Then you *die*, Trevor! Then you ... die," I finished my emotional explosion on a sob, shocked I finally voiced the word that we always danced around and never actually said.

"I know how hard my job has always been on you. You didn't sign up for this, but you still have to live it. But I can't sit idly by when people are dying on the street, RayRay. I do what I do to save as many as I can. What's going on at work right now is far reaching and very, very bad. The city is in danger. I can't tell you the details, but I'm as safe as I can be," Trevor's voice had a slight thickness, and he spoke in the low, gravelly tone he used when he slipped into protective father figure.

"I can't survive without you. Don't you dare die. Do you hear me?"

"I wouldn't dream of it. Who would do your nails?"

CHAPTER 33
Greyson

"Greyson, this doesn't look right," Mattie called with uncertainty as she pulled the pie out of the oven. "What did I do wrong?"

I wiped my hands on my apron and set down the knife I was chopping vegetables with as I peered over her shoulder at the dessert in question. There was something off about the pumpkin custard, and the curdled appearance made it clear there was no way to save it.

"I have no idea," I admitted. I'd never seen anything like it. I'd dealt with cracks due to overheated eggs, soggy crusts due to filling when it wasn't baked enough, and even curdling to a point, but this was extreme. "What exactly did you put in here?"

Mattie waved her arm across the mess on the counter and I spotted an empty cottage cheese container. No. She didn't.

"Not this?" I asked, unable to contain the giggle that escaped my lips. Mattie had wide eyes when she realized she'd made a catastrophic error and picked up her martini glass with a shrug.

"I'm guessing it was an incorrect ingredient?"

We looked at each other once more before we collapsed into laughter. Tears streamed down my face by the time Gavin abandoned the football game he was watching with Asher to see what the ruckus was about. Mattie and I laughed so hard we couldn't speak, and she just pointed at the stove where the offending pie looked even worse as it cooled. Gavin took in the hideous pastry and looked between the two of us as his gaze settled on me.

"Did you make this?"

"Of course not," I gasped, truly offended he could think for a moment that atrocity came from my hands. I immediately felt guilty and turned to Mattie to apologize. "I'm sorry, I didn't mean to sound like an asshole."

Mattie, who I had come to learn didn't let much bother her, waved me off and reached over me to refill my glass with the spiced cranberry martini she had made as the signature cocktail for the day. "It's true. It looks like dog vomit. Baking is not in my bag of tricks, but I can make a dope flower arrangement."

I nodded my agreement as my eyes swept over the white pumpkins artfully stuffed full of burnt orange and ivory flowers interspersed with red berries that were placed on the table. Mattie really was a master when it came to horticulture.

"Lemon Drop. How are you doing?" Gavin's voice brought me back to the conversation and I jolted when his lips brushed my cheek. I turned into him and pressed my palm against his face. He covered it with his and we had a moment without speaking as his understanding of my conflicted mood shined through his eyes.

"I'm good. Ish," I replied as I fought the wave of sadness. I didn't want to let it get to my eyes because it would cause a monsoon of tears I didn't want his family to witness. "Thank you. For doing Thanksgiving like this since it's just another Thursday for you."

"It is, but I can't generally spend our Thanksgiving with my family, so they loved the idea of us all celebrating together. Why don't we plan on doing a repeat Thanksgiving dinner once Trevor is back on regular assignment?" Gavin offered, and my heart squeezed in my chest.

"I'd love that," I spoke around the lump in my throat. "I miss him so damn much."

Gavin knew that. He knew I cried every day that passed without word on my brother. He was there to see me freeze every time the phone rang until I knew it wasn't someone telling me Trevor was dead. He had unending patience when it came to my fluctuating moods and stayed on the phone for as long as I wanted when he was on the road, regardless of how exhausted he was.

"I know it's not the same thing, but Gavin recorded a message to each of us before he left for his rookie year," Mattie said from behind me, where I'd forgotten she was standing. His family was aware Trevor was working, but they didn't know enough of our story to understand why I was so precarious emotionally.

"That sounds like a very Gavin thing to do," I replied with a smile, falling against him when he pulled me into his arms. Rina and Freddie walked in the kitchen from the deck, where they had been taking a bubble in the hot tub.

"What does?" Rina asked. She opened her mouth to the funnel Mattie had ready to pour alcohol down her throat.

"The Falcons bears with his voice messages," Mattie answered. "I was saying how maybe Greyson's brother could do something like that for her, to make it easier when he's away."

"I still listen to mine," Freddie piped up as she dried off in the kitchen. Gavin stared disapprovingly at the scraps of fabric that made up his sister's bathing suit, undoubtedly full of rage at the idea other people, specifically men, ever saw her wearing it. "Even though we talk almost every day, there are times I just need to hear my brother's voice when he's not available."

"I know for a fact Callie took hers to college when she left a couple months ago. We all did," Rina said, as she toweled off her hair. "Would your brother be open to do something like that for you?"

"I'm a little old to need a teddy bear from my brother ... aren't I?"

"You're never too old to need your brother," Freddie said gently. She leapt forward and captured me in a hug that left me completely soaked. I reciprocated for a handful of moments and let my tears fall when the remaining Halstead sisters joined in to hold me in a protective embrace of familial love. Gavin waited patiently to the side, his eyes locked on me as Asher bounced into the room and looked over us in confusion.

"What kind of a party am I missing in here?"

"One you aren't invited to," Mattie answered as we untangled ourselves from each other and she hip checked him hard enough to make him stumble forward a step. "Want a drink?"

"Is the answer to that ever no?" Asher replied. He glanced at me then shot his gaze to the ceiling. "Not that I'm looking, but you're advertising a wet t-shirt contest, Lady Halstead."

Gavin punched Asher and moved in front of me as he pulled me out of the kitchen and upstairs to his room. He yelled over his shoulder to his sisters to 'put some damn clothes on' as we exited. I felt vulnerable and exposed, tired of crying all the time. I was tired, period.

When we were safely alone, I inhaled the masculine scent of his room. Gavin locked the door and stood with his back to me, fists pressed against the wood and head down. Silence stretched uncomfortably, and I shivered against the wetness of my shirt.

"Gavin?" I finally managed meekly. When he turned and advanced quickly I gasped into his mouth when he captured mine in a fierce show of affection. His lips covered mine and his tongue nudged my mouth open. I recognized this, and it usually meant a leisurely evening getting my mind blown in every way imaginable. When he knew words wouldn't help, he turned to other ways to comfort me. I would never complain or turn it down, but I was acutely aware of his sisters and Asher one floor below us, and I'd come to realize I was not quiet in the bedroom. "We can't. Your parents will be back any second and your sisters are—"

"I need you, right now. It'll be quick."

"Why?" I had already lifted my arms as he peeled off my soggy shirt and tossed it aside with a plop on the floor. He lowered his head to my chest as he discarded my bra and when he pulled my nipple into his mouth, I hissed at the sensation of the warm wetness that contrasted my goosebumps. He hummed against my skin, the vibration sending a shot of electricity between my legs, and I no longer cared why he was so worked up. He guided me to the bed with his hands on my hips, and I pulled him down on top of me as I laid back, freezing for a moment when my head fell where the pillows were. Well, where they should be.

"They're gone," Gavin panted, his hands hurriedly pushing my pants down my legs. His intensity was outrageous, and while I knew we needed to hurry before we were missed, I really wanted to slow it down and enjoy this side of him.

"Why?"

The word finally got his attention and he pushed himself over me, resting on his forearms.

"Because. I won't have you afraid or uncomfortable by anything when you're with me. Ever."

I unbuckled his belt and shoved his jeans down his legs. When he reached over to open his nightstand drawer, I caught his wrist and swallowed hard. "No condom. Just you and me."

"Are you sure? I mean, I know I'm only your second. You trust that I'm ... are you sure?"

"I trust you," I whispered, the statement falling over us like a weighted blanket. "I want to share this with you. Unless you don't."

"I've never. With anyone. This is ours, and nothing can ever change that," Gavin whispered. He positioned himself at my opening, and after a final nod of confirmation from me he sunk inside with a groan. His eyes were closed, lips stretched into a loose smile. He was completely still and when I tried to move he shook his head and slowly peeled his eyes open.

"Can you ... hold off for ... just a second? I need a second."

"Is everything okay?"

"Too okay. If you move, I'm going to come. Seriously. Just a second, I promise," Gavin murmured with a bashful grin. I bit my lip to hide my smile and gave him as much time as he needed. When he ground his hips against me, I moaned, and he covered my mouth with his hand, before quickly pulling it back.

"Sorry. Just, try to be quiet," Gavin whispered, instead using his lips to swallow my sounds of appreciation. I remembered the house full of people directly below us, the thrill of being naughty heightening the experience. We made fast work of it, and when my orgasm climbed up my legs, I guided his hand over my mouth and sunk my teeth into his palm hard enough to make him wince, quickly followed by a dirty grin.

"I like it when you bite me," he growled against my cheek. "How do you want me to finish this? On or in?"

"What?"

"Your innocence is so sexy," Gavin replied as he nipped at my earlobe. "How do you want me to come? On you, or in you?"

"Oh! Um, however ... however you want," I stammered as my cheeks heated in embarrassment.

"Absolutely not. It's how you want. Always."

Was this real life? He even asked me *my* preference on *his* climax.

"In then. I want you to come in me." I could not believe those words just came out of my mouth. "I'm on the pill."

Gavin nodded and groaned, and I could tell he was close. "Good. About the inside part. I couldn't care less if you were on the pill."

He collapsed on top of me in a heap when his release overtook him, and I was breathing hard with the exercise and the totality of the statement he had just spoken. He'd effectively just told me he wouldn't care if I got pregnant. Which felt like a major development.

"That was insanely amazing," I said quietly, instantly missing the warmth and weight of him when he rolled off me and laid like a starfish across the bed.

"Mmmhmm," Gavin agreed as he laced his fingers through mine. He was almost fully clothed, with just his jeans pushed below his knees. It was a stark contrast to my fully nude body. "Sorry it didn't last that long."

"Maybe we can spend a little more time getting used to going without a condom when you drop me off tonight."

Gavin sat up on his elbows and nodded vigorously. "Yes. Yes please. Let's please do that."

I smiled under his lips when he moved back on top of me and whined in disappointment when he shook his head as I spread my legs under him. "Not yet, Lemon Drop. I want you thinking about my bare dick inside you for the next few hours so when I can do something about it, you're just as excited as I am."

"I can say with certainty I'm not going to be able to think of anything but that for the rest of the day," I replied as I scooted to the end of the bed. I regretted the decision to stand when the remnants of our lovemaking ran down my leg, a side effect I hadn't considered. The look on my face caused Gavin to laugh loudly. He quickly pulled up his pants as he jumped off the bed and disappeared into the bathroom. He came back with a wet cloth and ran it over me until he was satisfied all evidence was gone. I redressed my bottom half and glanced at my sopping wet bra and t-shirt. I shivered and crossed my arms over my chest as I headed to his dresser to grab a sweatshirt. Even though I would look baggy and unkempt in his oversized clothes, at least I would by warm and dry. While I pawed through his drawers, Gavin emerged from the bathroom with a white lace bra and dark green sweater folded over his arm.

"So ... this is kind of weird, but I looked at the tags on some of your clothes so I could get you some things to keep here. I admit I bought the lingerie based on what I like. Sorry. But not really."

I was overcome by the gesture and could do nothing but gape at him while he held them out to me. I took the clothes and found them to be my size and my style. The price though ... that was way out of my comfort zone. While lace wasn't usually my first choice on bras because the dips and dents were visible under my work shirts, this one was both sexy and classy.

"Why? I mean, thank you. They're gorgeous. But why?"

"I know we aren't there yet, but when—if—you get to the point you're ready to spend the night, I want you to feel like you're at home. Like you belong here. Because you do."

I dressed quickly and perched on the end of the bed.

"I want it, so badly. I want to fall asleep in your arms with no panic biting at the back of my brain. The fear, it never backs down. I've tried everything. Breathing techniques, soft sound machines, night lights, hot tea, pills. It does nothing. I hate that you might think it has anything to do with you because it doesn't."

"I don't. I want to help you through it."

"I'm scared it won't go away. I'm scared you'll get tired of waiting for your love to glue the cracks in me back together."

Gavin reached for me, our fingers curling together.

"Even if it doesn't, we'll figure it out. When you feel ready to try, you can stay over and sleep in one of the guest rooms."

I truly couldn't believe my luck. This understanding, empathetic man was mine.

"You'd be okay with that? Me staying here, but not sleeping together?"

"It would mean you're under the same roof so yes, I'd be okay with that." Gavin knelt in front of me and took my hands into his. "My life will never *not* have you in it, ever again. If you need your own bedroom here that doesn't include me, that's what you'll have."

"I don't handle change well. Each tragedy in my life forced it in a way I wasn't able to comprehend. Now things are changing so fast, and while it's positive it still has me spiraling. Trevor is what's going to push me over the edge. I need to know he's okay. He's never been under this long."

"You know they'd contact you if anything was wrong. And I know that doesn't make it easier, but he's a badass and his team is too. I'm sure they've got it under control."

"Have you met his team? Besides Jace, I mean," I asked, confused.

"In passing," Gavin replied. He chewed his lip and wore a guilty expression. "We were introduced at the police station."

"Police station? Oh no. Did Trevor have you brought in? Did he threaten you?"

"Not exactly." Gavin looked pained as he sat back on his heels and peered at me. "I've got to tell you something that might make you mad."

I'd cycled way too many emotions for one day. My bliss from the recent orgasm evaporated completely as my brain flipped through all the things he might say.

"The morning after you told me, Trevor texted and asked me to come to the station. I should have told you. I'm sorry."

Trevor had barely been in the door at the bakery when I announced that I had told Gavin everything. It was the first time I had ever seen him speechless. It was zero percent surprising he had reached out to Gavin on his own.

"I mean, I wish you had told me right away but I'm not mad. Trevor can be intimidating. I know it was a lot to process," I paused and pulled Gavin off the floor onto the bed next to me. "Did he loop you in more than I could?"

"He did. He told me about the protection order."

Shame coursed through me and I looked away, embarrassed that I hadn't been the one to tell him about that.

"It's probably not necessary anymore," I murmured. "She's never tried to contact me. I mean, letters here and there that I never actually saw, but nothing beyond that. But it makes me feel better."

"Something he said made me wonder if she was closer than she should be. Or I guess, what he didn't say. If that's the case, would it account for his behavior lately?"

My heart skipped at the possibility and I jumped off the bed as I began to pace the room.

"It could. But if she was here he would tell me," I hated the uncertainty in my voice. Because I honestly wasn't sure. Half of me thought he would never keep that a secret, while the other half knew he would track her like a cat with a laser pointer if she were anywhere in the vicinity and keep me in the dark until absolutely necessary.

"He also told me you can't have anything covering your face. That's why I pulled my hand back earlier," Gavin nodded over his shoulder at the rumpled covers. There had been no momentary flash of fear when he had tried to quiet me with his hand, and his explanation now made me want to throw him down on the bed and start all over. Even in a cloud of hormones, he *only* cared about my comfort.

There was a knock on the door and Mattie's voice filtered through.

"Sorry to interrupt your coitus, but Mom and Dad are back!"

Gavin jumped off the bed and wrenched open the door, standing back so Mattie could see we were both fully clothed. She didn't need to know she was right, just late on the statement. She looked between us and read the atmosphere as she took two steps inside.

"What did you do to her?" Mattie shoved Gavin accusingly. "She looks more upset now than she did downstairs."

Gavin squeezed my shoulder. I absently reached for his hand, overwhelmed by the possibility my mom might actually be nearby.

"He did nothing but soothe me," I assured her. Gavin's grip tightened on me, and I knew he was thinking of just how soothing our decompression session had been. "I'm just really emotionally screwed up right now."

"Family will do that to you," Mattie said. "Your most important people and your biggest headaches, all in the same package. But hey, you've got more now."

"What do you mean?"

"We take care of our own," Mattie said delicately. "You're one of us now. Not just his. You're family to all of us."

"For infinity," Gavin confirmed, squeezing my hip as the three of us left the room.

I instinctively reached for my necklace and my heart fluttered at the term my dad used to use.

"My love for you is endless, whether I'm here, or up there. Touch this when you miss me. I'll know. My infinite sunshine."

Was it possible all my pieces were falling into place? It felt that way. Which left me to wonder when it would all come crashing down.

CHAPTER 34

Gavin

I'd been standing at the door for ten minutes, but my sisters and mom would not stop talking, hugging, and laughing with Greyson long enough to get her out the door. Dinner had been a great success, but I was ready to take her home so I could have time alone with her and let her scream my name as loud as she wanted with no worry anyone would hear her.

"We'll come by the bakery tomorrow, would that be alright?" my mom asked, and I took the opportunity of a slight break in conversation to step forward and help Greyson into her coat. The way she lifted her ponytail out of the collar and let it slip through her fingers had my brain going to a very dirty place, and I called on all my willpower not to wrap it up in my fist and tug her head back right then and there.

"Of course. I'd love that! I'll make a special cupcake. Maybe a pumpkin pie one." Greyson winked at Mattie, who snort-laughed in response.

"Only if it has cottage cheese filling."

"On that note, I'm taking Greyson home before I vomit," I interrupted. I opened the door and tapped my foot while she said her final goodbyes. We walked down the steps and across the driveway and Greyson stopped when we got to my truck, pulling me into her and kissing me hard.

"What was that for?" I asked when she released me, not wanting it to end while being in a huge hurry to get her somewhere private.

"For everything. For your family and this day and these clothes. For making me so happy I forgot to be sad for a while. For all of it."

"It was my sincere pleasure," I kissed her quickly before I opened the passenger door and held out a hand for her to step up. A black Maserati sped past my house and turned into a driveway a few houses down from mine, and I recognized the occupants as they tumbled out. Greyson watched the women wave to me before she turned her stare on me and ignored my outstretched hand, scrambling into the cab on her own.

"Friends of yours?" she asked. Apparently, it was rhetorical since she slammed the door before I could answer. When I hopped in the driver's seat, she ignored me and turned up the music. Every time I turned down the volume from the steering wheel, she turned it up from the knob, and I bit my cheek to keep from smiling at the teenage jealousy I was witnessing out of my girlfriend who never had the chance to act that way in high school.

"They're not my friends; they're neighbors who wave to me when they get home."

"Pretty convenient how you forgot to mention you live down the street from Barbie's dream house," Greyson replied flippantly as she twisted the end of her ponytail. She was nervous, and I wasn't going to have that. None of it.

"I've never spoken to any of them. I don't know anything about them aside from their last name."

Judging by her sour expression, that didn't make it any better.

"Oh, well that's so great then! Gorgeous twins who can probably see in your bedroom with binoculars, and it's fine because you only know their last name."

I shouldn't laugh, but her jealousy was so unnecessary it was amusing. "They aren't twins."

Greyson glared. "You sure know a hell of a lot for not knowing anything."

I backed out of the drive and headed towards Greyson's house as I gently pulled her hands away from the end of her ponytail. She relaxed slightly and let me hold her pinky in mine. She was so cute, letting me know she was still mad by not allowing me to hold her entire hand, only offering up one finger.

"Their last name is O'Malley and I know that because they own the dealership where I bought my car. When my salesman copied my driver's license, he told me his sister and cousins lived on the same street as me."

Greyson pouted a few more seconds before she let me take a couple more fingers.

"Also, I'm not into redheads, that's Drake's territory. I'm more of a brunette baker guy myself."

She dropped her head to the side and rolled her eyes as she presented me with the rest of her hand to hold.

"Flattery will get you everywhere, Canada."

I brought her hand up to my mouth and held it there before I dropped it to my thigh, where I held it captive the remainder of the drive. When we got to her house, Greyson turned her back to stick the key in the door when I spotted a large man move towards us across the lawn. Instinct had me stepping behind her and turning out, so I faced the person dressed in black with a hood pulled low over his face, and she was surrounded by my body.

"Gavin what the hell?" Greyson's voice faded as she realized there was someone else on her porch, and a protective rush of adrenaline flooded my veins. The man stepped closer, still without speaking, and I was ready to lay him out when he pushed the hood back and I recognized Trevor's partner. Greyson gripped my waist tightly when she saw who was there, and I felt the fear spike in her increased breath.

"Jace? No. Is he...?"

"He's fine. He's alright."

"Then why are you here?" Greyson shrieked as her fingernails dug into my skin. I allowed my muscles to slowly relax when I realized she wasn't in danger, as Jace pulled a folded sheet of paper out of his pocket and looked at me.

"I have to say, I like the way you just jumped in front of her. It would make Trevor *very* happy. You're like a dog protecting its master."

"Thank you? Even though that sounded like an insult."

"No. It's the farthest thing from it. It's a compliment of the highest variety. You didn't know who the hell I was and made sure I didn't get anywhere near her. Plus, your senses are on high alert. You saw me before I realized I'd been spotted. That's skill man."

"I don't take chances when it comes to her."

"I can see why Trev likes you so much," Jace replied.

I turned to Greyson and slid an arm around her waist. She stared at Jace with wide, wet eyes.

"We had a meet tonight and Trevor asked me to give you this. He knows how hard this is on you, especially on a holiday. I could have waited to bring it to you at Icing tomorrow, but I thought you might need it," Jace trailed off as he passed the folded note, which Greyson accepted with trembling fingers.

"Is he okay?"

"He's doing great. I know you don't want to hear this, but he lives for this shit, Greyson. Being someone else so he can take down bad people, it's when he comes alive," Jace replied as he pulled the hood back up around his head. She didn't want to hear it. She shrank into her coat and a tear fell off her cheek. Her mood had, obviously, gone downhill.

"Do you want to go inside?" I asked. She nodded and threw both arms around my waist as she burrowed into my coat. She was one more inconvenience away from her breaking point, and I was going to make sure that didn't happen.

"Thanks for this," Greyson's voice was muffled as she waved the paper around, letting go of me partially to allow Jace to hug her into him and whisper something private. She nodded before she attached herself back to me like a koala bear. Jace gave me a head tilt before he looked around and jogged down the street. I didn't know where he came from, or how long he'd been in the shadows, but he'd been waiting for her to get back home. Even though he was a cop and practically a family member, I didn't like the thought of someone waiting to peer through her windows the second she got home at night.

I got us into the house and locked up before I steered her into the living room. She shook so violently her teeth chattered and I decided against trying to get her coat off, instead pulling her into my lap.

"Do you feel better or worse?" I asked gently as I wrapped her in a blanket.

"What do you mean?"

"Did seeing Jace and having him tell you Trevor is okay make you feel better or worse?"

Greyson unfolded the paper in her hands and read the words silently before she met my eyes.

"Thank you."

"For what?"

"Not asking if I'm okay. It's a question that exhausts me. How am I supposed to answer it? Tell the truth? Trust me, I know there's only so many times people want to hear how unraveled I am. Jace's visit made me feel ... I don't know yet. Mad? Because he gets to see Trevor and I don't. Relieved? Because I know, at least right now, he's safe. Not better. Not worse."

She folded the note and leaned forward, placing it on the table, looking at me apologetically.

"Don't," I interrupted, before she could open her mouth. "Don't apologize for wanting to keep it private. You don't have to feel like you're doing something wrong by not telling me what it says."

Greyson's shoulders sagged as she shrugged out of her coat and tossed it over the arm of the sofa.

"I'm so thankful for you," she murmured. I kissed her forehead and wrapped us in a blanket as I turned on White Christmas. She smiled against me when the opening scene started, and I let her ruminate in the memories of her grandpa without trying to talk. She was talked out. She needed time to be in her own head with no interruptions, and we watched in silence for over an hour before I asked if she wanted some tea.

"Greyson?" I looked down to see her sleeping peacefully in my lap, perfectly relaxed. This was huge. Last Thanksgiving, she fell asleep because she was sick and full of alcohol-heavy cold medicine. It wasn't because she knew she was safe with me, or comfortable enough to do it. It was because she couldn't help it. It was possible tonight was just her emotional rollercoaster finally cruising to a stop and she was too exhausted to fight it, but I chose to believe it was more than that and I was going to savor it for as long as I could.

She had never looked more beautiful than she did while she was at peace. I wondered what she dreamed about when she was in a good place and hoped she saw cupcakes, glitter, and her dad. I finished the movie and stayed on the couch another hour, wanting so badly to stay. It would be easy to fall asleep and feign ignorance when we woke up. But she wasn't ready, and I wasn't going to trick her or stay under false pretenses.

Greyson stirred when I slid out from under her and gathered her into my arms. I carried her to her bedroom and tucked her tightly under her blankets and kissed her forehead.

"I love you, Greyson."

Before I left, I wrote her a note and left it on the coffeemaker so she'd find it before she showered. I grabbed the spare key she kept in the kitchen so I could deadbolt the front door. After Jace's surprise appearance, I wasn't super comfortable leaving her alone. The way he skulked around in all black made it seem like he had stayed hidden for a reason. It had crossed my mind she could potentially be in danger if Trevor's undercover work went south and his true identity was figured out, but I tried not to let that thought stay in the forefront for long and I most definitely did not mention it to Greyson. She didn't need anything else to worry about.

When I got home and changed, I went to the closet to pull out the pillows I'd put away. After she told me what happened to her I tried to sleep like she did. I wanted to get used to the idea of not having pillows on the bed for when she was ready to spend the night with me. I didn't realize how necessary they were to my comfort, and I couldn't imagine going to bed night after night, year after year, with no cushion under my head. It was no wonder she barely slept since it was in no way comfortable. But if I had to get rid of every pillow in my house to get her to spend the night there, it was a sacrifice I was more than willing to make.

I fell into bed and closed my eyes, not opening them until the next morning. I came downstairs to find Asher in the living room flipping channels.

"Morning," I yawned on my way past. I needed coffee in a bad way.

"Bring me a cup of coffee with some of that bitch creamer, would you?"

I called him a derogatory term before I made his coffee how he liked it, handing it over when I came to the living room.

"Eddie's interview is about to start." Asher nodded at the television, where I saw Greyson's friend. He was surrounded by his paintings, dressed in a white linen suit with a pink and yellow tie-dyed shirt underneath. He had leather sandals on his feet, with his long gray hair tied on top of his head in a knot. He was the epitome of an eccentric artist, and I grinned and flopped onto the couch. Greyson was so proud when he'd told her about the interview, and bummed she was going to be at work and miss it. I would bet my career she was in her office, live streaming it and taking a break with the baking.

"So, tell us the story of Ed Julson," the host started. Eddie grinned and leaned back against the couch as he stretched his legs and crossed his feet at the ankles.

"My life really only began six years ago. Like most stories, it all started with a woman."

"Don't they all," the co-host interjected. Asher snorted, and I gave him the finger as I increased the volume.

"I was homeless, and one day this angel appeared. She handed me a check and asked if I wanted a job," Eddie paused, his eyes full of love and memories. "You know that feeling, that flash you get in a moment, when you know everything is going to be alright? That was mine."

"How did that happen? A random woman saving your life?"

"Well, she wasn't random. I'd been on the streets for years before that day. Always getting myself arrested in the winter so I could at least be inside for a while. Warm up and get some food. The police knew me, and they knew I was harmless. It got to a point they just put me on a bench, gave me a sandwich, and let me go.

"One night, this rookie cop came in with a very surly teenager. You could tell from the body language they were family. I knew him a little, he brought me in a few times. Seemed like a good kid. He plopped her down next to me and told her not to move until his shift was over. Turns out, she was at a party she shouldn't have been at and big brother was the officer who got called to break it up. Ooowee was she nervous! We got to talking and realized we'd both been through a lot, in different ways. She had all the money in the world but was drowning in sadness. I had nothing but the clothes on my back and the smile on my face."

Asher set down his coffee and I leaned forward with my elbows on my knees, completely enraptured. Asher looked over and pointed at the television.

"Is he talking about—"

"Shut up, I don't want to miss anything."

"The next day I was at the camp I set up in, and a police car pulls up. Nothing too strange there, but out pops my new friend. This little girl with these big blue eyes, dragging bags of stuff over to me. She said she couldn't stop thinking about our talk and hated the idea of me cold and hungry. She had brought me a winter coat, a blanket, some cash, and some cupcakes. Her own recipe, that she'd named after me. Can you imagine? No one had ever cared about me like that."

"Holy shit," I sat back as Eddie's words confirmed what Asher and I had both suspected.

"When she left, she hugged me and told me she'd really like to keep in touch. We did, but then she went off to college and while I didn't forget about her, life went on. Then one day, she's back. Grown up and owning her own business! She handed me a check that was enough to get an apartment, and I started cleaning her bakery that very day. A month later I painted a little mural on the wall at her place, and since her baking is the best around, those little wings got a lot of eyes on them. She had people asking who painted them. Asking about *me*," he paused as a sheepish grin overtook over his weathered face. "She took orders for custom paintings before she even talked to me, the little sneak. Sat me down and said she didn't want me cleaning her bakery anymore. I thought I'd done something wrong. But she said I had a talent that needed to be shared, and she wouldn't let me squander it cleaning for her. I told her she could go ahead and close her mouth, because nothing would ever stop me from repaying the huge debt I owed her for saving my life. But she's stubborn as a mule and said she wouldn't allow it. Too bad for her, I already had a key and just kept showing up every night. She finally realized I'm more stubborn than she is, and she wasn't getting rid of me that easily. Bing, bang, boom I've got an online shop, a spot at the art fair, and enough money to live comfortably. All because a sad little girl got caught at a house party."

Asher turned with a look of shock. "Did you know about this?"

"No. I mean, I knew she gave him a job when he was down on his luck, but that's all she ever said. I can't believe this." I shook my head. "Actually, I can. The broken will always love harder than most. She saved someone else because she didn't feel like she could save herself."

I turned back to the interview and became emotional at Eddie's next words.

"That girl is like a daughter to me. She saved my life with her kindness and I get to live my dream one hundred percent because of her. I hope she knows I love her with my whole heart. Forever and ever."

Asher hopped up when the interview was over and took his cup to the kitchen. He patted my cheek on his way back by.

"That lady of yours is something pretty special. But you already knew that. Keep making sure she realizes it, too."

"I'm trying, man. I'm trying."

CHAPTER 35
Greyson

There hadn't been a break in customers since we opened the doors, but that wasn't unusual for Black Friday. People got tired after ravaging store shelves and trampling their fellow man and wanted to refresh with sugar and caffeine.

I'd woken up in bed, emotionally exhausted from the up and down of the day before. I was half asleep when I padded into the kitchen to get coffee and found a note from Gavin. I wasn't awake enough to recall the fact I'd fallen asleep on him, exactly a year since the last time. I spilled coffee all over the counter as I read his words, keeping my finger on the dispenser button long after the mug was full. I was in tears by the time I finished cleaning my coffee mess, and I clutched his note in my fist while I got ready for work. It came with me to Icing, folded and tucked into the back pocket of my jeans next to Trevor's. Two notes from the two men in my life.

I was grateful for the quiet in the kitchen when I measured out ingredients for a peppermint mocha cupcake. My thoughts raced as I sifted flour with espresso powder and tried to recall the moment I fell asleep. One second, I watched Bing Crosby and Danny Kaye dressed up like ladies dancing around with blue feathers, and the next I'm in my bed tucked in tight with my stuffed pig under my arm. There was no memory of fighting off sleep, no glimmer of being carried from the couch to the bed. I was reeling from those implications, although I shouldn't have been shocked at all. Gavin was my safe place, my smooth landing after a bumpy flight. There was no reason, besides past fear, I should have been surprised.

He could have stayed, but he was respectful enough not to since it wasn't offered. Just because I'd fallen asleep *on* him didn't mean I was ready to sleep *with* him, and he would wait for an invitation before he made that move. If I could get past my worry of disturbing him, I'd suggest we give it a try. But I couldn't quiet the thought that no matter what he said, once he witnessed what happened in the dark of the night, he'd bail. It was a lot to handle, especially for someone who had an incredibly demanding and physically taxing job that required regular, solid rest. He wouldn't get that if he was in a bed with me, and the first game his performance dropped because of exhaustion I'd blame myself and shut down.

"Grey, your in-laws are here," Jemma yelled obnoxiously through the door. I really liked the sound of that. Being part of a big family was something I hadn't realized I wanted until I'd gotten a taste of theirs.

When I pushed through the doors and entered the bakery, I motioned them to the Consultations counter so they could bypass the insane line of people ahead of them. They ordered one of everything in the case and told me they'd promised Gavin they'd bring him a cupcake when he returned home from practice, so I packed an extra lemon one and added a sugar dipped strawberry just for him.

They had just left when Donovan alerted me to first-time customers. The couple that met me at the consultation counter were full of smiles in their matching plaid shirts and puffer vests.

"Hi there! Welcome to Icing!"

The woman beamed at me from under her husband's arm.

"This is such a cute place! I love those wings!"

My gaze strayed to the wall, and my heart tugged in wanting to get back to my office, where I could pull up a repeat of Eddie's interview. I slid a card across the counter.

"The artist always loves new customers," I said. "If you're interested, here's his info."

She looked at the card and then at her husband, as she tapped it against her chin.

"You know, this is the same artist that did the piece in Marshall and Siobhan's house. The cross? I remember the name," she winked at me. "I got up close and personal to check out the signature."

The hair on the back of my neck prickled for a reason I couldn't pinpoint, and I fought the urge to snatch the card back and protect Eddie's name. I did not like these people. I wanted them out.

"Um, so what can I help you with? Donovan said you haven't been in before. What are you in the mood for?"

The man smiled, perfectly innocently, but my stomach turned anyway.

"We're from Indiana. Just came into the city for some business. We're having dinner with our new neighbors tonight, and noticed a magnet for this place on their fridge. Figured they must like it, so thought we would stop in since we were in town."

"That's awesome," I replied enthusiastically. "Are there any particular flavors you're looking for?"

I battled within myself to stay focused while simultaneously wanting to get them out of the shop as fast as possible. Ten minutes later, they were bundled down with a variety of cookies and cupcakes, and I stopped at Donovan's side as they exited.

"Were they ... off?"

"Meaning what?" he asked, as they climbed into the back of a waiting Range Rover.

"I don't know. Just a weird vibe."

"Aside from their matching suburban soccer parent outfits

and unnervingly white teeth, they seemed fine to me," Donovan shrugged. I gave it a final thought and pushed through the kitchen door as the start of a migraine flared behind my left eye, and I pressed two fingers against my eye socket.

Thirty minutes later, I was nauseous and miserable. I grabbed my purse and headed out the back door after alerting my staff I was taking the rest of the day. I debated driving to Gavin's house to ride out the headache, but if it became a multiple day situation, I would need to get rest. When I got home, I shot him a text message that simply said *"Migraine. Will text later."*

I silenced my phone, grabbed an ice pack, and fell into bed. After the ice was positioned against the back of my neck, I closed my eyes. I attempted to push away the uneasiness that had settled in the back of my mind.

It was just exhaustion.

Right.

CHAPTER 36
Gavin

"Don't Get Your Snow Off the Street. Buy From Your Office Dealer, Like a Civilized Adult ... but seriously. Don't Do Drugs."

I read the caption from Biscuits in the Baskets' latest post. They had become focused on more than Chicago hockey, and now covered the city in general.

"Are they for real?" I asked with a shake of my head.

Asher set a platter of garlic bread on the table as Delaney shredded parmesan into the salad bowl.

"The story is valid and actually well written," Mila argued. Of course, she had spent two hands full of nights with Jay Montgomery and had noticeably started defending Biscuits. "It's just the headline that could use some work."

"You think?" Cohen pulled the lasagna out of the oven as Greyson dumped fettuccine noodles into the strainer in the sink. "They make it sound like a joke."

The news had been ablaze with coverage of the recent spike in overdoses around the city. It didn't seem to matter what drug, either. The deaths were spread across all types, from pills to heroin, and recent stories hinted at the inclusion of fentanyl in known street drugs.

"Can we please talk about something else?" Greyson spoke for the first time, her voice carrying across the room as she tossed the noodles into a bubbling pot of homemade alfredo sauce.

The shelter she provided baked goods to, and where Eddie had frequented when he was on the streets, had been hit particularly hard by deaths of regular visitors. Almost every day, she had been in tears after Eddie left with the boxes. Because he would come bearing bad news, another soul lost to the opioid crisis. Earlier in the week, someone had collapsed on the sidewalk one door down from Icing. Other tenants on the block were pissed about the optics. Greyson was heartbroken for the person who had fallen into drugs, and ultimately lost their life. She did the only thing she knew how to do and created a special for opioid awareness. A simple vanilla cupcake with a purple fondant ribbon, she donated one hundred percent of the profits to the department of public health and the shelters that passed out drug testing strips.

Her mood had been off since, and no amount of distraction in the way of orgasms had gotten her balanced. Add in the constant worry about Trevor, and she was one minor inconvenience away from a full mental collapse.

"I'm sorry, Lemon Drop. I shouldn't have brought it up," I murmured, as I pressed a kiss against her temple. Greyson gave a slight shake of her head.

"No need to apologize. I just ... can't."

Asher walked up to the stove and replaced the tongs in her hand with a glass of wine.

"Women, retire to the table and cocktail before dinner. The men folk will finish in the kitchen and serve you like the queens you are."

Delaney gagged good naturedly.

"How do you even walk through all that bullshit?"

"I've got tall boots," he winked. Greyson rolled her eyes and laughed, and a piece of me relaxed.

After dinner, we moved to my basement theater. Mila and

Cohen argued over which movie to watch while Delaney and Asher fought over the 'good' seat in the corner of the room. Greyson went to my room to change, and the chime of the doorbell floated down the stairs.

I hopped up them and turned on the hall light, pulling in a breath as I peered out the window.

"What the fuck," I muttered, then pulled open the door "Uh, hi. Can I help you?"

My neighbors smiled back at me, seemingly oblivious to how strange it was for them to show up at my doorstep at nine o'clock at night. Considering we had never officially met.

"Hiya! Is your girlfriend here?" One of the matching set of redheads asked cheerfully, looking around me into the house. I blocked her view, and folded my arms across my chest as Greyson's warmth pressed against my back.

"Gavin, who is it?" Greyson's head came around me as the women on the porch lit up at the sight of her.

"Oh, she is here! Fecking brilliant! Do you know how to make Porter Cake? We need *help*."

I watched Greyson's expression go from guarded, to confused, to intrigued in a matter of seconds. The women on my porch waited for a response as we both stared at them like they were from another planet.

"Uh, I do ... it's pretty simple ... but, and I mean this in the nicest way possible ... who are you?"

"Oh, *duh!*" The shorter one smacked a hand against her forehead. "I'm Vanessa O'Malley, and this is my cousin Kayleigh. We've meant to come introduce ourselves like a million times, but it's a little weird to just knock on the door of an NHL player."

I raised a brow as my arms fell from the closed off pose they'd been in, and I offered a hand to shake.

"It's nice to officially meet you. I'm Gavin, this is Greyson," I paused. "But it seems like you already knew that."

Kayleigh guffawed as she pumped my hand and looked at Greyson.

"Guilty. Your bakery is fierce. I pop in constantly when I bunk off from the dealership."

Greyson scrunched her forehead, as if the woman was speaking a foreign language.

"Anyway, my cousin Erica, Kayleigh's sister, always makes the Porter Cake for Christmas. But she's out of town for work and we don't know when she's going to be home," Vanessa cut in. "My aunt already had a fit that it hasn't been started. Kayleigh and I are not what you would call talented with the baked goods. Is there any possibility we can convince you to help us?"

All of Greyson's suspicion melted off her shoulders.

"Absolutely! Let me get my coat!"

I smiled at my neighbors as I held up a finger.

"Can you excuse us for just one second?"

I guided Greyson away from the door by her elbow.

"Don't you think this is just a little bit insane? You don't know anything about them! I'm not comfortable with you going into their house at night. Or ever."

Greyson gave me an exasperated sigh.

"They live in a mansion. I'm sure they are not murderers."

"Plenty of criminals live in nice neighborhoods, Greyson! Trevor would not be okay with this."

It was a low blow, and the effect of the words made me wish I could suck them back into my mouth. She deflated, the enthusiasm of helping new people with a baking crisis flattened like a balloon.

"You're right," she mumbled, and moved back to the door. "Why don't you two come to the bakery tomorrow? You can hang out in back with me while we make your Porter Cake."

"Seriously? That would be incredible," Kayleigh exclaimed.

"We will pay literally anything," Vanessa confirmed. "It's a really big deal to get it right and I do not want it on me."

Greyson waved away the statement.

"If you pitch in, I'll only charge for the cost of ingredients. I'm happy to help."

Kayleigh leapt forward and hugged Greyson against her body.

"You are the best example of human! We'll see you tomorrow!"

They were gone before either of us reacted, and we stood and watched them run back down the street.

"That was ... odd," I remarked as I closed the door.

"Add it to the list."

CHAPTER 37
Greyson

The ingredients were spread out in front of me, and my fingers itched with wanting to get started. It had been years since I'd made a Porter Cake, but I had not stopped thinking about it since the O'Malley's random pop-up on Gavin's porch the night before. If he hadn't witnessed it, I would have thought I made the whole thing up.

I can admit, when I descended the stairs from his room and saw them at the door, the fury that flashed through me like lava was more than a little concerning. My entire self had been suspended between bliss and battered in the past weeks. I had plenty to be happy about; my relationship was like it was pulled out of the pages of a romance novel, even if Gavin had become almost too overprotective, my business was beyond booming, and the network had just pitched us on a baking competition show.

But the other side—the parts I gave into at night, when I was awake next to Gavin—were crushing me. I felt like I was a half step in front of an avalanche. Far enough ahead not to get completely buried, but close enough to feel the danger at my back. Gavin was being weird. He was practically forbidding me to go home at night, and every time we went outside, he looked around like he was expecting someone to jump out of the bushes. The resulting sex was incredible, with his outpouring of aggression channeled into my orgasm. But it was stressing me out, and he wouldn't talk about it. Trevor was still gone, radio silence on that front. Jace had barely communicated, either. He responded to my texts with short, two- or three-word responses, and when he actually answered my calls, his voice was clipped and tight. I had also spotted an undercover car parked down the street from my house, which I made sure not to mention to Gavin. If there was a car on me, either Trevor or Jace felt I could be in danger. I spent the entirety of every therapy session repeating myself, since I had yet to figure out a way to stay calm about any of the upheaval. It was necessary to have something to focus on, and the new task from the O'Malley's gave me a break from the monotony of the day to day I had grown accustomed to.

I knew enough about Porter Cake to know it was a traditional Irish dessert, highly personal to each family, and customizations and additions were commonplace. There was no way to know how the O'Malley's made it. Luckily, I had pretty much every possible ingredient stocked in the bakery, but the beer was a huge question mark. While the name of the cake indicated it would be made with a Porter, plenty of recipes used a particular Irish stout. I was not fond of either type just to drink, so I did not want to have a huge variety waiting around for the O'Malley's that would end up going to waste. Donovan was on standby to run and get whatever they said we needed.

He came breezing through the doors, two petite redheads in his wake. They all had shopping bags in both hands. I breathed a sigh of relief to spot a bottle sticking out of the top of Vanessa's tote. It also made me like them just a little bit more.

"Hey there, Cakes," she dropped her supplies on the work table with a clatter. "How hot is he?"

She hitched her thumb at my employee, who was living for the objectification.

"You're not so bad yourself, Red," Donovan drawled. I rolled my eyes and pointed at the front of the shop, mouthing *out.*

Kayleigh and Vanessa began unpacking their bags, as comfortable as if they owned the place.

"We brought some of the stuff. I realized after we left that I didn't get your number, and Gavin looked less than thrilled by our visit. I didn't want his cherub face to slip if we came back with a list," Vanessa said. My face apparently gave away my annoyance at that statement, and she held up her hands. "We don't blame him. It was weird of us. No disrespect."

Kayleigh turned a bag upside down, and packages of dried fruit tumbled across the table.

"To be honest, we've wanted to meet you for months."

"You mean Gavin," I looked over the recipe Vanessa had slapped in front of me. It was straightforward, but the beer was not something I had even heard of.

"No, you," Vanessa waved away my response. "What would we have in common with a professional hockey player? A badass female entrepreneur, however, we are here to force your friendship."

I balked, actually completely confused.

"Erica being out of town for Porter Cake assembly was the perfect excuse to get to know you," Kayleigh grinned.

"Why?"

"Your rapport with your friends on *Eat It* reminds us of us," Vanessa said. "You guys clearly have so much fun, and the inside jokes and dirty food entendres give us life."

Kayleigh flopped onto a stool in front of the work table as we started to put together the Porter Cake.

"My sister has a massively stressful job. When she has time to relax, we all settle into our living room with a bottle of Jameson and big ass bowls of popcorn and binge your show. It's been our ritual for years."

I thought of my brother, and our own relaxation sessions. While it was seltzer, nails, and the Real Housewives on our side, the similarity caused an ache to bloom in my chest. The pain was so real I brought my fist to my sternum to rub away the knot.

"I'm honored to play a part in that," I murmured. "What does your sister do?"

Vanessa and Kayleigh exchanged a quick glance.

"She works for the government."

"Ah. I've got one of those in my family, too. It sucks."

"It really fucking does, doesn't it?" Vanessa replied.

I felt a piece of something slide into place with these veritable strangers, and by the time we had completed their family tradition dessert—with an extra, just in case—we had exchanged phone numbers and made plans to hang out. A part of me knew I had just met people that would impact my life.

For better or worse, though, that was the question.

That was always the question.

CHAPTER 38
Gavin

I rolled over and tossed my arm across a cold bed.
Damn.
I had not expected her to bail.
Again.

The first time was almost a given. Her first night in a different house, a different bed, with another person was a recipe for restlessness. I was prepared, and we handled it together. She had taken my offer on the guest bedroom down the hall from my own, and I tried my best not to take it personally when I heard the firm click of the lock from the other side of the door.

The times that followed were frustrating but halfway expected. I continued to assure her it was fine, that having her in the house was enough for me. Because it was.

Also, because I did not want her in her house alone at night.

But I couldn't tell her that.

The guilt over what I had done clawed at me every day, but it was better than fearing her safety.

I thought things were going to be different tonight when she had situated herself into the curve of my arm. I knew she was exhausted, with the weight of the holidays on her shoulders. She had fallen asleep before I did, or so I had thought. The absence of her in my bed now made me realize she had faked it, just like the night at her house.

The soft light of my bedside clock indicated it was two-thirty in the morning, and even though she would be up soon anyway, I went to check on her. My stomach fell to my feet when I saw the door of the guest bedroom still stood open.

I flew through the house, checking every room. Lights were thrown on in the other bedrooms, bathrooms, even the closets.

"No. No, no, no," I jumped down the stairs, quickly verifying she wasn't in the living room or the kitchen. That's when I found the note.

> *Don't be mad at me. I just needed to sleep at home. I've got so much going on at work, and I just am not ready for this, every night. It's not at all you. I didn't wake you because I knew you would convince me to stay. I love you to infinity, Canada. But I need to be at home. Fingers crossed you slept all night before you see this.*

I was in my truck and halfway to her house before I realized I hadn't even put on shoes. Calls to her phone went unanswered, and I had sweat through my shirt by the time I pulled up to her house. The kitchen light was on, and she pulled open the door with a confused look when I pounded on it incessantly.

"Gavin, what are you doing?"

I looked around in the darkness before I put my hands on her waist and pushed us inside the house.

"I just wanted to make sure you were okay," I huffed, aware of the look of suspicion on her face. In this moment, she looked unnerved. By me.

"Did you see my note?"

"Yes."

"Then you know I'm fine?" her voice ended on a question.

"I'm not sure I like this, Gavin. You've been acting ... primitive. Like I can't handle my own life without my big strong man. What is going on?"

I sucked in a breath of air through my teeth. Greyson waited, not giving an inch. It was clear now, the tension and worry I thought I had hidden so masterfully was obvious to the woman at the center of it. I had hoped I could keep it quiet, a necessary evil I had performed to watch over her while Trevor was unavailable. I saw now, that was not going to be the case.

"Let's get some coffee."

Greyson blanched, the words igniting some instinct in her. She knew I held onto something that was going to be painful to hear. When I reached for her, she backed away and held her palms out like a shield.

"You're scaring me."

"We need to talk," I said softly.

Greyson's hands flew to her mouth, and she shook her head repeatedly.

"Oh no. Nope. I don't want to do this. Whatever you are about to say, keep it in your mouth," Greyson's voice wobbled, and her throat bobbed with a hard swallow. "I can see it on your face. Whatever it is ... it's going to hurt me. Did you ... no ... you wouldn't. Did you ... che—?"

"Absolutely not," I interrupted. I couldn't even allow her to ask if I had been unfaithful. "It's nothing like that."

"What then? What could possibly bring on 'we need to talk' if not that?"

I dropped my head and pressed my knuckles against my forehead. I wanted so badly to touch her, but she had already started to close off. Her arms were pulled across her chest and one hand rubbed her pendant roughly.

"Your mom," I blurted out.

Greyson's arms fell and she curled her nose in confusion.

"What about her?"

"She's close. She lives in Gary."

"And?"

"That's literally thirty miles away, Greyson! It's not safe!" I exclaimed. She looked at me like she didn't understand what the problem was. "Doesn't that worry you?"

"No? I told you; she has never tried to contact me. She could be five miles away and it wouldn't affect me, because I don't care to know. Unless she's violating the order, I don't give a fuck," Greyson paused and narrowed her eyes. "Wait—how do you know where she lives? *Why* do you know?"

I winced. This was the part I dreaded.

"I wanted to make sure you were safe."

"You've mentioned that a couple times now. What does it mean?"

My heart pounded against my ribs as I pulled at my hair with both hands. She would understand. She had to. Silence stretched long and heavy, as I worked up the courage to confess.

"*Gavin*," Greyson hissed. She stepped forward, her hands balled into fists.

I swallowed hard. My throat felt like it was stuffed with cotton.

"I hired a private investigator," I whispered. Greyson's head snapped back, as if I had slapped her across the face. Her chin trembled as she looked at me with wide, unbelieving eyes. Nothing in my life had prepared me for the betrayal I saw etched across her face. The pain in my chest was as real as if I were having a heart attack.

"You hired a private investigator," she repeated, her voice thick. "How dare you. How *dare* you."

"You have to see why I did," I protested, moving forward, and gripping her arms. She wrestled away, dipping under my hand and scrambling down the hall. "He found things. Dangerous things."

"I have to see why you did? I see your fixer mentality. Your compulsive fucked up need to mend everyone. Because to you, I'm less than."

"That is so far off base," I started. Greyson's eyes closed

tightly, and she covered her ears. "I wanted to protect you. Since Trevor can't."

"Shut up!" Her scream pierced the eerie silence throughout the rest of the house, and I gulped air that was as thick as soup. "You did this for yourself. You think I need to be saved. I don't. I need to be loved. I thought you knew that, but I see now I'm just a project to you."

"Greyson, please," I spoke around the lump in my throat. "That's not true. I love you more than anything."

When she met my eyes, hers were almost black. The warmth was gone, replaced with cold, unfeeling, nothingness.

"You love being needed. You love to swoop in and be the hero. Chicago's Dad. Have you ever wondered why you're so focused on everyone else's problems? Because you can't face your own feelings of failure. And there's nothing anyone can do to help with that. That's on you."

Tears gathered in my eyes as I realized just how serious this was. She was shutting down in front of me and there wasn't a damn thing I could do about it.

"I was worried. Trevor said he keeps track of her, and he can't do that now. So, I thought..."

Greyson shook her head and laughed without humor.

"I told you the worst parts of my life. And instead of just holding that knowledge, you decided I needed you to do something about it. As if I haven't been living with it every day of my life since it happened."

"I know you can take care of yourself. You're one of the strongest people I've ever met," I said.

"You say that, but your actions speak differently," Greyson seethed. "I admit, it has made me feel really fucking good when you get protective over me. But that's so different than this. That's in front of me, something I see when it happens. You went behind my back, and never would have told me if I hadn't come home tonight."

Her eyes flew open, wide and furious.

"Wait just a fucking second. That's why you've wanted me at your house, isn't it? Because of your reports from your hired detective. It had nothing to do with being with me. Unbelievable!"

"I'm sorry I didn't tell you, but it's my job to keep you safe."

"You do not get it, do you? Your job is to play hockey. I'm not your *job*, Gavin. I'm your partner," she said with a shake of her head.

"I know that. But with Trevor being gone, the responsibility of your safety is on me."

"You are not Trevor. Trevor literally saved my life. He's my brother. His overbearing protection is due to our shared childhood trauma. Something I can't do anything about. I can't break up with *him*."

My blood ran cold, as if ice water had been flushed through my veins.

"What are you saying?"

"Get out of my house," Greyson spoke clearly, with menacing calm.

"Greyson..."

"Goodbye, Gavin."

CHAPTER 39

Greyson

Six days.

That was how long it had been since Gavin appeared at my door at three in the morning and told me he had hired a detective to find out about my mother.

Six days since I had seen his face crumple in front of me, and I felt nothing but fury.

Six days since my heart had shattered.

I had ignored his attempts at communication, not even opening half of the messages. I had been staying at Trevor's house, since I knew Gavin would continue to drop by mine to get me to see his side. I would have rather stayed with Delaney, but I couldn't bring myself to tell her or Mila what had happened, since that would force me to tell them the truth about my mom. I had even stopped going to work. Well, that wasn't entirely true. I went in on Falcons away game days. There was no way he could show up if he wasn't in town. But I barely baked, instead hiding in my office and claiming paperwork and filming meetings. My staff could sense the shift in my mood, regardless of how many times I faked a smile and told them everything was great. I pretended not to see their shared looks of concern when I delegated new customer consultations to Donovan or Jemma. They saw through my 'fun new plan' to assign a different employee to come up with a special for the day.

I was empty.

This was the problem with keeping secrets. When your life imploded due to them, there was nowhere to run. No one to confide in, to tell you that you were being a major dumbass and were sabotaging the best thing that ever happened to you.

"Knock knock."

I jumped in surprise, startled out of my wallowing by Vanessa's appearance in the door of my office. She flopped into the chair and settled her feet on the corner of the desk.

"Make yourself comfortable," I zeroed in on the soles of her boots, watching for melted slush to end up on my work surface. "You know this is a food service establishment, right? There's probably dog shit on your feet."

Vanessa gave an exaggerated roll of her emerald-green eyes before she removed her feet. Her boots hit the floor with a heavy thud.

"It's not like I'm writhing nude on top of your display case."

"That would bring in an entirely new set of clientele, I'm quite certain," I replied, as the hint of an actual smile fell over my lips. "What are you doing here, anyway?"

Vanessa was slouched against the chair, her feet spread and one arm thrown across the back of the piece of furniture. She was dressed in olive green cargo pants, black combat boots, and a tight t-shirt that read 'feeling a tad stabby today.' With her black stiletto nails, tragus piercing, and sharply winged eyeliner, she looked like a complete and total badass.

I was surprised to feel that tingle in my brain, the idea of a new recipe taking shape. Even though it hadn't been a full week, going days without any creativity had felt like years. I quickly scribbled notes for a malted chocolate cake with Irish stout frosting onto the edge of a therapy invoice.

"I'm here to find out what the fuck is going on between you and Gavin, and to help you fix it," Vanessa said.

My mouth dropped in shock, before I could remind myself no one knew anything was amiss. Officially, anyway.

"I don't know—"

"Yes, you do," Vanessa interrupted. "And lying is such a lame move. Especially because you *suck* at it."

I wasn't sure if I should be proud or offended by that. She was right. But how was I supposed to confide in a woman I barely knew, when my own best friends had been kept in the dark?

"Okay. I'll start. I'll tell you what I know," Vanessa ignored my silence. "Gavin is miserable. He does nothing but run when he's at home. All day long, back and forth, over and over. You haven't been over there for a week. And also, you look like shit."

"You're just full of compliments today, aren't you?"

"There's no room for kid gloves when it comes to tough love," Vanessa sat forward and pointed a tattooed finger at me accusingly. "Talk. I'm not leaving until you do. I've got two older brothers and come from a family of Irish women. I promise I'm more stubborn than you are."

"It's nothing," I mumbled. Vanessa slammed her hand against the pile of paperwork in front of me, and I half jumped out of my chair.

"What did I say about lying?"

"You're kind of scary, do you know that?"

"Whatever gets you to talk," Vanessa shrugged. My shoulders sagged in a combination of defeat and exhaustion.

"I think we broke up."

For all her grandstanding and alpha posturing, the admission shocked Vanessa. She leaned her elbows on my desk as she scooted her chair closer.

"That's not the greatest start, but we can still work with this. More information, please."

"Oh, now you're being polite?"

Her features softened and she reached for my hand, and when moisture slid down my cheek, I realized I was crying.

"I know what it's like to be drowning in your own head," she said gently. "I'm being pushy because I see it in you. I saw it the night on Gavin's porch. I saw it when we made the Porter Cake. I see it double now. Keeping it all inside doesn't make you some pillar of strength. There's no award for silent suffering."

I swallowed hard, focused on the tattoos that adorned the backs of her hands.

"I keep secrets. I've never been fully open with anyone. I don't know how to trust that people will keep my confidence, so I just keep it all to myself."

"Ah. Well, aren't you familiar with baker client privilege?" Vanessa asked. I looked up with an amused raise of my brow.

"What's this privilege you speak of?"

"I'm disappointed you don't know of it. In your profession, you really should. Any information shared between a baker and a client in the commission of the pastry creation is privileged communication. Neither the baker nor the client can speak on it outside the boundaries of the kitchen. If they do, it's a felonious act," Vanessa nodded, her hands folded primly on top of the desk.

"I'm pretty familiar with the laws in Chicago, and I'm fairly sure that is bullshit," I replied.

"It's federal," Vanessa deadpanned. "Trust me. I'm pretty familiar with those laws."

I pressed my lips together.

"Even so, our baker client relationship concluded with the completion of the Porter Cake," I debated. I could speak like a lawyer, too. "Anything we discuss now does not fall under the same purview."

Vanessa grabbed her purse off the floor and dug around until she pulled out a designer wallet that probably cost more than one of my mortgage payments. She unzipped it and pulled a crisp hundred out of the pocket. She slid it across the desk with her middle finger.

"Would you believe, I need cookies for dinner tonight," she glanced carelessly at the Rolex strapped to her wrist. "Looks like the bakery is closing soon. So, we can continue our discussion in the sacred walls of the kitchen, and our privileged relationship continues."

"I have plans this evening," I lied.

Vanessa arched a perfectly sculpted eyebrow. The ring that was pierced through it disappeared into the pink cashmere of the beanie pulled low over her forehead.

"Again with the lies," she clucked. "Baker's choice on the cookies. Let's get to work. On the dough and the truth."

With that, she breezed out of my office into the kitchen. I followed automatically, not even considering the fact I was allowed to tell her no.

CHAPTER 40
Greyson

"You can set them down over here. Thank you so much for this. For all you do. The residents truly look forward to your baked goods. For some of them, it's the only constant, good thing they have."

The shelter director's words would have brought me to tears on a good day. But on this day, they were enough to make a sob bubble up into my throat. I caught it just before it escaped, and swallowed it hard. My eyes had been wet from the moment I had walked in to the memorial service, clinging to Eddie's arm as if he were a life raft and I couldn't swim.

So many of the regular residents of Eddie's old shelter had been victims of the drug epidemic ravaging the city that they had decided to do a memorial service for all of them. When Eddie asked me to accompany him, I of course agreed. I also volunteered to provide refreshments, because I felt absolutely useless, and that was something I knew I could do.

Even though I had never met any of the people who had passed, knowing they were important to Eddie made them important to me. My heart broke a little more every time he told me about someone else that had succumbed to bad drugs. I hoped like hell the police could figure out who was behind what was starting to feel like serial murder. People bought drugs for a lot of reasons, and it wasn't my place to judge anyone's circumstances. No one deserved to die over it.

I scanned the full room, and my heart stuttered when my gaze connected with the warm brown eyes that made my knees weak. He was standing alone just inside the front door, hands shoved in his coat pockets.

"What is he doing here?" I asked Eddie, my voice low. He turned to me with a look of surprise.

"You didn't know? He paid for this."

My chest constricted, making breathing difficult. I smoothed my hand over my throat, finding my pendant. Of course he did.

"I don't mean just the memorial, either. He paid for them to have proper burials, too," Eddie continued. "That man is one of the good ones."

I hadn't taken my eyes off Gavin for the duration of the conversation, and I half felt like he knew what was being discussed. I tore my eyes away and settled them firmly on the floor as I made my way to him, forcing the nerves that clawed at my throat down into my stomach. I was a foot away when the familiar scent of him hit me and brought a rush of comfort, even as my eyes flooded. I took a deep breath and willed myself to speak without tears.

"Hey," I said quietly. "Eddie just told me what you did. That's … so incredibly you."

Gavin swallowed hard and shot me a pained grimace.

"I hope I didn't overstep. I'm not trying to be a hero, I just wanted to make sure they all had the chance to be laid to rest with dignity."

He didn't say it with malice, but the words made me feel two feet tall.

"I meant it as a compliment," I whispered, unable to meet his eyes. Gavin stepped closer. He did not touch me, but he stood close enough I had to look up if I didn't want to be staring at his boots. My chin trembled as we stared at each other. I had so much to say. So many things he deserved to hear. Starting with I'm sorry.

Just as I got the courage, Eddie strode up to Gavin with his hand outstretched and pulled him into a tight hug. When he stepped back, he gripped Gavin's shoulders in both hands.

"I don't have the words to thank you," Eddie's watery eyes conveyed his heartbreak. I watched Gavin closely, and saw the glassy sheen of unshed tears in his own. "You have to sit with us."

Gavin's gaze flicked to me quickly.

"I'm fine in the back," he replied, a forced smile plastered to his face.

I lightly touched his arm, and his eyes dropped to his sleeve before they searched mine questioningly.

"Please, sit with us," I paused. "With me."

Gavin slowly nodded, and he walked silently next to me to the front of the center. When we took our seats, he kept his hands flat against his thighs, clearly taking care not to make physical contact with me. While it was gentlemanly and appreciated, I ached for his touch. I focused on the memorial and became more emotional with every moment; I couldn't wrap my head around the loss of life, and by the time the entire list of names was read I was shaking with silent tears. An arm snaked around my shoulders, and I jolted at the familiarity of the gesture. Gavin leaned over, his breath on my neck causing an involuntary shiver.

"I can't see you suffer and do nothing. But if I'm making you uncomfortable just say the word."

Rather than respond, I leaned into him and let the tears come.

CHAPTER 41
Gavin

y knee bounced nervously against the bench, and I was completely tuned out of the pre-game meeting. Although Greyson was coming to the game to fulfill a promise to her new friends, my neighbors, she asked if we could go for coffee and a walk by the lake afterwards. To talk and 'clear the air.' I was unsure if that was a good sign or a bad, since we had not gotten into anything the day of the memorial. She leaned on me for support throughout the service and allowed me to hug her when I left. I didn't think I imagined the way she held on longer than I did.

Asher knew the stripped-down version of the blowup, that I had done something out of bounds and Greyson cut off all communication. Even though he was *my* best friend, the way he was ready to pound me into the ground for hurting *her* made me love him even more. If she refused my love, at least I knew she would be surrounded by other people who would throw down to defend her.

The worst part of the entire situation was that I wouldn't change a damn thing about it. I did what I had to do to make sure she was safe. If it meant she hated me for eternity, at least I knew I had done everything I could to protect her from the monster that had given birth to her.

I tried to keep my focus on the ice when we came out for warmups, but I failed. I was barely out of the tunnel when my head swiveled towards her seats, where she always was. Warmups were one of her favorite parts of the game. My stomach and my optimism dropped when I found three empty chairs.

"Still early, don't lose hope," Asher chewed on his mouth guard and knocked his shoulder against me. "You're at work, Gav. Don't forget that alright?"

I passed him a puck as we skated together to our side of the ice. He had been firmly reminding me to keep my head in the game the past week when I would fly off the handle and end up in the penalty box. I had more minutes in the box in the previous three games than I had the entire season. It was easy to see the correlation.

"I got it," a flush of embarrassment covered my face. "I haven't been acting like a captain. I'm sorry."

"You're right. You've been acting like a human going through some shit. I'm here for all of that, always. You just need to figure out a way to compartmentalize it until after the game is over. Or channel it into your game for good, not evil," Asher shot to Cohen, the puck hitting his glove with a heavy thump.

"Now that I know what it's like to love her, I don't know how to survive without it," I admitted. "She's like oxygen to me, man. I feel like I'm suffocating without her."

Asher passed me a puck and nodded over my shoulder.

"Well, looks like you should be able to take a deep breath now."

I turned my head to see Greyson making her way down the steps with Vanessa and Kayleigh in tow. She wore the jean jacket that identified her as a WAG, and the relief I felt about that made me light-headed. They slid into their seats as warmups ended, and Greyson was getting settled when I skated past. Vanessa pinched her, and I caught Greyson's look of irritation before she looked up and smiled shyly. The new friendship with my neighbors was unexpected, but I could see they were good for her, in a way I couldn't explain. Greyson motioned me to the glass, where I focused on her mouth to read her lips.

"Still on for coffee?"

I nodded emphatically.

"Absolutely."

Her response made me smile for the first time in a week.

"Better win those face-offs."

Unfortunately, that didn't happen.

The game was a complete disaster. With three minutes left in the second period we got slammed with two unanswered goals which left me in a violent mood.

When we came back out for the third, I took the opening faceoff and noticed her watch me long enough for me to think we were fine before she looked away. I purposely iced the puck two times in a desperate attempt for her attention before Asher skated around me menacingly, like a shark with blood in the water.

"Don't you dare fuck with the team because you feel like an asshole about whatever it is you did. Icing to get her attention in a faceoff circle? Are you serious right now? Get your fucking head in this game, *Captain.*"

It worked for another shift, until I got called for a bullshit slashing penalty and ended up in the box, where I slammed my stick repeatedly against the bench and cussed out the box attendant just for doing his job. Greyson finally gave me what I was after, her undivided attention with a look of pensive frustration. She mouthed the words *total horseshit*. I needed to focus on the ice, since Asher had very pointedly reminded me I was at work. But for every two seconds I spent watching the plays, another four were spent on her. I hoped she understood the apology I sent with my eyes.

I was less than halfway through the penalty when I was hit with a full body wave of dizziness. I blinked uncontrollably and demanded a packet of smelling salts from the attendant as the world swayed under my skates. I'd just broken the pack and waved it under my nose when I looked up and realized Greyson's entire world was about to shatter. She saw it on my face, a furrow of her brow that culminated in a startled jump when a heavy hand fell on her shoulder. I could make out Jace as he knelt next to her seat, flanked by two uniformed officers. She instantly shook her head and gripped the lapels of his jacket, as if the force she exhibited holding onto him negated the words that came out of his mouth. I jumped up in the box and watched helplessly as Jace held her face in his hands and spoke into a vacant stare.

"Greyson!" I shook off the attendant, who was trying unsuccessfully to push me back down on the bench while I pounded on the glass. "Get *off* me."

"Have to sit out the full two, Gavin. You know the drill."

Across the arena Jace gathered Greyson's belongings and held onto her arm as she stood from her seat. Her legs immediately gave out and she crumbled on the stairs. The spectators around her jumped up to help, but Jace and the other officers showed their badges and waved them off. I pounded both fists against the glass and shook the box, disruptive enough to gain Asher's attention. He looked over and mouthed *what the fuck?* I pointed my glove across the ice, and he witnessed Jace scoop Greyson off the floor and wrap her around his body. I watched as he ran up the steps two at a time while Vanessa and Kayleigh looked on. The entire scene took less than ninety seconds, and I took off like a shot when I was released from the box.

I abandoned my place on the line and skated straight to the bench as I ignored the coaches and teammates who yelled at me in confusion. Vanessa met me as I entered the tunnel and I stared up at her through the metal bars.

"Her brother. It's bad. It's ... really bad," she spoke the words we all knew could come at any time. My frantic gaze landed on a security guard at the top of the stairs and I called him down.

"Get her to the locker room. *Now.*" I demanded, as panic invaded my brain. I never thought this would be reality, but now that it was the only thought I could form without blurred edges was the need to get to Greyson. "Meet me down here, I'll drive."

Asher appeared behind me in the tunnel when the game was on a television timeout. He hugged me hard against him and dropped a towel over our helmets, so we were shielded from confused fans and media.

"Go. I'll be at the hospital as soon as this is over. I'll handle everything."

"I messed things up so bad."

"And you're going to make up for it a hundred times over now, when she needs all of you to take care of all of her," Asher paused with his hand on my neck. "I think ... Olive has been trying to tell you something is up. You haven't understood it, but now that you do—prove your worth."

"I'm scared."

"I know. Be strong for Greyson, and you can fall apart with me. Go. I'll be there as soon as I can."

The noise of the stadium faded as I ran to the locker room where Vanessa and Kayleigh stood huddled together next to the security guard.

"What happened?" I asked as I sat to unlace my skates. I hurriedly stripped all my gear and stepped into a pair of sweatpants and a plain white t-shirt.

"All I heard was shot. We didn't even know her brother was a detective. Then Officer McSexy told us to stay and tell you what happened, but then Greyson said it's not your problem to handle, but I know what's going on with you two and that she really fucking needs you, whether she'll admit it or not."

I froze with my hand in my locker as I reached for my keys. If Vanessa knew about our issues, they had gotten a lot closer than I realized.

"Where are we going?"

"Rushview."

I shoved my feet into my shoes as I drug them through the parking lot and into my truck. We were halfway to the hospital before Vanessa looked at me, my jaw clenched as tightly as my hand on the steering wheel.

"He's going to be okay, right, Gavin?"

I looked over and drew on every ounce of strength I had to lie to the woman next to me.

"Of course. He's going to be fine."

CHAPTER 42
Greyson

It felt like I was on the way to my execution as Jace pulled open the car door and helped me out. The glowing red EMERGENCY sign above the sliding doors shined like a beacon straight to hell. The soft whoosh of the door welcomed me to the reality of what had happened.

Jace kept his arm tightly around my waist as the eyes of everyone in the emergency room fell on me. He cleared a straight line down the hallway and pushed through a door where the carpet and wood of the waiting room gave way to harsh fluorescent lights and sterile white walls.

"Is the floor back here tile so it's easier to clean off all the blood?"

Jace stopped short and turned to me with wide eyes.

"What kind of a question is that Greyson?"

"It's a very valid one, I think. It's all cozy out there." I pointed back to the waiting room, where my body desperately wanted to escape to. "I like it better out there. I want to go back out there."

"I know you're scared. I know this scenario is one you've thought of a million times and always pushed away. But it's real, Grey. You have to face it, and we," Jace paused and swept his arm down the hallway lined with uniformed officers and plain clothes detectives, "are here to face it with you. You are *not* alone."

"This wasn't supposed to happen. You were supposed to keep him safe."

Jace clenched his jaw and dropped his head as he ran both hands roughly up the back of his scalp.

"He was recognized. The FBI was closer than we were, but it still wasn't fast enough."

If it was possible for your heart to stop beating and stay alive, I was sure it just happened. I tried to swallow but found it impossible. The exact scenario I wondered, fretted, and bitched about was the reason I stood in the hospital, unsure if my brother was in a room or the morgue.

"The FBI? He was working with the Feds? Why? Recognized how?"

Jace shifted uncomfortably.

"One of the people he was watching brought their girlfriend around the neighborhood. She ... was an old acquaintance."

The implication wasn't lost on me, and my eyes narrowed onto Jace as I stepped away from him.

"Who is she?"

"It's not important right now."

"Don't you dare tell me what is and is not important when it comes to the reason my brother is laying back there dying," I screamed. Silence washed over the room as a tall woman pushed to the front of the group. Her curly copper hair was unruly over her green zip up, and I zeroed in on the blood that stained the white t-shirt underneath.

"I'm Special Agent Erica O'Malley. Trevor was undercover with me. I'll tell you everything."

"*Porter Cake*?" I growled, near hysterics. Special Agent O'Malley took a step back, her eyes wide.

"Excuse me?"

"You're her! I had to make your damn Christmas dessert

while *you* were not keeping Trevor safe. What the *fuck* is going on here?"

My name rang out from the other side of the room, and Gavin ran towards me, flanked by Vanessa and Kayleigh. They stopped short at the sight of Erica, clearly just as confused as I was. If I had any question they knew about the specifics of Erica's assignment, that was gone now. They were as in the dark as me.

My anger and hurt from Gavin's boundary crossing over my mom fell away as he cupped my cheeks in his hands. I just needed something, *someone*, familiar. Safe. And that was always him.

"I'm so sorry," Gavin's arms moved to circle my body and held me so tightly it felt like he was crushing my bones. "What happened?"

I couldn't take a deep breath, and I pushed against his chest to get a little room.

"His cover was blown. That's all I've been told. Your neighbor was just about to explain what exactly has been going on the last month, since apparently, she's involved in all of this," I waved my hand at Erica, who was being manhandled by her family. They pawed at her clothes, inspecting her from head to toe. My stomach turned at the realization that the blood covering her skin belonged to my brother. Gavin's head swung towards them, his eyes narrowed in confusion.

"Wait. Is she a cop?"

"Special Agent," I corrected. "FBI."

"What the fuck."

"My thoughts exactly," I sighed. "Look Gavin, about before—"

His eyes were soft but sad as he squeezed my hand.

"We don't need to talk about that right now. I'm here to support you, but I understand nothing has changed. I crossed the line and I have to own that."

I opened my mouth to respond, to tell him I overreacted to the whole thing, to beg him to confirm he still loved me like he said he did.

"Greyson, can we go talk? Privately?" Erica approached, her sister clinging to one hand and Vanessa to the other. My heart twisted with jealousy that she could hold *her* family. I instinctively reached for Gavin. He curled his fingers around mine after a beat of uncertainty.

"Whatever you have to say to me, you can say in front of him."

He turned his head, and the look we shared spoke volumes. We would be okay, if he wanted us to be. His lip quirked and he gave my hand a gentle squeeze.

"Alright then. We've been working on a drug ring operating out of Indiana. Most of the drugs have been hitting the streets here, and my team needed information. That's where Trevor came in."

My stomach dropped to my feet. The drugs. The death. He was working the case.

"He's the best detective I've ever seen. Our joint task force with the Chicago Police Department was created specifically with him in mind. We needed his brain and his knowledge to take these people down," Erica continued.

My fists clenched, and the hand that still held Gavin's was shaken gently. He watched me closely, likely to see how close I was to complete eruption.

"I really don't need to hear your compliments about how good my brother is at his job," I said through gritted teeth. "Because it seems like you're shit at yours. He was never shot before he started working with you. And God help me, if another member of my family dies at the hands of the FBI..."

"Don't threaten an FBI agent," Gavin leaned into my ear and whispered, his ever-present voice of reason. "At least not to her. You can say it all to me."

He was right, but I did not want to hear it. I wanted to knock Erica O'Malley into the ground.

"I appreciate your anger, and all I can say is I'm sorry," Erica placated. I recognized the tone of voice, that gentle cop tone that must be part of their training. It did the opposite of calm and soothe me.

"How did this happen? Who blew his cover?"

Erica closed her eyes, as if she were reluctantly reliving a nightmare.

"The whole thing was messy. We ... we fucked up."

Gavin moved so quickly I didn't have time to leap forward and choke her out, like I was in the process of doing. His body jumped in front of me, and his eyes looked so deep into mine I felt his words in my soul.

"Lemon Drop. Let her talk. You're going to hear things you don't like, but they are necessary to get the entire story. No one expects you not to be upset, but you have to try to stay calm. Can you do that? For Trevor?"

Without breaking eye contact with him I nodded, determined to stay strong.

"For Trevor, I'll do anything."

"Yeah, you will. It's your turn to step up now. For him. You've been training for this, and I know you've got it in you," he murmured.

I loved Gavin more in that moment than I had ever loved another person. More than my dad. My grandpa. My brother. This was my person, and I resolved in that second to be the woman he deserved. No more letting the fear control my life.

"I'm okay," I assured him. "I'm ready to hear it."

He stepped back and reclaimed his position next to me. Vanessa and Kayleigh had moved a few feet away. They tried to appear as if they weren't listening to every word. It was a nice try.

"Neither of us were thrilled with being away from our families," Erica said. "We shouldn't have added personal touches to our undercover house, but we were sloppy. It's the holidays and we both have traditions that are important enough to mess with our focus. Trevor brought a magnet from your bakery. He couldn't have a photo of you, obviously, but he just couldn't be without you completely. We thought it would be fine, it was stuck against the side of the fridge, but ... it was dumb."

An uncomfortable sensation prickled at the base of my skull, a memory I knew I did not like, but could not force to the forefront.

"My sister and my cousin," Erica waved to the women who had become important to me, huddled together in the corner. "They bought me a painting for my birthday last year. I love it. But I knew I couldn't bring it with me under. Your brother had a similar piece done for me, so we could hang it in the house, and I wouldn't feel so lost."

"That sounds like him," I said softly. "All he cares about is how other people feel."

Erica nodded, and a tear fell down her cheek. She swiped at it violently, as if it were a hornet threatening to sting and she was deathly allergic. It was telling. I knew then that this woman who pulled Trevor into this dangerous situation, who was the reason he was hovering between life and death, was more than a colleague.

She was in love with him.

And she held more guilt than I could ever place at her feet.

"Things were fine for weeks, and we were making headway. But then the artist that did the painting gave a televised interview, and that's when shit started to collapse."

My heart stood still as I slowly absorbed the words. Gavin's hand loosened in mine and when I turned to him, his widened eyes and pale face told me he had made the connection like I had.

"Eddie? Wait ... the Irish cross ... oh ... oh God," I swayed, and the floor under my feet seemed to fall away. Gavin caught me before I hit the ground, and I was surrounded by police and FBI agents in an instant. Gavin and Jace led me to a chair, where I practiced the breathing techniques my therapist made sure were drilled into my head so I could work through a panic attack.

"Yes. The couple who run the organization watched the interview and put some things together. They had been at Icing, and gotten Eddie's card."

"Oh no. No, no no," I moaned. "Gavin. I'm going to be sick."

He moved swiftly and drug a wastebasket to the front of my chair at the same moment I leaned over and lost the contents of my stomach. Gavin twisted my hair in a loose hold around his fist and rubbed my back while I finished being sick in front of fifty people. If I wasn't so close to full mental collapse, I would have been completely mortified.

"It's my fault," I whispered, my throat raw and sore. "I waited on them. I gave them that card. You're Siobhan."

Erica's expression softened as she nodded an affirmative.

"Yes, that was the name I was using. But none of this was your fault, Greyson. You did what you always do, and looked out for your friend. You tried to steer Eddie some business and there is *nothing* wrong with that. This is all on us."

"I got a bad vibe from them. They made me feel squicky. I knew something was wrong but I didn't know what."

"Your instincts were correct. But again, not your fault. We might have been able to swing it if it hadn't been for—" Erica paused. She looked around the room and got a slight nod from Jace, who had been in the conversation since I sat down. Bile rose up my throat.

"Just say it," I said weakly. I couldn't take much more of this. I needed the story to be over.

"Your mother is involved with this trafficking ring," Erica said bluntly, ripping the Band-Aid off in one painful motion. "She blew his cover."

CHAPTER 43
Gavin

The number of police officers in the waiting room had increased exponentially in the hour I had been there. There was still no word on Trevor, and now that Erica had dropped that parental bomb on Greyson, she was eerily calm. She had absorbed the news without so much as a hitch in her breathing. But she also hadn't spoken a word since, and her body was perched stiffly in the middle of a chair, unblinkingly staring at the double doors. I knew better than to try to push her into talking, so I went to the coffee machine on the other side of the room and made her a cup, setting it next to her where I was sure it would remain, untouched.

I had called Mila and Delaney, and when I spotted them approach, they weren't alone. Mila clung to Asher and Cohen held Delaney's hand tightly. My heart flared at the sight of them, this group of friends who had somehow become a tight knit family that dropped everything when another member was in need. Asher pulled me against his chest, roughly pressing his fist against my back.

"How is he? How is *she*?"

I swallowed hard as we both turned to look at her, frozen like a statue in the chair.

"Not good," my voice broke as I watched Mila and Delaney drop to their knees in front of her. They each took one of her hands, but even that didn't break her out of the trance of self-protection. Asher, Cohen, and I moved towards them, and when their shadows fell over her, Greyson finally looked up, blinking as if she were confused as to where she was.

"Thank you for coming," she whispered. Cohen squeezed her shoulder and Asher brought her clasped hands up to his mouth.

"You're family. Where else would we be?"

Two matching columns of tears slid down her face, and she shook her head.

"I don't deserve you. None of you."

"That's not true, Grey," Mila replied. "We're family, and family circles tighter when the chips are down."

"Not mine," Greyson said. "Mine tries to kill each other."

Mila and Delaney exchanged a knowing look, and Asher and Cohen looked to me with questions in their eyes.

"I've lied to you the whole time I've known you," she continued. "My mom isn't dead. She tried to kill me when I was a kid. And now she's the reason he might die. And I've kept it a secret because I'm ashamed that my own mother didn't love me. So how the hell could anyone else?"

Delaney sat up on her knees and cupped Greyson's face in her hands as Mila stroked her knee.

"We know, baby. We've always known."

Now that was not something I expected to hear. Greyson cocked her head and looked between her two best friends, the blank look never leaving her eyes. Mila cleared her throat and squeezed Greyson's leg.

"Delaney and I were curious about you when we met in school. You were so blasé about the fact you came from a famous family, and we knew less than nothing about hockey. It was obvious it was important to you, since you watched every single game, and we wanted to understand. So ... we looked you up."

A lump wedged itself in my throat as Mila and Delaney

confessed to this secret. Asher stared at me until I met his eyes, and I gave him a barely perceptible nod, confirmation I knew about this.

"You never talked about your family besides Trevor and your grandpa, and we would never want to ask you something that would upset you, so we decided we would fess up whenever you told us about your past, but not bring it up before then," Delaney said gently. "Then the years passed, and you never did, and it just became something that didn't matter."

"What do you mean it didn't matter," Greyson cried, as she looked between them with wide eyes. "My mother tried to smother me with a pillow. I can't sleep around other people. I push away anything that makes me happy. I'm a mess of issues, and you think I can be a true friend?"

She lifted her eyes to me, and her face completely crumbled as she waved her hand at me.

"Fuck, I destroyed my relationship because he tried to protect me from ... this. This scenario. That woman," she shook her head as she wept. "I'm so sorry, Gavin. I'm so fucking sorry. You deserve so much better than I've given you."

Now all our friends were staring at me in surprise, since we had not discussed our fight with anyone, aside from my broad strokes with Asher. It was difficult to explain when the reason behind it all was a secret. Or so we both thought.

"We will always be us, as long as you want there to be an us," I assured her. "You have carried around so much guilt, so many secrets, for so long. It would affect anyone. I love you and I always will. We all have baggage. Because of you, I realized I haven't dealt with mine."

The family confessional was interrupted when the doors swung open and a man in black scrubs emerged. Everyone seated snapped to attention, and Asher and I each slid a hand under her arms. We helped her out of the chair to face the doctor who had the potential to destroy her life.

CHAPTER 44
Greyson

"Who is the family?" The surgeon's serious face scanned the room.

"Me. I'm his family. I'm Greyson, his sister," I replied. His eyes softened, like he was looking at his own child.

"Greyson, I'm Dr. Dubois."

"Do I still have my best friend, Doctor?"

"Trevor suffered some very severe injuries. In addition to the gunshot wounds, he had a depressed skull fracture that resulted in a subdural hematoma. We've released the pressure on his brain, and he's resting comfortably. But I can't say he's in the clear yet. We're going to monitor him closely for a few days, but the next twenty-four hours are the most critical."

"Can I see him?"

"Just for a minute. He won't be awake, but I can't say whether or not he'll know you're there."

Gavin squeezed my hip and gently pushed me forward. I steeled my feet against the floor and tightened my grip on his arm. "No, you have to come with me."

"Just you," Dr. Dubois was gentle, but firm. I forced myself to shuffle after him, like a kid on the way to the principal's office.

When I looked over my shoulder as we reached the door Gavin gave me a small, reassuring nod.

Dr. Dubois held the door and I meekly followed him down the harshly lit hallway to a recovery room with a uniformed police officer stationed outside. The reality of everything hit me in that moment, when I had to literally get through a guard to see my brother, and my knees buckled before I crossed into the room.

Dr. Dubois was quick and grabbed me under the arms before I hit the ground. He calmly talked me through the fact my brother looked different than I was used to and not to let his appearance take over my emotions. I took a handful of deep breaths before I lifted my eyes off the floor and onto Trevor. I instantly regretted it.

"That is not my brother."

"I know it's jarring."

Jarring was most definitely not the correct word for the black and blue monster hooked up to tubes and machines that laid before me. Trevor's face was so swollen I couldn't make out any of his individual, discernible features. A section of his hair was gone, shaved for the surgery to relieve the pressure on the brilliant brain that had solved so many of my problems. There was a bandage wrapped around his head and I couldn't have counted all the wounds on his body if I tried. The gown draped over him made him seem like a fragile doll, and the fact I knew there was evidence of a gunshot wound underneath made my stomach roll. My feet were as heavy as concrete and I couldn't do anything but stare at the bed.

"He looks terrible."

"Yes. He does. It's going to take a lot of time and work to get back to normal," Dr. Dubois replied as he gently pushed me closer to the bed. "Touch him. Hold his hand. Let him know you're here."

"I thought you said he won't know," my voice cracked as I softly laid my hand over Trevor's, which was completely still and surprisingly warm. I wasn't sure what I expected, but the temperature of his skin made me feel marginally better, as if the fact he wasn't ice cold was proof he wasn't dead.

"He may, he may not. The brain is an extraordinarily complex place, and every case responds differently. It never hurts to talk. Wouldn't you rather say it all in the off chance he might hear than say nothing on the possibility he doesn't?"

"He's all the family I have."

"Based on the support in that waiting room, I don't think that's true. I'm going to leave you with him now. If you have any questions, let a nurse know. They will get a hold of me. Don't worry about disrupting me. You won't. I work for Trevor, and in extension, you."

"Thank you, Dr. Dubois. For saving my brother's life."

When he left, I stood awkwardly at Trevor's bedside for a handful of minutes. Each time I moved closer I stopped when I was close enough to touch him and backed up until I was almost out of the room. This was so wrong. Trevor wasn't helpless, and he sure as hell wasn't weak. But as I saw him laid up in a hospital bed, unconscious and unable to move, I was reminded he wasn't a superhero.

He was just a man.

I folded my legs underneath me as I sat next to the bed and rested both elbows on the muted green blanket tucked under the mattress. Trevor's chest moved up and down, and I focused on the predictable movement rather than look at the battered face I couldn't believe belonged to him.

"I don't know what to say," I started. I felt ridiculous and hoped the cop outside couldn't hear me. At the thought I stood and walked to the door. When I popped my head into the hall he looked over and confirmed I could slide it shut for privacy. Once I was safely insulated, I sat down again and gathered his hand into both of mine as I laid my forehead down.

"I'm so sorry. I know I couldn't have done anything, but I should have known." I wiped a tear and watched him closely, deflated to see no reaction. I knew better than to expect anything, but part of me still believed my strong brother wasn't lying helpless as he fought for his life. "I promise, when this is all over, I'm going to be a better sister to you. You've spent long enough worrying about me, instead of living your own life. That's over now. I won't be selfish anymore. I swear."

A throat cleared behind me and I jumped out of the chair, shocked to see a nurse in purple scrubs with her hands clasped in front of her. I hadn't heard the door open, and I wasn't sure how long she'd been listening.

"We're going to get him moved upstairs soon. Once he's settled, we'll bring you up."

"Can I stay?"

She hesitated and gave me a sympathetic smile. It was obvious the answer was no, but she didn't want to break my heart and say it.

"His condition would prohibit overnight visitors, but I'll check with Dr. Dubois for sure, okay?"

I nodded in appreciation and gave Trevor a light kiss on his forehead before I followed her back into the waiting room. Gavin moved forward automatically and wrapped his arms around me.

The entire group was moved upstairs into a private waiting area, and I made sure Trevor was settled. Gavin hovered outside the room when I emerged and wrapped his palm around the back of my neck. He pulled me headfirst into his chest and I let his heartbeat soothe me into a semblance of calm.

"I'm here, Greyson. For everything that's coming, for whatever you need while he's still here. I talked to management. I'm on personal leave indefinitely."

It took a handful of seconds for his words to fully sink in and when I looked up, I found everything I'd ever needed in his eyes. He had rearranged his entire life for me, before we had even ironed out the issues that had kept us apart.

"I can't ask you to do that."

"You didn't. We're a team. We're stronger together," Gavin

replied with a grim smile. "Asher went to get some clothes from my house for both of us. I'm not leaving you here."

I had never trusted my feelings to lead me to a safe space. But as I stood in a harshly lit hallway that smelled like astringent and bleach and faced this man who fought through my fear to get me to accept his love, I knew my soul had found its mate.

"I..." I paused and cleared my throat as my voice gave out. "I'm not confident he's going to wake up. How do I go on if he dies and the last conversation we had was a fight?"

Gavin's hands moved to my cheeks, and he focused the full weight of his stare on me. It was as heavy as a pile of bricks, and I buckled under the pressure.

"Your dad will not let him die."

"Gavin," his name came out on a whisper, and every tragic moment of my life flashed through my mind. "My dad can't protect him now. He's gone. If Trevor goes too ... I want you to be happy, and if he goes ... I won't be me anymore. I won't survive."

Gavin was rough when he pulled me against his chest, and his fingers bit as they dug into my back. "Don't you dare say that Greyson. Do you hear me? You think he'd want that? You think he'd accept you throwing in the towel? No way."

"I don't know how to be the strong one. It's always been his job, whether it's fair or not. How do I do this? What if he isn't Trevor anymore? If he doesn't know who we are, or he can't walk or talk, or feed himself? What if—"

Gavin pressed his lips to mine. The shock of it knocked the wind out of me. In the two weeks since he had last done it, I had forgotten the instantaneous way his kiss salved my soul. My fingers gripped his shirt, desperate to pull him closer, to hold him against my heart where I never wanted him to leave. When he pulled back, he wiped my wet cheeks with his thumbs. "Then we deal with it. You and me, Eddie, Asher and Cohen, the girls, Jace and the CPD. Together. As a family."

"As a family."

"For infinity."

CHAPTER 45
Gavin

J ace returned from the cafeteria and handed me a much-needed cup of coffee. I took a gulp of scalding liquid and held in the curse that wanted to fly off my tongue. I was tired, uncomfortable, and needed a shower. I knew this hospital was my home for the foreseeable future and had no idea how to navigate the situation. I hated being out of control, and this was as far out of my comfort zone as I could get.

Greyson rubbed her hand over the back of her neck, which jolted me out of my thoughts. I immediately replaced it with my own, eager to do anything to ease even a fraction of her stress. She dropped her head and closed her eyes while she accepted the massage with a sigh. Her shoulders relaxed and she reached out for my coffee. She didn't react to the temperature after a long sip and handed it back before she fell against my shoulder and closed her eyes.

"I'm so tired. How am I going to get any sleep here, Gavin? I can't leave. I *won't* leave. But I can't even sleep around you, how am I going to sleep in a hospital with a hundred people milling around? It's going to be impossible," her voice trembled, and I smoothed her hair back from her forehead with a kiss on her temple.

"I'll take care of it," I promised, not sure how I was going to work it out, but happy to have a purpose. She shivered against me, and I texted Asher to see how long he was going to be. It had barely been sent when I spotted him down the hall, an overnight bag slung over each shoulder.

"Thank you, Ash," Greyson managed weakly as she unzipped her bag and pawed through. She pulled out an oversized sweatshirt and shoved her arms in as she burrowed into it. "I feel better already."

"Anything for you Gigi," Asher replied with a ruffle to her hair. He turned to me and curled his nose in disgust. "You smell like you ate the asshole out of a dumpster, man."

I shrugged and pulled deodorant out of my bag and swiped it under my shirt. "I had something more important on my mind than showering. I just wanted to get here."

Greyson furrowed her forehead and leaned over to sniff me. She made me self-conscious when her facial expression confirmed I smelled less than fresh, and I folded my arms over my chest like it would stop the body odor that poured off my skin.

"I love you for literally walking out of a game to be here for me, but you can go home."

"Not going to happen," I replied instantly. "I'm not leaving this hospital unless it's with you. I'm here until you're not."

"You need to shower," Greyson replied gently as she rested her hand on my thigh. "Now that it's been called to attention, you don't smell amazing."

I flushed in embarrassment and decided I'd head to the bathroom and do the best I could with hand soap and paper towels. I turned to let her know I'd be right back, and she pulled my head next to her mouth.

"Just so you know, for future reference, I like it when you don't shower and just take me when you're still in game mode. I swear, I can feel the aggression from the game sweat. It turns me on hardcore. To me, you smell like a future incredible orgasm. It's not bad, it's just not for now."

Although it was an incredibly inappropriate conversation for the situation and I knew she was wavering between numb disbelief and pure shock, the words filled my heart. Because I knew, without a doubt, we were back together, and going to be okay.

"I appreciate that. A lot. I'm going to go clean up and change, and then I'll figure out a way to get you some sleep."

"I don't deserve you," Greyson whispered as I wiped one errant tear off her cheek. I kissed her hard as I stood with my bag.

I hustled to the nearest men's room and left her with Asher on one side and Jace on the other, Mila and Delaney seated on the floor at her feet. Her support system was strong and intense, and I wasn't concerned to leave her for a handful of moments since I knew who was there to watch out for her.

I quickly cleaned myself up before I texted Mattie to tell her what happened. She surprised me when she answered instantly, since it was only five in the morning. What wasn't a shock was her offer to hop on the next plane to do anything we needed her to. Instead, I asked her to relay the information to the rest of the family. After that, I took a moment to myself and gripped the sides of the sink so hard my knuckles turned white. After a few deep breaths, I gave myself a pep-talk in the mirror before I went back to the uncertainty and fear of the waiting room. Here, in the calm of the men's room, with nothing but squeaky floors and bright lights, I could pretend everything was normal. Although I knew it was possible, I never considered anything could happen to Trevor that would throw Greyson's precarious mental scale off balance and leave her on the brink of disaster. I'd watched her quietly from the background for years but now that I was front and center, I didn't know what to do beyond hold her and let her know she wasn't alone. This was a test I wasn't sure I was prepared for, and I hoped like hell I wouldn't fail miserably.

When I got back to the waiting room it felt like no time had passed, nothing different aside from slight shifts in the positions of the people who waited for news. Delaney was now lying in Mila's lap, while Mila had one hand wrapped around Greyson's ankle. Jace's hands were clasped in front of his mouth, his elbows on his knees, and Asher had his arm around Greyson's shoulder with her head against his chest. A nurse approached the group, and Greyson jumped up.

"Is he awake?"

"No," the nurse replied gently. "But I spoke to Dr. Dubois, and he decided you can stay with your brother tonight. He cleared your boyfriend, too."

Greyson turned to me, her expression hopeful.

"Will you stay with me?"

"Of course," I replied automatically. "I'll be wherever you need me to be."

After she told our friends they could leave and they all told her they weren't going anywhere, we followed the nurse into the private room. I sucked in a breath before I could stop myself when I laid eyes on Trevor for the first time. The sight put into full focus just how serious the situation was. Greyson walked to the edge of the bed and squeezed his hand. I set our bags on the floor next to the couch and looked around. The television on the wall was on, the volume muted. There was a rocking chair next to the bed, and a pillow and two blankets stacked on the windowsill behind the couch. I picked up the pillow and tucked it into the closet.

"The couch pulls out. It will be tight for both of you, probably not very comfortable," the nurse sounded apologetic, as if we expected Four Seasons accommodations.

"This is perfect, thank you," I said. After she left, Greyson stepped away from the bed and looked at the bathroom.

"I just realized I haven't peed in like eight hours. I'm going to go remedy that before I make a mess of the floor," she bit her lip and glanced at Trevor. "Will you sit with him while I'm in there? I don't want him to be alone."

"You got it, Lemon Drop."

Our hands met as we moved in opposite directions, and our pinkies linked. Things felt normal. Well, as normal as possible. I dropped into the chair and forced myself to look at Trevor. He had always been intimidating, giving off an aura of 'I don't give a fuck and don't try to fuck with me' so seeing him like this was disconcerting. There was no preparation for this scenario.

"I tried to do right by you, Trevor," I started, my voice cutting out. I rested my elbows on my knees and dropped my head. "I'm sorry I failed. You asked me to do one simple thing, and I fucked it up."

"What are you talking about?"

I hadn't heard Greyson come out of the bathroom, so when her voice appeared over my shoulder, I damn near jumped out of my skin. I stood to face her and looked back at Trevor, as if he would come to my rescue.

"Hey, feel better?"

Her lips thinned into a straight line, and she brushed away the hair that had escaped from her messy bun.

"Don't try to change the subject. You know I heard that. What did you mean by he asked you to do one simple thing?"

CHAPTER 46

Greyson

avin pulled his phone out of his pocket and opened it to a text thread before he wordlessly handed it over. I scanned the top to see my brother's name, and scrolled to the beginning of the conversation. Trevor initiated it the day he went undercover. Judging by the time stamp, he had barely been out of Icing when he sent it.

TREVOR

I'm going to be out of touch for...probably a while. I need you to take care of her, Halstead. Promise me you'll keep her safe.

GAVIN

Of course I will. But is there something she needs safety from? Is it your mom?"

TREVOR

She's too close for comfort. Make sure she stays away from my sister.

GAVIN

How?

TREVOR

By any means necessary. Do not let me down.
I'm counting on you.

GAVIN

You've got my word. I'll do anything I need to
do. She will be safe.

I looked up to find Gavin chewing his lip. He seemed nervous, like this information was going to cause me to rip his head off. I couldn't blame him.

"Why didn't you tell me?" I asked, reading and rereading the messages.

"I would have," Gavin trailed off. I tore my attention off the phone and onto him. I read his implication loud and clear.

"But I didn't let you," I finished, as I gave him the phone back. He held onto my hand, and I looked at our intertwined fingers. "I messed things up so badly, Gavin. I'm so sorry. It's not enough. But it's all I have."

Gavin led me to the sofa, where I could still see Trevor. When we sat, he tried to release my hand but I clung to it, as if he would vaporize if I weren't touching him. He gave me a gentle squeeze.

"I don't need an apology. Because you were right. About everything."

"No, I wasn't," I protested. "You did what Trevor asked of you. Knowing this, it makes complete sense. This wasn't your fault. It was mine."

"But it isn't. Yes, he asked me to keep you safe. But hiring an investigator, that was all me. And to be completely honest, I don't regret it. I'd do it again. She's dangerous," Gavin paused, with a quick look at Trevor. "I guess we all know that now."

I wasn't given all the information of what had happened, so my mind had gone wild on scenarios. Had she been the one to pull the trigger? I knew she had no qualms when it came to attempted murder of her children. Or had she simply told someone else who he was, so her hands were clean? Either way, she was responsible, and I was dying inside.

"Still, I said awful things to you. Things that you did not deserve. Things that—"

Gavin leaned forward and captured the guilty words on my lips with his own.

"Things that made me think about my own unpacked baggage," he murmured, as another soft kiss dusted my lips. "After Olive died, I vowed to myself I would never let anything bad happen to another person I loved. Logically, I'm aware there was nothing I could do for her. But that seed of trauma planted early and the roots got deeper the older I got. When I fell in love with you, and learned about your past, that instinct reared its head in a way I had never experienced. When KJ attacked you ... fuck, Greyson, I seriously considered murdering him. Like ... really. It scared me."

"That wasn't your fault, either."

"No, but it was a time I failed to keep you safe, and I decided that would never happen again. Not on my watch."

"You sound just like Trevor," I said sadly, my gaze locked on my brother.

"I wonder if his trauma responded like mine. To what happened to you, to what she did. Because from what I've seen, his main focus is protecting the people he loves, too," Gavin said. "I should have told you about that text from the day I got it. I don't have an excuse, aside from wanting to protect you. I should have told you about the private investigator. But I promise you, Greyson. From this day forward, all lines of communication are open. I will never keep anything from you, ever again."

I turned back to him and swallowed hard. The only sound in the room was the steady beep of the monitor attached to Trevor.

I was tired.

"I promise not to push you away. I've spent my whole life running from happiness. I don't want to do that anymore."

Gavin held me against him as the last of my adrenaline dissipated through my bloodstream. I laid down with my head on his thigh as he unfolded a blanket over me. He crossed his feet at the ankles as he extended his legs in front of him and draped a second blanket over himself.

"Close your eyes. You might not be able to sleep with me in a bed, but we know you can sleep in my lap," Gavin found what he was looking for on television, and I smiled to see Bing Crosby singing about snow on a train car. "If you feel comfortable enough to sleep, that's great. If not, we'll watch White Christmas and then I'll go sit in the hall for a few hours so you can get some rest."

"Damn, how I love you," I said, as I lowered my eyelids and promptly fell asleep.

CHAPTER 47
Greyson

I hovered at the door; my purse slung across my chest like a shield. Every step I took towards leaving had me sliding two steps towards Trevor's bed. Gavin watched me from the rocking chair, an amused look peering up at me from his backwards Falcons hat.

"You have to get out the door to make it to the parking lot, where you'll have to make it into my truck to get to Icing."

I shot him a look before my focus settled on the bed, where I swore, I saw Trevor smirk. He still hadn't opened his eyes, but according to the staff, he was 'out of the woods.'

I called bullshit.

Until my brother could speak my name and tell me he wanted a White Claw, I wasn't believing one damn word.

"I should stay," I said, as Gavin reached his hand out. I scooted around the bed and fell into his lap, resting my head on his shoulder.

"I've got this, babe. If he wakes up, I'll call you before both eyes are open. The shop is ten minutes away. You can be back in no time," Gavin squeezed my hip as we both stared at Trevor. The bruises were healing, moving from deep purple to a hideous yellow-green. I was no longer waiting on pins and needles about if he would wake up. Now it was a waiting game. *When* was the question.

"I can't do it, Gav," the finality in my statement was clear, and I slid off his lap. "The furthest I can go is the cafeteria, which is where I'm going now. Those breakfast hot pocket things are actually amazing. You want?"

He sighed with a nod.

"I can *feel* the vibrations coming off you, Lemon Drop. The need to work is physically manifesting itself on your body."

"Don't start," I warned. "It's not that I don't trust you. I just … when he wakes, he needs to know I'm here."

"One with sausage, one with bacon. And a coffee," Gavin winked as he dropped his head to his book. He knew he wasn't going to win, and his quest to get me to do pursue a 'normal' activity was abandoned.

The line in the cafeteria was longer than it had been in a week, and when I approached Trevor's room with a bag of food in one hand and a tray of drinks in the other, I heard a familiar rough laugh that made me stop in my tracks. Gavin's voice filtered into the hall, and I held my breath outside the room.

"So that's a yes?"

"Of course, Halstead. I'm sorry I caused a rift between you two. Honestly, I never thought anything would push her to cut you off. She waited for you for so long, it never crossed my mind she would get so mad."

I hurried into the room, my eyes falling on the bed, where Trevor sat up against the pillows.

"RayRay," he smiled bashfully, and I didn't even try to hold back the tears. "Come here, you. I'm okay."

Gavin came and took the food from me as I advanced forward. Trevor scooted over, making room for me to climb into the bed next to him. I wept against his hospital gown, hot tears soaking straight through.

"I'm going to make some calls, let my family know you're awake," Gavin said, with a squeeze to my ankle. Trevor lifted his chin and nodded, smoothing his large palm over my hair.

"Thanks, Halstead," he said, his voice scratchy with disuse. I looked back with a watery smile and a mouthed *I love you*. When Gavin pulled the door closed behind him, the room was instantly silent, aside from the beep of Trevor's monitor.

"We should call the nurses. Tell them you're awake," I said, my head firmly against his chest. The beating of his heart soothed me, a predictable rhythm that told me my brother was with me.

"They can wait," he replied. "I'm so sorry you've had to go through so much because of me, RayRay."

"Trevor Hudson Park. You shut up."

He laughed, immediately followed by a wince. I carefully shifted, not to jostle his wound.

"It's been awful," I admitted. "But you're the one it happened to. How are *you?*"

He sighed, absently running his hand over my hair.

"I don't know yet," he said. "How much have you been told?"

"Agent O'Malley told me enough to force me to tell everyone in my life the truth about Mom."

He shook his head and scrubbed a hand down his face.

"Shit. I'm so sorry, RayRay."

"Did she ... was she the one who shot you?" I asked hesitantly.

"No."

I let out a breath, surprised to find myself relieved by that.

"I don't believe it was intentional. I knew she was living in Gary, but I had no intel that suggested she was involved in the operation," Trevor said through clenched teeth. "We went to a Christmas party at the neighbors house and in walks Mom. She was dating the father of the head of the trafficking ring."

"Of all the gin joints," I said weakly. Trevor laughed humorlessly.

"Right? She was just as surprised as I was, I think. She said

'Trevor? Is that you?' I said she must be mistaken, but she kept pushing, starting to cause a scene."

"That sounds like the mom I remember."

"Erica—Agent O'Malley—came over and asked if I was alright, using my undercover name. Mom flew off the handle when she told her she had the wrong person. Screamed 'I think I know my son's name!'

"I might have been able to save it if her boyfriend—that sounds so wrong, by the way—didn't pop off and say 'the cop?' There was a gun at my head before I could even form a thought."

My stomach fell at the picture in my head of a gun pointed at his.

"I met them. The neighbors. They came into the shop and I gave them Eddie's card. I started this," I said quietly. "I could have warned you somehow."

Trevor shook his head and tightened his grip on me.

"I knew. They came to dinner with a box from Icing. There's been a car on you since that night," Trevor paused as I looked up sharply. "Protecting you is my number one priority, even if I can't do it myself."

I knew he hadn't had time to process any of it, and the come down of the experience was going to affect him in a serious way. I wasn't sure I wanted any more information, but it was up to him if he needed to talk about it.

"Trev—"

Trevor swallowed hard, a war in his mind etched over his face. "Things were precarious from the jump. But we got everything on video, so if nothing else, we took them down. The rest, I don't think you need to hear, and I'm not so sure I'm ready to talk about it."

"If and when you want to—*need* to, I'm always here. And if you don't want to talk to me, I know a good therapist," I joked.

Trevor dropped his head against the pillow with a weak grin.

"Go ahead and call those nurses. Now that I'm awake, I can tell how much everything fucking hurts."

That was when I took a breath, and felt, for the first time since Jace pulled me out of the Falcons game, that my brother truly was okay.

And that meant *I* was okay.

CHAPTER 48
Gavin

Greyson insisted I get back to the team once it was clear Trevor would survive. As much as I wanted to refuse, she turned those eyes on me, batted her lashes, and used her feminine charms to get her way. I'd managed to not completely give in until after the second blowjob, when she'd kept her eyes locked on mine as she pulled back and swallowed. At that point I would have promised her I'd grab the moon out of the sky and present it on a platter made of golden glitter. So, there I was, in the visitor locker room in Miami after a grueling game that had me physically exhausted, when all I wanted was to still be on leave and available for anything she needed from me.

That night in the hospital had changed her, in more ways than one. After she exposed her past to everyone, her entire aura had lightened, and it was like a new Greyson had been born.

I'd just finished getting dressed when a call from her lit up my phone, and I answered with a smile as I zipped up my bag.

"Hey baby. Did you get Trevor settled?"

"Yes. Honestly, I'm glad he's staying at Erica's because he was being a dickwad. If I had to be the one nursing him back to health, he might not make it."

When the plans were made for Trevor's recovery, the full

NICO DANIELS

extent of his and Erica's 'fake' relationship was realized. There was
not one fake thing about it, and almost dying had made both of
them realize there was no excuse to waste time. Erica wanted
Trevor to stay at her house where there was always at least one
person who could be available in the event he needed something.
Her bedroom was on the first floor, which made it easier for him
to move around than at his own home, and she was right about
having someone around. Greyson had been impatient to get back
to the bakery once Trevor was awake and demanding to get back
to work, so to have the chance to do that was something she
accepted with open arms.

"He's continuing his run of being a stellar patient then?"

"Gavin, I swear. If their relationship withstands this, that
woman deserves a gold-plated vibrator that delivers orgasms like
pizzas."

"Or she could just get her orgasms from her boyfriend."

Greyson gagged and paused as I heard a familiar beep through
the phone. My heart stilled at the possibility she was where I
hoped she was.

"That's truly disgusting and ruined my appetite, darling man
of mine. Speaking of, if you're up for a late dinner I was thinking I
could have something waiting for you," Greyson paused and
cursed under her breath as the beep got louder. "Since I'm sure
you've already gotten the alert that I'm breaking into your house,
can you shut this damn thing off?"

I smiled to myself and opened the notification from the security company to verify it was a legitimate entry, and the line
quieted around her. My dick was suddenly very impatient to get
to Chicago, and I adjusted myself at the thought of her in my
house. I could almost smell the lemon sugar scent that followed
every move she made.

"I'll be very hungry for you when I get home," I murmured
softly, as I shoved my feet into my shoes while I held the phone
between my shoulder and ear.

Greyson laughed, the sound full of sexual frustration and

need. "So, I shouldn't bother to cook? You just want me laid out on the table?"

"You and cupcakes are all I need," I dropped my voice, even though none of the guys were around. "I can't wait to get inside you and bring in the new year with a *bang*."

"I sure hope you make it," Greyson sighed, as soft music filtered through the line. "The weather is awful. I'm worried you won't be able to get into Chicago."

I hadn't considered that, and the idea I might miss another New Year's kiss with her made me feel like I swallowed a bowling ball.

"Nah, we'll make it."

"I love you for your optimism Gav, but you aren't seeing what I am."

She switched to a video call and I was met with a winter wonderland out of my front door. The snow swirled so roughly it looked like a white tornado.

"Well, I'm going to say I'll be there in two hours until I hear otherwise," I answered as I slid my arms into my coat. "Be ready to get ravished."

She blushed, and I sent every prayer I had up to the sky that I'd be able to get home on time. The last few weeks had been bizarre to say the least. Going from a blissful relationship to breaking up was emotional enough. Then, the situation with Trevor, the opening of the book of Greyson's past with everyone in her life, and the uncertainty of what was going to happen to her mom, and I was spent. When it was obvious Trevor would recover Greyson started to leave for a few hours at a time to go home to shower and get some rest. The entire trafficking ring had been arrested, resulting in a deep breath out of everyone who had been quietly keeping tabs on her. After Trevor woke up and they had a chance to speak, she had confessed that she had noticed the tail he'd put on her. It seemed like we all had an inkling she could have been in danger, but kept it to ourselves so as not to alarm each other. There were no more secrets, and once it was clear safety had been established, everyone relaxed.

At the tail end of the week long road trip we were on, I was tired. Tired of the emotions, tired of missing her, tired of the uncertainty. The only thing I hoped for out of the new year was for life to go back to normal.

"Call me when you get on the plane, okay? I want to know when to start my countdown. If you get in the air on time you should get home with a few minutes to spare before midnight," Greyson said softly. "Thanks for being you, Canada. I couldn't have made it through this without you."

"You'll never have to face anything alone again, Greyson. I'll call you in a bit. Get naked. I love you."

I'd barely hung up and made my way to my seat on the bus when she texted to tell me she'd be getting naked exactly two minutes before I got home, because there was no way she was going to sit around the house with razor sharp nipples for two hours. When we got to the airport it was immediately communicated we would not get to Chicago on time, and to settle in for a delay of at least a few hours. Fucking fabulous. It was already almost ten, and we wouldn't take off until at least one in the morning. I sighed in defeat and lifted my phone to my ear to deliver the bad news. Greyson answered with excitement and was almost giddy, which made me feel like shit when I had to tell her I wasn't boarding the plane.

"Looks like your clothes will be staying on longer than we hoped," I ground out, frustrated with the universe. She was quiet for a beat, and I wondered if there would be tears in her voice when she spoke, but she surprised me yet again when she clapped into the receiver.

"Perfect! Oh, Gavin, this is *perfect!*"

"Elaborate please? I was kind of under the impression you were as impatient to see me as I am you."

"Obviously," Greyson clucked with exasperation. "But this is good. I'm so tired. You're probably tired. If I get a solid three hours of sleep now, I can be up and caffeinated by the time you land in Chicago. I'll be ready to *go* when you get here."

It wasn't a bad plan.

Five and a half hours later I was in my car as I drove through a damn blizzard on my way home. I was both concerned and excited when I couldn't get her on the phone. Part of me thought she had given into fear about staying over and gone home. The other part was worked up as I thought of her spread out on the kitchen table as she waited for me to have her for dessert.

It took three times as long to get home as it should have, and I was over the entire night when I turned onto my street and passed the O'Malley house, lit up like a Christmas tree. My own house was dark aside from a lamp in the front hall. The garage door rumbled and a full smile crossed my lips when I saw Greyson's car settled in the middle bay.

I dropped my bag inside the door and kicked off my shoes as I raced down the hall. By the time I got to the kitchen I had unbuttoned my shirt and was surprised to find the room empty. There was a lone cupcake in the middle of the counter, illuminated by the under-cabinet lights. When I got closer, I noticed the piece of paper shoved under the wrapper, the standard explanation card Greyson wrote out for every cupcake flavor displayed at Icing.

A NEW BEGINNING:
In Spain, the new year is celebrated by eating twelve grapes at midnight. This tradition brings prosperity and luck to the coming year. While we aren't Spanish and we couldn't celebrate the chimes of the clock together, this grape cake is my interpretation of the prosperity I've already found by opening my entire heart to you. I'm giving you all of me, tonight and forever.

I've heard the second part of this tradition is that you have to consume the grapes while wearing red underwear, and if you'd like to eat someone wearing red underwear, you can

find me upstairs. (I'm blushing like a maniac writing this.)
Anyway ... I love you Canada. Through all of this you've
proven you're in it, and while I knew it before, now I trust
it. I trust you. With everything.

I picked up the light-yellow cake and held it to my nose as hints of Moscato and citrus filled my nostrils. The top of the cupcake wasn't as domed and puffy as I was used to from her cakes, instead topped with a crunchy sugar crust and a dollop of yellow cream in place of the usual artistic swirl of icing. I carried both the cake and the card as I headed to the steps and groaned at the luscious lemon that exploded on my tongue when I licked the cream. As I burst into my room my smile fell and faded into full and total shock to find my beautiful angel. Asleep. In my bed. Fully relaxed, her chest rose and fell in a hypnotic rhythm, and her head rested on my side. The thing that made my breath catch in my throat, however, was the pillow she had her head on. I had never seen anything more beautiful than her asleep, her hair spread out like a halo on top of the fluffy pillow. I watched her for a moment before I moved to leave the room. I'd stay in a guest room so she could sleep peacefully and undisturbed. I'd just turned my back when her soft voice called out.

"Where are you going?"

I turned slowly and found her as she watched me with darkened eyes full of emotion. She tossed back the covers to expose her red silk nighty, the cups that held her chest lined in red lace and the hem that rode up her milky thigh as she stretched her leg out across the bed.

"I wasn't sure you wanted me to stay," I replied hoarsely as I crossed the room and set the cake down on the nightstand. I reached for her and ran my thumb across her jaw and under her chin.

"I guess my note wasn't as clear as I hoped," Greyson sat up on her knees and wrapped her hands around the back of my neck as I planted mine against the smooth silk that fell over her hips.

"I'm ready for the next chapter of my life, Gavin. With you. I'm not going to let the fear hold me hostage anymore. I know that as long as I'm in your arms I'm safe, and that includes the darkest parts of the night."

I swallowed around the lump in my throat and my nose prickled at her declaration. She watched my eyes glisten and leaned into my lips. Our tears mingled as we moved into the next stage of our lives in that one moment.

"This is the best gift I've ever been given," I said against her mouth, suddenly in no hurry to get her undressed. This was better, and I wanted it to go on as long as possible. Greyson rested her forehead against mine. She pressed her thumbs into my cheeks as the heat from her body radiated through my shirt.

"It's hard to believe it's only been three months since we became us. Throw in the ten days of separation, then Trevor, and the changes that have happened in my life since September have been extreme. But your love has been the only constant," Greyson smiled sadly, a slight upturn of her lips. "Day to day, I wasn't sure what the news from the doctor was going to hold, but I knew with certainty you would be there, for whatever it was. To be held, to yell, to cry. Any of it. Some days, all of it. But your dedication to me never wavered. I love you with everything I've got and I'm going to spend the rest of my life proving I'm worthy of your devotion."

Greyson reached over and pulled something out from behind one of my pillows. It was wrapped in blue and gold glittered paper, and she sat back and waited expectantly for me to peel back the wrap. The vision of her in that negligee with her hands clasped in her lap as her upper arms pushed her cleavage together had me somewhat distracted, and it wasn't until she dropped her head to the side in an unspoken question I snapped out of my daydream. I unwrapped the gift to find a throw pillow, dark blue with stars covering the soft fabric. Flowing script covered the front in a saying that made my heart stand still. "Stars Can't Shine Without Darkness." I clenched my jaw and looked up in shock to see her fiddle with her pendant as she chewed her lip. I traced the words that had been Olive's mantra, so stunned I could do nothing but stare at the words I hadn't heard spoken in sixteen years.

"What is this?" My voice came out sharp, and when she frowned, I hoped I hadn't ruined the beautiful moment.

"I thought a pillow would be a super meaningful gift to show you how much I trust you. I'm sorry, did I mess up?"

"No. Not even close," I assured her. "This is perfect. But the saying ... how did you know about the saying?"

Her confusion was evident as she looked from the pillow to me and back again. She had no idea what I was talking about. Yet another indicator she was my soulmate, and that Olive had sent a sign to let go of my guilt and finally live my life with happiness.

"It just felt right when I saw it. Because nights are the hardest, and you've been my shining star since we met. My light in the dark."

I moved forward and knelt on the mattress as I pulled her against me possessively and set the pillow carefully against the bed.

"This is something Olive used to say. These were," I paused and choked up as I remembered the day she became a part of the universe she loved so much, "her last words. This was the last thing she said, and somehow you found the quote and felt such a strong pull to it you chose it for this truly amazing gift."

Olive had been the calm and collected one throughout her entire illness, always the one who made everyone else feel better when they came to visit. The last moments were spent with me forcing my tears to stay in, because I would not have her feel like she needed to keep me together in the final minutes of her short life. I clearly hadn't done a very good job because she had laid her head on my chest and reached for my hand. She told me not to be scared for her, and whenever I needed advice to look up to the sky at night because stars can't shine without darkness.

I realized I was crying when Greyson pulled my head to her

chest and held it there. The steady beat of her heart brought me back to the present, to the reality of the night, and what my life was now. We were a team, made stronger together through the challenges so we appreciated the good times.

"I like to think my dad found Olive in heaven, and they helped us find each other," Greyson murmured softly, a smile evident in the tone of her voice. "They were our biggest fans, right? Well, they helped us find our true happiness, the only way they could."

I nodded against her chest, overwhelmed by literally everything.

"Can I make a request that might scare you, but I think will be accepted considering the commitment we've laid out here tonight?" I asked, my voice muffled against her skin.

Greyson hesitated and pulled back, looking at me with uncertainty before she nodded.

"After we're married, and we're ready for babies, and we get pregnant ... if it's a girl we name her Olive, and if it's a boy we name him Hudson?"

A tear slid down her cheek and she rubbed her pendant while she nodded emphatically.

"Yes, Canada. Yes. To everything. Now can we go to bed? Get tired before we go to sleep?"

"Absolutely. Every night."

"Forever?"

"For infinity."

The lights of the buildings twinkled against the water, and I sighed in contentment. Gavin walked quietly next to me, his hands jiggling in his pockets.

"You okay, Canada?" I hooked my arm through his elbow as he looked sideways at me. The Falcons had fallen in the conference finals, and he had been distracted since. Not unhappy, exactly. He was proud of the team, but getting that close to the cup without ultimate success was always a disappointment.

"I'm perfect, Lemon Drop. Why do you ask?" Gavin's eyes were focused over my head. I turned to see what he was looking at, but saw nothing but trees against the darkness.

"I don't know. You just seem ... nervous."

Gavin gazed down at me and his serious expression softened. He smirked, and that dimple in the corner of his mouth melted me.

"You can see right through me."

I hooked my arms around his waist and looked up into his eyes.

"What are you nervous about?"

He took a deep breath and blew it out loudly, as he looked up to the sky. There were more stars than I could ever remember seeing. Gavin smiled at the universe, and when he looked back at me, his confidence had returned.

"I'm not. Not anymore," Gavin reached into his pocket and pulled out a box. My heart stopped when he snaked a hand behind his waist to unhook my own and dropped to one knee. I clutched my chest, until I felt the beating inside, then kneeled down with him. Gavin threw his head back and laughed.

"You're not supposed to be the one down here," he teased. Tears welled up in my eyes as I popped back up.

"Oh, right! Sorry! Go ahead!"

Gavin lifted the lid of the box and peered up at me with the promise of the future in his eyes.

"I have loved you from the moment I watched you walk through the doors at Icing with flour on your face and icing on your shirt. I wasn't sure I would ever get the chance to wrap you up in that love, and then when I did, it was the best day of my life. Until the day after, and the one after that."

Gavin paused, and brought a shaking hand to his face to wipe away a tear.

"When I thought I had lost you, I literally felt like my soul had been shredded. I learned a lot about myself. Most importantly, that your love and companionship is something I physically need to breathe.

"I pledge my love and devotion to you, and I promise to be your sounding board and your confidante. But not your bodyguard or your overbearing protector. I'll fight every battle *with* you, not *for* you. Unless you want me to handle it, in that case I'm all in."

I could barely contain the sobs that threatened to wrack my body. Wet drops fell off my face onto my dress.

"So, what I'm asking is, will you do me the immense honor of agreeing to be my wife? Will you marry me, Greyson Park?"

It took several deep breaths before I could compose myself enough to speak. When my voice finally cooperated, I could only get out one word.

"Duh."

Gavin grinned widely and jumped off the ground, lifting me off my feet and into his arms.

"I take it that's a yes?" Gavin asked against my lips. I nodded endlessly, and found his mouth. The kiss I shared with my *fiancé* was magical and not at all appropriate for public viewing.

"Get a room, will ya?" Asher's voice floated through my love drunk haze and I spotted him emerging from the trees. Cohen, Mila, and Delaney flanked him wearing matching smiles. From the opposite side of the trees, Trevor and Erica casually held hands and Jace leaned against a lamp post with Vanessa and Kayleigh. Eddie sat on a bench, a sketchpad in his lap.

"You did all of this for me?" I asked incredulously. "My entire family is here."

"I couldn't imagine doing something so important without them by our sides," Gavin replied. He gently set me down as we were swarmed by the people we had chosen as family.

"Let's see the ring," Mila demanded, and held up my naked finger. I realized Gavin hadn't even slipped it on, and he shrugged with a blush.

"I got carried away," he apologized. He plucked it out of the satin and slid it on my finger, the diamond glittering against the soft glow of the lights that illuminated the shore. The perfection of it took my breath away, and Mila and Delaney leaned in with simultaneous gasps.

"The center stone is round and a custom setting to look like the North Star, and it's surrounded by an infinity twist made up of smaller stones. They're held in a cupcake setting," Gavin explained. I heard the pride in his voice, the care that went into creating this truly perfect piece of jewelry.

"This is ... my life in a ring," I spoke around the lump lodged in my throat. "You've outdone yourself. But I'd marry you with a ring pop. The only thing I *need* is you."

"You've got me," Gavin murmured. "You always have."

"And you've got me," I said. "You always will."

National Domestic Violence Hotline:
800-799-7233
Text START to 88788

Acknowledgments

First and foremost: thank you to you, the reader, who has made it this far with me. I wrote this book to prove to myself that I could, and I am eternally grateful you shared your time with me in reading it. I hope to see you again soon.

A close second, J. I couldn't have made it here without you. I love you and your encouragement, your opinions and help with scenes. You're the best partner I could imagine. Love you to the moon.

Q, you're my best work and my proudest accomplishment. I love you beyond words.

Mom and Dad, I owe everything—literally all of it—to you. I hope you're as proud of this as I am. Love you more.

Shami, you're my best. The late nights and early mornings, the simultaneous IG and text convos, the 'screw it' when I'm feeling like the kid left out on the playground. I'd be lost without you. The best friend, I love you forever and always. Pack the car. The trip is on.

Renee, what can I say beyond 'Believe'? You've been my right hand throughout this entire journey. Look at us now- we did it! But don't think that photo is retired. It's the only thing that keeps me going. That, and your encouragement. You're the best example of human.

Brandi, my birthday twin. Thank you for your work, your encouragement, and your friendship. Beer and pretzels are on me next time.

Jana, Michelle, Heather, thank you for finding the issues my tired eyes and bleeding heart couldn't. Because of you, this book is better than it was before.

Helena, you brought me into a world I never knew existed. Thank you for your mind, your heart, and your friendship. I was ready to give up and you gave me an entire Saturday, a video call and a country away. Your knowledge and willingness to share your time made all the difference. I'm so thankful for you.

I could go on forever. Everyone who encouraged and supported, I love you so much.

Keep your eyes on the stars, and never stop reaching for the moon.

About the Author

Nico lives in Iowa with her husband, son, and rescue dog. When she isn't writing, she spends her time binging true crime podcasts, watching The Golden Girls, dancing around the kitchen to Fall Out Boy, and asking her pit bull who the cutest boy is. (Spoiler alert: it's him.)

For a bonus scene and a sneak peek into what's coming for book two, sign up for my newsletter!
www.nicodanielsauthor.com

facebook.com/nicodanielsauthor
instagram.com/nicodanielsauthor

Made in the USA
Middletown, DE
29 June 2023

34113722R00227